D1052989

imaginative biography about this unusual figure, who carved out a distinct place in post–WWII Hollywood."

—Publisher's Weekly

"This amazing book is all heart....Chip Jacobs blends the skills of an investigative journalist, the glitz of Hollywood, and the smooth storytelling of fiction to weave a profile of his larger-than-life uncle that will leave you crying, laughing, and gasping in wonder, often on the same page. Bravo!"

—Denise Hamilton, bestselling author of The Jasmine Trade

THE ASCENSION OF JERRY

"Brilliant....A delightfully off-kilter true-crime tale....Jacobs' ear for a good story is pitch perfect....The Ascension of Jerry isn't an old song in a new key, but an entirely new song about crime, fear, and a weird kind of redemption that could only happen in the general vicinity of Hollywood."

—Ron Franscell, bestselling author of The Darkest Night

"This is not just another Hollywood Whodunit. In the end we find it is really about one man's search and struggle to find his own personal truths and redemption. Well written and highly recommended."

—Steve Hodel, bestselling author of Black Dahlia Avenger

"A terrific book—I couldn't put it down."

—Stephen Jay Schwartz, bestselling author of
Hollywood vs. The Author and Boulevard

ARROYO

ARROYO

A Novel

CHIP JACOBS

RARE BIRD BOOKS

LOS ANGELES, CALIF.

THIS IS A GENUINE RARE BIRD BOOK

Rare Bird Books
453 South Spring Street, Suite 302
Los Angeles, CA 90013
rarebirdbooks.com

For more information, address:
Rare Bird Books Subsidiary Rights Department
453 South Spring Street, Suite 302
Los Angeles, CA 90013

Set in Warnock
Printed in the United States

10 9 8 7 6 5 4 3 2 1

Publisher's Cataloging-in-Publication Data

Names: Jacobs, Chip, author.
Title: Arroyo: A Novel / Chip Jacobs.
Description: First Hardcover Edition | A Genuine Rare Bird Book |
New York, NY; Los Angeles, CA: Rare Bird Books, 2019.
Identifiers: ISBN 9781644280287
Subjects: LCSH Pasadena (Calif.)—History—20th century. | Progressivism (United
States politics)—Fiction. | United States—Politics and government—1913–1921—
Fiction. | Bridges—California—Pasadena—Fiction. | Pasadena (Calif.)—Buildings,
structures, etc.—Fiction. | Dogs—Fiction. | BISAC FICTION / Historical / General
Classification: LCC PS3610.A356418 A77 2019| DDC 813.6—dc23

To the hometown that still bedazzles me, and Auggie (the original wonder mutt), who delivered joy that greatly exceeded all the worthless objects he munched.

"Far better it is to dare mighty things, to win glorious triumphs, even though checkered by failure, than to take rank with those poor spirits who neither enjoy much nor suffer much, because they live in the gray twilight that knows neither victory nor defeat."

—Theodore Roosevelt

NOTE TO READERS

THIS BOOK IS A historical novel. Although the majority of characters are fictionalized, some were actual people, and I've created scenes and dialogue based on what I've discovered about their lives over the course of my research. Nearly everything written here about the Colorado Street Bridge—and Pasadena—is accurate. A portion of my book proceeds will go to my local humane society and suicide-prevention groups.

PROLOGUE:
MR. INCIDENTAL

NARROWED IT DOWN, HAVEN'T you, buckaroos?

You see a wheezing old man in a tuxedo and top hat, acetylene torch in hand, and the choices seem obvious. I'm either a dapper escapee from a mental asylum, or a geriatric thespian shooting the album cover for an avant-garde band. Either way, you peg me as a pathetic dinosaur out for attention in this well-accomplished town.

You're all wet, but I forgive you. Wrinkles can deceive.

My story, or rather *her* story is a razzle-dazzle whodunit from the cusp of the tailpipe age. If my knees weren't so arthritic, I'd be down on them in gratitude, thanking the cosmic bread crumbs for shepherding me here. Now I can croak full of life, a disruptor with an AARP card.

But I digress.

Having been away so long, I'm proud to report our lady remains as enthralling as ever—lithely posed, majestic from her studded crown to her floating toes. Forget age. She's as mysterious as a fog bank, epitomizing classic beauty despite the predictable skid marks.

What, you think I'm laying it on too thick? That my Sears-brand hearing aid runs on New Age crystals? Then inch closer for a peek. She won't bite. Just don't get too comfortable, for the old gal, on this her eightieth birthday, has depleted her tolerance for the bullshit myths garlanded around her. Whitewashed glories, forgotten heroes: she can no longer bite her tongue, assuming there's one in there.

Ever since that young man's visit, my descent into miserable decrepitude has reversed into the determination to rise above self-pity. Put pep in my hobble. Why? I now appreciate that unseen forces drafted me—me, the crotchety fossil that detests bingo, *Seinfeld*, and sports visors giving headwear a bad name—to connect the firefly dots around our silvery empress.

Who killed the brightest lights this side of Busch Gardens, when Pasadena was a wonderland of possibility? Permitted our thirst for pretty objects to callus us? Let me tell you: neither an illustrious reputation nor a knack for pageantry is a force field against sin.

Appearances. It's always about appearances in this damn place. No one wants to confront this bugaboo: that "history," as one skeptic laid bare, "is a pack of lies about events that never happened told by people who weren't there."

Well, I *was* an eyewitness, back when Orange Grove Boulevard was a macadam thoroughfare for our resident tycoons, and tamale-cart vendors made killings on blue-collars' paydays.

First things first: you'll notice our lady in question has had some "work done." Blessedly, the patrons who financed the procedures refused to allow a gauche Botox job to wind back the clock, knowing a trout pout on her would constitute criminal disfigurement. Imagine Lauren Bacall, or, for you whippersnappers, Michelle Pfeiffer, with a weeping goiter.

Consequently, she hasn't been so much "refreshed" as restored, jowls tightened, calves bolstered, along with more intimate intrusions best detailed once the children are asleep. Let me also stipulate that none of these nips and tucks were required to warrant her spot on the pedestal of all-time greats. Her unflagging grace, revealed when party animal Woodrow Wilson ran America and you could only find one decent brand of mayonnaise, earned her stature long ago. If a person can adore someone of her physical grandeur—no offense, Sally, my beloved—color me enchanted.

Allow me to confide a few darker twists. For every blandishment lavished on her, for every popping flashbulb and cream-puff story, she rarely enjoyed a red-carpet existence. By her mid-twenties, in fact, some of those who exalted her as "magnificent" and "hypnotizing" clamored for her summary obliteration. They woofed that she was obsolete, a statuesque has-been replaceable by the next hot number. She'd done her duty. Now, take a dirt nap.

You think she brooded at the conspiracies to topple her, by metal teeth no less? Never. She stood proud, shoulders back, that proverbial good sport willing to let painters brush-stroke her and middlemen over-commercialize her while selling Chryslers on television. She even refused to slap defamation suits against the rumormongers who smeared her as a pied piper for ghosts and a stoic murderer of the helpless. Brace yourselves, folks. It was her human masters who superimposed that alter ego on her.

Trust me here: the Arroyo Seco's queenly bridge and I go way back.

Judging by the hippopotamus camped on my chest, I don't have much time to convince you, either. Bribing a cabdriver to taxi me from my lasagna-Tuesday, Lysol-ed nursing home to the hardware store and then here almost did me in. With heart disease, high cholesterol, gout, anemia, and more, my blood chemistry is a biohazard.

Miraculously, though, I persevered, with places to go at 0.5 mph. Hunched forward on my walker, I clacked toward the scene of my future defacement, the august Rose Bowl (and cosmos-probing Jet Propulsion Laboratory) to my right, asphalt subdivisions to the left. I brushed my hand up against her fluted railing in reacquaintance. Pure jazz!

Not to gloat, but I accomplished this feat in the same fucking penguin suit that used to constitute my trademark get-up, when I owned the San Gabriel Valley's finest haberdashery. That I collapsed backward gasping for breath upon reaching my destination, a bench inside one of the bridge's romantic sitting areas, was, admittedly, less dignified.

Again, feel free to decry the vandalism I'm plotting against this nationally recognized landmark afforded all manner of federal protections. Know I'm hoping to win your absolution in the end—a liver-spotted firebrand in a sundowner canyon. It was in reading about the public festivities surrounding her grand reopening that I realized I had my opening. There'd be indulgent layers of decorations you could've camouflaged a Marine Expeditionary Unit behind.

Personally, the trimmings harken childhood memories of the syco-phantic extravaganza staged for presidential visits: the overkill floral ar-rangements and congratulatory banners; the ritzy, color-coordinated table settings and special refreshments. Thank you, city fathers, nonetheless. Your bridge party is allowing me to be the asshole I need to be.

Now, excuse me while I try not to die.

Phew. That was a pain. Not that I was ever agile with power tools, but I have a suggestion for whoever manufactured the acetylene device I just lit to slice through a section of the iron, suicide-prevention fence: you might mull lightening future canisters for us elderly deviants.

No such gripe with my leather, side-shield sunglasses, which I recently fished out of my keepsake trunk to recycle into welder's goggles. Like history, fashion is circular. Shades popular with biplane pilots and Progressive Age motorists are de rigueur again as "steampunk aesthetic."

The person at the epicenter of this gave them to me as a child, along with the surprise in my bag. My hope is that they'll persuade him to speak truth to concrete; that he'll remind Pasadena that for all its old-money probity and cultural firepower, it's the light in our collective eyes that counts more than our rosewater vanity. Last time he saw me he called me cuckoo, so I have my work cut out for me.

Another absurd truth dawns on—oh, crap, here comes the fuzz. It's go time.

⫶⫶⫶

HE'S GANGLY AND BALDING, this fifty-ish cop, with an aura of resigned diminishment in his drooping shoulders and scrunched-together features. Roughly thirty feet away, he's approaching from the east, visibly annoyed at his day-wrecking development: me.

"Excuse me, sir, but mind telling me what you think you're doing? That fence you just destroyed is public property." He's speaking in a loud husk, assuming my waxy face also confers deafness.

"Yes, officer, I'm quite aware of that. There's no need to yell."

"Good. Then stop."

"Not to split hairs, but stop what? Cutting the fence or not revealing my thinking?"

My glibness is poorly received. I know this because the cops' nostrils flare and his palms stiffen in double-halt formation above his night-blue uniform. He must be working morning security for the rededication bash following the queen's $27 million structural/seismic rehab. Poor sap's probably visualizing telling his captain that this geezer outflanked him.

"I'll clarify," he says. "Lay down the torch. That's an order. You could hurt yourself, or someone below. You wouldn't want that on your, uh, conscience." Under his breath he mumbles, "Jesus, of all days for a 5150." That's police code for nutjob unloosed; he's confused me for a jumper. "Whatever is eating at you, there's help available."

He's roughly fifteen feet from the bench now, with the forecast calling for a high chance of another life-is-precious cliché. Soon he'll have the bead on me.

"Officer, I can assure you I pose no threat to public safety or myself. I'm here to set some records straight. Nonviolently."

"Aha. I knew you were educated. And I'll tell you what. Since you're dressed like Alfred from *Batman*, I'll be your Commissioner Gordon. First thing I did when I was assigned here was drive past the mansion behind you they used as Wayne Manor. Sergeant Daniel Grubb requesting permission to approach. And you are?"

"Name's Mr. Incidental."

My curveball annoys him. He scratches the tip of an ear the size of a soap dish, still plotting to charm me into surrender. "Is there someone we can contact? Someone looking for you?"

Officer Sneaky has further narrowed the gulf between us. "Why, yes," I respond. "There is one particular individual you can track down. But I'll need time to explain it all first so you don't think I'm certifiable."

When I dip my head and wink rakishly to accentuate that point, my top hat tumbles onto the sidewalk in front of where I sit. Embarrassing. "Leave that where it is," I add.

"Let me propose a bargain?" he says slyly. "You desist from further tampering with the fence, and I'll agree to your terms. This doesn't have to escalate. Big event starting here later today: the mayor, speeches, giant scissors. The works. Fair?"

Fair? Really? Fair would be sparing the Branch Davidians from burning to death in Waco, Texas, or those innocent kids from being gunned down here on Halloween night. Fair certainly isn't blaming yours truly for defending himself after a pimple-faced shoplifter punched him years earlier. "Exhausted as I am, sergeant, I can't. If, out of principle, I have to sever a hole in this fence and drop a few things on the vulgar condo below I will."

"No, you won't. I'm going to counter-offer you, one gentleman to another."

As a retired businessman, I've seen this move. Compliment, disarm, and then blitz. "Don't test me," I say, though I bet he will. "I still have my reflexes."

With a flick, I reignite my Orchard Supply torch in my white-gloved hand and tug down my side-shade sunglasses. The nozzle hisses a burnt-orange stream of fire, which I briefly aim at him. Then I run the flame over the lower part of half a dozen fence posts, whose upper ends I previously sliced. After a little more melting, one good whack will probably detach it, sending a roughly three-foot-by-three-foot section crashing downward.

Grubb's mouth plops so wide I count three fillings. "That's a fucked-up move," he snarls. "I thought we established a dialogue."

"They're not mutually exclusive."

He's done reasoning with my feisty-curmudgeon routine. "Dispatch," he says into the Motorola walkie-talkie clipped near his right epaulet. "Sergeant Grubb requesting backup to the Colorado Street Bridge, and probably the department shrink if she's around. Copy?" *Sssssssssssss.* "I said, 'you copy?'" Evidently, no one does. He wrenches down on his Motorola to bring it nearer to his mouth. "Dispatch, dispatch," he says louder. Nope: still static isolation.

The flatfoot, even so, has drawn closer. Once he bum-rushes me, he won't even require handcuffs to subdue me, just a decisive hand around my grizzled neck. For a lifer likely a decade from his pension, Grubb has moves.

Then again, so do I.

When he lunges at me, I release the torch, which clanks metallically on the bench. My weapon of choice is less formidable, outwardly anyway. It's my walker. The action-reaction is karate-esque. He barrels my way. I bash him in the temple with one of the walkers' space-age-light aluminum arms. *Kiai!*

Down goes the sergeant. Down in a heap at my polished Italian loafers. For the first time in years, I'm a senior in control.

He comes to quickly, perpendicular to me, discovering that he's pinned down on the deck. One of my walker's green-tennis-ball-tipped-legs presses on his throat. The other squishes his crotch. While old age has shrunken me, I'm still six-feet two-inches, so my legs fit easily over the top of the walker to keep the pressure on.

From the concrete, Grubb sputters statutory threats: about how I'm guilty of assaulting a law-enforcement official; how I've ratcheted a minor vandalism charge into a felony; how my walker "better not have fucking cracked" his Ray-Bans, the location of which, like his police cap, he's unsure. He's a squirming human alligator, ashamed at his predicament, madder by the second.

Anxious about what I've done—hey, even us old fogies saw the Rodney King thumping—I subpoena every stringy muscle to continue immobilizing him. I grunt. I channel applied physics I heard at a free Caltech lecture. I ask God why he's led me down this preposterous road, and to spare me physical agony once the officer thirty years my junior breaks free.

That shouldn't be long. Heart palpitating, I wonder about releasing him. Pleading for mercy; blaming the antidepressants, a dead wife, despair over my evaporating social relevancy. Anything.

Then, faster than the hot winds blow, to quote from those gods of classic rock, I sense a change in my combatant's degree of resistance. His writhing is slowing; so, too, have his hands, which before were scrabbling for leverage.

Sergeant Grubb, whom I'll soon learn transferred to Pasadena after the 1992 Los Angeles riots made him question humanity, has stopped fighting because he's worked the math. He's calculated that he wants to hear my far-fetched yarn a few integers more than he desires to club me within legally defensible police guidelines.

"Sonny Jim," I say, "let me ask you something. Do you believe in second chances?"

He eyeballs me from his back. "Depends on what kind?" he says. "For a codger quicker than he looks?"

"No. The kind, and this will sound worrisomely eccentric, that Shirley MacLaine would applaud. Life repeats."

"Not really. I'm Catholic. We believe you go up or down. Not around. But if you can spell it out before any of my colleagues see me like this, imprisoned by a glorified cane, I'm open."

"Deal. Imagine a past when—"

THE BIRDS OF PASADENA

S AY WHAT YOU WILL about his morning pep and cowlick, his galling diet and corny pride. No one ever rode Mrs. Grover Cleveland, the animal, quite like Nick Chance.

Already the speediest one in the yard, she shifted into another gear whenever Nick sank down on her fluffy mane and whispered encouragement. Promised a treat. Today, as she folded her black wings into her white chest to blow ahead of the competition, you might've expected smoke coiling off her hooves. They didn't call her the "feather cannonball" unwarranted.

Nick's companions breathed her dust, but on this four-mile pleasure dash anything was possible. Adept a rider as their front-running chum was, they knew he often grandstanded in the lead, and sometimes took harrowing spills he was fortunate to walk away from with only bruises and a laugh. So, they pressed their boots into their own steeds, whooping to themselves *this* wasn't over.

The three good-timers raced under the trees atop their six-foot-tall birds, whose feathers were guaranteed retail gold. Moving at a blurry clip, in a canyon being auctioned off by the day, the group rooted up dust onto a pathway trimmed with imported shrubs and plants where gauzy light laced through the veiny branches. Everyone, human and beaked, wished the jaunt could stretch into dusk.

Their valley trail was pristine, so far as trails go, and empty, with no snobs around to bewail what they couldn't comprehend: two-legged animals being ridden saddle-less, low to the ground, where hands served as reins. The steeds, cobra-necked creatures more prehistoric roosters than horses, high-stepped in this amber light, their clawed feet *pahrump-ing* on the terrain.

Mrs. Cleveland was particularly delighted to be away from her monotonous day job being sheared for the textile business. She cranked her pimpled mouth to telegraph this.

Awk-awwwwwwww. Awkawwww. The ostrich's shriek of joy carried a wild edge.

The posse next burst into a shamrock-green meadow, clopping past mossy ponds filled with ducks and swans, then grasslands, and then chubby sheep too busy grazing to observe this unusual bunch.

Nick, a dark-haired free spirit in a white, collarless shirt, was also ready to whoop. Rotating his torso back, eyes electric, he shouted at his pursuers: "If either one of you idiots says life can get better than this, I'm stealing your wages. I swear it." The best part for him still lay around the bend, due north, though he didn't advertise what others might call obsession.

Waldo Northcutt and R. G. Crum nodded in agreement, snapping mental photographs of their lunchtime joyride away from Cawston "World Famous" Ostrich Farm where they all worked. Someday, they might be retelling escapades about how they mimicked cowboys, if only for a few hours a week, on the backs of quicksilver beasts native to South Africa. Reverie over the burning competitors in them tried closing the gap, even if was merely for show.

Around them now flew hillsides blanketed in myrtle and ivy, tarweed and wild oats—vistas of fauna and flora so pervasive they provided thirty gardeners full-time employment. Before long, they came to the perimeter of the more formal section of the grounds. This part of the great wash was brushed with stands of willows and redwoods, wisteria and camphor, cacti and oaks. Each were meticulously planted to shade park benches and picnic areas, or simply to conjure whimsy.

A master horticulturist from Scotland, with a $2 million budget, crafted this nature preserve and semi-private park, consumed by the tiniest detail. Robert Fraser spaced the jacarandas and birds-of-paradise so they didn't upstage the citrus groves. He researched what type of mulch to shovel into the scented flowerbeds for durability.

Every inch of these thirty acres was actually his boss's backyard, and America's beer king demanded nothing shy of arboreal perfection. "Make it beautiful!" Adolphus Busch commanded, probably with German-accented bravado. "Make it different—regardless of expense." His Scotsman listened.

The three riders, all raised here in the foothills of the Sierra Madre mountain range, appreciated the transformation of the ravine from "tin can dump" and animal graveyard to botanical eye candy. Since Adolphus began "wintering" in Pasadena in 1904, his gardens were graded and hoed, contoured and planted into the unofficial "eighth wonder of the world," all courtesy of his staggering wealth and ferocious imagination.

Blindfold the trio and they could still pinpoint the fairy-tale nooks, where terra cotta replicas of Little Red Riding Hood, Hansel and Gretel, and other mystical beings awaited children's squeals.

Fast upon them was the baby elephant statue, then to the right the thatched-roof Old Mill home with spinning water wheel, the latter a residence that Adolphus converted into a playhouse for a daughter. Nice childhood, if you were born into it.

Even so, it was the sunken gardens—a dreamscape of grassy veld terraced in circular patterns over banks and swales—that could spur the cruelest heart to skip. Trails to explore them dipped and rose around planters and benches, a canvas of variegated green finer than the world's priciest golf courses. Optically, it was as close to heaven as mortals were permitted. The three compadres and their amber-eyed ostriches, Nick's Mrs. Cleveland, R. G.'s Mr. Mahatma Gandhi, and Waldo's Maggie, had cavorted here before.

They galloped along the familiar path, just beneath the first steppe, batting around sarcastic jibes characteristic of twenty-seven-year-old men hesitant to fully grow up. Busch Gardens was theirs, this being mid-September, except for a few couples gripping maps sticky pink with cotton candy.

RG, freckled and fair complected, was the first to hear the intrusion of a black motorcar puttering to their right on a trail-hugging road. Being in the rear of the pack, he initially paid the gate-crasher no mind. Then, as the car persisted alongside, he recognized he must. The automobile, a shiny, black Ford Model T with its top down, appeared intent on making a statement. Animals were quaint, but engines were California's new apex predator, even in a rockery chattering with birdsong.

Behind the wheel was an older man in a charcoal suit, who had bushy eyebrows akin to a supercilious owl. RG didn't dislike him entirely, amused by watching how the driver's gray hair and shaggy mustache quivered in the wind like wild grass. A minute elapsed before RG noticed something alarming. Rather than a delirious grin about being in Adolphus's oasis, the man's expression was competitive.

Pinkies to lips, RG whistled to Waldo ahead, next hollering, "We got company." Waldo's eyes bulged after the Model T man chugged past him and toward Nick. Between the driver's puckered face and lead-foot pace, it was obvious he was egging for an impromptu race between, as it were, metal and feather.

Waldo pinched Maggie's lower neck, coaxing it to slow from gallop to canter. RG pulled up next to him on Mr. Mahatma Gandhi. (Maggie was named for a character in the comic strip "Bringing Up Father;" Mahatma because the pacifists at the farm revered Gandhi, and this bird had his eyes.) "Should we attempt dissuading Nick?" asked RG. "I fear this could culminate with a priest over someone."

Waldo, with windblown black hair and a cleft chin, asked back: "How?" You intend on catching Mrs. Cleveland without a motor?"

Nick, now forty yards ahead, probably wouldn't have heeded prudence anyway. Over the years, he leapt from waterfalls to assure the more timid it was safe; tongue-tied a president; stuck his hands into smoldering machinery vital to his employer's bottom line. His middle name wasn't reckless; it was Augustus. It just sometimes felt that way, especially with dares.

The narrow path they were traversing was ripe for one, too, an unusual straightaway in serpentine Busch Gardens. Dead end aside, it was ideal for a race if you added testosterone.

When the Model T man flashed into Nick's peripheral vision, Nick twisted his head, first puzzled, then irritated. Yet the provocateur changed that. He communicated wordlessly, jutting his chin several times toward an imaginary finish line ahead.

Nick squeezed his tongue into his cheek, tallying pros and cons, triumph versus discretion? *You only live once*, he thought. *Take him.* Two head dips broadcast his assent.

The driver stamped the accelerator, pushing ahead a few lengths in a spurt of black, fizzy exhaust. Nick's ostrich, named after her human doppelganger, Frances Folsom, a handsome First Lady with a pronounced brow, took offense inhaling the crud. She puffed up her neck, gyrating the flexible muscle around 180 degrees toward Nick to register her complaint.

"Nip me back at the farm," Nick said. "Let's show that motorcar what you can do."

Maybe it was Nick's inflection, or her premonition of a blood orange for reward stimulating her pea-size brain. Whatever the incentive, she was now a fowl with a purpose, afterburners engaged, not unlike her fellow birds in the Tournament of Roses' ostrich-chariot races. She tucked her wings further into her oval torso and straightened around her head. Behind that breezy, slightly bowlegged lope was sheer velocity. *Pawrump, pawrump.*

Mrs. Grover Cleveland made up so much ground on the Ford you might've suspected that one of its whitewalls frayed. Nick rocked forward, tucking his chin into the base of her neck. Her speed was thirty-nine miles per hour, sub-Cheetah, but still plenty fast. Tied with fifty yards to go, Nick already knew the race's outcome. Nobody bested Mrs. Cleveland's stretch kick. It's why Nick gave his spontaneous opponent a two-fingered salute blazing to victory going away.

"Here, here!" Waldo hooted from behind. "Atta boy."

Nick, however, couldn't get too bigheaded, for that could get you killed. He focused on deceleration, lest he plow headfirst into a flower bed a hundred yards from Adolphus's cliffside mansion, "Ivy Wall." A tug here, a boot nudged there, and Mrs. Cleveland, the feather cannonball, extended her wings for drag.

Nick's opponent brought his Ford to a rolling stop, gnawing his bottom lip in disgust. Atrocious idea; he never should've listened to that salesman who crowed the automobile could take a Kentucky Derby champ.

After he spun Mrs. Cleveland around, Nick dismounted, hoping to shake his competitor's hand. The sore loser would have none of it, refusing even eye contact. He snatched his black cap from the passenger seat, scrunching it over his rumpled hair. The dog-leg-shaped veins bulging from his temples were exhibits of humiliation.

His attempted exit from Busch Gardens provided a second dose of it, as well, for he allowed himself scant room to navigate a U-turn. Needing to back up before he could blast out of there, he threw the knobby gearshift into reverse. This, though, only propelled the Ford unartfully over a low curb dividing the road from the parkway. Stranded neither here nor there, he grinded gears while Nick and company watched him struggle to achieve traction for his polished automobile.

Finally, the Model T lurched onto the road, nearly sideswiping Mrs. Cleveland on its pebble-spitting departure. As it did, the driver, an affluent brick manufacturer, fantasized about barbecuing the ungainly critter on his backyard spit. Mrs. C brayed *Aw-aw-awwwwww* at him.

"You sure taught him a lesson," RG said. He'd ridden over to Nick, who stood at the finish line scratching his bird's chest. Waldo joined them on his ostrich, pocket watch in antsy hands.

"She did, anyway," Nick said. "That fella will be seeing her in his nightmares for the next month."

"And forgetting to tell his wife," RG added. "Henry Ford may soon be receiving hostile correspondence recommending he add horsepower to the next version."

"Don't think Ford will be sweating too much," Nick said. "Read the other day we have more motorcars in town than any other city. There's thousands."

"More than New York? Or 'Frisco?" said RG. "I don't believe it."

"No, per person, or something mathematical. Point is we better relish this time while we can. Next thing we know ostriches and, heck, horses will be nostalgia. Not that I'm opposed to progress."

Waldo twirled his pocket watch by its chrome chain around his finger and reversed direction in a wider orbit. "I hate," he said, "interrupting this illuminating dialogue about the course of civilization, fellas, but perhaps we can request our local universities to pursue it."

"And why's that?" Nick was chomping a piece of straw he extracted from behind his ear, grinning that cheeky way of his.

"Because we best be heading out. Check the time. You know the sticklers these new owners are about punctuality. Neither RG nor I are favored sons like you, Nick. Heck, we're barely management."

"Oh, please," Nick said with a laugh.

"My stomach is going to be rumbling all day on account of your lunchtime gallops," RG said with a titter. "Going to be crackers and a stale apple, if I get lucky."

"You're already lucky, if you catch me," Nick said, stroking Mrs. C's fleecy side. "Look where you are. I won't be too much longer myself, in case anyone asks."

"Can't resist a gander this close, can ya?" RG said. "You chose the wrong profession."

"I have plans. Now hit it, goldbrickers. We're coming back next week, ready for all takers."

Soon enough his friends and their mounts, Mr. Mahatma Gandhi and Maggie, were receding south past upper Busch Gardens, toward the woodlands. Once the Raymond Hotel, a sprawling, European-style hotel on old Bacon Hill was in view, they'd be within shouting distance of Cawston.

Nick swept the bangs from his eyes and inhaled the buttercup nectar in the air. He looped his arm around Mrs. Cleveland's neck, which alerted her he was hopping on and not to buck. "One more stop, girl. Then it's home. Extra grain for you tonight."

They plunged north through timbered landscape that, from a leasable hot-air balloon, resembled a Christmas tree with a crooked trunk. No out-of-state millionaire with an estate on the bluff yet commandeered this scruffy part of the Arroyo Seco as a passion project. Not yet. The branches from the tangle of wild trees here were so densely intersected it could've been midnight at noon.

In the dark, you needed hometown soil in your blood to know that the trail paralleled Orange Grove Boulevard, Pasadena's glitziest residential street. It bisected roads with English-Lord-sounding names—Arlington, Barclay, Bradford—a few hundred feet above the ravine to the east. Here, California Street segued to Arbor Street, Arbor to Clay Street.

Of course, Nick didn't need to triangulate to get where he was headed. His ears were his compass, the distant banging and sawing his magnetic north. Knowing he was close, he pushed Mrs. Cleveland to a light trot through the thinning canopy of oaks and sycamores.

And there it lay, barely a quarter done, already resplendent. Nick's brain went woozy, basking in the scale of Pasadena's astounding creation.

To him, the three finished arches protruding over the gorge could've been the chassis of a luxury ocean liner under construction in dry dock; the open spandrel columns bracing them suggested cathedral windows only missing stained-glass; the scaffolding crisscrossing the next span was the lattice of an Atlantic City roller coaster, albeit between the Arroyo's granite walls. This must've been how Parisians felt watching the Eiffel Tower monopolize the French skyline. The bridge was a New World declaration: reinforced concrete could conquer anything.

As Mrs. Cleveland stood there dumbly, Nick sat listening, enraptured by the cold-slurry colossus. It was a dreamer's percussion: carpenters pounding nails into wooden frames, wire cutters snipping rebar in snappy clicks. Around them, horses whinnied as they levered into the air telephone-pole-size timber required for framing. The diesel-powered mixer churning gravel, sand, and cement into soupy concrete was sweet music of its own: *chunka chunka chunka*.

Nick yearned to get closer. Needed to get closer. Intended to get closer. But a boy on the hill couldn't contain himself.

The kid, pallid and shaggy under his tweed cap, stood next to his mother, disinterested in Pasadena's ambitious roadway. He yawned watching its robotically operated dumpcart ferry concrete to men perched on planks a hundred feet up.

His mother, who wore a black, Victorian dress and stacked her ash-brown hair in a bun, tried engaging her ten-year-old, anyway. She asked him if Jules Verne, whose stories of stealthy submarines and whirlybird airships the child read by oil lamp, would approve of such derring-do? Stiffly, he answered, "I guess," and took an indifferent lick of his chocolate ice-cream cone.

After an absent-minded glimpse into the ravine, he was a different boy. He started pointing at the valley floor, feet dancing in place. It was an ostrich that turned his ennui to giddiness—an ostrich ridden by a smiling man. Had that dumpcart sprouted wings and flown toward the sun, Icarus-like, he wouldn't have cared.

"Mother, over there! *Look*. That's, that's uh, uh, an ostrich, a real-life ostrich. They say they can outrun horses. You showed me one in a picture book."

"I suppose it is, love," his mother said.

"Is it from the farm you promised to take me to once I got better? Pretty please: may I ride it? Who knows if the creature will ever return?"

"Reginald, you'll do no such thing," she said sternly. "You'll finish your treat and we'll catch the trolley home and wait to tell your father the happy news."

Terming Reginald's news "happy" did no justice to its enormity, though that's the way parents spoke to cocoon terror. What they learned that day was a monumental relief, ten thousand prayers answered. Reginald did *not* have tuberculosis, which his mother trembled he did when he coughed up yellow loogies for the last few months. It was only mild bronchitis.

"Be grateful," said the jug-eared pediatrician, after he listened to Reginald's chest through his stethoscope and barraged his mother with questions about whether he suffered nocturnal sweats or weight loss. "The Sword of Damocles spared your son." His examining room was inside a medical boardinghouse operated by the altruistic Emma Bang. The humble, two-story building was perched off Orange Grove on an embankment diagonal to the bridge.

But Reginald wouldn't be consigned to it, separated from his family to recover, if possible, in the antiseptic, "busted lung ward" Mrs. Bang ran on the upper floor. He needed only fresh air, ginger, and parental decompression. Buy him a cone to toast what should be a normal life span, the doctor said. After nearly hugging him to death, his mother did.

Her hot tears of bliss were dry memory after Reginald caught wind of Nick's ostrich. Without asking permission a second time, he tore away from her, careening down the trail toward the clearing where Nick was watching men swinging from ropes. In his zeal for a ride, Reginald was barely conscious of dropping his ice cream, or his mother's panicky screams.

"Hey, hey, hey, mister," Reginald shouted, arms flapping, getting close. "Can I have a turn? How hard can it be? I'll be careful."

Mrs. Cleveland, afforded a human voice, would've said, "Stay the hell away." Not only was she drained from the day's exertions but those incessant hammers and rumbling machines made her jumpier than the trains unloading tourists at Cawston. Her love of Nick notwithstanding, a construction zone wasn't her idea of pasture. It was her idea of a madhouse.

Reginald's approach, hence, was her excuse to dash off, and she bolted west toward a clump of overgrown oaks with a first step that Olympian Jim Thorpe would've admired. Nick could only swoop his arms around her neck to keep from being thrown backward. "Whoa, whoa, whoa, *whooooa*, girl!" he pleaded to negligible effect.

By the eighth "whoa," she was rocketing toward a shady picnic area west of the bridgework, where she had pecked before for seeds, leaves, and other morsels for her gizzard. She'd sedate herself there by eating her feelings; though, it should be noted, that ostriches, the planet's largest bird, are as perpetually hungry as they are dimwitted and incapable of flying.

Problem was, Mrs. C was coming in too hot, despite Nick jerking on her neck to reduce her speed. *Whack.* The pinewood picnic table she collided with only vibrated. The large, wire cage resting on top of it—the one imprisoning thirty-seven South American jungle parrots—was lighter. The impact bumped the cage off the table, pitching it into the dirt. The latch door immediately busted open, and the phosphorescent-green, strident-throated parrots capitalized. They flew the coop in a jailbreak, soon forming into an arrowhead-shaped formation circling the bridge.

A hunched-over coot in a ratty jacket jogged over, zipping up his pants after taking a leak. Realizing his black-market profits were gone, he shook with anger. "You just cost me fifty dollars, you simp," he yelled. "Those parrots didn't wander in." He threw his arms around his head, then stomped a muddy boot. "I'm expecting remuneration. Unless you want to be coughing blood."

Nick, unsure of what he interrupted, sat dumbfounded on Mrs. C's back. The animal trafficker was less passive. He reached down and extracted from his sock a ten-inch Bowie knife.

"There's no need for that," Nick said, goading Mrs. C to retreat ten yards. "It was an accident. And you don't want to rile her. She's got a mean kick."

"Don't think of scampering off," he said, spittle on his lips. "The transaction you ruined was months in the making."

"Apologies, sir. We didn't mean any harm. A boy spooked her."

"Your varmint, your trouble," he said. "I ain't an aristocrat. I gotta eat." To underscore his wrath, he reared back and flicked his wrist, chucking his glinting hunting knife at Nick.

By the time Nick ducked behind Mrs. C's reedy neck for protection, the blade hooked to the left, landing in an azalea bush. Either the coot misaimed it on purpose or something else, a sudden gust, perhaps, saved Nick from being impaled. This wasn't his time of dying. "Thank you, God," he mumbled.

Another man now appeared from the grove. The coot's partner in crime was considerably younger, with a weasely nose and a cooler demeanor. "That should teach you to respect others' property," he said, trying to justify his associate's knife-throw as a warning shot. He picked up the empty parrots' container, in which a tuft of dislodged feathers remained, and then dropped it. His clientele, quirky rich people who paid good coin for non-indigenous species, would be disappointed.

"Bunky," he said to the coot, "I'd like to get my mitts on him, too, but we mustn't draw undue attention to ourselves."

"So we're gonna let him off, him and that pug-ugly—what is that, a giant chicken—without getting square? And the name's not Bunky, it's—"

"For hell's sake, man, I know your name," the younger animal-trafficker said, cutting him off. "I don't want *him* to know it in case the police nose around. Those parrots will make a nuisance of themselves if they loiter. Let's cut our losses. You, mister, can buzz off."

Nick pondered offering them free passes for a Cawston tour to make amends. Still, why play nice with crooks when one might've just tried slicing his jugular? He directed Mrs. C in the opposite direction and they trotted off. Nick sensed icy stares boring into him from behind.

Reginald's mother, clutching the hem of her now-silty dress, was at the dusty patch where the incident began when Nick returned. She already chastised her son for both leaving her side without permission and scaring a volatile animal. Yet Reginald was as giddy as before. "You must let me ask him, Mother," he said, with smears of that nickel cone crusted around his chin. "I just know he'll say yes."

The scarlet pique in her cheekbones was draining to pink as she recalled the day's bigger revelation. Eventually she acquiesced. Reginald, she said, could ride him, for five minutes only, provided Nick agreed and her son apologized.

Under Nick's control, the 289-pound bird trudged figure eights as if she were a mare consigned to pony rides ahead of the glue factory. At least she was calm.

"Blooming, eck, Reg, you had me scared stiff you were going to break your neck. You're *never* to duplicate that!"

"Yes, Mother. You already told me," Reginald said, engrossed by Mrs. C's two-toed hooves. "Do you think my friends will believe what I'm doing, Johnny especially? He's such a braggart."

"He better, love." She turned to Nick. "Pray tell, he hasn't caused you much grief. He's an excitable lad. I suppose they all are at that age."

"Not a bit," Nick white-lied. He also feigned ignorance when Reginald asked him whether he observed those "quirky, green birds" flying overhead. "I notice your son doesn't share your brogue. Are you English?"

"Through and through. From a proud, musical family in Staffordshire, West Midlands, north of Birmingham."

"And guess where the ostriches are from, Mother?" Reginald said. "Guess!"

"*Hmm.* I'll have to revert to my schoolgirl days for that one. Somewhere in Africa, I'd say."

"Actually," Nick said, his fingers twisting the straw back in his teeth, "South Pasadena."

A CERTAIN HEAVINESS OF FEATHERS

Nick had a good rationale for lunchtime trots atop Mrs. C. They called it morning.

At Cawston Ostrich Farm, managing three-hundred-plus birds of varying temperament and appearance was a manpower-munching, six-day-a-week grind. "One of the strangest sights in America," the New York press corps described the area's top employer. Sensationalism like that sold newspapers but that's about it. The banking collective that acquired the enterprise from its burned-out namesake had a profitable venture to maintain in an ever-changing world. Need a cushier job? Apply to Pasadena's watchmaker—or its coffin factory.

Junior executives like Nick accepted the long hours and other unsavory elements for the paycheck and the challenge. Light as silk, adaptable as glass, the farm's prize-winning feathers ensconced Cawston as a household name in its niche, on par with Dove soap and Ford cars. Around town, it was an economic powerhouse, and a tourist destination to boot.

It took dedication and camaraderie to mesh all the parts. Nick reminded everyone of this, including himself, as he wiped at dye stains on his trousers and battled pressure headaches before deadlines. Slavish hours and sleep deficits were routine. Despite the sacrifice, he thrived here, a feather man with a sunny future, even if he never pictured this as his life's vocation. At what some dubbed the most "glamorous" ostrich-couture production house around, you didn't punch the clock. It punched you. That's why he needed those midday outings through

Busch Gardens or around the Raymond Hotel: his accumulated stress had to be jettisoned someplace.

A Martian visiting this era might've wondered where feathers *didn't* show up. After all, they ornamented ladies hats, boas, muffs, plumes—both French and Duchesse—and stoles. They were peddled at big-city boutiques and in mail-order catalogs. Durable and chic, they made dressing stylishly easy. The upper crust considered them musts. The wives of kings and concubines of kingpins wrapped their powdered necks and fancy hairdos in the satiny material. High-paid Broadway actresses and burlesque dancers alike performed in the ticklish fluff. Ditto for women posing for racy, soft-light portraits.

The feather industrial complex was savvy, ensuring its bird-wear wasn't confined to the privileged. Housewives on gas-lamp blocks from Boston to San Diego owned feathers. Ponytailed girls implored Santa for smaller versions. Souvenir collectors were never forgotten, either, what with ostrich tchotchke replicated on silver, wood, and paper.

Cawston itself inscribed its name and its notable ostriches everywhere thinkable: on pocketknives and letter openers, watch fobs and lockboxes, even calendars and measuring tapes. Barren mantelpiece? Try a painted hollow Cawston egg the dimension of a coconut.

Mass production by shearing *Struthio camelus* was genius. The inventory always grew back.

Nick was fresh out of the University of Southern California when the company hired him, and it didn't take management long to appreciate his intuitive smarts and natural charisma; that he was a keeper worthy of being groomed. Asked how he was faring getting into work, he often replied, "On the upside, you?" More than his contemporaries, the farm's marketing motto, which preached to "always advertise your distinctions," resonated with him. As Nick emphasized to tourists and reminded distributors, only select-male feathers made the cut, not the inferior stock "other manufacturers" hawked. Every sale also carried a money-back guarantee. Moreover, customers could buy with clean consciences, for Cawston policy forbade child labor, animal cruelty, or other shortcuts around its golden geese.

Recently promoted to co-assistant manager, Nick had a load on his shoulders, and could perspire a quart on hectic days. Rotating from station to station, troubleshooting mishaps, or attending to special orders, he sometimes hoofed miles before the sun peaked. Glossy brochures did little justice to how expansive the enterprise was.

Cawston was a minib city unto itself, a humming assembly line inside a warren of buildings. Specialization ruled. There was an egg-incubator house and fireproofed storehouse, dye room, and catalog-fulfillment department. On the periphery were a gift shop, rare bird aviary, and Japanese teahouse. Off-site were retail stores in downtown Los Angeles, New York, and Chicago, as well as a four-hundred-acre breeding farm in the eastern prairies of Riverside County. Visitors here to snap photos, watch a shearing session, pet tamer birds, or stroll were always impressed. The grounds were kept so tidy that you'd more likely see a dead ostrich's apparition than mounds of un-shoveled guano.

Nick, who rotated to every post, excelled most at the mechanical- and sales-brainstorming side of the job. Having the ostriches trust him as much as the wranglers only improved his cachet. Conversely, time in the dye house, where monochromatic colors came to rainbow life in a miasma of nauseous stink, was torture.

When the sixty-hours-a-week sacrifice turned his bones heavy, when he couldn't handle another production crisis or malcontent employee, he reminded himself his work was preparing him for his real future: popularizing solar energy.

It was the industrious Aubrey Eneas, an English-born inventor/gadget-noodler, who tapped Cawston, of all places, to demonstrate the planet's first commercial solar-powered motor. The engine he installed debuted to fanfare in 1901. From then on, it was running, generating energy that helped feed, water, and house Cawston's assets with near-magical dependability.

Nick, a history buff, was hooked once he learned that the ancient Chinese and Romans inspired Eneas's creation. Its predominant feature was an immense, ribbed dish that resembled a metal umbrella turned inside out. Lining it were eighteen hundred small, beveled mirrors that collected the sun's invisible heat with visible precision. Nick, in a letter to his mother in Indiana, described the red-hot beam condensed by the mirrors as "liquid fire being trapped."

It was the mirrors that were the linchpins, for they channeled heat from the sunrays into a large boiler containing a thousand gallons of water in a deep-water well. After the subterranean fluid reached a boil, the steam it generated powered an engine capable of pumping fourteen hundred gallons of water—per minute.

Still, Eneas's revolutionary technology didn't run on gee-whizzes. It required a decent understanding of astronomy as the Earth's star arced through the sky ninety-three million miles away. To adjust the dish to capture optimal sunbeams, the Englishman borrowed a solution from astronomers. Some of them yoked their space telescopes on "equatorial mountings," which swiveled on greased, ball-bearing tracks producing relatively easy movement. If it was good enough for scientists exploring the Milky Way, including some on Pasadena's mountaintop, it was good enough for a quill factory.

Nick, awestruck whenever Eneas dropped by, oversaw his solar machine on a daily basis. Unlike Eneas, he was a non-technical type who marshaled his deductive skills whenever there were cables to untangle or boiler valves to replace.

One midmorning, he squatted on his haunches, sprinkling dirt from his hand after he angled the dish. The same daydream was hijacking him again: gleaming solar mirrors on roofs electrifying *all* of Pasadena. Unbeknownst to him, Waldo was sneaking up from behind with a message he planned to deliver with comical fright. He got the sun behind him, and then flapped his arms so the outline resembled a hawk swooping down. Noticing it, Nick jolted out of his trance, covering his head from any looming talons.

He sprang up when he saw it was Waldo, knocking the clipboard out of his hand. "You better store an extra pair of pants here when I jump out at *you* because you're going to wet yourself in fright."

"I'll give that some consideration," Waldo said with a snicker. "I popped over to tell you that I'm unable to make it today. I've got a roof-full of drying feathers to oversee."

"Product in, product out," said a recovered Nick. "I suppose I'm going solo."

⸎⸎⸎

NICK AND MRS. GROVER Cleveland, together again, had their heads lost in different galaxies. Nick's was tilted forty-five degrees, watching a man in overalls impersonate a lunch-pail Tarzan. Up seven stories, the carpenter was swinging by a waist-cinched rope to zip around and hammer nails into forms for the bridge's next soaring arch, as if there was nothing to it.

Mrs. Cleveland, flame-red lips curled in a pout, had her attention pointed downward. She was nibbling baby lizards and tasty pebbles after earlier gamboling around Cawston's yard on this bone-dry October day. As Nick must've lectured a thousand tourists, it was a wive's tale ostriches stuck their heads in the sand when frightened. They did it to forage.

The sun's position alerted Nick they should head back. "Whatever you're chewing will be here next week," he told Mrs. C, spinning her away from the structure increasingly looming over the canyon's boulders and trees. He pushed her into a trot.

Unlike their previous excursion, it wasn't a competitive Model T or Reginald's exuberance injecting distraction this time. It was something weightier yet also lighter: the giggling of ten white-shirted kids sitting cross-legged in a horseshoe pattern on one of Busch Garden's manicured hummocks—kids amazed to watch Nick bop by on his ostrich before the trail back to Cawston dipped into the woodlands. Hearing the group laughter behind him, Nick halted Mrs. C, wheeling around to pinpoint the source.

The youngsters hailed from local hospitals, sanitariums, and Mrs. Bang's boardinghouse, each with a spirit-pummeling diagnosis that shackled them mostly inside. Tumors, missing appendages, swampy lungs, hemophilia, encephalitis, bone decay, leukemia: that was their childhood. One little girl required an attendant just to stay upright.

The thickset nurse in charge wished the rider either gave them a cheery wave or never materialized at all, for it seemed cruel to tease those sweet, shrunken faces with such a bewitching sight when all they knew were unfair surprises. Like dying before adulthood. "Don't be sad, sweeties," the nurse told them. "How about we sing a song? Those not well enough, clap."

Clap? That's all they have? Nick, hoisting himself up off Mrs. C's back by grabbing a tree branch, got a notion. A moment later, he burst out of the tree line seated *backward* on his ostrich, waving his beanie carnival-barker style. *Paw-rump.* "Greetings, ladies and gentlemen," he called out.

"Ready for your entertainment?" Back he came for another pass, this time reclined sideways on his mount like she were a mobile chaise lounge.

In his last run, Nick attempted an untried stunt, shifting his butt from the bird's withers to over its left wing. Mistake. Fabulous as slapstick, it left Mrs. C unbalanced and touchy. In reaction, she cut a sharp right off the path in front of their audience, bee-lining for protective shade. Her twitchy motion caused Nick to lose his grip and eat it, tumbling and rolling to a standstill on Busch Gardens' gravel. *Awk-awwwwwwwww,* Mrs. C screeched when a hobbling Nick retrieved her.

The audience was in hysterics as Nick bowed. Some of the kids even tried imitating his clumsy fall. They mistook his crash for a theatrical finale, and why spoil that? "Ahem, my good lady, where are your manners?" Nick said, hambone. "You've neglected to curtsy for our crowd?" Now pecking at an acorn, she disregarded him. The rolling chortles continued as Nick cast his eyes upward in faux pique.

And, when he did, he noticed a distressing presence: a billowing mushroom cloud of smoke from an apparent brushfire north of where they were. Layered in gray and black, the plume coiled up a thousand feet. Nick sniffed the air, smelling a woodsy char hinting that hundreds of trees were aflame. He bowed again, spun Mrs. C around, and remounted. He had no plan, only a compulsion to know if what he was eyeballing might rampage east into Pasadena as a city killer.

"Everybody up, nice and calm," the nurse told her charges once she, too, understood a potential disaster was at hand. "We can sing inside Mrs. Bang's."

❦ ❦ ❦

HE KNOTTED A GREEN bandana around his mouth and dug his boots into the crumbly hill on his town's side of the upper Arroyo. From his belt loop, Nick unhitched the retractable mariner's telescope he'd purchased at Vroman's Bookstore to zoom in on bridge construction. Squinting, he peeked through the brass eyepiece, hoping for optical clarity but only feeling exasperation. An impenetrable wall of smoke and buzzing embers that looked like a million drunken bees was all he could discern. He spent oodles of time as a child around here, so at least he had a mental map to access.

On the canyon floor below, he knew, were the flatlands and farmland of unincorporated Linda Vista, where the Sierra Madre mountain range tapered away into the Crescenta Valley. Here, the present-day—ice delivery, telephones lines, legal services, electricity—was subservient to the agrarian past of citrus belts and sleepy, red-tile ranchos there; farmers, working their plots in a checkerboard layout, harvested and exported lemons, blood oranges, tomatoes, grapefruit, tangerines, mandarin apricots, and twenty other cash crops. Question was: would these flames render them all scorched history?

To truly know meant edging closer; meant being a risk-taker isolated with an agitated ostrich. The hot Santa Ana winds swirling were already making Mrs. C stomp her hooves, and Nick could empathize. The gusts, as always, carried an ominous energy of Old Testament consequences. When they jostled the oak branches around him with that shushing sound, the hair on his forearms bristled.

This is too important to miss. After a pat and a treat to reassure Mrs. C, he remounted her and rode down the trail toward the ashy canyon. A mile or so away was Devil's Gate Dam Park, where local ghost stories flourished, and a man was recently blown into a tree testing an experimental motorcar. No one else was around.

They stopped at the trestle bridge that Myron Hunt, Pasadena's architectural prodigy, designed to deliver passage from one part of the valley to the other. Few traversed it much anymore; in a couple years, no doubt, it'd be scrap wood from the bygone horse-and-buggy era. Crossing the Arroyo by foot or hoof anymore was going the way of the porkpie hat.

But the bridge's end post would come in handy tying off Nick's jittery bird. "No wandering away," he said, tossing her an orange. "I'll be back before you digest that."

He jogged along a dirt road that took him to the nape of the fire-gnarled hills. Along the way, he coughed and tamped his watery eyes with his bandana. It wasn't until a prolonged Santa Ana gust blew away a lower veil of smoke that the moonscape destruction revealed itself. Up on the summit, orange tongues of flame spiked thirty feet into the sunless murk.

This was bad. Uncontained, the brushfire could plow west into La Crescenta, the backside of sleepy Glendale, or worse: it could leapfrog east, taking out Pasadena's exclusive Prospect Park neighborhood. Nick reminded himself not to stand there, ogling destruction; not to stand there listening to chaparral sizzle. But that's what he was doing when a mighty oak snapped mid-trunk and log-sledded downward toward a trailhead. He assumed it'd slide to a stop a safe distance from him. He was wrong. It slammed into a boulder twenty yards away.

When nothing more barreled down, he sidestepped up the blackened slope to investigate the damage. Above him, small battalions of separately organized men, perhaps a hundred total, swung picks, shovels, and hoes trenching firebreaks. Some wore Pasadena Fire Department uniforms; others were civilian volunteers. The rest were Mexican laborers troweling away at unburned vegetation, barely acknowledged. Even so, he could see the motley firefighters were making good progress. He was preparing to turn back just as an angry voice hollered upslope: "You little cretins should be ashamed of yourselves. *Go!*"

On the other end of Nick's telescope was a bearded fire captain gesturing at a cluster of laughing, prepubescent boys skipping away. The captain shook his fist at them, and then climbed back toward his men. Nick adjusted his lens, trying to fathom what the boys did, and then came upon one of the ghastliest visions ever.

The heap of dead and dying jackrabbits and rattlesnakes was about two feet high and three wide. The forest animals must've been loping and slithering away in panic as the wildfires torched their homes when the hooligans ambushed them with clubs and sticks for their sadistic gratification.

"Their mothers should make them sleep next to live snake holes for that," said a woman who Nick didn't see come over, riveted as he was by the scaly, furry death mound.

He lowered the eyepiece to view a skinny woman about his age—a curious gal with a masculine jaw, warm eyes, and wavy, light-brown hair.

"You part of the crew?" she asked with a spunky voice.

Nick tugged down his bandana. "Nope. Just came to size up how far this thing was spreading."

"A voyeur? I wish someone was watching my property when it kicked up."

"And why's that?" Nick said, hacking twice.

She pointed toward acreage still domed in grayish-charcoal smoke. "The fire flattened one of our greenhouses this morning before any help arrived. We lost half our picked crops."

"My sympathies. Here's hoping you can rebuild. I'm Nick, by the way. Nick Chance."

"Pleased to meet cha. Name's Hattie Bergstron." They shook hands, Hattie with a wiry grip. "I have to rebuild. A girl has gotta earn her keep."

When Hattie doubled over to cough herself, Nick peered again through his telescope at the animal corpses. He regretted it, for he saw a baby jackrabbit trying to wiggle loose before a diamondback on its last gasp bit him. Nick collapsed his scope after that.

"Did you say Bergstron? Wasn't there an article about you recently?"

"Yeah, if you call that yellow journalism an article. Just because we run a vegetarian colony here that nobody bothers to understand, those reporters labeled us a coven. Accused us of lesbianism, witchcraft. We're none of those things. We're pioneers."

"I'm not judging you," Nick said, thick-tongued. "I thought your name sounded familiar."

"We live simply, grow food to sell. We still have our fun, though." She winked.

Up behind Hattie walked a tall, waifish woman whom Hattie introduced as her friend Maude. A bandage covered part of a pink burn mark on her hand.

"Hopefully, they'll have this doused by nightfall," Nick said to reorient the subject. "Anybody else lose any property?"

"They sure did," Hattie said. "Some of the richest people anywhere."

Nick was stumped. The only wealthy, hillside property owners he knew lived on Pasadena's eastern banks near the bridge, not these tree-packed lands.

"You ever hear of Henry Huntington?"

"The railroad baron? Who hasn't?"

"He owns something in the order of three thousand acres. Another fat cat just bought in, too. He's planning to build a mansion, then a public park to outdo Busch Gardens."

"Only a fool would attempt that. No replicating Eden."

"Call me a socialist, but I'm leery of millionaires buying up local nature to feed their vanity. What about the rest of us?"

Nick saw Hattie's animated face starting to pinch. "Say, what do you grow? Specifically?"

"Nuts, heirloom tomatoes, radishes—anything without a mother. We don't bother with citrus. There's too much competition, and too little water with so much pumping going on. Can I interest you in any singed walnuts?"

"Tell you what. We meet again I'll give you my business. I better skedaddle now, though. I got a vexed ostrich waiting for me. Best wishes rebuilding."

"An ostrich?" Hattie said with a tired smile. "I hear they're peculiar."

"They are."

Twelve minutes later in that smoky air whooshing around the valley, Nick found Mrs. C bucking against her rope, and with good cause. Not far away, Myron Hunt's Linda Vista Bridge was smoldering. They took the long way home to Cawston.

‡‡‡

FLEET BURDETT WAS THE most entertaining jokester Nick could've ever befriended. Having attended grade school, Pasadena High School, and USC together, where they studied and caroused in equal measure, they were closer than Nick was with RG and Waldo, however fond he was of those work goofballs.

Fleet, with his pale eyes, maize-colored hair, and self-proclaimed "Viking blood," was an original: a science nerd with a cutup personality. Now a second-year student at the USC College of Medicine, he also was loyal as a Bassett Hound, a friend for all occasions. He was there through Nick's darkest nights and brightest successes. Just think twice before inviting him to a public funeral.

Pasadenans had flocked to a high-beamed Unitarian church on Marengo Avenue to honor the laudatory life of builder John Drake Mercereau. He had died, just shy of his fiftieth birthday, with another man in a horrific motorcar accident two weeks earlier, when his vehicle somersaulted two hundred feet off a ridge near a dam his company was erecting north of Los Angeles.

Nick, though never meeting the man, was here paying his respects, for it was Mercereau's firm assembling the bridge he considered his hometown's legacy achievement. He cajoled Fleet to attend the Saturday service with him in the misguided assumption he'd button his politically cynical lips in the high-ceilinged house of the Lord.

"He's in the hereafter now," Fleet said in a loud whisper near the memorial's end. "You think Mercereau cares two cents that people know wires were pulled to land him the job?"

Nick elbowed him. "Next time you're at school, find out if there's elixir for diarrhea of the mouth. You can't indict someone with no proof—at their own wake."

Fleet clucked his tongue. "Why do you take everything about the city so personally? I'm only asserting that the lapdog press should've mentioned the coincidence involving the dearly departed. Nick, the man submitted the winning low bid when someone with nearly his exact name, from the same home state, was a Pasadena commissioner (councilman) until a few years ago. *Harrumph*."

Up at the pulpit, a speaker described Mercereau as a "man of the highest integrity." Back in the pews, Nick would see his contrarian pal loading more ammunition.

"Indict him for sinking the Titanic and Pasadena's fly invasion, while you're at it," Nick said, muffling a smirk. "There's not a shred of evidence those two Mercereaus were related, let alone in cahoots. They spelled their names differently, so they weren't siblings, either."

"Well, I have a lab mate with loose lips, and his uncle is in the One Hundred Percenters club—you know, the bankers, the moneymen that work the levers, along with those gents at the Board of Trade. Let's just say they're certain rooting interests at city hall."

"*Shhhhh*," said a shiny, bald elder in the pew in front of them. "Be respectful or leave. A man died."

"Rumors aren't facts," Nick murmured a respectful pause later. "Let's examine your scruples. Aren't you bedding a dowager to assist with your tuition?"

"Yes," Fleet murmured back. "We have an arrangement. But that's hardly germane to a bridge some have duped themselves into believing was born from Immaculate Conception. You know what Mark Twain, your favorite writer, would say?"

"That I should sucker punch you and toss you in the Mississippi?"

"That politicians and diapers must be changed often, and for the same reason."

This time, the elder contorted around to give the two his stink eye.

J. D. Mercereau, as his eulogizers attested, was a man geared to self-reinvention. After migrating here from New York to invest in real estate, he promptly lost his savings in the 1886 land depression/scandal that nearly destroyed Pasadena, then only a dozen years old. To scrape by, he and his family tried reselling orange-tree seeds. When that failed, he grabbed a pencil, sketching engineering designs on wrapping paper.

That was the ticket. Small-bridge contracts flowered into work erecting piers at local beaches, then a breakwater, and then county assignments. The roadway over the Arroyo would've been Mercereau's crowning accomplishment.

The minister requested everyone stand to sing "Nearer My God to Thee." The way the sun poured through the stained glass made you think he was close, too. Nick and Fleet rose with the hundreds there, Fleet whispering, "Death is proving to be JD's champion public relations man, no?"

Nick failed to hear it. He was in the sudden orbit of a higher force.

Drinking her in from across the aisle, his head swapped some oxygen for helium. It was her eyes—luminous, hazel eyes that that weren't just dazzling but knowing. It was her wheat-colored hair and strong chin, the pixie eyeteeth, the ruby-shaped face. And it wasn't only her beauty that captivated him. It was a self-possessed aura that declared her a planet unto herself.

The vision in the belted, black taffeta dress wasn't from here; Nick, the get-around bachelor, knew that much. Nor, either, was she oblivious to his attraction. During the hymn's verse about the "sun, moon, and stars," the woman lowered her hymnal to locate the origin of the heat field directed on her. She found it in Nick's open-piehole expression, and then redirected her steely gaze forward.

Bowled over by her, he couldn't wait to clump down in the pew to start breathing normally again. So much for the composure of a guy able to chat up Rose princesses and other head-turners that made his buddies stammer monosyllabic come-ons. Once he was composed enough to point her out, irreverent Fleet didn't miss a beat.

"A funeral," he whispered, "is no place for lust. It's a place where we seek absolution from sin. Pasadena, confess."

FIREBALL PALS

ASK NICK *THE* PLACE for Saturday night culture, and he'd tell you it was Clune's Theater before you completed the question. The best grocery: Nash Brothers. Books and photography supplies? No contest: Vroman's. But if you were ravaged with hunger, and pork-and-parsnip stew served on starched linens at the Maryland Hotel didn't tantalize your palate, there was a single gastronomical name to memorize: Buford L. McKenzie, wizard of meat.

Buford, fifty-one, was blond and balding, with a gut that pooched out over a normal frame as if it were forever gestating a food baby. He'd been a long-suffering civilian chef at a humid naval base outside New Orleans until a year ago, when his bosses ordered him to stop serving his homemade recipes—lamb stews, gumbos—for Sunday suppers, which deckhands scarfed with gusto. Stick to the Navy menu, they insisted.

The soft-spoken dean of the mess hall refused. Seamen defending their country, in a world about to introduce battlefield chemical weapons, deserved better than bland fare, he argued. Superiors huffed that was insubordination and presented him an ultimatum: he could revert to protocol or resign. The chef quit the Big Easy in style, dumping a pot of jambalaya on the shoes of an imperious lieutenant commander.

Out in dry-air California, Buford toted with him a genius for marinades and a yearning to be his own master. With savings he concealed in an empty Crisco jar, he opened a food stand cobbled from pine and tar on

Fair Oaks Avenue. Damn Buford McKenzie. Cows must've felt honored appearing between his bread.

For Nick, Buford's Special, a mouthwatering, grilled-meat sandwich layered with sautéed onions, garlic-mayo, special herbs, and fixings, was as much addiction as sustenance. Throw in that vinegar-drizzled coleslaw and "Poor Man's Banana Pudding" and you knew why the noontime crowd could run twenty deep. Rival lunch counters would've gladly paid Buford's train fare back to the Bayou—the gator-infested part.

His exodus would've devastated Nick, one of the shack's best customers. On arduous days at Cawston, when he couldn't slip away for a ride, Nick would either snack on saltines and salami he brown-bagged from home or scrounge for leftovers from the farm's teahouse.

This Friday was different. Cecil Jenks, Cawston's mild-mannered general manager, insisted that Nick take the afternoon off and to skip his normal Saturday shift, too. He fretted his star underling was burning the candle toward exhaustion; the company couldn't afford to lose him ahead of the holiday rush for feathers. "You're not welcome here until Monday," Cecil said. "Go digest a full meal."

Nick intended to do that and then some with the eighteen cents jingling in his palm. At Buford's scuffed counter, he attempted a risky maneuver: he ordered *two* belly-busting plates: one to eat at a table behind the shack, the other to nosh in Busch Gardens enjoying bridge-workers' acrobatics.

Buford, the soft-spoken roly-poly, grinned hearing Nick's request. He then shoved nine cents back.

"What?" Nick asked. "You out of grease?"

"No," Buford said with a diluted Cajun twang. "I don't condone ambulatory dining."

Nick blinked. "You know there's food trucks on Colorado Street, right?"

"There's also venereal diseases, but you don't line up for them."

"Can't you make an exception, Buford? I see ostriches in my sleep. Catch me?"

"I can. And as much as I like you, soggy bread and cold meat ruin the soul of my sandwiches. What do you have then?"

"An appreciative patron?"

"No, you have mush."

Back and forth their good-natured spat went. As it dragged on, customers behind Nick started grumbling for him to hurry along; they could smell the aromatic smoke coiling from Buford's grill. "You're not the only one famished," a trench-digger bitched at Nick. Buford finally mopped his sweaty brow and proposed a compromise. Grudgingly, he'd bundle Nick's to-go sandwich in a white paper bag, provided Nick consumed it no later than two o'clock to ensure the meat's integrity.

Nick agreed and got busy, dispatching his first sandwich under a shaded table in three minutes flat. He took his time with the slaw and pudding.

These were working-class grounds: this stretch of Fair Oaks Avenue near Pasadena's border with tinier South Pasadena. Sure, it was no longer a barren patchwork of clapboard Victorians, brown dirt lots, and mom-and-pop stores. But it was a world away from cosmopolitan downtown Pasadena. Up there, the button-down dealmakers and motivated civic groups, the awning-fronted stores and Saturday night crowds telegraphed unstoppable ambition.

Nick, ready for lunch-part-two, brushed the crumbs off his dye-blotched trousers and strolled north on the new, concrete sidewalk. From here it was a fifteen-minute walk to Busch Gardens, and not once did he fear being stalked by a criminal. But he was—by a thief whose nose smelled opportunities in parts-per-million.

The malnourished crook survived by begging for handouts or scavenging in restaurant alleyways. Based on his distended ribcage, his nutritional intake was a starvation diet. His head was poking around inside Buford's side trashcan when the scent of Nick's juicy, to-go sandwich wafted his way. That changed that: he forgot all about digging out day-old biscuits and gravy and set his sights on a snatch-and-run feast.

The thief tailed Nick for a block, plotting his timing. He needed to grab the bag just as his mark's hand dropped to its nadir in the stride. The stakes were high. If the wrong person apprehended him, he might not be long for Pasadena, or anywhere.

The dog, whose fur was a shade lighter than caramel, had this shtick humming today. His black muzzle snatched the bag out of Nick's oblivious hand with one yank, and his paws took it from there. He was twenty yards away before Nick saw the leaking, white bag in the dog's teeth. Nick didn't deliberate a moment before giving chase. He earned that second sandwich. There was ostrich stink in his bloodstream to prove it.

He's nimble, but he's no Mrs. C, Nick thought after ten steps. The mutt ran with a jackrabbit lope, which disadvantaged Nick in black, clodhopper work boots. So he pumped his arms vigorously, dashing south on Fair Oaks toward the ornate Raymond Hotel. Had he looked back, he figured he would've seen Buford's customers slapping their knees at the spontaneous pursuit, and probably cheering for the sandwich bandit.

Farther down the block were the enormous, open doors of a yellow-brick, Pacific Electric railcar maintenance "barn," which was set back twenty-five yards from a Red Car stop. If the dog were shrewd, Nick thought, he'd haul butt inside, cut through a service rack, and race out the other side to the open field. The meat-sniffing hoodlum adopted that very tactic, sprinting toward the repair shop's entrance en route to his hunger-quashing salvation.

But then he pulled a fast one. He skidded to a stop on his overgrown nails in front of the facility. Was it the pungent reek of oil that gave him reservations, the noisy machines? It couldn't have been moral etiquette. *I'm getting my sandwich, so help me.* That seemed more probable after the animal unexpectedly released the slobbery bag from his jaws. From the rail-barn's concrete apron, he now stared into the depths of the building, floppy ears pointed up, furry brow wrinkled.

No human, Nick or otherwise, could appreciate what his instinct did.

Inside there, a boxy transformer next to a gasoline drum was hissing. From it, a shower of white sparks began arcing like a Roman candle toward the open wood rafters. Nick's outstretched hands almost reached the bag holding his Buford's Special when a grease monkey inside the barn yelled: "I've tried—I can't stop it! *Run.*"

A hard shaking that rattled the shop floor spread to an interior wall holding tools on a pegboard and a time clock. The noise that followed was more portentous: the shrill whistle of an overheating machine and the snap of metal rivets popping.

Kabuuuush!

The malfunctioning transformer exploded with the ferocity of an artillery burst. A hellish, vermillion fireball punched a gaping hole through the open, V-shaped roof. Flames crackled inside. Angry boils of black smoke spit out from the barn's doors halfway across Fair Oaks Avenue.

Rather than incinerating Nick and the opportunistic hound where they were, the shock wave, for some inexplicable reason, launched them skyward, up possibly ten feet. Rocked by the blast, Nick's organs felt whipped inside out, as if inverted by the violent pressure changes. How he even was conscious to register that spearing, dagger-esque pain, never mind the furnace-hot temperature up there, wasn't even the most bizarre aspect, either.

During the seconds he was airborne, time became a trickster that slowed everything to a molasses drip. Fragmented chunks of brick, steel, rubber, and wood fluttered and rotated lazily past his eyes. Another debris field floated next, presenting wires and hinges as well as a severed human arm and most of that uneaten second sandwich. Also in Nick's sightline was the dog whose legs were pedaling cartoonishly, like he was trying to outrun what would assuredly be a fatal landing.

Nick's last two thoughts, before his own presumed demise, were more mundane than metaphysical: why did death sting so fucking badly, and; why was the cloud of sparkly amethyst enveloping him going to be the final thing his mind recorded?

◆◆◆

HE CAME TO FLAT on the sidewalk, gazing into the faces of bickering strangers. Over him, a man and a woman were quarreling in hushed voices about what hospital he needed to be rushed to: the one that admitted only whites, or the color-blind one specializing in emergencies?

The post-blast pandemonium, where folks were running every which way to extinguish the oily fire and check for the dead, danced on the edge of his awareness.

Nick passed out again, and when he cracked his eyes his head was propped up on somebody's itchy needlepoint purse. Best he could tell from his fuzzy inventory, he'd retained all four limbs. But the back of his skull ached, probably from thumping into the ground, and a sprained right wrist throbbed in rhythm with his pulse.

He remembered nothing of his airborne journey. Not the excruciating pain or leg-pedaling dog, not the detached arm or the purple fog consuming him before going lights out. Nothing. Even so, this wasn't how a well-earned lunch was supposed to unfold.

"Hello, kiddo. Good to have you back among the living," said a bushy-browed man in a merchant's apron bending down at his side. The shopkeeper was the one arguing before with the lady about which hospital should treat him.

Nick, at that moment, didn't know good fortune from duck soup. "How long," he asked groggily, "was I out?"

"Can't tell ya. I ran over after the street shook something hellacious, and here you were."

Nick couldn't stay roused in that brume of smoke and clatter of footfalls. His world spun, and he slipped out of it with the Good Samaritan watching over him. When he awoke an indeterminate time later, Buford was crouched where the merchant was, inspecting Nick's puffy wrist.

Nick squirmed seeing him. "What gives? I can't stay awake. It's surreal."

"What gives is that the Pacific Electric building is no more," Buford said. "Help's coming."

The former Navy chef and his avid patron weren't far from where people were lobbing pails of water at an inferno reducing the bricks-and-mortar structure into a roofless shell of slag and debris. Inside were the remains of railway mechanic Joey Grimble. The fireball he was unable to escape, the fireball ignited by that faulty transformer, lopped off his arm and mutilated the rest of him. The flames were too intense for anybody to venture in to ascertain if there were other victims.

The last thing Nick recalled was observing the shower of white sparks inside the darkened building. But he sensed how close he came to buying it, and a tear leaked and his face bunched. "Buford," he said, sniffling. "My head, it's blank. Are other people hurt?"

Buford stroked Nick's hair, which still had its cowlick, and wiped a blob of oil from Nick's cheek. "Don't fret about that. Stay here."

Nick exhaled hard, trying to gather himself. "What choice do I have?"

"Feisty. Good sign." Buford ran toward his shack in his filthy smock.

Lying there, Nick tried punching through his brain fog by listening to the commotion: the fire department bell clanging in the distance, the tinny sound of buckets being filled by a measly hose. Harsh smoke and the whiff of flesh swirled.

Buford returned shortly, bandaging ice to Nick's wrist with a soapy dishrag. "*Ouch*," Nick said. "Busted?"

Buford shook his head. "Nope. Seen worse after shore-leave brawls."

Nick flexed his legs in trial movement. Though his body was rag-dolled by the explosion, he wanted out of the turmoil. It wasn't like he was seeing stars. "Help me up," he said. "I'm okay. Just sore."

Buford scowled disapprovingly. "Don't be proud. How 'bout if I tilt you up until you get your bearings."

Nick agreed, so Buford knee-crawled behind him and curled his arms under Nick's armpits, folding him into a sitting position with his legs outstretched. Nick smelled marinade on his helper's palms.

"In your prayers tonight," Buford said, "say one for that cur that purloined your lunch."

Nick swiveled his head side to side to loosen it up; the gyration made him twinge. "I forgot all about that scalawag, he said. "Why waste a breath on him?"

"Because without him," Buford said, his palm supporting Nick's back, "they might be shoveling pieces of you into a wheelbarrow."

Nick yanked down on his earlobes, checking his hearing, and then he tested his jaw. "Without him? He got me into this. He must be dead, anyway."

"Not exactly," Buford said. He pointed to the side, where two people were caressing the wounded animal's head. He lay on his side, eyes closed. "Your wrist any better?"

"Peachy. What do you mean he saved me? Providence did."

"Not if you ask the trench-digger behind you in line earlier. He claimed watching that varmint drag you away from the building not ten seconds before the second boom hit. It knocked me into my grill."

"Sure he did," Nick said, fantasizing about getting into bed. A brutal headache was starting.

"I'm only telling you what I heard," said Buford, standing up. "Someone's fixin' to take you to the hospital. I'll circle back. Gotta make sure my livelihood isn't on fire."

"Go," Nick said. "I'm intact."

"Next time, no double-orders."

Nick wasn't ready for catastrophe humor yet. And he doubted what the trench-digger said about the supposedly heroic dog. In the murky aftermath, he only trusted his eyes, and he twisted around on his butt in the direction of the former rail-barn. The flames bounding out of the demolished roof and charred sides were making him sweat.

The *ding-ding-ding* of an arriving trolley on Fair Oaks prompted folks to turn their heads, surprised to see it. Four-alarm disaster or not, the northbound Red Car had a schedule to maintain. Its next stop was Green Street, Nick's home street. When its bell clanged again, it reminded him of a buoy in pea-soup fog.

The only passenger to disembark was a rangy man with mutton-chop sideburns and a notebook. He began machine-gunning questions to any passerby who stopped to listen. "You here when this blew? Know about casualties?"

Nobody answered the reporter. A moment later, a florid man, whose belly strained against his uniform, hopped off a spit-shine Seagrave fire engine and blocked him. "And you are?" asked Fire Chief Dewey Morgantheau, whom gossips long compared to Pasadena's Ulysses S. Grant in manner, girth, and predilection for alcohol.

"Frank Yochum, Pasadena Star. I heard the eruption a mile away, Chief. What do we know?"

"*We*? Tell you what, Mr. Yochum. You let us execute our job, and I'll refrain from flinging you and your premature questions into the gutter."

"I'll stand where I want," the scribe said, shaking his notepad. "I'm the public's eyes and ears."

"Right now, you're being their jackass. Remove yourself until we douse this."

Nick felt his mood shift hearing the confrontation. He wasn't going to any hospital for bumps and bruises. He was going home on that Red Car before it departed. Up on his tingly feet he went.

He walked over to the larcenous dog, why he wasn't certain. A twenty-ish pickle-cart salesman was the only one still kneeling by him. The mutt remained on his side, panting, though his eyes were now open. His observable injuries were worse than Nick's: a laceration over an ear, a gash on a hind leg, and an oblong scorch mark on his black-splotched tail.

Nick tapped the pickle man on the shoulder. "Mind if I step in? I'll ferry him to a doctor."

The food vendor with a large birthmark on one cheek looked up in confusion. "Mister, weren't you conked out fifteen minutes ago? You should be on a stretcher."

"Nah, I got my wits," Nick said. "The best thing is not to dawdle with the little guy. Do me a favor and lift him up?"

Against his better judgment, the street animal man went along. When he deposited the skinny, thirty-pound stray into Nick's arms, the dog whimpered and Nick's bad wrist javelined pain into his shoulder.

The Red Car conductor, a graying man in vest and straw hat, dinged the final bell, eager to separate his trolley from this fiery, if required, stop. Nick hurried over, still unsteady, walking around the fire department ladders and hoses to board it. He sat in the front with the dog sideways in his arms, feeling as brittle as glass. There were only four other people onboard.

⊕⊕⊕

NICK HURT ALL OVER: head, wrist, belly, leg, even a right buttock, where there was a magenta-colored bruise shaped like Idaho. It was seven at night, roughly six hours since he and the guest asleep on a blanket in the corner straggled into the courtyard of Bungalow Heaven West. When Nick rapped on Fleet's door across the walkway, Fleet set down his textbook describing the nuances of the human liver and led him to bed.

His examination confirmed Nick's assessment that hospitalization was unnecessary. How his best friend was capable of taking the Red Car and walking from the depot to here, carrying that load in his arms, was an ode to adrenaline; well, adrenaline and shock.

During Nick's post-concussion siesta, Fleet dug into his doctor-to-be medical bag to triage him. He splinted Nick's wrist, disinfected a forearm abrasion, and probed for signs of internal hemorrhaging, of which there were none.

Still, Nick awoke in pain, and Fleet handed him three Bayer aspirin and a finger of "strictly therapeutic" Irish whiskey. The chunk of ice Fleet put in one of Nick's clean socks rested on his neck.

"How's the criminal doing?" Nick asked, once he could lean up in bed. He scanned over at the dog, whose singed tail was gauzed and lacerations dabbed with hydrogen peroxide. Fleet also converted Nick's favorite cereal bowl into his guest's water dish.

"Like you: battered pretty good, but nothing broken. I patched him up. You've sure been tempting fate lately"

"What can I say? I crave excitement."

52

"And I'd like you in one piece. Do you remember anything before being knocked on your keister?"

Nick tilted his head back, which made him dizzy, so he tilted it back. "Only bits and pieces. Mainly chasing that thing after it snagged my sandwich, and then waking up in the center of bedlam."

"While I was checking the pooch, by the way, I found a scrub oak leaf in his paws."

"That's nice. Can you stop talking so loudly, or at all? My head!"

"Sorry. Aren't you intrigued to hear my brilliant deduction?" Fleet stretched his arms; he'd been here for hours, mostly in Nick's hardback desk chair.

"Not really."

"Too bad. Your visitor is a canyon dweller. He's got hillside musk all over him. He must forage in town to steal food from suckers like you."

"Gosh, that is brilliant," said Nick. "What's next? You deduce fleas?"

"Funny—for you. I'm assuming you don't recall what you babbled when I got you to bed and asked you the story about the dog. You mumbled something about someone seeing him drag you away from peril."

"Oh yeah. I did forget that," Nick said, kneading his temples. "I don't believe it, though. I merely felt sorry for the thing."

Fleet cocked a patchy eyebrow. "Then let me introduce you to the evidence. Lean up."

Nick wanted to say no thanks, but Fleet had a persistent intellect to go with his inappropriate mouth. "Okeydoke. Make it snappy." He bent forward with a grunt, and Fleet wiggled two fingers under Nick's grimy, ash-streaked collar. They touched skin. "Feel that?"

"Unfortunately. That's my best work shirt."

Fleet helped settle Nick back against his headboard. "Those two holes, old man, are from teeth, or rather, canine incisors. His. I checked. I believe he did rescue you, unless you have an alternative explanation for the teeth marks. That animal executed something superhuman. Question is what are you going to do?"

Fleet got up and walked to Nick's stove, setting the teakettle to boil. His dark-wood bungalow was identical to Nick's. They were newly built, chockablock with Craftsmen amenities, including a water closet, a leaded-glass window, a pantry, a closet, and built-in shelves.

"I don't know," Nick said. "I wanted to murder him before. But I guess I owe him. What kind of creep would I be if I booted him, especially hearing stories about strays disappearing off the streets?"

Fleet set out two tea mugs. "I heard about that, too. It's repulsive. I hope it's not some maniac on the loose. Then again, our landlord might chloroform *you* if he discovers you're violating the lease by keeping a pet here. He spent ample money on this place."

Nick sank into his comfy bed. "True, though he doesn't have a key, does he? And he hasn't swung by for an inspection yet. I'll give it a whirl for a few weeks. How much damage can a scrawny canyon dog instigate?"

After tea, Fleet returned to his bungalow and liver diagrams. Nick followed the dog into sleep-land.

◈◈◈

THE NEXT DAY WAS Sunday, and Nick and the boxer-Labrador mix he decided to call Royo, on account of his past home in the Arroyo Seco, were on the mend. His right wrist only hurt when he moved it, which made him glad he was a southpaw and had more aspirin.

It was his stomach requiring attention, since he'd eaten little after his infamous to-go sandwich went up in flames. He needed to go to the market to restock, because his accidental companion had already devoured the meager rations Nick had around: raw carrots, apple slices, sugar cookies.

Nick returned home from Nash Brothers with two bags of groceries— and the realization that underfed Royo was making up for missed meals. In the ninety minutes he was away, the scavenger ransacked the bungalow. He snagged a near-empty box of Nabisco crackers that Nick kept on his pantry's bottom shelf as well as the beef jerky he forgot about in a coat jacket. He teethed the legs of Nick's varnished dresser, as clear by the wood chips on the floor, and capped off his impromptu buffet by munching part of a small ostrich quill he plucked from Nick's desk.

Nick was miffed. Royo was alert.

He walked over toward the dog, who Nick could tell had jumped on his neatly made, pine bed while he was shopping and returned to his blanket before he'd comeback. "You and me, boy," he said, crouching down to wag a finger in the dog's taupe and black face, "need to agree on who runs the show around here, if I decide to keep you. Catch me?"

Royo listened to Nick's ground rules, cocking his square head and perking his triangular ears. Nick took that as acceptance, and then checked the abrasions that Fleet slathered in ointment. They didn't appear inflamed, so Nick tousled Royo's mangy fur. When Nick did that, however, the dog bared his teeth and growled.

"Watch it," he said. "And display a little gratitude. You can trust me."

Nick tried a different approach, letting Royo sniff his hands before he cupped the mutt's chin in them and scratched his whiskers. This time, Royo didn't snarl. His brown, saucer eyes stared penetratingly into Nick's. Something must've clicked.

The dog angled his squiggly-browed forehead down, as if it were a friendship invitation, and Nick went with his instinct, which had advanced him this far in life. They touched foreheads. While it hurt his ginger neck, the skin-to-fur contact brought an overwhelming sensation of familiarity, of brotherhood.

Nick retracted his head, stunned. And Royo mouthed his first unbidden word: *Roooh.*

"Was that hello? I don't speak bowwow."

Ruuuuus.

"If you're as industrious as you are ravenous, you'll find a way to communicate. Just refrain from any further pillaging. I need this lease."

Nick unpacked his groceries and then flopped facedown on his bed. He shook out of a light nap thirty minutes later, feeling Royo's sandpapery tongue giving his cheeks an introductory lick. From then on, Royo abandoned his corner blanket, commandeering the wall side of Nick's bed as his.

Coverage of the rail-barn explosion in the papers reinforced Nick's gratitude to be alive. Lower down in the stories, after references to the dead railcar mechanic and passerby who tried extinguishing the fire, was a mention of an "injured pedestrian and dog" who disappeared before the ambulance arrived for them. Nick was relieved to go unnamed, knowing Cawston's new bosses were sensitive about unsanctioned publicity.

Later that day, before turning in, Nick grabbed his catgut-strung acoustic guitar to see if his recovering wrist could bend. He strummed a few chords from an Al Jolson song, and Royo, un-spurred, hopped down from the bed. "A music enthusiast," Nick said to him. "Shame you don't play snare drum."

Royo padded over to the corner facing him, listening. Nick switched from Jolson to one of his meandering originals, "Pasadena Sun," and could hardly fathom it when Royo performed his own original act. Pressing his mane against the wall, the dog managed to rise up on his hind legs and, unbelievably, walked eight tottering steps. *Eight.* As he did, his dark, rubbery lips upturned in a way you'd associate with a smirking teenager. Nick was so flabbergasted he stopped playing, which seemed to spur Royo to drop down onto all four legs. Could he have been trained at the circus, and escaped the Big Top for a vagabond life? "That was astonishing," Nick said. "You can move upright."

Royo, for the first time, next approached him, wagging his bandaged tail with that leer still on his lips. He wanted his butt rubbed and maneuvered himself to be scratched. Nick obliged, thinking he should immediately alert his friend about the trick he just witnessed. Then he recalled something Fleet remarked earlier: "If that runt could tug someone more than five times his weight to safety, other mysteries must reside in him."

THE GIFT SHOP

Six weeks later, Nick—for the price of a greasy sandwich and that fireball—had in his new roommate both a plaything and uncanny attendant.

Despite his itinerant past, Royo had no trouble adapting to being a domesticated dog in a city that prided itself on its benevolent treatment of animals. He learned to shake hands with his paws and play dead on the first try. He'd spring high to catch bouncing tennis balls and entertained himself by staring in the mirror. To Nick's dismay, he continued gnawing furniture, but how could he stay cross when Royo revealed his inner spirit at Busch Gardens by chasing swans and hurtling ceramic elves?

Yet, he was more than a rascal, one that knew not to crap in the bungalow when Nick cooped him up during the day. He was a periodic butler. After a stressful sixteen-hour shift from which Nick was ready to keel over, he fetched Nick's starchy nightshirt from underneath his pillow. When Nick returned home with a wrenched back from repairing Cawston's solar-powered water pump, Royo was on the case. He negotiated his snout into the low glass cabinet storing the minty camphor rub and woofed.

And that was for starters, because Royo had some Saint Anthony, finder of lost objects, in his frisky soul. Misplaced keys, a missing boot, a mislaid gasket: Nick simply cursed frustration about their unknown whereabouts and Royo would commence his search, poking his head underneath heavy objects, behind doors, or wherever need be to locate the vanished items. To indicate he found them, he splayed on his belly and swished his tail, metronome-esque.

"I should take you to the old Devil's Gate gold mine," Nick said after recovering a pen. "You find a vein and it's goodbye ostriches."

His colleagues recognized there was something unique about the dog whenever Nick brought him to the farm as his tagalong. The loud, yummy gurgling Royo emoted rolling on his back in dry grass was a Victrola of ecstasy; his perceptive head tilt observing the ostriches' strange mating rituals and pack-trotting suggested data collection. That Royo would stick his cold nose under Nick's armpit to shake him out of his daydreaming further engrained the impression he was different. "He's as irregular as a bearded lady," a feather-drier once said. "Only smarter."

Nick's boss, Cawston general manager Cecil Jenks, told Nick he could continue bringing him, as long as he didn't disrupt production. Nobody else received such special dispensations, but, honestly, they weren't "going-places Nick." A recent *Scientific American* article gave him prestige to burn within the company. (Not that he confided to Jenks, or anyone at the farm, that he and Royo nearly burned to death on Fair Oaks Avenue.)

The flattering cover story was the best publicity the farm could drum up absent a Madison Avenue ad campaign. And this was free. Cawston's groundbreaking employment of sun power, the article said, was reaping fat dividends, a gamble its competitors were too timid to attempt. Along with descriptions about the budgetary advantages of solar-to-steam energy were mechanical diagrams about the equipment, as well as photographs of curious ostriches peeking around the farm's most popular tourist prop: scale-model Egyptian pyramids. Aubrey Eneas was portrayed as an adaptive genius, Nick the hometown product who kept the machinery humming.

Cecil, whose wispy blond hair was dwarfed by a large, trapezoidal forehead, was uncharacteristically giddy about the story. He appreciated what an endorsement from *Scientific American* meant: leverage, even relevancy. His higher-ups were green-eyeshade sorts working out of a Spring Street building in downtown Los Angeles. Cecil long suspected that they'd fire-sell the business in a downturn. Someday, the ostrich-fashion bubble would pop, as all fads do.

That wasn't now; the proof was in the ledger. Once the "Sunrays in Feather Town" issue reached the stands, mail-order sales tripled. For

Nick, those column inches devoted to him were career pixie dust, or, at a minimum, grist for a raise. Many around Pasadena, where residential, solar-fired water heaters were already in vogue, read it.

As such, it was tragicomic how swiftly Nick's positive notoriety backfired in his sanguine face; almost farcical how a month after the article appeared, he was knelt down on the gift store roof, feeling lower than guano.

It was here, through a skylight, where a cat burglar busted in. Any literate crook could've done it. Indeed, Nick's explanation to *Scientific American* about how he persuaded Cawston's to install a pair of four-foot-by-four-foot glass-panels to further reduce the farm's electricity bill was an instruction guide. The burglar, armed only with a screwdriver and rope, lowered himself into a virtual Tiffany's of stealable loot.

Nick, confronting his biggest professional blunder, was dejected, though not distraught, having learned to compartmentalize his troubles to remain the eternal optimist he was. The issue was what to do: seal up the skylight to thwart future break-ins or reinforce the panels? He stood up, thinking/hoping that company insurance would cover the losses. It *was* only money, and he was fortunate to be breathing. He also was fortunate to find levity from this elevation; from the roof, he could see a group of white-turbaned Shriners teasing what they believed was a real ostrich. It was stuffed.

RG's two-pinkie whistle snapped him back. Nick shuddered, knowing RG only used that signal to herald problems (including the time he locked himself in the outhouse on a one-hundred-degree day). Nick dismounted the roof ladder as he always did: leaping backward over the last rungs.

"You're white as a sheet," Nick said. "Who died?"

RG, still wheezing from the run over, shook his head. "Not the best figure of speech today, Nick."

They soon were darting across the yard toward the main paddock. When they reached there, a gaggle of workers stood inside the dim light looking despondent. Stunned. Some were even crying and hugging. Cawston had lost an icon. Mrs. Julius Caesar was gone.

Nick hunkered down next to her, stroking the bird's limp, pointed head. For years, she was the public face of the operation as Cawston's most commercialized, recognized, photo-shot bird. But Father Time didn't kill her; gluttony did, as evident from the three-inch-long construction nail protruding sideways through her narrow esophagus. After a lifetime of hatching profitable baby ostriches and thrilling the masses, Mrs. Julius Caesar asphyxiated alone in her hay-floored chute.

"She must've gone out thrashing," said Gus, a wind-burned wrangler. "It's dismaying. She was such a character."

"Anybody have any notion how these escaped our attention?" Nick asked, projecting calm when he wanted to break something. He held aloft another long nail that his fingers stumbled over.

"You tell us. You're the one Mr. Jenks put in charge," said Otis Norwood, stepping forward from the grain barrels stacked along a wall. Nick's onetime friend was one of those people with the facial geometry to be classically handsome—far-spaced eyes under thick brown hair, lantern jaw—if his perennial scowl didn't nullify it. "But I suppose you're spread mighty thin, what with your solar doohickeys and magazine interviews."

Otis's barb set off grousing from other mourners in the barn. Two onlookers in high boots drifted out, back to their chores. Nick held his tongue, bringing Mrs. Caesar's head into his lap, contemplating her funeral.

"We should bury her behind the paddock," he said. "Let's pour some of those red pebbles she enjoyed gobbling in the hole."

"And the photograph of her with Teddy Roosevelt," said Agnes, a raspy-voiced maintenance woman who'd worked at Cawston forever. "Those two had a connection. She nibbled his mustache when he visited."

"Good idea," said Nick, speaking up. "We've suffered a real loss here, people. No getting around that. It's all right to feel blue. The best way to honor her is to ensure there aren't more nails around that could jeopardize her friends. Can someone please go through the whole area with a rake?"

After two workers volunteered, Otis not one of them, everyone else started filing out. The mood was so glum you could hear straw rustling under their boots.

The next afternoon, Nick sat awkwardly in his boss's office in the same wicker chair he'd worn a groove in during the past three years. From it, he and Cecil planned seasonal goods, troubleshot problems. Only two months ago here, after Cecil praised Nick for doing "a crackerjack job" following a record quarter, they polished off a quarter bottle of absinthe. Today that wicker dug into Nick's flesh.

Cecil's forefinger stabbed a copy of the *Scientific American* article. Indictment-style, it was pointed to where Nick gloated about "the beauty of the skylight" for the world (and underworld) to read. Nick knew Cecil was furious because Cecil was itching under his collar, which he did instead of yelling to keep his hypertension under control.

"I warned you before the journalist arrived not to say anything that could harm the company," he said through gnashed teeth. "You've never been one to brag, Nick, you did let yourself get cocky."

"The thrust of the story was about the sun, so I showed him how we were parlaying it," he said quietly.

"Do you think it's wise back-talking me before I inform the CEO that twenty percent of our best inventory disappeared because of a self-inflicted error?"

Nick's chin fell. "No, sir."

Next up for Cecil was the demise of the farm's photogenic ostrich, who presided at Cawston longer than her Roman namesake had sat on her throne. "This gaffe," he said. "I'm not attributing to you. That lamebrain was bound to die of her own piggishness. If there's any employee to single out it's Otis. He oversaw the reinforcements we made to the paddock, and the cleanup. Anything to add on that front?"

"I'd prefer not to comment on him. I'm just grief-stricken about Mrs. Caesar."

Cecil's tone softened. "You're still young. You'll appreciate death is generally ridiculous. Nonetheless, I want your guarantee there'll be no further embarrassments. And that you'll board up that skylight."

"You have my word," said Nick, relieved Cecil didn't say boo about the wireless solar lamps and solar projector he obsessed over in his off hours. Or that no one connected him to those nuisance parrots, which squealed and squawked like a contentious couple almost every dawn. "Anything else?"

Yes, Cecil said, there was. He was docking Nick's salary twenty dollars and placing him on probation to highlight the importance of discipline. He slipped the "Sunrays in Feather Town" article in a desk drawer before adding a final thought. "If you desire a future here, stay in the present."

Walking out a little numb, Nick summoned Royo for the trip home to Green Street. While he was getting chewed out, Royo sat in front of the administration building's flowerbed, smacking his lips and tasting the different flowers the way Nick did some food.

⊪⊪⊪

He eyeballed his alarm clock sideways when it shook at five fifteen in the morning. He allowed himself a single yawn.

It was three Mondays since Cecil's rebuke, and Nick had no intention of adding another. With spry movements, he blazed through a morning routine that commenced with a cleansing whiz and shave and concluded with Royo demolishing his breakfast; the dog had packed on the pounds since moving in. Nick, again, planned to be the first manager into work and the last out. No Buford's Specials for him.

They were in Busch Gardens, which they used as a shortcut to Cawston, by six. Down here, Victorian Age serenity—fountains tinkling under grand willows, gardeners troweling colorful plants—made no concession to building cranes and steely pistons in the cities. Still, Nick regretted not stopping for coffee. At this rate, they'd arrive at the farm an hour before the gates unlocked.

Why Royo, who always clung to his heels, suddenly flew off toward a thicket of sycamores Nick had no clue. A dog capable of strutting on his hind legs, approximating human expressions, and finding lost items shouldn't be capricious. When Nick caught up to him, he was doing something else odd. He was pawing at the door of the replica Gingerbread Hut, outside of which a sweet, ceramic grandmother stood holding a tray of fake cookies.

Nick wrenched him away by the collar before his nails scratched Adolphus Busch's property. Royo, with that Boxer-breed sinew, though, waggled free and resumed clawing. "For a bright animal, you're acting the moron," Nick said with a chuckle. "The whole thing's make-believe. There's no lamb bone inside with your name on it."

He turned sideways against the doorframe to re-grip the collar, which he bought at a dry goods store. In doing so, Royo's antics became *Nick's* hassle. A belt loop on the back of his trousers snagged over the hut's antique-replica door handle. Now, he'd effectively trapped himself against the doorframe with little room to maneuver. No matter how he tried to untangle himself while restraining Royo, he couldn't jimmy himself loose. Minutes passed.

Think, Nick. He did by letting go of his dog's collar, unbuttoning his doorknob-ensnared pants, and then stepping out of them into his skivvies to shiver in the crisp air. After he unhooked his trousers and redressed, he flicked one of Royo's ears in irritation.

Once they were back on the southbound trail to Cawston he checked his pocket watch, sure they had gobs of time. *Sonofabitch.* He was forty-minutes late, and two miles away. Two possibilities: his alarm clock malfunctioned, or he forgot how to read the hour. Only Royo knew the third option.

Nick tried acting nonchalant reaching the yard in a light sweat after jogging half the distance. "Morning, Waldo," he said, rotating his head side to side, searching for a certain boss.

"Relax. Cecil is en route to a meeting downtown. You oversleep?"

"A fairy-tale hut accosted me. Don't ask."

"Not even if you're on the upside?"

"Not even."

Nick walked his usual rounds by midafternoon, finding everything running smoothly; his tardiness was a hiccup just Waldo noticed. Cawston's assistant manager now leaned against the gift shop counter, tallying the day's haul. Shoppers enticed by ads and discounts that Nick suggested were bumping into one another for the hot sellers. So brisk was the spending that clerks twice emptied the cash registers' jingling drawers to make room for fresh cash. That heinous cat burglar would soon be a memory.

Nick snapped rubber bands around greenbacks and entered numbers in the ledger. Lucrative day so far: $480, the highest non-holiday total ever. He took a breath and glanced out the window. There was Royo, capering with a baby ostrich in a pen while tourists howled in laughter.

Yet two hours from quitting time was two hours too long. Otis was here, pushing aside the curtain separating the gift shop from the stockroom. He used to supervise this store, a plum job reserved for management up-and-comers. That was before Otis curdled into a dark version of himself. It wasn't only his beef with Nick, over one of Nick's inventions, that warped him. It was the chronic sinus pain torturing him.

Nick hoped that he would spin around and leave. He didn't; Otis sidled up next to him to chew the fat. "I don't know what it is about these cock-amamie animals, but people can't seem to stay away," he said, all civil-like.

"Seems so," said Nick, who'd resumed counting bills to discourage conversation.

"Of course, that won't bring Mrs. Caesar back. Everyone's putting that on me."

"C'mon. That's not true."

"Yes, it is. And speaking of the truth, I should jump on the loudspeaker right now to recount *this* farm's history. Customers should know Edwin Cawston, our revered founder, stole the very ostriches he used to create this venture from South Africa. In the dead of night, in cages: that's a fact they don't tout in the brochures."

"You well know there's more to the story," said Nick, eyes downward. "Incidentally, aren't you supposed to be drawing up the next paddock improvements?"

"So serious. I'm only talking shop with a valued colleague."

"Please, Otis."

"Don't get your knickers in a knot. Tell you what: I'll disappear if you lay out what happened to your father; may he rest in peace. Cecil always reminds us we're family."

Nick slapped down a roll of quarters on the counter. Otis continued on.

"Was it true what the scuttlebutt said? That the train that struck him launched him thirty yards? All the way into the fields?"

Nick flexed his recovered wrist and exhaled. *Don't take the bait.*

"That must've been messy. Closed casket funeral, I'm assuming."

Nick, without looking up, said in a still-poised voice, "You're not going to provoke me with despicable insults. We all have a vested stake in how much these people buy."

Otis scooted closer so both of them stood shoulder to shoulder with their backs to the customers. "I can't describe how elated I was watching you knocked down a peg for the burglary."

"And I can't tell you how perplexing it is that someone who rode lunchtimes with us, who inspired me when I wanted to fling my tools, is behaving like this."

Otis leaned in. "You know the source of my displeasure with you. And I know your father was a suicidal wreck. Let's hope you're not the fruit of his deranged tree."

Nick didn't flinch or threaten. He calmly shut the ledger and tucked his fountain pen into his shirt pocket. He then bobbed his head—and socked Otis under his left eye with his right elbow. Nobody else saw the lightning blow. So much for not being baited.

Otis patted where Nick clobbered him and grinned. Coolly himself, he pushed Nick's shoulder and connected with a sharp right hook to his jaw. The punch sent Nick backward into an unsuspecting cashier, a chatty, gap-toothed woman who nearly tripped into a spinning cabinet of miniature glass ostriches.

"*Holy smoke*," Otis said with yippee. "That felt good."

The feather-shop donnybrook was on. Skills-wise, pugilist Jack "the Galveston Giant" had nothing to fear.

The combatants shifted from behind the cramped counter space into the browsing area. Nick, who hadn't been in a fight since seventh grade, popped Otis in the nose, driving him into the "Affordable Boas." Customers backpedaled against the wall, some appalled, some rapt. There were gasps, a solitary: "What are you ignoramuses doing?" Mothers snatched their roaming kids. Registers ceased ringing.

The squeamish might've fled but the two careened into a wire rack holding souvenir postcards near the door. This toppled the rack, spraying images of ostriches in men's hats or with celebrities across the floor. The basket of small, individually sold feathers that rested on top of the display went sailing, too, filling the gift shop airspace with floating plumes you'd either imagine from a stardust dream—or a barnyard atrocity.

They twirled next into a shelf containing a row of Cawston pens and ink refills. Several of the vials exploded when they struck the floor. One splattered the trousers of an erudite-looking man with matted brown hair, leaving his trouser cuffs an archipelago of streaky black. Round three was less compelling, if still a must-see. Otis grabbed Nick by his tattered collar, Nick grabbed him back, and the two whirled into another tchotchke rack of ostrich key chains and pillboxes. Tuckering out, they threw feeble punches the other easily dodged. Every time they stepped, they crunched merchandise that an hour earlier was carefully arrayed.

The three-minute bout ended when two haggard ostrich wranglers separated them. Few customers bought much afterward.

❖❖❖

CAWSTON'S GOING-PLACES JUNIOR EXECUTIVE was going places all right, south mostly. Nick knew it listening to Cecil enunciate terms like "inexcusable actions" and "appalling judgment." Nick, with his split lip and scraped chin, slumped in that familiar chair.

For Cecil, it wasn't the skylight-break-in or the demise of Mrs. Julius Caesar that induced him to chug pink bicarbonate before informing Nick of the obvious. It was the fact that Nick lost his temper on the same day that Pasadena Mayor William Thum had traveled to Cawston to discuss a company storefront at a prime locale on Colorado Street.

"Congratulations, Nick," said Cecil, itching under his collar with no restraint. "You couldn't have picked a more opportune juncture to sabotage that opportunity if you tried."

Thum, Cecil said, requested the meeting be pushed up two weeks, something Nick would've known if he were "present at the morning briefing today instead of being God knows where." Wasn't he aware of how "supremely busy" the mayor was overseeing the bridge and a half dozen other municipal projects? Thum was a businessman himself, co-inventor of the popular Tangleet-brand flypaper, making him "the one dealmaker with whom the farm needed to curry favor."

Nick tried blaming his faulty watch, his stretch of bad fortune. He played the honor card, saying any decent son would've slugged someone spewing the type of "reprehensible slander" that Otis did.

"Stop," Cecil finally said. "It's too late."

"With due respect, it shouldn't be," Nick said in a snippy tone while sitting up. "The sum total of my contributions, from improving the solar pump to streamlining how we bring feathers to market, should allot me reconsideration. Whenever you put me in charge of a task, I've delivered. Doesn't that buy me something?"

Cecil angled forward in his chair, pushing the bicarbonate bottle to the side. He wasn't itching anymore. "What it buys you is severance and an open invitation to ride Mrs. Cleveland when she's not in service. You're obviously free to take your solar ideas unencumbered."

"Tell that to the bill collectors," Nick muttered, rubbing an inflamed knuckle. "Forgive me if I'm being curt."

"During your fisticuffs with Otis, whom I've already fired, did you happen to notice a gentleman wearing wire-rimmed spectacles and a tartan vest?"

"Not really. I was occupied."

"You should have. That was William Thum, Nick. *The mayor.* Unlike you, he arrived early for our discussion, and was browsing in the gift shop when you and Otis resorted to playground tempest. It was his pants that you spoiled with our best ink. We begged him to let us pay for his dry cleaning, but he was too magnanimous. Quite the spectacle you gave him."

The room went silent as Cecil pretended to flyspeck a sales report and Nick hung his head. After a minute, Cecil got up, walked around behind Nick, and placed his hand on a shoulder that Otis nearly dislocated. "Glance out there," Cecil said, pointing toward a line of ostriches being sheared. "This isn't the tightknit venture you joined out of USC. It's cutthroat. The bankers that control us would slaughter our entire stock and sleep soundly that night for the right offer. We're on borrowed time."

Nick squinted through the glass, seeing baskets packed with brown, black, and white feathers that'd be sold across America. "Is that supposed to make me feel chipper on my last day at a place to which I've given my all?"

"No," Ceil said solemnly. "It's supposed to jog your memory of what I told you when I promoted you. You're bound for something bigger than peddling quills for snobby hats."

THE FIRST LADY OF BUDWEISER

THE JOBLESS ONE SPRINTED off the line of scrimmage, head-faked Fleet, and ran clear, momentarily forgetting about his whirlwind destruction of Cawston's souvenir shop. Into his outstretched hands Waldo dropped a teardrop pass on a blanket of emerald turf. Another long completion, another laughably easy touchdown: Nick's "team" was now ahead twenty-eight to fourteen in a game fueled by Budweiser.

He was still trotting ahead in celebration when he twisted around to trash talk Fleet. "You call that defense?" he yelled back. "That was simpler than stealing licorice from Helen Keller."

Fleet might've gotten beat, but Lady Karma wouldn't. Nick never saw the ceramic dwarf in his path. Not on this moonlit night in Busch Gardens. His waist smashed into the gnome, somewhere near its rakish, alpine hat, and Nick somersaulted over him onto the grass. A body that'd taken its lumps on Fair Oaks Avenue, on Mrs. Grover Cleveland, and in his scrape with Otis added a borderline hip pointer to its chart.

"I'll gladly yield another score if you duplicate that," Fleet shouted. Like the others, he was shoeless, with cuffs rolled up, and shit-faced. "How's your pelvic bone?"

Nick picked himself up and hobbled back. "Better than your coordination." He vowed to return tomorrow to repair the decapitated gnome with bonding glue, if he remembered.

He then lofted the leather football to his quarterback. Waldo, who had a rifle arm, was a crummy receiver, especially in the dappled light.

He tipped Nick's throw so the ball bounced straight up and came down, naturally, on RG's head. Everyone snorted, except for Royo, who fetched the ball in his chops. Gregory "Gilly" Brook tried grabbing it from him, but the animal juked him, daring him to try again. Sandlot football wasn't normally this hysterical.

Gilly, at thirty-seven, was older than the other four. As a veteran Busch Gardens' landscaper, he was entrusted with caring for the expensive geraniums and yellow roses. He was a bony, everyman sort with receding brown hair and a missing right pinkie from a childhood accident at his father's Nevada sawmill.

Nick met Gilly when his Elks Club toured Cawston. There, the two discovered a common passion: after-work suds and fun. While Gilly's club-mates in fez hats made fools of themselves around the ostrich pens, Gilly confided to Nick about how he jerry-rigged an inexhaustible supply of beer—and, no less, in a city patrolled by a temperance movement that'd love nothing more than for the Anheuser-Busch Company to go belly up.

Few employees, Gilly said, knew about Adolphus's private stash; how the tycoon stored Budweiser reserves for parties in barrels kept in a refrigerated shed between his Ivy Wall mansion and the canyon bluff. Learning the vats were replenished with little scrutiny, Gilly devised a plan. One night, he tapped a vat by connecting it to a soldered drainage pipe. After he flushed out his so-called "beer pipe" with bleach and water, he camouflaged it in ice plant downslope into the gardens and installed a valve. Gravity was the barkeep. Turn the nozzle to imbibe workingman champagne. Smartly, Gilly appropriated only small amounts.

Meeting for the first time tonight, Nick's old friends became Gilly's new ones. They decreed him Adolphus Junior for his sneaky idea. And Buford: what do you call him besides a munificent sandwich savant? Before they liquored up ahead of their unauthorized game, they traveled to his shack and brought back dinner to eat *al fresco* at the gardens' "Snow White" table. (Knowing what he did about Nick's close call, and now learning about his termination at Cawston, Buford raised no stink about packaging these sandwiches to go.)

While appreciative to all, Nick mostly owed Fleet thanks for arranging the Friday night tomfoolery. Two days earlier he burst into Nick's curtain-pulled bungalow, announcing that the deadline for Nick's sulking was expiring. He suggested they ride up the Mount Lowe railway for some fresh air head-clearing. At that, Nick raised his stubbled chin. What about, he countered, an 'Everything's Okeydoke' party. I am an idealist, after all."

"Dilly," Fleet said. "Let there be bacchanalia."

When the group tired of guzzling Budweiser from tin cups, they slurped it directly from the beer pipe, which gunned amber lager into their mouths at high velocity; Royo lapped up his foamy share from a pie pan. Soon their shirts were damp from overflow, and the second half of their "game" deteriorated with every predictable stumble and klutzy tackle.

The final play was controversial and cross-species. Gilly snapped a four-fingered hike to RG, who dodged a blitzing Waldo for an intended bootleg. Just as Nick closed in to deck him, RG at the last second pitched the ball to Royo. He caught it in his teeth, looped around, and outraced Waldo for the winning score.

"Doesn't count," Waldo protested. "Your halfback's paw stepped out of bounds."

"Like you're sober enough to tell," RG cracked. "Concede defeat, sport."

Grass-stained and flush, they put their jackets back on in the November night and chugged some more. Afterward, they sat down to admire Pasadena's nighttime sky. They were in drunken slumbers within minutes.

Right before he joined them, a disturbing thought occurred to Nick. If word leaked about what happened at Cawston, to say nothing of his role unleashing those voluble parrots, he might well have to bail town to join the people of the corn in the flatlands his forefathers fled: Indiana. Wouldn't that be circularly ironic?

⯗ ⯗ ⯗

His blackout dream was a spinning carousel of unexpected encounters, commencing with the goddess that spellbound him at J. D. Mercereau's wake and continuing with meeting eccentric Hattie in the blackened hills of Linda Vista. How that round tip from an unknown object was involved wasn't evident. Whatever its role, the pointy thing was rocking his chin back and forth. "Go away," Nick slurred from his Budweiser sleep cave.

His dream resumed with animals, and he saw himself kneeling next to the nail-perforated Mrs. Julius Caesar and next, playing guitar while Royo swaggered on his hind legs.

But that pesky tip returned, this time speaking with a European inflection. "Excuse me, you need to wake up."

Nick rolled onto his side.

"*Schnell.* I cannot leave you here." To emphasize that, the interloper stopped harassing his chin. The tip now rubbed directly over his mouth, and it reeked of shoe polish.

"*Yooo-hooo.* Wakey, wakey, Rip Van Winkle."

Ah, crimminy. Nick shook awake in the netherworld between post-inebriation and pre-hangover. The sleep killer—a woman's gray, colt-skin boot—lingered over his face like a dark zeppelin.

"Please, sir, my foot is tiring," the stranger said. "It cannot taste very good."

Nick hoisted himself onto his elbows. Needles jabbed his eyelids. "No, it didn't," he said with reasonable lucidity.

"I was afraid the police would discover you," the old lady obviously from Germany said. "After the recent burglaries, including at my own house, an officer patrols the gardens every night. He's quite strict. Youthful mischief would infuriate him."

Nick, who knew all about the area's cat burglar, stood up damp and shaky. The evening's debauchery traced to him, and he slyly tried locating his accomplices that the woman had yet to discern. Using the moonlight and the garden's spaced-out ground lights, he saw that Waldo was asleep, hugging a shrub twenty yards away. RG was farther away, snoring face down by a family of clay foxes in wedding garb. Knowing Fleet, he had probably crept away, gulped black coffee, and returned to his med-school studies.

"I appreciate your gesture, ma'am," Nick said. "I hope I'm not, um—" He fumbled for verbiage that wouldn't boomerang in court. "Not trespassing."

"You are. I will not tell, though. I'm married to the property owner. And if my nose is correct, you enjoy his products."

How fitting. Pasadena's wealthiest doyenne, Lillian Busch, busting Nick in her husband's storybook park. She extended her hand in introduction, revealing a weighty diamond ring probably worth more than Argentina's gross domestic product. Mrs. Busch was continually in the news for her charitable giving and extravagant lifestyle. Nick mumbled his name, just a second before a crunchy rustling from the bushes diagonal from them.

"Oh, my heavens." The petite woman in her late sixties covered her elongated mouth. "I hope that's not a mountain lion pursuing somebody's pussycat. Or us."

Nick knew the stirring was no cougar. It was Gilly crawling up the hill in a job-preserving retreat. Should she uncover his beer pipe, Gilly would likely be standing by Nick at the next soup line. "Why take the chance with our welfare?" he said. "Let's stroll toward the lamp. Nocturnal creatures detest light."

She bought it, and they walked the opposite direction on a path of decomposed granite. What a pair: one was an unemployed, would-be inventor in a fog of liquor and uncertainty; the other was the archetype of a catalog grandmother whose family basically owned St. Louis, parts of Germany, and some of Pasadena's most prized real estate.

"Try one of these candies," she said, digging a wax-papered confection from her sweater pocket. "They're scrumptious."

As repulsive as candy sounded, Nick realized he coulndn't demur. He unwrapped what appeared to be a caramel, depositing it into his cottony mouth. "*Umm*. What is this?" he inquired with a manufactured smile. "It's not chocolate."

"Marzipan. Wonderful, aren't they? We order them special from Berlin."

"They're special all right, Mrs. Busch." Nick thought he might puke on her colt-skin boots.

"Here," she said. "Have another."

Nick chewed it under the yellow lamplight's chemical halo, yearning to spit it out. After they sat down on the bench beside the light, Lillian stared at the pink-lavender bruises on his face.

"Did you injure yourself tonight, doing whatever it is you were doing?"

Nick touched the cheekbone that'd made acquaintance with Otis's right hook. "These? No. A disagreement with a former colleague turned heated, you might say."

"Ja, Ja, I mean, yes, yes." She examined him closer. "Say, I've seen you before. I'm certain of it. You ride an ostrich through the gardens, no? On some Saturdays, you perform tricks on it for the affirmed children. You make it fun balls."

Nick was tempted to correct the doughy-featured woman that she meant "balls of fun." Conversely, she could have him arrested for trespassing, and the negligent homicide of an innocent gnome.

"That's me; those kids can't get enough of it when I ride her backward, sideways, anyway I can. They're especially fond of when I get thrown. I call my act an ostrich rodeo. Anything I can do to make them smile, I will."

"You excel at it," she said. "Though I'm more partial to our family peacocks. Their tail feathers remind me of cheerful times."

Nick, whirling in disbelief that this woman recognized him, smiled. When he was starting out at Cawston, the Busches celebrated their fifty-year wedding anniversary here with a ring-kissing spectacle never seen before. During the festivity, she sat on a throne studded with diamonds and pearls. Well-wishers came bearing gold—as in gold flower baskets, a gold-ruby calendar and, in the case of then-President William Taft, who once toured the gardens in a motorcar, an uncirculated twenty-dollar gold coin.

The Busches' next major event was an American Medical Association convention that set records for attendance. Thousands swarmed into the gardens for an elaborate, south-of-the-border-themed jubilee where troubadours and Mexican nationals served tamales in sombreros. As added flourishes, trained ducks waddled at guests' feet and a meadow was specially planted with white carnations.

Her husband, Adolphus, a goateed, five-foot-five livewire, had in these fanciful grounds a sanctuary from corporate pressures and the hard-knuckle politics of keeping American alcohol legal. Pasadena, he spouted, was "the grandest place in the world." He was forever raising his chalice praising its aura.

"Not to offer unsolicited advice, but you might consider wine next time," Lillian said, directing her long-lashed eyes at him. "Between us, Adolphus refers to his product as 'dot schlop.' He prefers the grape or Dom Perignon."

"I don't foresee much bubbly in my future," Nick said, gazing up at the Milky Way. "Every time I blink, a black cloud's hovering. Which is humorous for someone who covets a vocation in solar energy."

Lillian buttoned the top of her sweater. "I've heard of such things. Some houses in town heat their water with the sun, no, on their roofs?"

"They do indeed. I want to spread my ideas wider."

"Ostriches, ailing children, lights, wanton drinking: you're a distinctive person, Nick Chance."

Distinctive and desperate. Before he knew it, he was telling the baroness in pearls about his woebegone last few months. Despite the travails, he said he'd never give up on the sun-charged inventions that he invested hundreds of hours and countless all-nighters perfecting.

Lillian listened earnestly. When Nick was through, a smile upturned above her dimpled chin. "Since you're mechanically inclined, I have a proposition, a job proposition. Adolphus usually does our negotiations. He'd call this mutually beneficial."

Nick leaned forward, forgetting about his drunk, comatose friends. Here was her offer: Lillian said she'd ply connections to secure him a job on a "prestigious" public works project, provided he agreed to her "extra terms."

Nick filled with appreciation, if not low expectations. The only city employment he knew had vacancies was in Pasadena's waste disposal system, which outsiders described as "ingenious" because they weren't stuck there. In this system, some of the citizenry's collective shit was piped underground to collection fields miles away. There, the excrement was converted into fertilizer essential to grow foodstuffs—foodstuffs that Pasadenans consumed in a grotesque digestive cycle. This wasn't a shiny future. It was a career tromping in acres of human feces. "The sewer?" he asked tremulously.

Lillian stifled laughter. "No, no, Nick. I hope you're not afraid of heights."

"I'll change streetlights for a paycheck. I thank you and will—."

"Dear, Nick. Stop guessing. On Monday, I'll speak to someone at the Mercereau Construction Company. They have to listen because of my last name."

Nick was almost shaking. Tumblers were clicking. "You mean on the bridge, the Colorado Street Bridge?"

"Correct. You must promise me that once I recommend you, you'll be, what's the word, conscientious. And that you'll continue riding that silly ostrich for the children, and at the Easter egg hunt I organize for those without."

"I accept," he answered, probably too quickly. "I might just have an idea to share with the company, too."

"You're enthused. Good, good, good," she said. "This has been a productive evening." Lillian gave Nick the name of her contact, directing him to be at the man's tent at seven on Tuesday. "Before I say goodnight, we do have one additional piece of business to conduct. Please follow me."

Nick couldn't fathom what it was. He hoped it wasn't that elf he shattered.

They walked the trail to near where Mrs. Cleveland bested the Model T. After a bit, they stopped at the base of a knoll overlooking some of Busch Gardens' more arbitrary embellishments: a Glider swing, a Grecian pergola, prickly cacti imported from Arizona (where Aubrey Eneas now spent his time on a new solar endeavor). To the west were the terraced steppes at the park's western perimeter.

"Lilly," as she insisted Nick call her, lifted the hem of her "hausfrau" dress and walked up the mound toward a flowerbed of special import. It was planted there to remind visitors what bankrolled this renowned parkland. The Anheuser-Busch emblem, a large capital "A" capped with a gold star on its high point and an eagle through its center, was inlaid in the grass in browns, reds, and yellows. The insignia measured a gaudy seven feet.

Lilly directed Nick's attention to one of the flowerbed-eagle's talons. The light here was weak, emanating only from Japanese lanterns strung from adjacent trees. Nick sidled closer to understand what she wanted him to view.

Damn! I knew I forgot something. Nick's *zzzz-ing*, inebriated mutt lay there asleep. "Oh, Mrs. Busch, Lilly, apologies. He's mine. An independent animal, to be sure."

"I discovered him tonight before I found you. Do you get your pets intoxicated often?"

"First time," he said. "We won't repeat it. Again, it was a particularly dismal week."

"As I gather. Now rest up. And thank you for brightening this old woman."

Under clouds scudding around the moon, after he shook hands with Lilly-the-lifesaver, after he awoke Royo, Waldo, and RG, he lumbered up the switchback out of the gardens with a bum hip and his still-wasted dog in his arms.

Physically, he was a punching bag. Psychically, he was a man anew. His misadventure at Cawston opened a door to a job on a wondrous bridge the entire world would soon be lionizing. *This* was his destiny-bender.

Outside the upholstery shop a block from his Green Street bungalow, Nick set a sobering Royo onto his paws. Nick had no choice, for his stomach was yanking the ripcord on its contents. After he hunched over to vomit and dug out a stick of Wrigley's Spearmint, he turned his head. His intuitive dog was grinning at him, again.

◍◍◍

Schematics in hand, future at stake, Nick swayed outside a crisp, white tent roomier than his cottage. Hung above the flap of the entry was a bold-print sign: "J. D. Mercereau Bridge and Construction Company: Management ONLY."

Foremen in splattered overalls, some cradling mugs of steaming coffee, rotated in and out to receive the day's marching orders in five-minute intervals.

"Next," a voice bellowed. "Snappy now. Concrete mixing in thirty minutes."

Nick puffed his cheeks and ducked under the flap, striding in assertively, only to bobble his designs when they brushed a tent pole; cat-quick, he grabbed them off the dirt floor. The man sitting behind a paper-jumbled desk offered no greeting.

"Excuse me, sir, I'm Nick Chance."

Marcus Stonebreaker lifted his swarthy head and lowered it, continuing to annotate the edges of a structural blueprint. "Give me a second," he said with a gravelly voice. "From what I heard, you've got no other pressing engagements."

The company's forty-five-year-old construction czar had kinky black hair, deep-creviced features, and hairy ears. Nick's first impression: the man had the finesse of a grizzly, which, parenthetically, Pasadena boosters stressed no longer roamed the mountains, making meals out of hikers. After he finished writing, Marcus flashed Nick a scowl. "Mrs. Busch tells me you're a gem, and a local," he said. "All that gets you here is a sniff. List your qualifications."

He stuck an unlit cigar in his mouth and crossed his arms, waiting to be impressed. Nick could tell he was husky, well over six feet tall.

"I have management experience and a USC business degree," he said. "I've been an ardent fan of your bridge since—"

"Sycophants need not apply," Marcus interrupted. "And this isn't our bridge: it's Pasadena's."

"Right," Nick said, gulping. "I'll be quick. The city's light standards, from what I've read, should throw off decent candlepower on the bridge deck."

"And?"

"But there's nothing to illuminate the adjoining hillsides. At nightfall, it's pitch dark on the peripheries, which won't be beneficial for drivers. Or safety."

"And an ex-ostrich plucker has a solution to a backburner oversight?"

Yeah, he's a grizzly. "As a matter of fact, I do. And it's not pricey." Nick unrolled his schematic on the table and twirled it around for Marcus to analyze. "At Cawston, when I wasn't overseeing the solar-powered water pumps and assisting running the place, I devoted myself to engineering and trial testing this."

"Yeah, yeah. What am I looking at, exactly?"

"A new type of lamp that utilizes mirrors to channel heat from sunbeams into dark glass and obsidian. At night, the heat is released into a globe bulb coated with phosphorous. That, in turn, activates a filament generating a silvery glow that lasts all evening. My lamps don't require much maintenance either. It's mainly swiveling them every equinox to compensate for the sun's seasonal path. Nothing to it."

Marcus scrunched his face into the diagram. Nick's rendering presented a tapered, two-foot-tall device with small, angled mirrors surrounding a floodlight-size bulb. The rounded base was where the crumbly heat-storing material sat.

"Damn thing reminds me of a metal petunia," Marcus said. "Mirrors for petals. Am I wrong?"

Petunias? "No, good comparison. Admittedly, the wattage produced isn't nearly as robust as the new lamps on Orange Grove Boulevard, but they cast surprising illumination. And they require no wires or hookups."

"Tell me why I should gamble on an amateur, particularly when our budget is stretched to a breaking point. Wireless electricity seems pie in the sky."

"Actually, it's pie available now."

"That's big talk, Chance. If you were so gangbusters about your invention, you should've brought a prototype."

"I would've, but we don't have a deal, do we? This is a million-dollar concept, and I'm protective about it. If you think I'm blowing smoke, contact my former colleagues at Cawston who've seen it work. I bled for this." Nick upturned his palms, exhibiting hands crisscrossed with scars and nicks.

Marcus related to that. "Go on. You got yourself a few more minutes."

Nick guided him through the particulars of his device, including its weight, voltage, beam radius, and weather durability. Marcus next asked Nick to mark up a landscape plot plan to indicate where a dozen lamps "might be seated." This Nick did, having already anticipated such a request.

Marcus rocked back in his chair and lit his stogie afterward. Above his tent, a whistle blew to announce the start of the morning shift. "Tell you what, though. I'm still on the fence about you. Those unlit slopes are troublesome, so I'll pencil in your contraption as a probationary project. You get two lamps operating as advertised, and we'll discuss adding another ten."

"Okeydoke. I'm confident."

"Good. I respect that quality in people who need to prove themselves." City Hall, Marcus added, would pay for the materials out of its discretionary budget, since the lights technically weren't part of the contract. The Mercereau Company would finance Nick's salary.

"One more condition," Marcus said. "If things work out, you agree to do odd jobs whenever sought. Running errands. Lending a hand on the concrete hopper. We like to think of ourselves here as a baseball team, where everybody pitches in wherever needed."

"So long as I keep the rights to patent my lamps, I can live with that," Nick said. "I'm a quick learner."

"Fine," Marcus replied. "Guess this wasn't a complete waste of time."

NICK'S METAL PETUNINIAS

A T THE MESS TENT the following day, after he filled out his employment papers and requisition needs, Marcus introduced Nick to some of what he tabbed the job's "bridge rats." They were a rough-hewn bunch, hardened like coal miners (minus any "Black Lung cough"). No one could doubt the men's tradecraft.

There were the two Colorado brothers (yes, Colorado, like the street), and two John's (Visco and Moseley); there was Ed Erickson, and J. Mulaney, C. J. Johnson, and foreman R. Reynolds. The most memorable name: B. Mum. Marcus told Nick he'd meet the project's onsite executives, lead civil engineer C. K. Allen, of the design firm of Waddell and Harrington, and F. W. Crocker from Mercereau, later.

"Try not to embarrass me with the suits," he said. "You're still an asterisk."

For the next three days, Nick was all eyes and no mouth, reminding himself not to gawk too much at the bridge's majestic contour.

Before he got rolling, the company needed to order the parts. His pint-size lamps bore no resemblance to the much larger, conventionally powered ones that'd shine from pedestrian alcoves jutting over the deck's sides. Once installed, they'd be beauts: forty-six fluted, cast-iron lampposts, each one hung with five fishbowl-shaped globes pinched together like grapes. Equally attractive would be the inlaid benches and urn-supported balusters that'd be carved out at the end. Everything about the viaduct shouted class.

And, speaking of class, Marcus put Nick through his own, reminding him he needed to be "a student of the bridge" in case he was asked to emcee a VIP tour as one of the few college-educated grunts. "Jot this down," he ordered, in a first-week lecture. "This is your 'Star Spangled Banner.' Commit the details to memory."

Nick scribbled Marcus's words in his trusty, moleskin notepad. "She'll be 1,480 feet long and twenty-eight-feet wide end to end. Height: twelve to fifteen stories above the ravine's floor. Grade east to west: 2.65 degrees. Design: eleven open-spandrel arches, nine of those parabolic. Footing gets complicated, so just say she rests on boulders and gravel capable of handling up to 166 pounds per square foot."

Nick's left hand was smeared with black ink before Marcus's didactic was halfway done. This bridge, he gloated, was to engineering what the Titanic was to cruise ships (before she sank in April): "monumental." She'd consume eleven thousand cubic yards of concrete, plus six hundred tons of reinforcing steel.

"Now for her real singularities," Marcus said, fake shining his nails. Besides its ultra-efficient construction and striking aesthetic, which was inspired by structures in Spain, Greece, and Italy, the bridge was being curved at an unusual fifty-two-degree angle to shorten its distance over the highest section of the gorge—a design, Marcus explained, that required a heftier foundation but less expense. "They tell me she'll be the highest and longest of its kind anyplace. You don't need a measuring tape to recognize she'll be a beauty queen."

The Colorado Street Bridge's price tag, as Nick already knew, still angered some, strong economy and all. At inception, the tab was ball-parked around $235,000—an exorbitant sum in a time the public demanded limited, penny-pinching government. It took flesh pressing and deal making by Pasadena's Board of Trade, its proto-chamber of commerce, to goad voters in 1911 to approve a $100,000 bond issue, money matched by Los Angeles County. An additional $13,000 was being ponied up in onetime payments from the city and wealthy interests in unincorporated San Rafael Heights across the Arroyo. Pain, in other words, spread around.

"Avoid talking dollars if you're ever around muckety-mucks," Marcus advised. "Distract them with the bend, how she fits into the canyon hand in glove. Stay away from the other sore points, too."

"Other sore points?" Nick asked, looking up from his notepad. "Isn't all the controversy over its path settled? The city was trying to do right by everyone, I heard."

"Some free counsel, Chance. Stay clear of local politics. They can be gangrenous. I'm not from here. I do know your town grew weary of watching so much blood and mayhem when people in wagons flipped over navigating those steep trails in and out of the gorge. What was the slogan used to sell the bridge: motorcars, not horses? The whole country is going to own automobiles in ten years. Harp on that."

Marcus's thrust, while gruffly enunciated, resonated with Nick's conviction in progress. The lives that'd be spared by this roadway, the time economized once drivers could reach Los Angeles, the beach, and points west with a minute ride over the Arroyo more than justified the cost.

How serious was the bridge's whip-cracking grizzly about Nick's trivia retention? Serious enough that on Nick's third day there, after he returned to base camp from planting small yellow flags to evaluate locations for his trial lamps, Marcus hollered at him to come over. "Rookie," he said, standing above one of the subsurface footings that gripped the Earth like the leg of a claw-foot bathtub. "Tell me about the primary spans."

"Two sets of parabolic ribs, squared in form, connected by tie beams. The spandrel columns on top carry transverse and longitudinal beams."

"Not bad for someone who didn't know a tie beam from Ty Cobb before. You got a decent memory. The road surface?"

"Nine to eleven inches."

"Project dates?"

"Started in July. Finished by spring."

"Almost. Gonna take a tad longer to snip the ribbon. We're estimating summer now."

"Okeydoke," Nick said.

"You know what? You're ready?"

"For what?"

"Not to be a virgin anymore."

"Pardon, sir?"

The next day, Marcus brought Nick to meet foreman Harold Prescott, "Wink" to his friends on account of an eye twitch. Wink took him someplace he only fantasized about: onto the barebones deck.

"Stay sharp every second up here," Wink shouted over the diesel engine churning sand, cement, and gravel into wet concrete from the eastern bank. The smoky machine spun with a cyclical racket that vibrated Nick's boots. "Distracted people don't last."

Nick then followed Wink into a makeshift tunnel, which was created by the elevated trestle track for the concrete-bearing dumpcart; wood supports propped that rail high over the deck. Looking west in the slatted light beneath it, the bridge appeared to stretch into golden infinity.

"Keep your ass put while I check on today's pour," Wink yelled.

"Done," Nick shouted back, feeling official.

Stomach-curling to others, the altitude didn't bother Nick. While Wink ventured out, vanishing into the tunnel, Nick spread his boots for stability. These coordinates sure beat gawking at the bridge from Mrs. Grover Cleveland's mane. It also changed his perspective. Some locals, for example, compared the company's tight orchestration to a beehive. Nick, standing where he was now, realized that was the wrong insect metaphor. It was more tantamount to an ant colony.

From his locale, he watched heavy trucks dump their gravel payloads at an outcropping close to where he performed his ostrich rodeos, during which he now wore sunglasses to infuse showbiz flair for the kids. He heard bridge rats communicating from different levels of scaffolding, truncated lingo and whistle sequences. He observed horses, grouped in teams to hoist the timbers needed to mold concrete members, nicker under the stress. When they levered up packs of rebar—long, rods inserted into the drying concrete to strengthen it—they wiggled midair, reminding Nick of giant pencil mustaches.

Lastly was the snow-globe view, for off the deck's flanks was a breathtaking panorama. Take your pick: the Mount Lowe Railway, Busch Gardens, Los Angeles's nubby skyline, the squiggly lines of the blue Pacific, scrub forest. You could lose yourself up here. And Nick did with his dreamy expression.

"*Hey*! What'd I tell you about keeping focused?" Wink hollered from twenty feet away. "Maybe I should've described how a cracked skull looks."

"That's not necessary," Nick called back. "I'll do better my second time. Promise."

They lingered for another ten minutes, squatting as the dumpcart rumbled slowly overhead. After the vehicle reached the far edge of the deck, Wink described how workers raked the chunky, oatmeal-ish slush from it into a pivoting tin chute called a distribution hopper. From there the goop was funneled into wooden forms known as "falsework." Once the concrete inside those molds dried, it birthed another structural bone. Steel-welded troughs were hauled out to transfer concrete to the lower levels.

"Time to go," Wink said. "I'll notify Marcus you didn't shit yourself."

۩ ۩ ۩

"Come in, my dear Nick," Lilly said, looking insubstantial in the foyer of her Orange Grove manor. "You must be pooped. A tall glass of lemonade should do you wonders."

Though he'd prefer a Budweiser and a washcloth for a French shower, he said, "Count me in."

It was Saturday, and he spent the morning tramping around the rutted hillsides, revising lamp locales for maximum sunbeam collection. That his socks now were peppered with prickly foxtails or that he tripped over a buried rock mattered little. Marcus needed to be dazzled.

After his half-day shift, he rode Mrs. Cleveland, who RG generously brought up from Cawston, for another ostrich rodeo. Today there were twenty children in attendance. This being his fifth show, he allowed little Reginald, whom he ran into earlier at the soda fountain, to arrange the hoops and small jumps he added to make the show livelier. And it was. Now he felt whooped.

Lacquered in sweat, he followed Lilly into the depths of the city's most talked-about residence. "After me," she said. "We'll relax in the parlor."

Ivy Wall was paneled and upholstered, decorated in Old World luxury with crystal chandeliers and valuable artwork. Every inch of hardwood floor was buffed flawlessly, every Persian rug priceless. Her husband's personalized Pullman railcar was reputed to be similarly resplendent.

They passed walls hung with photographs of the imperial-bearded, barrel-chested Adolphus—doppelganger, perhaps, for the future "Rich Uncle Pennybags" on the Monopoly board. Lilly's hubby had hooded eyes and, now, a beard that lengthened as his hair thinned. The photos showed him hobnobbing with presidents Roosevelt and Taft, the head of Harvard, even rival Frederick Pabst. In some shots, they posed with the clubbiness of poker buddies.

"It's good to have friends in high places," Lilly chirped, noticing Nick's bulging eyes. "Did you know that Adolphus predicted that Andrew (as in Carnegie) and JP (think Morgan) would covet houses here after he showed them around? He was correct, though sometimes I wish he hadn't said a peep. I wanted to keep Pasadena our secret."

Nick, who always considered the city's "wintering tycoons" more of a curiosity than emblematic of what spawned Pasadena's exceptionalism, tried not hyperventilating. Every ten steps, it seemed, were fresh flowers in costly vases. How could this be, he marveled: him here weeks removed from his drunken escapades in Busch Gardens? He'd bumbled upward.

Strolling to Lilly's parlor, they passed a side window out of which loomed another sumptuous property radiating palatial ambience. This was "The Blossoms," which Adolphus purchased from tobacco magnate George S. Myers for a then-home sales-price record: $165,000. And what did the Busches do with it? They converted it into a guesthouse. But when you're president of the company producing the "King of Beers," selling more than a million barrels a year, you can spend as a king would.

Adolphus, one of twenty-two children, emigrated from Germany, entering the brewery business in his early twenties. St. Louis, home to many of America's first-generation German immigrants, was an obvious place for him to settle. Those Germans knew their beer, and Adolphus wanted to win their loyalty. Love Lilly as he did, his marriage to her was strategic. His father-in-law was veteran brew-meister Eberhard Anheuser.

After Adolphus joined his company, he set about crafting a hard-to-make, crisp lager that'd appeal to his native countrymen and Americans alike. By the 1870s, he was making headway, partly by rewriting the rules of beer-ology. Under him, Budweiser became the first United States-produced beer to be pasteurized and distributed nationally on refrigerated railcars, which were replenished by icehouses along the tracks. Besides ensuring his product didn't spoil, he also mastered brand marketing, product giveaways, and opened his plant to public tours.

Budweiser's little big man was a different sort of new money tycoon, flamboyant and philanthropic, bombastic and unvindictive, except when it came to backstabbing politicians. He was unrepentant about flaunting his wealth but also enjoyed fraternizing with working stiffs. Nick recalled that a few locals carped that he'd thrown his money around to snap up excessive acreage. The majority felt otherwise, swooning for Busch Gardens, even if it sat in a city founded by teetotalers and only was open part time.

Adolphus spoke with a diminishing German accent in a booming, often blustery voice. What he rarely talked much about, though, was the myth that he bootstrapped his way to the top as an immigrant who began without two nickels to rub together. This simply wasn't true. Even so, he deserved his place as one of the planet's mightiest businessmen.

Something about being in Ivy Wall reminded Nick's of an anecdote about Adolphus's sway. Supposedly, he once abandoned guests, among them an aide-de-camp to German Kaiser Wilhelm I, at an affair here to seethe in private over what he considered President Taft's personal betrayal of him: Taft's decision to publicly denounce alcohol for the crime and moral decay of the American male. So pervasive was Adolphus's clout that the Kaiser's man couldn't complain about being snubbed, and Taft, a jolly, hail-fellow sort, scrambled to make amends.

Not that Nick questioned Lilly about any details.

"Sit down," she told him, pointing toward a Queen Anne chair in her sun-kissed parlor, which overlooked the upper gardens.

"You sure, Lilly? I'm gamy."

"Nothing baking soda won't address later. I have sons. Now, tell me: were the children amused by your larks today?"

"Yes, if their mirth was any barometer. They implored me to attempt a handstand. I was contemplating bringing my new dog next time to distract them."

Nick's benefactor giggled as a servant rolled in a sterling silver tray with two glasses of iced lemonade and finger sandwiches. Next to them, horrifically, was a crystal dish of marzipan candies. He tamped down his cowlick and swigged lemonade. "Mrs. Busch, sorry, I keep forgetting, Lilly: I cannot thank you sufficiently for helping me to line up this job. To know I'm contributing to the bridge, well, I could die happily."

"All I did was place a call. You took it from there. But, I must confess to harboring a stealthy reason for inviting you here this afternoon. I have another favor to request; I hope it was all right passing you a note to visit me here through the (Mercereau) company."

Here it comes; more terms. "Think nothing of it. I'm in your debt," he said after swallowing a mouthful of cucumber sandwich. "Anything you require."

"This won't take more than a few hours. Have you heard of the Pasadena Perfect Committee?"

"I can't say that I have."

"You're about to, then."

The committee, she explained, was tasked with compiling the city's application for America's "Most Beautiful Small Town" competition, a contest loaded with entries from the Atlantic seaboard. She volunteered to be a cochairwoman and was assigned to memorialize the Arroyo's history tracing back to Pasadena's founding "Indiana Colony." What she was too polite to articulate: the effort was becoming a vanity project that gobbled everybody's time.

"See those papers?" she said, brow crinkled. "It's my personal Alps. And that's from the last six months."

Across the room, Nick spied a Victorian table buckling with documents, folders, and reports three-feet high. A baby ostrich could've hidden behind it. Lilly pressed her chin into her beaded collar, frazzled at the sight of the paper mountain.

"Since you told me you grew up here, I was hoping you might help the assistant I retained to organize the material into a quick city history lesson. My chauffeur can drive you two, so there'd be no walking, just talking. You thrive at that."

Nick, on his third tea sandwich, covered his mouth. "I'd be honored."

"Good, good, good. Don't let my assistant's quiet demeanor mislead you. She's extremely bright and efficient at her job. She's from Chicago and, how can I put it, unfamiliar with her new setting. Studying old reports is no substitute for hearing it from a native son. A few hours pointing out representative sights are all I ask."

"Piece of cake," Nick said, thinking he lifted a weight from her. But, he realized a heavier one lurked in her baggy eyes.

"Much appreciated, my dear Nick. Would it be a bother for me," she paused, "to share an admission difficult for me to divulge to others?"

"Of course not," Nick said, unsure what to say.

"My attention is elsewhere. Adolphus, my darling strudel bear, is not well. Not well at all. I'd be with him in Germany today, but he forbade me from traveling there because he refuses to distress me. His lungs are awful. It's cruel enough we lost our boy, Peter. I fear Adolphus may join him soon."

Nick went still. Peter Busch was a prodigal son who died under mysterious circumstances; there was gossip that he contracted a virulent infection after being pricked by a girlfriend's hairpin. "I'm certain your husband has retained the best doctors."

Lilly's fingers quivered gripping her lemonade. Her other hand was loaded down with a bracelet enameled with that Budweiser eagle. "Yes," she said, "the finest doctors money can buy, and yet none can quell his cough." She cleared a sudden frog in her throat. "I doubt he'll ever return here. Oh, how he cherished chasing his grandkids around Hansel and Gretel in the gardens. *Ich bin gebrochen.*"

"Pardon."

"I'm brokenhearted. If he goes, we'll be a ship without its captain."

Aha. She's suffering. I must remind her of a son. "Lilly, don't give up hope. Your husband has defied the odds his entire life. The Rockefellers aren't like that. I'll pray for him."

Nick felt horrible. One minute, Adolphus's Pullman was smashing the land-speed record, arriving here from St. Louis in a blurring fifty-eight hours; the next Lilly is contemplating a funeral cortege aboard it.

"Bless you, my boy. Maybe my daughters are right when they assert I get ahead of myself."

Movement from the parlor's entryway broke her sadness. A woman in a veal-colored dress wiggled her derriere into the partially ajar French doors to open them. She was taller than diminutive Lilly. Nick couldn't glimpse her face as she backed in to unload a fresh armful of documents on the committee-designated table.

"My regrets, ma'am," she said. "I was unaware you were entertaining. I wanted to alert you that I finished."

"So quickly? I assumed it'd take you a week to sort through that stack?"

"It wasn't that onerous. I have a system."

Lilly's Girl Friday wheeled around, and Nick mouth fell open—again. It was *her*, the knockout from the church service from which Fleet nearly got them booted; the one who temporarily paralyzed Nick's capacity to speak. Now she looked through him. Nick chugged the last of his lemonade to steady his composure.

"Jules Cumbersmith, please make the acquaintance of Nicholas Chance. He's a fine young man who works on the bridge and hails from here. Of all the people I've considered to educate you further about Pasadena, he's the best."

Nick popped up to shake her hand with a clammy palm. She offered back a fish-cold hand, more of a side pinky than grip, and a courtesy smile. "Pleasure," he said overeagerly for someone trying not to act eager. "Weren't you at the memorial for Mr. Mercereau?"

"Yes," she answered in a one-word shutdown. "Lilly: does this appear suitable?" She handed her a one-page summary of something on onion paper.

Lilly ran a bauble-loaded finger down it. "Superlative. I say that every time. You can scoot home."

Fiery-eyed Jules gave Nick a titular nod and spun in such a rush it fanned her dress behind into a frilly bell. Nick hadn't moved from where he stood.

"You can sit down," Lilly said, looking cheerier. "If you can hear me."

"Whoops," he said. He parked his sidetracked self in his chair.

"Can you amplify further on what you'd like me to—?" Nick lost his train of thought when Jules appeared through the picture window outside the parlor. "Uh, what was I saying? Oh, yes, the educational tour."

"Nick, my dear, I wouldn't raise my hopes."

"Hopes, about her? Nah. I was pondering on what side of town to commence. I prefer brunettes, anyway."

"Your expression says otherwise."

By the time Nick departed Ivy Wall, he came away knowing more about the woman he pretended was of no interest to him. Jules, Lilly let slip, was twenty-seven, educated at Northwestern University. She was a diehard suffragette, cryptic about her off time and past, and a literary aficionado of Upton Sinclair and the Brontë sisters.

"She's singular, that one," Lilly said, escorting Nick out. "I'd stick with local girls. Can you be here next Sunday for the tour?"

Nick yearned it were tomorrow. "I can squeeze that in."

◖◖◖

THAT EVENING INSIDE NICK'S bungalow, where Royo smacked his lips impersonating a hungry Nick, Fleet pitched Saturday night dinner at the Hotel Maryland to celebrate Nick's new job. Rose-covered pergolas, brass spittoons, elaborate sauces.

"I don't know," Nick said, reclining perilously back in his desk chair. "My spats are at the dry cleaners." He suggested Debussey's, a tasty deli up the road from Buford's.

"Pass," said Fleet, who leaned against a sink nowhere as tidy as Nick's bed. "We just autopsied a bilious food inspector who basically ate himself to death."

"Relevance?"

"Debussey's sells cottage cheese in big scoops, and it reminds me of cadaver cellulose."

Nick fast-balled a gasket at Fleet, who ducked just in time. "Why do you always have to be *so* specific about your revolting dissections when you know it nauseates me?"

"I apologize. Apologize for not sending you an embalmed cat after you hid a live toad inside my baked potato last April Fool's."

"'Kay. Point taken."

"What about this place?" Fleet performed a curt bow, hands in praying position. "Understand?"

"You're a real credit to your race, you know that? Let's go."

They soon were ladling wooden spoons into miso soup at a far corner table at Manako's Japanese restaurant on upper Fair Oaks. Under paper lanterns, customers worked and fumbled chopsticks, scraped dishes, and dropped steamed rice into their laps. The bow-tied Japanese waitstaff laughed about it in private.

Fleet was peppy now that he had some walkaround money from the dowager paying him for sex, meaning he no longer needed to borrow so much from Nick. He emptied his miso in throaty slurps. He and Nick next laid waste to everything set before them: soy cucumbers, sesame chicken, and possibly squid they didn't order.

Between bites, Nick told Fleet about his encounter with Jules Cumbersmith and Lilly's serendipitous favor.

"You including the Hotel Green on your itinerary?" Fleet asked.

"How can I not?"

Nick immediately regretted saying this. Fleet enjoyed a semi-photographic memory that enabled him to recite blocks of text he read years ago and score well on medical school exams even if his subject mastery was so-so. Whenever he could razz Nick about what he revered—the hometown whose cape he draped himself in—he did.

"You should entertain this Chicago dame about what happened at that hotel," he said. "It's history, too."

Nick twirled chopsticks while Fleet recounted the debacle. Only years after its inception, Pasadena tried impressing the first president to visit it, Benjamin Harrison, with a swanky, two-hundred-person dinner. On this anticipated night at the Hotel Green, high rollers clinked glasses and gave toasts amid polished cutlery buffed to Emily Post standards. What could go wrong? Liquor. Behind the kitchen doors, "colored" waiters hired from Los Angeles uncorked the hooch reserved for later. Hors d'oeuvres, as a result, were stalled, follow-up courses sidetracked. The help left a path of empty wine bottles in their wake.

"Should your Ms. Cumbersmith not be amused," Fleet said, "I'd revisit your infatuation with her."

Nick hated admitting it. Fleet, in all his obnoxiousness, made sense. "Benjamin Harrison is in then."

Fleet, later in the meal, did something uncharacteristic. He turned sincere. "Look. I know we express ourselves by teasing, but I'm proud of you. Wiring cash to your mother, standing up against Otis, staying faithful to your lights, well, that's mettle in my book."

Nick slow-punched Fleet in the shoulder, affection for emotionally constipated men. Then he saw he left a cube of tofu in his soup. He spooned it up and beamed his pal a knavish look. "Should we try again? Tonight could be our night for a soy free throw."

"We do have juvenile reputations to uphold," said Fleet.

He slanted his head back and opened his mouth. The last time they attempted this, the gelatinous blob ricocheted off Fleet's nose and onto another customer's table, which the diners there didn't find terribly farcical. This time Nick gave it better arc. The tofu landed directly on Fleet's tongue.

They erupted in laughter, which now caused half the restaurant to gawk at them. Nick lofted his menu to shield his blushing face; Fleet almost choked getting the cube down. By the time they caught their breath, a woman in a crude burlap dress and Indian necklace was sashaying toward them. She sat down at their table, self-invited.

"The initiative us businesswomen have to take," she said. "Heya, Nick. You still interested in nuts?" She raised a brown paper bag she brought over from her seat.

"Yes, I think. Meet my friend, Fleet Burdett."

"Pleasure, Hattie Bergstron." For a farmer unfairly maligned for witchhood and lesbianism, she made burlap look respectable. "What do you say? For a nickel, these almonds will nourish you as nature intended."

"I promised." Nick dug a nickel from his trousers. Hattie dropped it in her cleavage.

"I hope I'm not intruding on you rapscallions." She said that she and Maude were sampling "traditional city food," minus any meat, after selling out all the nuts and fresh produce from their stand at the intersection of Orange Grove and Colorado Street.

Intruding? The instant sexual alchemy between her and Fleet was as thick as their goo-goo eyes over the table's soy sauce. Hattie couldn't wait to regale him with her story about her commune's migration from Pennsylvania to the hills outside Pasadena, and how it was ostracized for eschewing dairy, spices, and war. She was an animated talker.

Fleet kicked Nick under the table to signal he intended to pursue this vegan Annie Oakley. "So," he said, "no one inside your group consumes eggs or starches, either? I ask this purely out of nutritional curiosity, being a future doctor."

"Nope. We do cultivate grapes for homemade wine. As a scientist, you ought to observe the fermentation process."

"I definitely should."

Nick prophesized where this was going: impending nudity. Fleet and Hattie agreed that they needed to dispose of that wine tonight, lest it spoil in another victory for the city's moralizing prohibitionists. Up rocketed Nick's hand for the bill.

While he waited for it to escape this hormones-derailed dinner, Fleet tried further impressing Hattie, who was boyishly cute for a woman and definitely self-assured. He regurgitated the Hotel Green story.

Not to be outdone, she told her own presidentially themed tale. About six weeks ago, she explained she noticed that someone stole a little-known, gold-embossed plaque near her stand. Inscribing it was Teddy Roosevelt's warning to city politicians during his 1903 visit to the Arroyo Seco. Hattie knew neither the identity nor motive of whoever removed it. But she remembered its phrasing, which she theatrically repeated: "Mr. Roosevelt said, 'what a splendid natural park you have right here! Oh, Mr. Mayor—'"

"Don't let them spoil that," Nick said, completing the sentence. "I heard him say that in person."

As soon as his words died out, Fleet's expression turned impish again. Just like that, Nick recognized he stepped into a self-loaded wolf trap. He didn't need Fleet dredging up his long-ago brush with Roosevelt. Ever. Now, *he* kicked Fleet under the table, and Fleet took mercy on him.

Hattie didn't notice it; she just finished her memory about the mysterious plaque. "I'll never forget when I saw it went missing. It was the very second that I heard the explosion from that grim accident at the Pacific Electric facility."

"*Check*," Nick said again, waving his arm. He didn't fancy rehashing that incident, either, even though it brought an inimitable dog into his life—a dog, Nick suspected, that could occasionally read his mind.

Meal over, bill divided, he moseyed along Colorado Street, where you often needed to pivot sideways to avoid colliding with nuzzling couples or messenger boys. When he entered his bungalow, there was Royo, reclined up against Nick's headboard like a person reading a book, except he wasn't reading. He had Nick's belt in his chops for a good chew. Shamed, Royo dropped his leather aperitif and brought his front paws together, as if bowing in contrition.

"Nice try," said Nick, who was getting used to this.

He clumped down at his desk to tinker in his Saturday night solitude with another gadget he wasn't ready to demonstrate to anyone. He popped in a stick of Wrigley's Spearmint of which he went through a couple packs a week. Royo, immediately, was at his legs, begging for his own stick. "There's no way," Nick said. "You don't chew. You inhale."

Nick changed his mind when Royo whimpered again. Yep: he could chew gum, too. "You're some kind of freak," he said, fluffing Royo's ears.

Over in Linda Vista, Fleet and Hattie downed Hattie's homegrown Cabernet at a fortuitous time. Most of the hillside colony had boarded a train to San Diego to scope out a potential new home. At midnight, the couple's incantations echoed so far that a homeowner in Prospect Park across the valley mistook the squealing for the annoying green parrots.

Ignorant man: didn't he know the chartreuse birds cawed *youch, youch, yeow-chhhh*, not a carnal *yes, yes, yes, yeeees*?

THE ROSIEST OF HISTORIES

H E SHOULD'VE KNOWN BETTER. A morning person like him never should've downed an entire kettle of coffee studying up to gab about one of his favorite subjects. Especially not to an enigmatic woman who made his palms sweat. Nick's exuberance vanquished common sense, and now his bladder would pay the price.

From the moment the Busches's luxury motorcar, an eggshell-white, brass-appointed Oldsmobile Limited, rolled off Ivy Wall's gravel driveway, he began talking. Or, more accurately, preaching his civic gospel of Pasadena while Jules sloughed in the back with more indifference on her cheeks than makeup.

"I'll keep it brisk," Nick said, spying her in the rearview mirror. "I don't want to overwhelm you."

"I can't wait," she said.

Nick paid her tone no mind as Sunday church bells rang out across the quiet town. He had a promise to keep to the wife of dying man. How much Jules absorbed was up to her.

Her crash course would start on the Pasadena's recently added eastern side.

On the drive there, he ticked off basics about California's third-largest city. "It was thirty thousand strong and growing," he said, "arguably the class of the San Gabriel Valley, no offense Monrovia.

"Heartland roots gave the place its essence, but its atmosphere (both cultural and geographic) attracted a surfeit of big personalities, among them astronomers, writers, inventors, philanthropists, and social reformers. Take Owen Brown, son of hanged abolitionist John Brown, the white man who attempted igniting a slave revolt in Harper's Ferry, Virginia. After years on the run, he landed in Pasadena, and never left.

"It was Midwesterners tabbing themselves 'The Indiana Colony' who first stuck their flag in this foothill plain nine years after the Civil War ended. As a whole they were educated, God-fearing people, scientifically minded and adamantly anti-alcohol. 'How dry we are!' one of their first banners read.

"Working for the Busches," Nick said, "you must know that not everybody concurs with the temperance movement hard-liners. I side with Adolphus there. Didn't he say people, not the government, should get to decide what they pour down their gullet?"

Jules didn't answer.

"Energized as the colonists were about being here, they had a crisis on their hands not long after arriving," Nick continued on. "First, a prolonged drought ripped through the citrus belt providing many of them employment. On its heels was a real estate bust aggravated by slick-talking speculators. They plied their targets with whiskey, women, and flimflammery about huge yields, sometimes negotiating over poker games. Lives were quickly poisoned, dreams with them, overpaying for land or buying parcels with misleading values. It was a dramatic beginning," Nick said. "A living parable. Thousands exited town disgruntled."

"If I may, every city has its trials," Jules said, speaking for the second time, head squished into the Olds' leather seat.

"Despite the setbacks, Pasadena, like much of Southern California, wasn't a hard sell to outsiders searching for a better life. The economic opportunity was wide open, and the progressive culture was tolerant of divergent views. But there was something else, something that couldn't be bottled: dry sunshine that boosters trumpeted in recruiting pamphlets and speeches." Nick unfolded a paper and listed the diseases the climate supposedly improved here: TB, malaria, cirrhosis, enlarged glands, insomnia, constipation, and phthisis. Even, he stammered, "female disturbances."

"Folks poured off the trains in the ensuing years, repopulating the town with migrants from every nook of America. They surged in from the Jim Crow South, the Dust Bowl, and the East Coast, particularly Massachusetts and New York. Naming a city with so many sterling attributes was no simple task. Some of the early contenders were screwy—New Granada, Indianala, Muscat, Kleikos."

"Wait. Kleikos?" Jules said. "Your city fathers were comparing themselves to Greece? Isn't that self-aggrandizing?"

"A little," Nick said, bladder ballooning. "Everybody, however, always says Pasadena is the Midwest in Mediterranean weather. Ultimately, leaders reverted to provenance. Pasadena translated as 'crown of the valley' in Weoquan, the Indian tribe that settled the lands before the white man. You probably already gleaned that from your research."

"How could I forget?" she said.

Obviously, this wasn't the juncture for Nick to mention that the Chances of Bloomington, Indiana, were one of Pasadena's original families, sandwiched alphabetically between the Bristols of Iowa and the Clapps of Massachusetts.

"By now the Oldsmobile had departed the concrete streets on the westside for the unpaved road on the city's eastern sector, where many of the town's domestics and less well-heeled resided. Here, the homes were spaced out, the commercial buildings few. They wheeled by Eaton Wash and passed Lamanda Park. They drove by Rosemary's Cottage, home to the 'slow girls,' and shotgun shacks from whose clotheslines hung long johns and hotel uniforms." Nick described the empty spaces and ramshackle blocks filled with non-Anglo faces as "a scrappy expanse that won't always be forsaken."

Jules, with her head still ratcheted back, volunteered her most trenchant observation so far. "I've seen what being neglected means for the disenfranchised in Chicago."

"And?"

"In the tenements, it translates into children playing marbles around diseased water."

Nick was tempted to joke about Pasadena's unusual sewage-to-fertilizer system; he aborted that notion, recognizing Jules lacked his zest for topical sarcasm. "Nobody," he said, "can alter what was. We can strive for what should be." *Not bad.*

"In mid-city," he pointed out the dusty grounds of Tournament Park, home to Pasadena's signature event: the Tournament of Roses Parade. "It relocated here, to California Boulevard, after outgrowing its original locale. Where the first New Year's Day events enticed only several hundred spectators, at twenty-five cents a ticket, thousands of fancy dressed, smiling people now flocked to it. Reviewing stands were erected for spectators to enjoy flower-bedecked floats in the morning and thrilling competitions in the afternoon. Tug-of-wars, foot races, horse races, chariot-style ostrich races, once even a race pitting a camel against an elephant, which the pachyderm won. January-first sporting welcomed all feet."

"Initially, tournament organizers from the exclusive Valley Hunt Club foresaw an annual football game as a central attraction. The first contest was such a rout, though, the University of Michigan walloping Stanford forty-nine-zilch, that the races replaced the gridiron action."

"So why are we here?" Jules said, somewhat Sphinx-like.

"Because this site is emblematic. It's our future. Pasadena," he enthused with all that caffeine pinging through his system, "was transforming itself from a tourist hotbed and agricultural juggernaut—one still packing railcars with thousands of tons a year of sellable cabbage, butter, olives, citrus, wine, and such—into an entrepreneurial-scientific economy. Nothing typified that better than the fact that the expanding Throop College of Technology (the future Caltech) moved next door to Tournament Park. The new meets the old."

"Duly noted," Jules said. "Anything more?"

Duly noted? "Just a smidge," he said, getting the message.

When Lilly's chauffeur swung them by the Hotel Green, Nick retold the Benjamin-Harrison-dinner-fiasco story, as Fleet suggested. *Boom.* It was the first time Nick heard Jules laugh. "Nearby was the elevated wood cycleway linking the giant hotel and points south. A plan to extend it into Los Angeles was scotched," he said. "Still, it gave road builders ideas."

Up next were a couple of Greene & Greene Craftsmen houses, whose woodwork was a near aphrodisiac for certain architectural buffs. But they elicited no reaction from Jules. The orphanage bankrolled by fat cats and the billboard decreeing Pasadena "Just Like Paradise" met that same listlessness.

Nonetheless, they went to Colorado Street, past Clune's Theater, by Vroman's, then the One Hundred Percenters' club building. At Fair Oaks, they dipped south so Jules could soak in the Raymond Hotel where blimps from the dirigible factory nearby hovered over the luxury building's tree-plastered hill.

Going this route involved passing Buford's and the Pacific Electric Railway maintenance barn, which Nick was dumbfounded to see was almost fully rebuilt. Gratitude, survivor's guilt: they all cascaded inside of him dredging up that fiery shock wave. He still had no lucid recollection of what happened to him between the blast and Buford's consoling face over him on the sidewalk. Fleet said disrupted memory was consistent with head injuries, and Nick accepted that, Fleet being a future doctor (and he being a master of compartmentalization).

The last stop on the Jules Cumbersmith educational tour was at the old Carmelita fairgrounds. It was at the intersection of Orange Grove Boulevard, north of where the Busches and other big spenders lived, and Colorado Street's dead-end dip into the Arroyo Seco. Over the precipice sparkled Pasadena's coming automobile bridge, the very quintessence of the city's concrete tomorrow.

"Mere yards to the north," Nick said, believing this was history Jules truly needed to appreciate, "was the rustic world of James W. Scoville. In the late nineteenth century, he built a private dam out of boulders and a hydraulic pumping station out of concrete to trap mountain-fed waters vital to irrigating the area's orange groves. Without them, or the well-trafficked carriage/footbridge over his complex, who knows how fast the city would've developed? Scoville's pay scale augured Pasadena progressiveness, too. He compensated laborers by the number of their dependents."

"If we weren't called Pasadena, we could've been named after him. Better than Kleikos, right?"

Today, Mr. Mercereau's creation dwarfed Mr. Scoville's. Nick hoped Jules understood that implicitly. Yet her engagement with anything was tepid, at best. In two hours, she uttered fewer than two hundred words, including "got it" and "duly noted." She did yawn eight times, the last after Nick described his hometown's hottest industries: real estate, law, and the roaring automobile trade.

"Some know-nothings gripe that Pasadena revolves around chic places like the Valley Hunt Club and Millionaire's Row," Nick said in closing. "That it's old money and priggish, too picturesque for its own good. To them I say, 'Remove your blinders.' Our stock-and-trade is decency. If we were a passing fancy, we wouldn't be risking our necks building a first-class bridge for the benefit of all. Any comment? Jules?"

He looked in the mirror. She was asleep, mouth open. Nick fake-coughed.

"What'd I miss?" she asked.

"Nothing," he grumbled. "Driver, I think we're done."

After they dropped her off, Nick asked Lilly's chauffer to pull over after twenty yards so he could run up somebody's driveway to whiz behind a hedge.

◈◈◈

He scarcely cared that his narration was a warm glass of sleep-inducing milk; that his city of kaleidoscopic flowers, five hundred bird species, and galaxy-plumbing telescopes was so colorless to her. Pasadena didn't need Jules's approval, and *he* didn't need to deceive himself that she was anything but a paycheck mercenary with dry ice in her veins. After all, he was employed on the most intricate piece of derring-do engineering in America while she shuffled papers for Lilly's vanity project.

In the last week, Nick had taken the components the Mercereau Company requisitioned for him and fashioned the two solar-powered lamps required for his audition. He also re-traipsed around the slopes on the bridge's eastern banks, obsessing over the ideal spots for his lights. This was the grueling side of being an inventor, and one where you needed to remain hypervigilant. One misstep in the irregular terrain could snap your ankle in a gopher hole. One distraction could plant your foot on the tail of a venomous Copperhead. Because of that, Nick always swiveled his eyes between the sky and the ground, ears constantly listening for rattles.

Five days after he played tour guide for Jules's benefit, Marcus stayed late with him on the bridge deck to assess how well, in Marcus's terminology, Nick's "little metal petunias" performed. Intimidate Nick as he did, there was no doubt that Marcus was astute. Even though Nick's inventions glowed as he vowed they would, Marcus said he'd reserve judgment until he returned the next morning at six to confirm they still were shining.

It rained that night, and any cheaply made devices would've malfunctioned if water leaked into the seals. But when a sleepy Nick met a grumpy Marcus at dawn, the devices were still casting their exotic, silvery light.

"I'll be, Chance. They passed muster," Marcus said. "I expected they'd fritz out. You're authorized to add another ten."

"I knew they'd work," Nick said.

"Hold on. All you did was remove yourself from probation. You get all twelve twinkling and then I, and I alone will decide whether to consider more. You flub it and your patron won't save you. Clear?"

"As a bell," Nick said.

Marcus scribbled checkmarks on the to-do list on his clipboard and walked off the deck, already preoccupied by his next headache.

╫╫╫

INSOFAR AS OVERALL WORKPLACE camaraderie went, the retail feather business was simpler to acclimate to than rough-and-tumble construction. Working offsite those first weeks, Nick barely had any interaction with the company's rank and file. When he did cross paths with the grungy, suspender-wearing crew, they reacted with cursory nods and wary glances.

He didn't begrudge them for mistrusting him, for whispering about him, for asking which crony greased his hiring. His rationale for being here—installing solar lamps when society was just beginning to plug appliances into electrical sockets—must've sounded flimsy in an industry where you proved yourself on narrow planks at ticklish altitudes. If he was going to fraternize, mess-tent lunches were Nick's best venue. Eating tended to soften folks up.

He tried to ease in already with the bridge rats by seating himself at the far end of their tables, committed to more observation than speaking. Today, he set his tray down in a center seat, ready for further contact. Another outsider, a pasty company accountant who tucked his tie into his shirt, pulled up a chair simultaneously. And how did the men react? Their gossip ground to an awkward halt.

"How's everyone faring today?" Nick piped up with studied innocence. "Same old, same old?"

A man in a rawhide vest, who managed the horses, bailed him out from the stony silence. "We were just grousing about the frost. Half the farmers around here are using smudge pots to combat it. In a few weeks we may need to employ some ourselves. My fingers are blueing."

"Yep, springtime can't come soon enough for me, either," Nick said, trying to spark dialogue. "I'm overworking my fireplace."

Had someone else joined in, Nick was ready with a corny joke about "what was so great about the so-called 'Great Freeze of 1912?'" No one did. This was worse than Jules's silent treatment. Technically, these were colleagues.

At a table diagonal to them—the mess tent had ten total, eight for the working stiffs, one for management, and another brimming with food—someone was being serenaded with a rousing "Happy Birthday." Whatever the division of labor at base camp, Nick intuited a comradeship that didn't welcome just anybody new with a smile and a lunch tray.

So, he recommitted to lunch, assuming he'd need longer to fit in than he calculated. Besides, while the fare here wasn't Buford's caliber, it was surprisingly good. Ham roll, corn on the cob, gingersnaps, iced tea: the management was savvy. Contented stomachs made for productive hands.

While he chewed, the bridge rats chatted among themselves, though they weren't shy about burping and farting for public consumption. When the tie-tucked bean counter left, more animated banter resumed. Nick exhaled, realizing *he* wasn't the conversation-killer. This could be his moment to connect, if he posed a more original question.

"Excuse me," he said to the general table. "What's it like on the scaffolding with no safety nets? Is it always trapeze walking, or does it become another day at the job?"

A rosy-cheeked man from Boston chuckled aloofly, as if only a wet-behind-the-ears nob would vocalize such a naive comment; his buddy, one of the Colorado brothers, elbowed him to stop. Nick cringed at himself as the seconds ticked by. He took a massive bite of ham roll, if only to stuff something in his mouth besides boot leather.

"Let me tell ya, it hardens the concentration," finally said Chester Filkins, a pock-skinned, carpenter/concrete-raker whose defining feature was a caterpillar-shaped scar threading down his neck. "You're petrified at first. One wrong move and it's curtains. After a while, you acclimate to imitating a Billy Goat."

Now I'm getting someplace. Nick nodded and chewed.

Chester wasn't done answering. "You got to harden yourself up there," he said. "You sure can't cry about the money."

"Amen to that," said rebar-clipper Harry Collins, raising his iced tea.

The Mercereau Company, as Nick was learning, paid its men more than typical contractors, up to $4.50 a day, depending on skill and experience, on account of the perils. Untested him was making three.

Now that he asked a decent question, he repeated his name for those who didn't know it, and the other seven men at the table introduced themselves, some with more juice than others. He wasn't intending to say anything more. Someone else did, though.

"Yeah, but Billy Goats don't hear what we do, do they?" muttered Darby Nixon, a beanie-wearing, oval-faced wirepuller with a dab of mustard on his weak chin.

"Quiet, Darb," Chester said, in a scolding tone. "Keep your damn voice down. Those suits got big ears."

"Hear what?" Nick asked, when he probably should've allowed the remark to pass.

Some of the table bridge rats glared at one another and pivoted their heads to check for eavesdroppers. Darby's comment, it seemed, casually injected an incendiary topic.

"Stick around long enough and you'll hear it, or feel it," Darby said at a lower pitch.

Nick crunched a gingersnap, trying to act unfazed.

"Best we can tell the action is coming under the deck," Darby added. "This thing's got a will of her own."

Chester, the table's tacit leader, lost it at that, plucking Darby's beanie off his head and jamming it into his lap. "Quit talking out of school. We don't know this fella from Adam."

Darby, humiliated, put his cap back on. "Yes, we do. He's noodling with those lamps. And don't touch me again, bub." He balled his napkin, picked up his tray, and tromped off in anger.

When the whistle blew for the afternoon shift, everybody else left the tense scene, too. It was now just Nick, Chester, and the elephant in the mess tent that Darby invited in. A minute passed while they finished their sandwiches.

"Darb's a reckless lug, but he's not wrong," Chester said in a muted voice across the table. The suits think the rattling and shaking we told them about is nothing. Claim any disturbances are from normal, concrete settling or creaky forms. I don't know. Never experienced nothing like it at twenty other jobs."

Nick snagged a stray piece of ham and abandoned discretion. "Would it be impertinent for me to ask, Chester, if anybody's calibrated this, scientifically speaking?"

Chester glowered. "Scientifically? You're a college boy, aren't you, greenie?"

"Yes. And I've read about objects vibrating rather strangely if their frequencies are the same as something else nearby that shakes first. It's physics."

"Physics, yeah, I should've thought of that," Chester said mockingly. While he wasn't as daunting as Marcus, the menacing scar by his jugular was a "proceed carefully" sign.

Despite it, Nick pressed on, unwilling to be bullied. "Just because you're a veteran doesn't invalidate my question, and Darby broached the subject."

Nick, new guy, wiped his face and scooted the bench away. A second later, Chester curled his finger for him to sit down, which Nick did, reluctantly.

"I didn't mean to snap at you. What do I know about science? I started working at fourteen. But I've been around, and I ain't never heard a bridge rattle like this, or talk."

"Talk? How?"

"Lean forward," Chester said, sweeping his paranoid eyes around the room again. "It goes *How-uuuuuuuu-kkkkk. How-uuuuuuuuuuuuu-kkk.*"

Nick maintained a neutral expression to mask his skeptical mind. He waited a respectful minute before answering. "That sounded similar to a whale I've heard off the coast at Redondo Beach. Those noises can carry surprisingly far inland."

"I suppose, I suppose," Chester said. "What about the wildlife gone missing?"

"Missing?"

"Raccoons, deer, coyotes: you don't see none of them anymore. Only things around are those lippy parrots. You got to get into Busch Garden ponds before there's anything with a tail."

Nick let that poppycock have its airtime. He didn't doubt Chester and Darby believed what they said, not unless they were fooling with him. Sailors, he knew, were often superstitious, and some bridge rats must be in the club. They were confusing frequency transfers or reverberating noises—whales, faraway building jobs—for campfire-story bunkum. As for the missing animals: it was winter hibernation time!

"Not to be argumentative," Nick said, "but I've ridden a Cawston ostrich here, and the only time she acted up was a day the hammers were really banging and a boy scampered toward her."

Chester shrugged as he rose, his sneer easing into a smirk. "If I were in your shoes, I'd be asking questions, too. But you might be surprised by what concrete can do."

Nick got up, as well, and shook Chester's hand. "I'll keep that in mind."

Striding out of the mess tent, however, Nick mind was already closed. Next time, he'd restrict his comments to the upcoming baseball season or the spectacular fire that razed another landmark, the La Pintoresca Hotel. Failing that, he'd amuse the table with stories of ostriches that resembled notable Americans.

SPRING STREET'S GRAYBEARD

S ATURDAY AFTERNOONS BELONGED TO him. They were Nick's me-
time, *his* greedy-time—his time to recharge the battery he depleted
five-and-a-half days a week sweating the details of his special lamps.
Jaunts with Royo into the hurly-burly of Los Angeles were his outlet, and
it only was a Red Car trip away.

Not that it was a cinch getting his dog aboard because, barring
emergencies, animals were prohibited on the Pacific Electric's spiffy trains.
Initially, Nick circumvented that regulation by purchasing three tickets
and sweet-talking the conductors. Lately, though, he'd been managing it
by buying only two fares, with no blandishment required. Royo would just
hop up the steps, grin at the drivers, and they beckoned him aboard. Nick's
former canyon dog was a charmer of humans, uniformed and otherwise.

Today they boarded at their usual spot: the Santa Fe depot near the
flyover bridge linking the Hotel Green's twin buildings. The trolley was
pretty full, and a few starchy passengers cast reproving glances when they
climbed on. To maintain a low profile, they walked to the rear to stand by
the brass grip-pole there. Everybody else ignored them, bound up in their
own worlds.

In front of them was a cross section of the times: parents dragging
fidgety children to department stores to purchase clothes they didn't want;
Fedora-topped businessmen headed for weekend meetings; scullery maids
gabbing with black men in red bellboy uniforms. Diverse as this mix was
to observe, Nick fantasized about spacing out for the next thirty minutes.

Well, no one ever gets everything they desire.

In the row ahead of him was Constance Prunell, a wealthy busybody belittling a slender Chinese lady in a dry cleaner's smock sitting next to her. Like Lilly, Constance was forever in the newspapers, except for more judgmental reasons. She was on the board of numerous civic organizations, most prominently as chairwoman of the Committee to Eradicate Eyesores, which advocated for the demolition of blighted properties it viewed as unseemly for a city of pronounced architecture. Edison Electric's rail-maintenance barn, pre-disaster, was Number Seven on the committee's list of proposed teardowns; Buford's stand was Number Three. To Nick, she was the worst strain of elitism: someone who freely took out her self-loathing on people with less "status" than her, someone who decided *what* was beautiful and what was vulgar. She didn't represent his Pasadena.

The ham-faced fifty-year-old with preternaturally round eyes was quietly pressuring the Asian woman to vacate the bench they were sharing so she could hog it to herself. Nick, from five feet back, heard her say, "I won't permit my clothes to be washed by your leprous kind so why should I have to sit near one now?" She topped that with something about "opium dens" and "squirrel-eaters." Her victim may not have understood English well, but she comprehended she was being demeaned as sub-human and was about to cry.

Uh-uh. Nick wasn't having this, not so much out of civic gallantry as personal irritation. He dropped Royo's leash and visualized how he wanted his mutt to roust her. Royo enacted it, too, trotting a few steps up the aisle and cutting right into the bench where Prunell was hectoring that woman. *Tada.* Constance bristled when Nick's "diseased mongrel" squished past her legs to nuzzle up against the object of her cruelty.

"He can't be here." Constance said. "This is an outrage! There are regulations."

"Oh yeah?" Nick said, tilting forward and flashing his dog's hole-clipped ticket at her. "Good news. There's an empty seat up front. We wouldn't want you catching anything."

"The nerve," she said. "I'm allergic, I'll have you know."

Constance trundled up the aisle, her round eyes sweeping the train for an eyewitness to corroborate her odious treatment. By the time she forced another passenger to scoot over for her, she was pledging to write authorities about this. And if there was anything she'd mastered, besides preemptive intolerance, it was the complaint letter.

The shaken Chinese woman scratched Royo's ears in appreciation. Before she alighted, she flashed Nick a wounded smile. He and Royo then moved onto the bench still warm from the confrontation, and Nick barely revisited the incident again. There was too much else spinning in his head.

It was on these adventures where he was trying to ascertain, by experimentation, if Royo truly could read his mind by culling his brainwaves. On last week's excursion, Nick gestured at a salted-pretzel vendor outside one of the Red Car stations, thinking, but not vocalizing, how he'd like to split one, if Royo were so inclined. Without any prompting, his dog jiggled his head. To determine if this was a fluke, Nick later pointed at something revolting—two crows fighting over a rat carcass in an alley—and mentally asked Royo his opinion. The dog leaned back against the trolley bench—and covered his eyes with his paws.

His clairvoyance, if that's what this was, wasn't an everyday power, just the same. Sometimes, he failed to react when Nick prodded him. Instead, Royo stared at him as if Nick was trying to force the issue, or neglecting the bigger picture.

Today was their fourth Saturday rompabout into Los Angeles together. On prior outings, they pedaled a glass-bottomed boat on a small, mossy lake in mid-city, and rode a bumper car at the Venice Plunge. They wandered around a snobby Hollywood art gallery, where a woman was aghast that Nick flipped Royo a wadded-up stick of Wrigley's, and even more offended when Nick pretended to speak French to him.

A trip to a MacArthur Park lion show, where an animal trainer rode a man-eater inside a cage for the audience, was the most mind-bending act they sightsaw. Motivated by it, Nick created a new bedazzlement for the ostrich rodeo. At this afternoon's show, Royo got a running start, leapt off a stool, and soared through a bamboo hoop that Reginald nervously held aloft. Where did Royo land: on *Nick's* shoulders as he trotted Mrs. C in a circle.

"Bravo, flying dog," the kids shrieked rhythmically. "Bravo, ostrich man."

Now, bumping along in the Red Car this winter day, Nick posed himself this. What constituted the greater spectacle: his communion with a wily, intermittently clairvoyant canine, when telepathy and séances were all the rage (and the focus of scientific studies), or the pandemonium of downtown Los Angeles, America's former murder capital? It was a toss-up.

Here on Spring Street, the crowds were thicker, the buildings higher, the ads gaudier than Pasadena. Here, the merchants' awnings were grimed in soot, and the black overheard wires tangled like spiderwebs. Its busy intersections, where trolleys, carriages, automobiles, and bicycle messengers vied for the same space as gladiators would, made Colorado Street at peak hours seem a backwater.

Where Pasadena, the Crown City, was tidy, insular, and Apollonian, Los Angeles was a merry-go-round of perpetual motion, brazen humanity, and sin-for-sale. Where Pasadenans cultivated literary salons and scientific orations, newsboys here hawked scandals (raided brothels) and municipal firsts (William Mulholland's coming aqueduct) with the timbre of rival Chihuahuas. Pasadena was beef tenderloin and white wine, its southwesterly big brother a sizzling hot dog and cold draft.

You even could get trampled here if you weren't alert. In their first seven minutes on the thoroughfare, Nick and Royo needed to squish in next to a barbershop pole to dodge the sidewalk masses—that covey of Evangelical women, chanting about repentance in poufy dresses; that clutch of businessmen nattering on about "venal landlords" fast behind them. Who needed vaudeville at Clune's, either, when the weirdos of Los Angeles ambled in the open air? In front of the alcove where they stood waddled four trained ducks; on their fluffy, white backs were painted advertisements for a health food store and a honky-tonk. Soon came pamphleteers promoting nickelodeons and "affordable land," then a quartet of curly mustachioed singers practicing harmonies for a gig.

For Nick, keeping Royo leashed at his side in this Dionysian setting required strong hands and bribery. "I told you'd it be a zoo," he said over the thrum. "Behave yourself and there could be a bratwurst in your future. Hear that?"

Royo's chin bounced.

The marquee of the theater across the street was itself pandering capitalism in bold-relief letters. A nickel bought you a variety act headlined by "juggling pituitary giants" or a peep show. Nick didn't covet any of that, certainly not without Fleet. He coveted a Coke, and Royo could use water from a drugstore soda fountain half a block up Spring Street. What luck, too, for not twenty feet beyond it was Cawston's national headquarters. Nick, exhilarated as he was about working on the bridge, was intrigued about the merchandise the company was hyping in his absence.

Yet, he should've been more careful, because on his fourth, energetic stride toward the soda fountain, his right shoelace caught a loose sidewalk board, and he pitched onto his knees. Royo's leash stretched taut when he tripped, spurring the dog to look back at its klutzy holder. People veered around him while he freed and retied his bootlace, no worse for the stumble.

It was in straightening up that Nick discerned a nattily dressed gent of about seventy observing him with an unnerving grin. A knowing grin. He leaned against a narrow storefront twenty feet up Spring Street, tipping his Boater at him. Classic con man: flattery before stealing you blind. *Let him rope another sucker.*

Nick, clutching Royo's leash, tried swerving around him on the people-packed sidewalk. That strategy tanked. The character snatched Nick by the collar of his winter coat and yanked him into the doorway, effortlessly.

"Mister," he remarked in a sonorous voice, releasing Nick's jacket. "That's one enchanted pooch you have there."

Nick tried getting away, but, strangely, his feet wouldn't budge. Like they were stuck in concrete. "Hey, what's the big idea?"

"Excellent question," said the man with the finely clipped gray beard.

"Let me go or I'll pop you in the beezer and find a cop."

"That won't be necessary," the graybeard answered. "Nor will this take long."

How's he doing this? with his boots still moored, Nick twirled his head, searching for explanations. A clue was right there in the storefront glass.

"Messages From the Other Side: Ten Cents" read a sign in indigo letters. "Readings by Guinevere Adler, acolyte of the Purple Mother." Everyone knew about the Purple Mother. Katherine Tingley was the spiritual theosophist hounded by the *Los Angeles Times* and other moral gatekeepers in the early 1900s for operating a so-called "spook's nest" near San Diego. She contended that her cocker spaniel was a reincarnated associate.

Nick scowled at the huckster that, he had to acknowledge, employed one talented tailor. His black, pinstriped suit was manufactured from such luminous fabric that its borders appeared to halo light. Must've been a fluky reflection from the afternoon sun. "You know, it's against the law to put folks under trances without their permission," Nick said. "What's your game?"

"This isn't a game, and you're not under any spell," the graybeard responded, eyes agleam. "The name's MZ and I've been expecting you, Nick."

"Hey, how'd you know my name?" he said snappishly. His feet weren't going anyplace.

"I know what I know," his captor said with a theatrical lilt. "I'd lack credibility if I called you Henry. My industry has its standards. You should feel honored I know your name. You're among a group of people selected to debunk history's greatest myth."

"What? That the abominable snowman is a guy in a costume?"

"Clever," he said with a dissolving smile. "I sincerely recommend you wake up to the role you've been designated to play, unless you want the cycle to chew you up and spit you out. My advice: tail the voice."

Nick assumed he was referring to Royo, who, for all his smarts, now was licking his privates as if there were steak drippings on them, oblivious to his master being shaken down on their Saturday jaunt. The denizens of Spring Street didn't care, either, blurring past them on their way to sales, shows, or a Coke, like the one Nick was supposed to be guzzling. "Who writes your material?" he said. "A sauced poet?"

"You'd be impressed if you knew. Anyway, if you fail to recognize me upon our next encounter, it means you're still searching for the light in the road. Good day now."

When Nick tried lifting his boots again, they were free, and he wasted no time hurrying across Spring Street with Royo ahead of an oncoming truck. They began scurrying back toward the train depot, but not before Nick turned for a final look at the graybeard. He was tracking him while also holding open his jacket for Nick's viewing pleasure. Inside the purple-velvet lining were dozens of sparkling pocket watches—props, obviously, to scare the unsuspecting about their days running out unless they paid him for intervention.

"How cornball," he said to Royo, who peered at Nick with eyebrows as narrow as Charlie Chaplin's. "His crystal ball must be in the repair shop."

Rather than taking the trolley to where they started out, the depot closest to Nick's Green Street cottage in Bungalow Heaven West, they rode the other Pacific Electric line to Pasadena. This route whipped trains around a hairpin turn and then over a white-knuckle trestle bridge at Garvanza near Highland Park. Many predicated a trolley eventually would sail over the side here, killing everyone onboard when it crashed, sardine-can-like, into the scrubland hundreds of feet below. Nick, believing the alarm overblown, usually watched passengers dig their fingers into the wooden benches as the train listed and *click-clacked* over the gorge. Today, after the phony mind-trip with the graybeard, he lost interest in observing fear ripple through the Red Car. He needed to glimpse the most scientific object in his universe: the bridge.

And before they de-boarded for that, Nick first needed to dissect a boot. So he removed one and, in the flickering sunlight through the trolley window examined its worn-down heel. Yep. As he guessed, there were a half dozen, exposed nail-heads that hidden magnets under the wood sidewalk could've latched onto as part of a rip-off. That huckster was cunning; the intrigue was how he knew his name, and there had to be a logical answer. By the time they disembarked, Nick wasn't nearly as unnerved as he was boarding.

He and Royo were at the top of a trailhead between Ivy Wall and Mrs. Bangs, preparing to amble toward base camp, when events again rearranged the itinerary. This time it was a distant rumble Nick could sense trembling his ankles. In lieu of winding down the embankment, they turned right. First time Nick ever heard of the shop now demanding to be heard.

He and Royo hugged the path that snaked around the Arroyo's eastern rim. With every step north, the vibration heightened and a rattling noise began surging with it. Five minutes later they came upon a garage-size building overrun, or concealed, by thick, brown vegetation. Nick swatted away the branches, battling through the prickly brush until they reached a nondescript, windowless structure. "A. J. Pearson's Industrial Testing: By Appointments Only," said painted letters over the door. Nick had never heard of the shop before.

He pressed his hand against the outer wall. It quivered so intensely it almost tickled. Some type of heavy machinery, something perhaps for a newfangled truck, was blasting full throttle inside and convulsing the surrounding terrain. Nick banged twice on the door. No one answered, which wasn't surprising. You could've run a herd of wildebeests into that wall and no one would've noticed.

Ruuuuun. Errrrrrrrrrrrr. Ruuuuun. Ka-ka-ka.

Homeowners certainly would've protested this insane noise and juddering if the place wasn't so isolated from development. For his part, Royo cared little about zoning. The industrial racket made him revolt against his leash.

"Give me another minute, boy," Nick thought, hoping Royo picked it up over the clamor. "We're on to something."

Ruuuuun. Errrrrrrrrrrrr.

Nick decided to skip any close-up view of the bridge and walk home after his accidental discovery. By Orange Grove Boulevard, he'd put the Spring Street fraudster behind them. A bigger mystery was solved: the bridge *was* a victim to the wails and frequency vibrations from this overlooked machine shop.

"There's your ghost, Chester," Nick muttered to himself. "Physics."

BOOT CAMP FOR BRIDGE RATS

WHEN HE WASN'T ON the deck squinting through his pocket telescope, or in the field scribbling notes for his lamps, Nick was a student of cutting-edge construction. His first lesson: in 1912, no sharp minds built with Old World brute force anymore. They worked with Progressive Age economy of motion.

Consider the gravel needed to batch concrete for the bridge's prodigious appetite. It'd be wasteful trucking the stuff in from distant mining pits when the pebbly rocks were abundant near the jobsite. Workers swinging pickaxes and shovels to excavate it from the slopes bookending the construction zone solved that problem. Resource optimization wasn't sexy. It was just smart.

The diesel-powered mixer, which churned that gravel, cement, and water into concrete, was another example. It spun its mixes next to where the driverless dumpcart ascended its oval trestle track. Doing this shortened the time needed to deliver the mush, so bridge rats weren't waiting around to channel it into the wooden forms. Retaining the flexibility to add a second dumpcart was another inspired advancement.

To Nick, if there was anything paradoxical about the Mercereau Company's ultramodern approach, it was his realization that assembling something of this magnitude was to buzz-cut a small forest's worth of timber. Indeed, of all the stations at base camp, the sawmill area might've been the most decisive. It was there that lumber essential in creating the falsework used to shape the bridge's elaborate parts was prepared with fussy precision. No wood, no concrete bridge. Fortunately, Pasadena's bountiful mountains served as a lumber supply store.

Engineers schooled in geometry and trigonometry burned through pencils, slide rules, measuring tapes, and antacids in this process. They needed to ensure these wooden casts were sawed, milled, and bent just so. It didn't matter whether the falsework was for the soaring arches Pasadenans gushed over, or spandrel columns reminiscent of glass-less cathedral windows. Failure to get it precisely right, to translate the architect's granular specifications into three-dimensional reality, threw everything into a tizzy. Bungling meant do-overs where heads rolled.

Once the falsework was ready to be bolted together, horses became the freight elevators delivering the shaped boards to the bridge rats up on scaffolding. The horses trod the opposite direction of the structure, pulling ropes levering the wood to the proper elevation. In a decade, Nick expected, hydraulic cranes would replace them.

Given a chair and a Buford's Special, he could've watched this regimentation for hours. Cawston's enterprise was well organized; Mercereau's was fantastic choreography. Even the open-hearth furnace, which cooked the long, ribbed strips of rebar sunk into the wet concrete to fortify it, never roared a second longer than necessary to scrimp on fuel.

But Nick couldn't gawk. And he already tried too hard once to ingratiate himself with the crew. When he could locate no other place to sit for lunch one day, he took his place at the end of Chester's table, saying, mildly as possible: "Afternoon, fellas. All right to join you? Mess tent's chockablock today."

"Sure. Take a load off," said an amiable lumber cutter with sawdust in his scalp; at five feet seven inches, the giant crosscut saw he used appeared to operate him. "Say, that's some heaping of grub you have. You cross the Mojave?"

Keep it short. "Sometimes it feels like it after my tromping about."

Chester nodded curtly at Nick, and Nick nodded back. When he wasn't slopping chipped beef into his mouth, he kept it shut this time. Sage decision, for the bridge rats were gossiping again in hushed tones. This time the subject avoided the supernatural. The topic du jour was jobsite gaffes.

"Only a politician who'd never seen a grommet in his life would impose such a hasty deadline," said Chester, working a toothpick in his gums before he rolled a post-meal cigarette.

"Don't rile yourself up—Stonebreaker claims they're bringing in reinforcements," said carpenter Porter Hodge, a prissy-looking fellow in a remarkably unstained flannel shirt. "Old man Mercereau, RIP, must be clapping. I recall him spitting bullets when we fell behind getting those first footings sunk."

"Well, some things are worth getting riled up about," Chester replied, still picking his teeth. "Before he signed on here, our design architect, Mr. Waddell, had the emperor of Japan and Grand Duchess of Russia draping medals around his neck. That's what I read, anyway. Other cities fell on bended knee for his services. So what happens in Pasadena?"

"I'll play along," Hodge said. "What?"

"The pooh-bahs award him the job, argue with him over a measly five thousand dollars, and the city repays him by changing his blueprints. How's that for respect?"

Fleet, Nick knew, would've been backslapping Chester if he heard this. Repeating the fix was in. Needling him about one of the rare articles critical of the bridge, the one where county politicians expressed reservations about coughing up a hundred grand for the job because of rumors about "wire-pulling" in Pasadena's construction bidding.

Nick himself wasn't so delusional to believe the project was immunized from normal greed and ego. In his homer mind, it was a matter of relativity: Pasadena was downright antiseptic compared with New York's Tammany Hall, or Los Angeles City Hall. Ask Messrs. Van Nuys and Lankershim about how the powers-that-be there hoodwinked them out of their San Fernando Valley land holdings for the Owens Valley Aqueduct poised to deliver water from the Sierras.

"Our new friend must be asking himself again what he got himself tangled up into," said Darby, who sat far from Chester in case the hothead exploded again.

"*Aw*, he's being polite, as his mama taught him," Chester added. "That's all."

The men continued bellyaching about labor shortages and miscues securing patented building materials; they nattered on about how the nighttime freezes were affecting the falsework lumber and ill will among some property owners whose acreage the city condemned.

Nick kept shoveling chipped beef into his mouth, saying nothing. Walking away after lunch, he was glad he proffered nothing about how A. J. Pearson's engine-testing shop was the probable source of Chester and Darby's superstitions, or that he didn't counter the other grievances. Stubborn people tend to only listen to evidence that reinforces their slanted views.

✦ ✦ ✦

A FEW MONDAYS LATER Nick rose at four o'clock, a ball of anxious energy. The night before, he decided that was the smart hour to set his alarm clock. Royo must've been eavesdropping on his brainwaves, as he sometimes did unasked, for the dog awoke him with a sloppy lick to the eyelids at three fifty-nine on the dot.

Nick's movements were swift in this pressure-cooker moment. He splashed cold water on his face, pounded a bowl of cornflakes, and fed Royo scraps. He was out the door in sixteen minutes with cowlick hair and sleep dust in his eyes; out the door in a dark Pasadena before newspapers announcing the discovery of "cracked petroleum" and the possibility of Irish home rule hit the streets.

At Orange Grove Boulevard, Nick glanced up at a moon hanging low in the sky like a hazy silver dollar. He smiled at it, and lit out toward the banks. He didn't need to run, other than being amped up about re-inspecting his lamps again before Marcus rendered judgment. That he was here last night at ten doing the same obsessive thing was of no consequence.

Once he checked every one of his twelve lights again, he scaled the bank, passing the splattered concrete mixer onto the deck. Could he ever use caffeine: his pocket watch read five. He swayed on his heels, thinking, for some reason, of his father.

"Fancy meeting you here, Chance," Marcus said, slapping a meat hook on Nick's shoulder from behind five minutes later. Nick practically leapt out of his skin, feet from the edge of the bridge. "*Sheesh*. Don't have a heart attack. You didn't hear a big galoot like me coming?"

"No, sir," Nick answered, trying to de-shock his system.

"Guess not." Marcus stood with a steaming cup of Joe, which Nick wanted to steal, and a battered clipboard. The saggy bags under his eyes were matchbox-size. "Let's get this done. I got new bridge rats starting today that I need to interrogate. Can't lie: I enjoy it."

"Yeah," Nick said. "I get that."

"Careful, wisecracker."

Marcus placed his mug down on one of the two-by-four railings, which served as temporary safety buffers along the open sides of the deck. He withdrew a stubby pencil from behind a hairy ear and walked to the south side of the roughly two-thirds-done bridge. Nick stayed where he was, his stomach in knots. First morning light was slashing the horizon pinkish-orange.

Next, Marcus strode to the opposite side, the one that looked out on the Sierra Madre range, to assess the six solar lamps there. "You passed," he declared matter-of-factly after a minute. "I'll make this quick. I'm okaying you to add another dozen around the existing ones. They could use some beefing up. Maintain the same configurations."

"In obtuse triangles?"

"Yeah, what you said. Make sure the light's aimed at where the motorcars will be entering."

"You got it. It's heady to realize this will be their debut."

Marcus picked up his mug and drank the rest of the coffee. "Look. I'm not a sentimental man," he said, wiping his mouth with the sleeve of his wool jacket. "To be honest, I was looking forward to firing you—you being foisted on us and all with zero experience. I can't reasonably do that, can I though, when your little metal petunias continue working. I still expect you to revise the site plan and estimate a completion date."

"That I can do."

"No lollygagging, either. We're busting our humps to complete this job."

"I'll get right on it."

When Nick spun to leave, Marcus once more clamped his fleshy hand on his shoulder. "We're not quite done, eager beaver. You may still be leading VIP tours. Reassure me that I can trust you."

And they say sadists have no fun. "Fire away."

"Altitude of the highest arch? Quick."

Nick's brain fought through fatigue. "Um, two hundred twenty-three feet."

"Why's she curved?"

"Unevenly distributed bedrock on the west, narrow on the east. Good footings need unshakeable ground."

"Not bad. The daily pour?"

"I know that. Up to one hundred twenty cubic yards per day, with an eight-man team."

"Concrete mix?"

"Four parts gravel to two parts sand and one part cement."

"Last one. How many road apples do our best horses crap in an average day?"

Before Nick could answer it was a trick question, Marcus rolled over him. "Why doesn't anyone think us roughnecks have a sense of humor?"

"I have no idea," Nick said, biting his lip.

⟐ ⟐ ⟐

AFTER WORK THAT TRIUMPHANT day, Nick didn't drag his exhausted body straight home. He scaled the path toward Ivy Wall to ask Lilly for a favor. They hadn't spoken since he played tour guide to her inscrutable Girl Friday. Lilly greeted him warmly, even so.

His question involved Royo, canine tornado. The dog's cabin fever, his hatred of being left alone in Nick's bungalow for hours on end, six days a week, was at a breaking point. While Nick was away, the stray chewed and then chewed some more. The carnage so far included Nick's hiking boots, two sets of schematics, a college photo album, and enough divots in the hardwood floor to start a new trend in the Arts and Crafts movement. Royo also figured out how to bypass Nick's pantry door to pilfer human food. Whether he was doing that because of a rapacious hunger or as insurrection, it didn't matter. This couldn't go on.

Was there any possibility, Nick asked from Lilly's parlor, if he could board Royo in the fenced-in pen, where her dog stayed, while he was at work nearby? The backyard space, which overlooked upper Busch Gardens, was roomy enough for twenty Royos. "He'll be good," Nick said. "I think he takes out his loneliness on my possessions, one gnarled object at a time."

Lilly didn't twist any knives as Marcus did when you needed something. "Delightful notion," she said. "Maty, my butter streusel, could benefit from the company. My staff can only attend to her so much."

She opened the doors, and they drifted out onto the square, grassy enclosure. Jules didn't seem to be around, and Lilly, thankfully, didn't broach her. A steel-gray schnauzer trotted over to say hello and beg a treat from Lilly's pocket. A giant opal on the baroness's hand winked sunlight as she threw the rag-mop a carrot. Maty crunched it and immediately returned to her spot in front of a custom doghouse mimicking Snow White's steep-roofed cottage. There, the dog a quarter of Royo's size resumed her compulsive behavior, alternating between licking her paws and nibbling lawn.

The schnauzer, Nick gathered, must spend all day there. Because of her lapping tongue, the grass was pocked with yellow encrustations where even new turf wouldn't sprout. Royo would need time adjusting to such a pampered, lazy pen-mate that didn't even bother terrorizing squirrels or barking at milkmen.

After Lilly accepted Nick's repeated thanks, she said she had "something I've been meaning to get you. Hold your donkey while I retrieve it from inside." Minutes later, he departed with a gold-embossed envelope.

In the weeks that followed, Royo settled into his fresh air, doggy-care with a new cohabitant still more preoccupied by her own tongue than playing. For him, the real benefit of being outdoors was freedom. Within days, he learned how to escape by squeezing through loose fence posts, using his liberty to romp about and explore Pasadena beyond luxurious Orange Grove Boulevard.

DORIS AND THE WRITER

THE WELL-HEELED GUESTS STRIDING into the main banquet room at the Hotel Green were astounded at the lengths party organizers went to recreate a hoedown in this historic chamber. Everywhere they looked were scarecrows and mason jars, banjos and hay bales, country punch and substantial farm animals.

"Wunderbar to see you," event chairwoman Lilly Busch said seeing a new face enter. She employed another go-to greeting for certain male acquaintances: "*My, my*. You look as handsome in overalls as you do in a tuxedo."

It was wise to butter up the attendees. She wanted their money.

Nick and his stag date, Fleet, watched her press the flesh with her donors from the back wall next to the pocket library. They were sipping complimentary Budweiser, preparing to hobnob with the upper-crusters, many of them awkwardly attired in cowboy hats, cowpoke skirts, and rawhide for Lilly's costume-gala fundraiser.

Between the pair and the pasty faces were twenty or so blue-and-red-checkerboard-covered tables on the parquet floor. Off to the side was a grub table heaped with fried chicken and other countrified fare.

"Knock Pasadena all you want," Nick said, "but you think you'd get this quality of people watching in Whittier?"

"No. Probably not," Fleet said. "Let's drink to that."

They clinked bottles.

"And you promise to be a good boy, correct? No talking out of school."

"Yes, mother," said Fleet. "No speaking of Gilly's beer pipe, your green parrots, or the Spring Street man who guessed your name."

"Anything else?"

"*Fine.* I won't mention the Benjamin Harrison incident. Don't I have First Amendment rights?"

"I'm suspending them tonight."

Nick, as Fleet knew, didn't wanted to be here, despite this venue being a ten-minute walk from his bungalow. And it wasn't only his distaste of artificial socializing. It was missing a double-barreled opportunity elsewhere.

Two weeks earlier, a former girlfriend who worked at the "Solar Observatory" on Mount Wilson, invited him for a sneak peek at the huge, steel-and-concrete dome under construction there. Once the French manufacturer milling the giant lens stopped botching the job, George Ellery Hale's telescopes could well revolutionize astronomy. They'd pack the optical firepower to peer tens of thousands of light years into the universe's past; maybe unlock the spectral mysteries of the sun. A former Austrian-patent already yearned to book time there.

Still, Albert Einstein wasn't in Pasadena like Nick, a layman with a fervor for science and a shot at romance on Mount Wilson. But all that evaporated with Lilly's invitation for him to "enliven the atmosphere" here with his vitality. He couldn't refuse.

What Nick could do was eyeball the head-spinning list of local millionaires or their kin on the event program. In alphabetical order, there were Armour Cochran (pig iron, coke); John S. Craven (Liggett-Myers tobacco); Henry C. Durand (groceries); Arthur H. Fleming (lumber); Eva Scott Feynes (publishing); David B. Gamble (soap); Anna Bissell McCay (vacuum cleaners); Lamon Vandenburg Harkness (Standard Oil); Henry Huntington (railroads, *et al*); Lewis J. Merritt (iron ore); Mrs. George Pullman (trains), and, Nick and Royo's favorite after the Busches, William J. Wrigley (chewing gum). They all either resided in Pasadena or "wintered" here.

"We better hope the ceiling doesn't cave in," Nick said. "The US economy would sink."

"True. You'd need," Fleet said, swigging on his Bud, "a morgue just to house all the zeroes in their bank accounts."

They entertained themselves observing this assemblage of wealth and privilege tipping Stetson's or showing off western boots fresh out of the box. A third of the attendees weren't in any hokey outfits they judged beneath them. They wore what they frequently did on Saturday evenings on the Pasadena party circuit: black ties and ball gowns.

"Is that," Fleet said, "who I think it is approaching us?"

"I can't read your mind," said Nick, whose dog frequently read his, "but yeah, if you're talking about Pasadena's White House connection."

Hobbling past them to the ladies' room was the aging Lucretia Garfield, widow of former President William McKinley, who was assassinated by anarchist Leon Czolgosz in Buffalo, New York, in 1901. After his bullets flew, Teddy Roosevelt assumed the presidency, which paved the way for Nick's intersection with him, and she relocated west to a five-bedroom Craftsmen. Wags called Mrs. Garfield the area's "lady in continual mourning," for no dignitary passing through town would dare leave without paying respect.

A minute later, it was Nick's turn to point. "Correct me if I'm wrong, but isn't that *your* dowager over there? I didn't know she was that rich to warrant an invitation. I sure hope Hattie isn't aware of your arrangement with her."

Fleet quickly hid behind Nick so the small-mouthed woman in a sunflower dress didn't notice him. "No, Hattie doesn't know," he said. "You try attending medical school with poor parents minus any helping hand; my side jobs only pay so much. I wouldn't have come if I thought I'd run into her."

"Well, don't even consider bailing now. Tug your cowboy hat down over your face."

Though twenty years Fleet's senior, the dowager, who lost her industrialist husband long ago, was actually a beguiling woman who just craved virile, younger men.

They'd just sat down at a table across the room from her when Lilly motioned Nick to come to the side of the stage up front. She was in a taupe Texas ranch dress accented with pearls the size of bonbons. Nick, by contrast, wore a black jacket-bolo tie costume over a white dress shirt; Fleet compared him to a louche, riverboat gambler.

"Stay right here," Lilly told Nick after a brief hug. "There's someone who wants to say hello. I'll go retrieve her."

Nick didn't dare let his mind wander. While he waited, he surveyed the inside of what locals nicknamed "The Castle." The Hotel Green was the size of a battle ship. It was a full block long, designed in a hybrid, Moorish-Colonial style, and painted in sand tones with red trim. Its hallmark turret fronted a plaza you could imagine Norman Rockwell painting. Unlike the La Pintoresca and The Raymond, its steel and concrete construction ensured it'd never burn down. Its glamorous spaces once served as the headquarters of the Valley Hunt Club and the Tournament of Roses.

Still, you wouldn't know that now from the job Lilly's decorators did transforming the banquet room from hoity-toity to barn shindig. Hay bales lined the walls; milking buckets offered guests wrapped candy apples and Lilly's hideous Berlin marzipan. The denim pockets on the scarecrows propped up in the corners were where everyone was instructed to deposit their charity checks and cash.

Some of the party accoutrements were alive, as an unexpected *moooo* by a Jersey heifer demonstrated. It and other barnyard animals were trucked in from San Gabriel Valley farms because what's a hoedown without critters? The bigger ones—two bovine, three sheep, one Shetland pony—were tethered by restraints. Hens, pigs, a sedated raven, and others loitered in an adjacent area, cordoned off by troughs.

Nick was sizing them up when Lilly returned. "Nick, " she said, "you must remember your high school history teacher. She recalled you when I mentioned your name at a committee function. She said you were at the *top* of your class."

Under the crook of Lilly's arm was a stooped over old woman with veiny arms and a twitchy neck not unlike a geriatric pigeon. She was half blind and even deafer.

"Miss Figgleberry, marvelous to see you," Nick said, pecking her on her powdered cheek.

"Nick, is that you?" she said in a quaking voice. "Lillian informed me about your current occupation. How invigorating it must be arranging lights across our glorious new bridge."

"I'm developing lamps, Mrs. Figgleberry," Nick said loudly. "Solar-powered lamps."

"Cramps?" she said. "I don't have cramps at my age anymore, sweetie."

An hour later, guests were in their chairs, finishing their entrees. Lilly spoke from a small riser through a bank of cigar smoke and social chatter, much of it about the dreaded imposition of America's first income tax. Lilly said it was everybody's responsibility to support needy children, as well as Civil War veterans who either visited or relocated to California. Subsidizing their admissions to Busch Gardens and assisting local charities was a modest start.

"In closing, dear friends, I ask you to give until your wallets cry in pain. Not to lecture such a distinguished crowd, but the Bible makes a point about rich men and eyes of needles. I say that, too, as a dreadful seamstress."

Uk-uk-uh-haw. Uk-uk. Evidently, the leased hen appreciated her punch line.

"Pardon the interruption," Lilly said, vamping. "She must be nervous, we're serving her cousin."

Nick hated acknowledging it, but he was enjoying himself. The guests at his table were friendlier than their initial scowls, except for the snob in a raw hide jacket displeased that Nick momentarily placed his elbow on the table.

Next were further solicitations by others for donations, and a reminder about the ongoing efforts by the Pasadena Perfect Committee. When a paper-clip scion quoted another of Adolphus's tributes about the city—that it was "a veritable paradise (with) no equal in the world regarding healthful climate, scenery, vegetation, flowers"—Nick saw Lilly gulp at the front table. Few must realize how sick Adolphus was.

The night was roughly two-thirds over as waiters prepared the coffee and a wire basket emerged for a raffle. A couple of banjo players set up for a square dance. This wasn't a group that stayed late.

The same heifer that mooed before—a seven-hundred-pound, cinnamon-colored Jersey cow—was done, however, being a compliant party decoration anymore. She snorted again in a call of the wild that made the crowd shudder. The animal didn't immediately repeat it, so most of the attendees went back to their cherry cobbler and check writing.

Almost no one heard what one of the livestock handler's said to the other seven minutes later. "John, Doris is loose! She's snapped her ropes. Trap her."

Too late for that, however, after the cow hurdled the hay bale supposedly sequestering her, stomped her heels, and released a moo that could've awoken a mummy. Now there was *no* barrier between her and some of America's richest people, many of whom were never so close to a beast like this before. Eyes bulged. Hearts raced. Bodies studded with diamond jewelry shook.

Nick, while slightly beer-brained, popped up to assess the situation. From his time around ostriches, he knew how easily some larger creatures became unhinged. He looked up front: nothing but magnates in country regalia. He looked to the side: just waiters in black. He gazed to the rear last, and there, by the kitchen door, stood one of Lilly's party organizers.

Apparently, Jules Cumbersmith's experience with cows in big-city Chicago was limited because otherwise, she wouldn't have been wearing a silky, claret-hued dress. Where she saw one shade, that heifer interpreted red, a red demanding it trample her.

Doris mooed another war cry that vibrated the cobbler plates. Then it was on: she bent her head and charged directly at Jules, who froze against the wall. The cow's hooves slipped after her first tentative steps on the polished parquet floor. Once she regained her footing, Doris was only third yards from Jules, and closing fast.

"Lady," a beanpole-thin handler yelled. "It's the dress. The color!"

"Now you tell me," Jules shouted back. She tried shoving open the kitchen doors to get away, but they opened out. Her only resort: kicking off her heels and scurrying toward the raffle table.

Fleet jumped up next to Nick. "You're a doctor, sorta," Nick said to him. "Got any tranquilizers?"

"Sure," he jibed. "They're in my pocket with my blow darts."

It was confusing knowing what to do as Doris chased Jules from the boundary area into the space between the tables and the stage. After this continued for a minute, what seemed like a slapstick turn of events was taking on the air of disaster. In panic, some of Lilly's guests bailed out the exit door onto Green Street. The two frailest attendees, Gilda Figgleberry and Lucretia Garfield, were escorted there. A dozen millionaires, meanwhile, helped their wives onto the checkerboard tables, which was comedy on its own.

Which wasn't to suggest that Jules was fully deserted. One of the animal handlers, dreading that she was fodder for a grievous head-butt, threw a lasso as the rogue bovine hoofed by; having rarely practiced, he roped a chair. A gent in a Stetson hat, who was either a Wrigley or a Gamble, threw his winter coat over Doris's neck. The cow shook it off in three strides.

Jules, after running and cutting, finally leapt onto the low platform where Lilly and others spoke to cower behind the black curtains. Lunatic over her red dress, the athletic heifer jumped onto the stage, too. Jules bounded out, racing down the center aisle. "Can *someone* do something about this she-devil?" she said, shaggy-breathed. "I'm tuckering out."

Unsure if the animal might charge them, fifteen or so guests too scared to risk running to the exit packed themselves into the railed orchestra stand, where the banjo players were intending to play. This left no room for Jules, though someone there shouted advice: "Play dead."

The other farm animals began editorializing with a nerve-rattling chorus of clucking, hawing, whinnying, and baying. Never had such an ado transpired in a hall where the pampered and chauffeured schmoozed during the hotel's thirty-year existence; not even the Benjamin-Harrison-dinner kerfuffle.

Nick pirouetted, trying to freelance a solution. Doris, evidently, wasn't going to be thwarted with a table or somebody's coat. His eyes focused on the food table, where he and Fleet twice loaded up on fried chicken, gravy 'n' biscuits, green beans, and potato salad.

Now, he let a remedy flow to him and, sure enough, a light bulb clicked on.

He relayed it to Fleet, who nodded his head without further commentary and rushed off to prepare. Nick then sprinted toward the buffet table, ripping off his jacket, bolo tie, and white shirt on the way. Distracting striptease? Better.

Nick dunked his dress shirt into the punchbowl of the vodka-spiked "Wild Cherry Country Punch." He didn't want Jules's blood on Doris's dark heels. Bare-chested, he ran back and climbed onto a vacant table in the middle of the banquet room. From it, he managed a two-fingered whistle, which RG had previously tried teaching him; most of the time it'd produced more spittle on his pinkies than a shrill blast from his lips.

Jules, with fear in her eyes, turned to him as he hollered his plan. "Fine," she said between pants. "*Anything*."

Nick pinkie-whistled again, and this time the heifer locked its furious eyes on him. "Doris, what do you think about *this* color?" he shrieked, holding up his red-punch-soaked shirt by its collar as if he were a matador. "Come and get it, kitty."

He hopped down from the table just as Jules, gown hem in hands, sprinted by him in her bare feet. The snorting cow, which had fallen behind after skidding on a napkin, abruptly forgot about the woman in the claret dress she wanted to pancake. Nick's red shirt was now her bull's-eye, so to speak.

Nick ran toward the rear of the hall with amused horror etched in his face. In his sightline was the Hotel Green's pocket library, which held a small, prized collection of works from esteemed California writers. Now it'd become something else, what with Fleet opening its mahogany door and hiding behind it.

"Get ready," Nick shouted as he raced square at it with Doris in pursuit. Right before he was about to smash into the library's doorframe, he lobbed his soggy, punch-red shirt in there and hopped to the side. The cow, unable to slow her hooves on the parquet floor, skidded into the little room, crashing into the back bookshelf. Fleet slammed the door shut, and Nick brought over a chair to prop under the knob.

Nick, with no shirt and sticky hands, and cowboy-hat-less Fleet hugged. The remaining guests, down to a quarter of Lilly's original audience, clapped and cheered for them in a chorus of "Bravo," "here, here!" and "quick thinking, lads."

By the time Nick saw Jules again, she was rushing into the ladies' room in tears.

Twenty minutes later, Fleet exited with his impressed dowager, who said his "bravery warranted a special cuddling." "Before I go," Fleet muttered to Nick, "what is it with *you* and animals nowadays? You're going to get yourself killed, and that'd be a shame. For me."

Lilly by then was speaking with the banquet room's frazzled event manager, who saw no levity in this as Lilly did. She reassured him they'd reimburse the hotel for any damages caused by Doris's antics and Nick and Fleet's impromptu incarceration of her. "It could've been worse," Lilly said. "What if she'd gotten into your kitchen?"

This she said while waiters and busboys were already sweeping up. Besides food, straw, and party favors in their dustpans were other telltale items, among them a monocle, a woman's dentures, and a liniment vial.

Blessedly, Lilly had barred any press tonight, or this would've exploded into a national punch line.

The previous uproar now was as quiet as the idle scarecrows, into whose pockets the Busches's friends stuffed seventeen thousand dollars. Only stragglers like Nick and hotel staff remained when Jules emerged from the bathroom, mascara smeared and formerly bobbed hair a bird's nest. She grabbed her discarded heels and trudged his direction.

"That was something," Nick said to her in a borrowed waiter's shirt. "Are you all right? You'll be avoiding milk for a while, I imagine."

Jules, the anti-damsel, smiled at him and pulled him to the side to converse. For a moment, Nick thought she might reward his heroics with a smooch. Lilly stood in the center of the trashed room reviewing the bill, though she occasionally glanced over at them.

"Avoid basking in this," Jules said, holding her plastic smile. "You managed a good deed in an unpredictable circumstance, and I thank you. But don't flatter yourself too much. I had an alternative rescue plan."

"What? Take the dumbwaiter?"

"Do you ever stop joking when the subject *isn't* Pasadena?"

"Okeydoke," Nick said, resentful of her tone.

Still smiling, she said, "Goodnight." And that was all.

When he arrived home at midnight, Royo offered him no victorious welcome, either. No, he was reclined backward on Nick's bed, again, with Nick's tennis racket in his teeth. Half the strings were ripped out.

"Oh, wunderbar," Nick said.

◆◆◆

NICK AND FLEET, WITH parents out of state, celebrated Christmas together by exchanging small gifts and inside jokes. They attended Pasadena's event-heavy New Year's Day, including the Rose Parade and ostrich races, whose outcomes Nick always predicted correctly. On the maiden night of 1913, they sipped cheap champagne. When Nick strummed "Auld Lang Syne" on guitar, Royo pirouetted on hind legs.

Three weeks later, on a hump day in late January, Nick sat alone on a Red Car inbound from Los Angeles. Between his boots rested a jingling bucket of metal parts for his solar lamps. In his hand was a business card pumping confidence into his chest.

Rex Gleason, an Edison Electric Company special assistant, handed him his card after Nick led him and two others on a rain-shortened tour of the bridge. Reginald Plant, who didn't have school that day, was also on the outing. The first of his many questions: "who'd bother taking this boring road after someone invents flying motorcars?"

Percy Fixx, a beady-eyed, broad-shouldered icehouse proprietor, was the Pasadena VIP of the bunch. The forty-something businessman served on the executive committee of the Board of Trade, among other organizations, and was known around town as a financial whiz and lady-killer. He didn't articulate much today, sponging up Nick's narration with a grin on his face. But there was something reptilian about how he looked at you, as if he was trying to determine if you picked up on his extra row of teeth. Nick mistrusted him from the second he shook his frigid hand.

After the tour concluded in the misty shadows under an arch, which Nick joked that Edgar Allan Poe should exploit as a backdrop in a future horror tale, Gleason told him he'd like a quick word. "We've been following you since you were at the ostrich farm, Mr. Chance," Gleason said. "What you achieved there and here, from what we understand, is nothing short of remarkable. If your schedule permits, we'd be honored if you'd meet with some of our technical people to expound on the science behind your lamps. We live to harness energy wherever it exists."

Gleason, a chunky man with an orange-hair comb-over that oscillated in the breeze, cited Edison's hydroelectric plant in Riverside; he mentioned the steam power it furnished to some Pasadena streetlights "before," he added, "your city decided, somewhat rashly, to charter its own electric utility."

Nick was gracious and noncommittal, telling Gleason he'd contemplate the offer that he had no intention of pursuing as he considered Edison Electric a predatory octopus. Even so, the solicitation was a pride booster. Proof that the octopus was scared of what he was refining; that his lamps could be his legacy. Who knows? Later this century, kids on field trips might trek to the banks of the Colorado Street Bridge to eyeball where the sun-power revolution began.

That's why he was still fingering Gleason's card while trying to balance his pail of bolts, wires, eyelets, and filaments on the trolley floor. He bought the components this morning at Tilly's Hardware Emporium store on Virgil Avenue with a purchase order he wrote out, too impatient to wait for the harried requisition clerk to do it.

Now those parts clinked hypnotically to the rattle of the steel wheels like a dreamer's song. This was a fruitful time for inventors like him to be asking the proverbial "why not?" Technological breakthroughs launched in the Gilded Age of excess were booming in the Progressive Era. Since 1900 the "firsts" were ubiquitous: the alkaline battery, the Brownie camera, the electric typewriter, the jukebox, color photography, an "all-purpose zipper."

A gentle, two-finger tap on his shoulder from a passenger behind him wrenched Nick out of his reverie. "Pardon me, sir," said the male voice. "Would you be able to recommend an establishment selling a hearty sandwich?" Nick turned his head ninety degrees, seeing the side of a man in a tweed cap. "Everybody I ask," the passenger continued, "directs me to one of your city's delis, which isn't suitable. My constitution can no longer abide the aroma of pickles, not after consuming their juice for a week."

Before Nick told the unknown gentlemen he was in luck, he said, "Mister, you drank pickle juice? On purpose?"

"Ridiculously, yes. Would you permit me to come sit next to you so I may be discreet?"

"Sure, why not?"

Nick nudged his parts bucket over with his ankles while the stranger settled in.

Holy Mackerel. It's him. Him: as in America's premier muckraker; him, as in the blue-eyed, thin-lipped literary star so distinguished he could go by his first name. And now he needed a sandwich recommendation.

Upton Sinclair introduced himself. "To finish my comment," he said, "a quack New York physician convinced me that dill-pickle juice was a detoxifying agent. The only thing it removed was my appetite."

"Your timing's impeccable, Mr. Sinclair. I'm disembarking in two stops for a late lunch at Buford's Meat Shack."

"Sounds morbidly unhealthy, and delicious. Tell me about this Buford's."

Nick couldn't help but wonder what those tycoons and scions from Lilly's cow-disrupted hoedown would opine about his seatmate? In Sinclair's blockbuster novel *The Jungle*, he exposed, within a morality play, the queasy realities of America's industrialization of food. Its publication hastened health and safety laws that saved people's lives and tested several presidents. His typewriter keys, in that bestseller and others, soon vaulted him into an everyman crusader.

Not that he was currently dressed like a public champion. Under his black coat he wore a white, V-neck vest and matching tennis pants stained at the knees. His smile was also inconsistent with his reputation for unflinching seriousness.

"If you're hankering for a belly buster, search no further," Nick said. "You're welcome to accompany me."

"Call me Upton and you're on." He tipped the beanie he depended on to stay incognito.

In the twenty minutes until they sat down with their plates, Upton, unsolicited, explained to Nick why he yearned for such a decadent meal. In sum, the socialist idealist had meandered too far down the rabbit hole of experimental dieting.

In response to deteriorating health—bad teeth, bronchitis, dyspepsia, insomnia, you name it—he penned a book about the virtues of caloric restraint. It wasn't the hot-selling novel his publisher desired, but that was its problem. He had a cautionary tale for his audience: the chocolate cake, buttery potatoes, and bread of his privileged youth led to dangerous eating habits as an adult. Worse, he believed, America's increasingly artificial food system—formaldehyde-preserved beef, anyone—was the fast track to an early grave.

It was sheer irony hearing about his gastronomic near-suicide being as they were within arm's reach of two unapologetically fatty sandwiches. But it was a story Upton was determined to tell. He claimed he tried everything to regain his health. He traveled to the wellness lands of Battle Creek, Michigan, to wean himself from modern food laced with sinister bacteria; he visited digestive resorts in the Adirondacks and Bermuda.

"Nothing was succeeding," Upton said. "I exercised vigorously and drank water by the bucket. I consumed only milk and raw foods. It was slow death."

"Something obviously worked," said Nick, half his Buford's Special already gone.

"Yes, it did. Moderation. Now, I hew nine days out of ten to an ascetic diet of puny meals. Broth, fruit."

"And the tenth?"

"I treat myself, and mitigate the internal havoc afterward with water and pomegranates."

"Smell the roses, so to speak?" Nick said, lamenting how schmaltzy that sounded in this town.

"Advocating for change against the powerful should warrant the occasional indulgence, no? Critics accusing me of spreading fads know little of which they speak."

Nick could've pinched himself, well aware of how his new acquaintance sparred with American giants named Rockefeller, Vanderbilt, Schwab, and Carnegie. Copies of *The Jungle* and *The Moneychangers* rested high on his own bookshelf, where Royo couldn't mangle them. But, as Upton's readership knew, personal turmoil had mangled him. Health issues, divorce, rumors of "free love" at the East Coast utopian compound he founded before it mysteriously burned down. Life slapped him around not in spite of his fame, but because of it.

Upton, a methodical eater savoring each bite of Buford's magic, said he was in Pasadena to further recuperate while marinating ideas for his next book. "Swinging my racket under your eternal sun, though, is spoiling me. And I'm monopolizing the conversation, too. Tell me about you."

Nick recapped his background and eventful last year, skipping the Cawston's gift-shop fight and rail-barn explosion just up Fair Oaks Avenue. Trying to impress the writer, he mentioned how the Edison Company was, if not spying, monitoring his wireless, solar lamps.

"You got them steamed up," Upton said, blotting grease from his slender fingers. "Don't stop."

"You did once say you could judge a man's contributions from his enemies."

"That I did."

"What are you chasing in the long run?" he asked, digging into his vinegary coleslaw.

"Another sandwich?"

For the first time, Upton laughed unrestrained, which gave Nick an unappetizing view of the future Pulitzer Prize winner's (and future California gubernatorial candidate) set of crooked teeth. "Then you'll never see forty," he said. "Which might not be such an awful thing."

Nick napkined his face and tried curbing his tendency for glibness. "What I want is to marshal the fire in my belly, to learn if the ancients were prophetic: that the sun we take for granted could be the antidote to propel modern civilization. This job in the Arroyo is my chance to, I guess, outlive my obituary."

Upton, thirty-five, rocked his head. He glugged water next from a canteen he kept in the cracked-leather satchel with his tennis racket and notepad. After he was done eating, he removed his cap and turned his face to the winter sky. In doing so, Nick noticed another dichotomy about him. Though tanned and alert, he presented the silhouette of a malnourished tripper, a kind of intellectual hobo.

Try as he might to remain unrecognized, it wasn't working. Every literate restaurateur knew the author of *The Jungle*; he was one of the country's most photographed men. Buford, the quiet Cajun, realized it was him in a heartbeat, and tried acting unruffled when he and Nick ordered their specials. Inside, however, he was a wreck, praying his celebrity customer didn't get a gander at his kitchen—the flies, the smudged aprons, the char on the grill. If he wrote about it, ever, Constance Prunell would have his stand bulldozed in a week.

In the patio area, fellow eaters slyly pointed at him. Buford himself waddled out after ten minutes, sitting down with a frequent customer to chinwag. This was just pretext, for his obvious intent was spying on guess-who. Nick giggled when he saw the pudgy-bellied chef sneaking glances at whether Upton was jotting notes.

"*Mmmm*," Upton said. "That was wickedly good." With his blood sugar revved up, he gabbed even more rat-tat-tat. He talked about his European journeys and his "incredible son." He spoke of his irritation with the blinkered New York publishing industry and, then, his habitual incapacity to relax. "When you're interested in everything, it's challenging to enjoy anything. It's my curse—that, women, and diet. So what happens? I travel to Southern California and discover myself in the proximity of elitists. Isn't one of your boulevards nicknamed 'Millionaire's Row'?"

"Yes. Just to the west," Nick said, visualizing the apricot liqueur/ladyfingers set that dominated there. "On the other hand, money does not a snob make. I've spent time around Lillian Busch, and she's inordinately generous. If you stroll through Busch Gardens, you'll appreciate the joy it brings the many, too."

"I have visited the gardens and found them therapeutic. But I am not an authority on her husband. From my cursory knowledge, Mr. Busch seems to be one of the more decent moguls. I have heard he's a political tiger, and tigers do maul their adversaries when provoked. I'd wager he wouldn't mind digesting some prohibitionists right now."

They chuckled at that imagery before Nick circled back to his point. "True as that may be, the Busches have welcomed deprived children onto their grounds. They support earthquake relief and orphanages. Be careful about lumping them in with your usual saber-toothed scoundrels."

Nick last's line contained a whiff of dudgeon. Upton recoiled, fretting he'd gone too far. "Apologies, Nick. When it comes to industrialists, I'm an incurable skeptic. Can I blame the saturated liver of a carpet-bagging visitor?"

"Yes, you may."

"*Phew*. At the risk of further offending someone who's been so solicitous, would you think me arrogant for saying that no matter how attached one becomes to a place, an institution, a cause, whatever, one must always be willing to peek behind its veils?"

Nick listened without comment, for this wasn't moralizing by sardonic Fleet. It was musing on class politics by a man deemed brilliant on that front.

"One last observation, if you can tolerate it," Upton said.

"I can."

"Pasadena contains a split personality. It's gorgeous and seemingly well administered; suffused with an aspirational ethos. I've even grown fond of those obstreperous parrots. However, the mansions along the canyon close to your bridge trouble me. They honestly do. They remind me of feudal castles upwind of serfs."

Did Buford sprinkle drugstore cocaine in his sandwich? Nick sat up ramrod on his bench. His heart was pounding. "Respectfully, Upton, Pasadena is anything but medieval. None of those big spenders cast much influence over us. Our roots are deeper. Have you ridden to Mount Lowe? Taken in a scientific lecture?"

"No, I haven't."

"Here's another for your list: next time you finish playing tennis at Annandale Country Club, strut out onto the bluff. At sunset, when purple light gleams off our mountain, you'll understand *what* we cherish."

Upton's expression was sincere, if a little sheepish. "You have my word, though I am uncertain about my next match. I so overdid it with my backhand that I visited tennis elbow on myself. A local physician, J. H. Wood, has me applying hot eucalyptus compresses. They stink so hideously I smell them in my sleep."

"If you drank pickle juice, you can tolerate that."

When they rose to leave, Nick waved at Buford, who allowed himself a relieved smile. Upton, apparently, wasn't going to expose his hygenically-iffy kitchen.

Out on Fair Oaks, bucket in hand, Nick said he needed to hustle back to base camp. Before he did, Upton had a final request. "Would you mind writing down your address? There's an invitation-only party I'd be enthralled if you could attend. It's not until summer, and I hope to still be here."

Nick, fresh from the lunch of a lifetime, couldn't believe he was gripping Upton Sinclair's Mount Blanc pen.

WHITE CITY IN THE SKY

H E UNBUTTONED HIS COAT outside the rear flap of the mess tent, exhaling a puff of steam in weather that made absolutely no sense. The first months of 1913 were extreme—subzero nights, drenching rain, coastal fog. Now it was snowing outside, and it was almost Easter. How shivery was it? Buying pliers in town yesterday, Nick overheard an old-timer moaning that the springtime goose bumps were a flashback to his Indiana youth of "cold coffee and frozen pickles."

The inclement conditions would've been politically treacherous for the Mercereau Company, whose project was already behind schedule and under pressure to open, had it not crafted a plan to accelerate production by adding manpower with a third shift. The mandatory workers' meeting, which Nick ducked into late, was covering this topic and more. Judging from the sound wave of applause he heard, the message was resonating.

"To repeat, you're ours for the next three months; that means three more months of paydays," Marcus said through a bullhorn atop a table at the front. "As our gal is taking a mite longer to complete than expected, you should all be here past the Fourth of July. We hope that provides some bankable assurances for you and your missises."

Another peal of applause swept the tent, a few beanies tossed into the air, as well. Seventy men crammed into a space designed for half that made it feel clubby. The scent inside—soggy wool, mass perspiration, and a hint of pork and beans from lunch—was less chummy.

"All effort, no backsliding, fellas," Marcus said in his gruff bellow. "Don't forget to help out the new men, either. We're reaching that finish line together."

"You keep employing like this, we'd help the *devil* and his Okie cousins," a blue collar shouted from the rear.

Marcus gave him a winking nod, trying to encourage camaraderie, knowing the assignment ahead would require maximum effort. "You better start scouring for a pair of horns, then," he added, "because all of you are getting the rest of the day off, with half pay."

"*Stone breaker! Stone breaker!*" workers chanted.

"Settle down. *Shhhh.* Settle down. We're not sending anybody out in a blizzard, not even the ugliest of you cusses. They're predicting the storm should be gone by tonight, so be ready to move double-time tomorrow. Any questions?"

People turned to one another to confer within their cliques, weighing the cost of publicly asking anything against this news of additional paychecks. A rebar-furnace operator tentatively stuck his hand up, and then retracted it.

Not Chester: there was no ambivalence in his flagged-up arm. When Marcus called on him, a tremor rippled through the audience. "Mr. Stonebreaker, I have an honest inquiry. Any truth to the gossip that we've been waylaid, partly anyways, because the next arches need to be reinforced in case they decide to run trains over the bridge? Henry Huntington's people kicked in money for the job. Only natural they want to further their interests."

The reaction was mixed—some gasps, a little jeering. Mainly there was pin-drop silence as everyone waited to learn if Chester's provocation was an active bomb or a juicy dud. The rumor about any train was certainly news to Nick. There was camp-wide chatter that a water line might someday be attached under the deck to hydrate the hills of Linda Vista and San Rafael just outside Pasadena's western limits. The other tidbit, which Nick heard about secondhand through a company engineer, was even more ludicrous: that the "peace-and-quiet loving millionaires" on the Arroyo's eastern bluff arm twisted the Board of Trade to champion a bridge *lower* than needed to maintain their unobstructed mountain views. If accurate, that would've leaked out. Been denounced. Caused a ruckus.

"No truth to it at all about Mr. Huntington," Marcus said, sans-bullhorn to conspiracy-monger Chester. "Zilch. This road will be for automobiles only. That's what voters paid for, and that's what we're delivering. Any other bogus scandals anyone wants to broach?" No hands spiraled up. "Now, before any of you leave for home to loaf off, talk to your foremen to see what you can do about battening down the hatches as we've done during other tricky weather. That's it."

People flooded out the two exits in cheerful moods. When Nick saw he was behind Chester, he swerved away.

Outside, the snow twirled in papery flutters. Flakes blanketed company tents and equipment in the gorge and dusted church spires and merchants' awnings in town. In the whiteout, the bridge resembled a slate-gray blimp levitating above the canyon. It was spooky not hearing construction racket banging from it.

Nick yawned, having been up since five. Funny, he told Royo, whom he confined in the bungalow today rather than walk him through the storm to Ivy Wall. Dreamers like him rarely get much sleep. Post-meeting, he started packing his tools away into a gunnysack near the requisition tent. Though recent frosts cracked two lamp globes, the overall results were reassuring. His lights still gobbled and stored enough sunlight in these extraordinarily cloudy months to beam through the long nights. He had three more to install before the next dozen were in place, after which Marcus would either shit-can him or authorize more.

And, speaking of: "Must be colder than a witch's tit for you California sissies," Marcus said with a snort. As an Iowa native, these conditions were nothing. As a journeyman construction boss, neither was the choking workload. He slept most nights on a cot in his tent, apart from his four children and asthmatic wife, warmed by a little fire.

Nick steeled himself for abuse or a bridge trivia challenge. "Yes, it is," he said. "Not that I've ever seen a witch naked." He was champing to get home to frolic in the white stuff with Royo and Fleet. Snow typically requiring a trek into the Sierra Madres to play in was now piling at street level. Kids freed from their classroom prisons were heaving snowballs in enjoyment. On Colorado Street, a resourceful hotdog vendor switched to selling hot chocolate heated by Sterno cans.

"I have a present for you," Marcus said.

Nick kept a poker face. "Another VIP tour?"

"Better. In appreciation for your efforts, so far, I'm sending you away."

Away? Like to Anaheim (home to more immigrant Germans than a Busch family reunion party)? "Where's that, sir?"

Marcus placed into Nick's shivering hands two tickets to another of Pasadena's famous enchantments. "Thank you," he said. "Weather permitting, I'll be up there Sunday."

"Enjoy. The company bartered for these. Your hard work merited them."

"And here I thought you were going to quiz me on weight tolerances."

"You can't help yourself, can you?" Marcus said. "One aside: I've noticed you at the chow table getting an earful from bridge rats I refer to as the Nellies, as in Nervous Nellies. Obviously, you can fraternize with whomever you wish, including Chester. Just take it from a grizzled pro. There are always gossipmongers on large-scale enterprises. Doesn't mean they don't excel at their trade, only that they're prone to extracting isolated facts and weaving them into fantasy. Understand my thrust?"

"I believe so."

"Us in management aren't deaf. We've heard the tittle-tattling about bizarre goings-on. You're a logical sort, Chance. Don't you find campfire tales blasphemous—to God *and* science? I do."

Before he answered, Nick visualized A. J. Pearson's thunderous machine shop, which he believed was responsible for the groans and rattles around the bridge deck that disquieted some of these Nellies. He didn't inform Chester about it before and wouldn't notify Marcus now. Doing that might be an acknowledgment he investigated the matter.

"Sometimes," Nick said, blowing on his hands, "it's smart to let people vent, regardless of one's own views. Truth's a splinter. It always breaks the skin eventually."

"See," Marcus said. "That's using the ol' noggin."

◆◆◆

Turns out Mount Lowe Railway's policy about allowing dogs aboard wasn't as flexible as normal Red Cars. The railway's humorless ticket agent was impervious to Royo's human-esque "let-me-on" simper. He crossed his uniformed arms when Nick lamented hammily: "we'll get you there *sometime,* boy, before you die."

A pair of George Washingtons needed to come to the rescue. "Just this time," said the agent in a muffled voice, palming the two dollars Nick slipped to him. "If he does his business, you'll be mopping it with bleach. Take the back row."

The math was still in Nick's favor. The round-trip tickets that Marcus awarded Nick retailed for six dollars on what promised to be a full trolley. Mere days after the freak snowstorm, Pasadena's spring weather was supposed to default to seasonal norm: clear skies and a seventy-degree high.

You started this three-legged voyage into the clouds at a depot at the top of Lake Avenue in Altadena, a wine-growing/farming highlands chopped from the forest and canyons northeast of Pasadena. It was eight in the morning on Sunday, with Nick peppy to show Royo what one of his hometown heroes accomplished. "Wait till we get there," he said as the more formally dressed passengers boarded, some of them frowning at Nick's black-muzzled companion. "You can touch the sky."

Transporting oneself to the piney fringe of the Sierra Madre range, which stuffed shirts rhapsodized as "The Alps of Pasadena" (or its "Granite Breasts"), required two hours of endurance. This first jag was a leisurely trip on a meandering route past poppy fields and avocado-colored waterfalls, spiraling over the Rubio Canyon wash. Here, the less adventurous could decamp for a hotel pavilion furrowed into the canyon walls. Barely into wilderness, there was dancing, dining, Japanese lanterns.

Those pressing on exited the cable-type car for an open-air funicular well publicized in magazines. Tourists compared it to a stylish "opera box," though Nick, who'd ridden it on multiple occasions, compared it more to a giant, fairy-tale sleigh cobbled by Santa's most ambitious elves. The funicular climbed the appropriately named "Great Incline" on a unique, three-railed track, clacking upward in places at a hair-raising sixty-two degrees. Passengers stayed relatively level, but the angle still tensed jaws and induced benedictions for the vehicle's emergency brakes.

This half-mile ascent could take forever, unless you were either new to it or a thrillseeker. As both, Royo was enthralled, with his nose sniffing terrain and his paws clamped over the side. Nick watched him, conjuring mental images of sausages to determine if he reacted by licking his chops— confirmation it was one of his mind-reading days. Royo didn't, so Nick communicated by whispering into his floppy ear.

The funicular clattered upward, over a ravine, easing to a stop at a terminus bittersweet for many Southern Californians. Ten or so years ago, they would've rushed off the cab to line up for the "White City in the Sky." Nick smiled elegiacally recalling its bygone layout, telling Royo before they got off. "When father would bring me here, he'd say this place 'erased the line between possible and impossible. Now imagine what you'll do.'"

Royo cocked his head knowingly. Yet he couldn't know *this* history.

Professor Thaddeus S. C. Lowe, the railway's initiator-financier, and civil engineer David J. Macpherson, his colleague, had tackled the inconceivable. They saw this mountain and conquered it, creating a resort above the city at an elevation that blimps had difficulty reaching. Before calamities obliterated most of it, the star attraction was the Echo Mountain House, a seventy-room, circular-decked Victorian hotel: Lowe's answer to San Diego's posh Hotel del Coronado. Built on a promontory overlooking the valley floor, the first-class hotel was a gemstone in Pasadena's emerging tiara. For distinction, all the surfaces were painted white, including the funicular visible from Busch Gardens.

At its outset, the White City never suffered for customers. Honeymooners booked it. Tourists mobbed it. Outdoor-enthusiasts saved for it. If the views didn't wow you, activities did. There were tennis courts, stables, an impressive zoo, curio shops, and a labyrinth of trails. During the Fourth of July and Christmas, the busy place could've used a turnstile. Reasonably affordable for the commoner, it was altitude with trimmings.

"Come here for a sec," Nick said, clapping Royo to his side after they exited the funicular. "You don't want to squander this."

They walked twenty yards toward the cliff. At the edge, Nick squatted and slung his arm around his dog. "See that pile of rubble over there? Let's say Professor Lowe's reach exceeded his grasp. He might've been the city's first scientist."

Long before George Hale traveled west from MIT to erect his space telescopes, Lowe commissioned one on his mountaintop that'd discovered ninety-five nebulae. White City also boasted one of the world's strongest torches: a searchlight whose Herculean beam could radiate thirty-five miles. You could shoot light all the way to the Channel Islands off the coast from it, or rile up horses in faraway towns. Some jokers once illuminated the private parts of skinny dippers at a pond below.

For those uninterested in that, there were hike-able gorges so deep that the sound-chamber effect boomeranged voices back myriad times. It was how Echo Mountain earned its name. Nick's personal record: seven repeats.

Rohw, gurgled Royo.

Gilda Figgleberry, Nick's now-ancient teacher, devoted a whole week engrossing her class with Lowe's vision, and Nick never forgot an iota. He decided right then if he ever had a son, Thaddeus would be his middle name. In his school report on the railway, Nick characterized it as "the stuff of legends, fashioned as much by sheer brawn as brainy innovation." To groom the complex track, mountainsides were dynamited and precarious crossings traversed. When pack mules defied their floggings, refusing to continue on the jagged, snake-filled slopes, Lowe's men hefted the backbreaking loads themselves.

Lowe never started off dreaming of this. Self-taught and industrious, he aspired to cross the Atlantic in a hot air balloon. When Abraham Lincoln requested he spy on Confederate troops from one instead, a military first, Lowe fulfilled his patriotic duty. Post-war, the handsome inventor bunkered in a lab, mastering something else extraordinary. He distilled hydrogen gas from charcoal and steam, which pushed refrigeration technology into the modern age. Later, he opened ice factories, founded Citizen's Bank here, and grew affluent enough in his adopted town to launch this rocky-top playground.

"But White City didn't last, as some things aren't meant to," Nick told Royo as they hurried back to the platform, where a new tram idled for them. Only years after the resort debuted, shaky finances started eroding the bottom line. Everything except the observatory sunk into receivership and, ultimately, new ownership. Ensuing trouble made you wonder if it was hexed. In 1900, fire consumed the hotel. Then an astronomer went blind. Then electrical storms and floods wreaked havoc, almost killing several children. Even Lowe's Grand Opera House on Raymond Avenue fizzled out.

Lowe died six months ago, at eighty, but in a sense he was already gone. "Was it worth it?" Nick muttered to Royo as they took their rear seats. "Should Mr. Lowe have spent his retirement counting his fortune until he was a doddering fool? Course not."

Quickly, Nick realized he needed to cork the nostalgic observations to his furry-earred companion. A respectable couple sharing their bench leaned away from them like they were contagious. Next, a man clutching a book behind them remarked to a fellow passenger (for Nick to hear), "Only a simpleton converses with a dog as if he were a person."

Simpleton? Nick immersed into thought, an exhilarating one, too. As soon as the Colorado Street Bridge was finished, he was establishing a solar lamp company and hotfooting it here. He could sell Lowe's successors a hundred units, easy, to bolster the track's spotty lighting.

From here on, the electric-traction railroad became a moderate-speed roller coaster. At first, the *zzzzz-zzzzzing* tram hummed smoothly past meadows, chasms, and granite walls. Up close, the trees and vegetation matting the southern side of the Sierra Madre shook alive in vivid colors; gazing up at them from Pasadena, they blended together over the ridges in speckled, blackish-brown patches and swatches of mossy green.

But the higher the tram ventured above the chaparral, the greater the frequency of corkscrewing bends on dozens of curves and bridges. Brochures never mentioned motion sickness currently turning some passengers green. A scarf-wearing old lady mouthed prayers crossing Las Flores Canyon and the drop over "The Cape of Good Hope." Nick, whose iron stomach handled heights and spices better than herky-jerky motion, wanted off.

At last the cab swung around its final bend, toward the sign announcing they'd reached Crystal Springs, altitude 5,600 feet above sea level. The hoarse-voiced conductor reminded everyone not to miss either of the departing trains. Those cliff-swinging turns would test courage at night.

Appearing before everyone was the largest structure around: the two-story, stone-and-wood Alpine Tavern. It was as homey as Echo Mountain was once sprawling. Nick jogged to the men's room first thing; Royo doused a redwood with what Fleet, who was occupied today studying clubbed feet and harelips, phrased as the dog's camel-size bladder.

Accompanying the tickets—which Nick recognized Marcus gave him to ignore the Nellies, as he was already doing—were two food vouchers. Some add-on. Lunch here wasn't like Mercereau Company's. It was veal tough as suede and stinky deviled eggs. Royo lapped up what Nick passed on.

You were cloud dancing, nonetheless, bracketed between Millard Canyon to the west and Eaton Canyon to the east. Behind Mount Lowe loomed three sister peaks: Mount Disappointment, Mount San Gabriel, and Mount Markham, the latter named after Pasadenan Henry Harrison Markham, California's dashing governor in the 1890s. The crisp air made it borderline sweater weather; Nick stored one in his worn daypack.

"Now what?" he asked Royo after that unsatisfying lunch. They were isolated on a touristy campground off-season with hours to kill and no White City to luxuriate in. So, they loitered inside the tavern dominated by a gargantuan stone fireplace and a vintage rocking chair, all of which whittled away five minutes. Nick examined a map highlighting caves scattered with Indian artifacts next. "Should we go?" he asked Royo. "Magnificent views, if you're agreeable to swallowing flies along the path."

They moseyed outside, and Nick's canine wiggle-waggled over to a board pointing toward "Mt. Lowe's Inspiration Point" and woofed. "Sold," Nick answered. "Just keep that veal breath to yourself."

Although the tram coming up was full, the overall crowd here was sparse. The exception was a gazebo whose "lookout telescope" Nick hoped to peek through. A large, boisterous group of cackling mothers, grab-ass adolescents, and fathers debating Yankees versus Cubs beat them there, though. Nick was tempted to yap that it was public property, not theirs.

At a bench behind the gazebo, he dove into his pack for diversions. He played tennis ball toss-and-fetch with Royo. He Frisbee-d saltines, tallying how many he could catch in a row (nine). He read deeper into *Great Expectations*. He started and crumpled a letter to his mother. His acoustic guitar would've been swell here.

When the gazebo-hoggers left, Nick and Royo jumped into it, chasing each other and wrestling under the roof; that was good for nine minutes. Afterward, Nick squished his face into the pivoting telescope for a gander at Pasadena's Mesopotamia: the Arroyo Seco. What else was there to do? Let Royo scarf a whole sleeve of crackers?

Nick let his eyes take a lazy trip from the canyon's start at the Red Box Saddle watershed onto the high, alluvial plain. They followed the wash, which demarcated upper Pasadena with the La Crescenta Valley, on its serpentine route around trails and old camps, into the Devil's Gate expanse and the Hahamonga area. The Arroyo then slashed downward past the Linda Vista hills, the Scoville pump house, Nick's magnificent bridge, and all the way into the Los Angeles River.

The ravine might've appeared peaceful from these heights, but city folks knew it could be schizophrenic. In the dry season, mountain waters produced either a trickling stream of residual snowmelt or a parched, riparian gulch. During hard winter rains and deluges, its personality was hardly gentle. Indeed, swift-moving currents often swamped the banks. The most potent mudflows would flatten most anything in their way, living or inert.

This raw power wasn't lost on Indians long attuned to nature. To the Tongva tribe, the roar of slapping waters downstream from Switzer Falls was the clamor of an otherworldly wager between the tributary and the Great Coyote Spirit.

It was along these banks where a Mexican land grant launched Rancho San Pasqual of early, unincorporated Pasadena. Fifty years later, members of the Indiana Colony aggregated south, on what was now Orange Grove Boulevard, to fashion a water-fed town. Talk about great expectations.

Or, for Nick now, great languor: the last time he was so bored out of his gourd was leading a Cawston tour for a convent of nuns that'd taken a vow of silence.

He tilted the telescope up to see if he could locate Catalina Island, but he overdid it, aiming the lens into the sky at nearly ninety degrees. For a few seconds, the lens caught the blazing sun dead center, which reflected the glare from the Earth's ten-thousand-degree star directly into his left eyeball.

Oww. He shut his eye, reeling away from the cliff like he'd just electrocuted himself by stupidity.

Under his eyelid, yellow dots buzzed in circular orbits, and a sharp headache cropped up with them. Squinting out of his right eye, he backpedaled to the bench where he was before, and sat down clumsily on it. Somehow, he was able to scrounge into his backpack to grab ahold of his Bayer aspirin and canteen. He shook out some pills and swigged water. Then he lay down, draping his arm over his jackhammering skull.

Once the whizzing dots slowed, he cracked his sun-blasted eye. Blurry vision was better than viewing only black out of it. Wherever Thaddeus Lowe was in the ether, Nick hoped he missed this. He massaged his temples and tried forcing himself to doze off.

Arf-arf-arf-arf-arf. Rohrrrrr. Rohhhh.

Royo's fusillade barking ended his nap after seven minutes. Nick popped up and saw, in fuzzy optics, his bigmouth dog up an embankment about fifteen yards behind the bench. Something in the shrubberies around a purple wisteria there was inciting him to sleuth.

An *achoo* rang out from inside the bushes next. There was a person hiding in there.

"Present yourself," Nick said. "My dog will pounce."

Nick, figuring it was one of those kids from the gazebo trying to prank him, summoned Royo back when no one answered. Royo didn't move though, and then three consecutive *achoos* rattled the branches. His Mount Lowe stalker was an allergy-sufferer.

He hopped onto his boots, noticing an object by the bench he could weaponize in case he'd underestimated the threat. It was a pinecone. "Jig's up," he said. "Get out here."

Royo now was poking his curious snout through the shrubbery, sniffing at whoever was crouching beside the wisteria's gnarled base. His tail was wagging propeller-esque, which he usually reserved for greeting Nick or chasing a Busch Gardens' swan. Soon, he vocalized recognition— *Oh-roh-yur ow*—at the intruder.

"Don't make me throw this, uh, rock," Nick said. "It'll hurt. Probably."

Displeased by the silence, he fastballed the pinecone against an oak near the wisteria, which exploded in a brittle burst. "There's more where that came from," he added.

A creamy female hand crept up in surrender. "No need for that," said the hiding woman in gray hiking pants and a lima-bean sweater rolled up at the arms. Jules Cumbersmith swiped through the bushes and emerged. "Spit it out," she said. "You must be crafting some witticism." *Achoo.*

Nick's afternoon was officially pear-shaped. "I tend not to make light when someone is spying on me," he said. "Not even someone experiencing a sneezing fit."

"May I sit down to defend myself?" she asked.

"That'd be sensible. One of the bushes you waded through was poison oak."

"Oh, grand," Jules said. She examined her forearms for rashes and trod sheepishly down to the bench, sitting at the far end from Nick. Royo, the traitor, immediately mashed his butt against her knees in a "rub-this" demand.

"Before you chide me for any nefarious intent, you should know I've been up here overnight on committee business for Lilly. "It's—*oww*. Ants are biting me with their tiny teeth." She pushed off the bench, swiping red dots off her neck.

If Nick weren't so cheesed off, he would've found that endearing. "On business?" he said once she sat down again. "Bunk!"

"It's the truth. She requested I conduct research at the Alpine Tavern. I was in there, rifling through an old diary, when I observed you two arriving on the noon train."

"And you decided you'd surveil me, in case you needed to inform her of any sordid behavior I revealed up here. That's one razor-thin alibi."

Jules didn't say anything. Her hands were active, though. When she wasn't scratching at her neck and her arms, she was rubbing Royo's bristly hind.

"At least you're switching it up. Normally you treat me as invisible. Every time I've waved when you're in Lilly's parlor, you either ignore me or draw the curtains."

"It's not out of," Jules paused, briefly fleeing into the cubbyholes of her own head, where she seemed to do most of her living, "out of malice."

"Whatever the rationale, I don't deserve it," Nick said sharply. His headache was ebbing.

"I had my reasons. I'm not gregarious like you, unrestrained in opinions. I'm an inward soul. You don't know me."

Big deal, her cheekbones could best any Rose princess's. "Nor you I. If you believe I wanted to spend a Sunday driving around with someone who literally fell asleep to my narration, you got another thing coming."

Jules stopped kneading Royo's keister. "I regret my indifference that day. I'd barely slept the night before. Since then, I've revised my impression of you."

"Yeah, downward."

"No, that's not accurate. There's a minor chivalry to you. When you bother to tame that cowlick, some girls might even say you're reasonably attractive."

Some girls? Dopamine butterflies executed loop-de-loops inside him. They throttled back, recalling how she treated him at Lilly's gala. "Cow? That rings a bell," he said sarcastically. "I'm going to move over there to the stone wall; it wouldn't be a trip to Mount Lowe for me without peeking over the edge of the horizon."

Nick left the bench, sitting down on the rampart paralleling the embankment; she followed. Royo walked over next, lying in the dusty gap between them with a sigh.

"Because you must think me a closed book, I'll share this about that night at the Hotel Green. I was ungracious to you not only because that vile animal frightened me. It was because I failed to extricate *myself* from a pinch, and I detested that. I apologize."

Nick swung his legs over the bank side to side. "So what's a closed book doing concealed in the shrubbery? You could've descended the mountain without me knowing you were present."

In the seconds before Jules responded, a zephyr kicked up a dust devil and quivered the branches of oaks spaced out along the rampart.

"Curiosity, I suppose. You may be nettled at me now, but I was infuriated at how you leered at me at Mr. Mercereau's memorial service, Nick. You were mentally unbuttoning my corset without knowing anything about me. Don't try refuting it. When men objectify women for their lustful fantasies, especially while denying us rights, I could scream."

"I'm not denying you anything," Nick said. "And regrets for thinking you're pretty."

Jules carried on. "As I said, I've softened my viewpoint. You're neither a pervert nor a glad-hander."

"Lord, help me," Nick said, grasping his chest in mock agony. "I've been buck-shot with faint praise."

Jules stroked her chin, returning to the citadel of her mind; life taught her not to give too much of herself away. "Please understand how protective I am of Lilly. She's more delicate than you realize. I needed to ensure you weren't manipulating her to further your aspirations."

Nick, typically composed, almost blew his stack. "Manipulate? Who do you think you are?"

"Someone who's learning. Just listen and you'll see. A few Saturdays ago, I watched you perform your ostrich act from Mrs. Bang's kitchen window."

"Mrs. Bang's?"

"Yes, I was in there plating cookies that I'd brought over from Lilly's for the children. That's where I heard that little girl with leukemia, you know, Edna Hollister, becoming hysterical in another room. Her parents had just informed her that she didn't have much longer. Anyway, she was outside later with the others, staring out despondently, while you rode your bird. After the show was over, you tried coaxing her to smile. You made Royo chew gum for her and do his somersault trick. He almost rolled down the hill."

"I recall," he said. "But I had no idea the boom was just lowered on her."

"I know. And I'll never forget what I witnessed next. When she began sobbing, you directed Royo to her, and Edna buried her face into his neck. I was myself watching that gut-wrenching scene from the window. Royo laid his paw on her shoulder as though he was consoling her."

"Yeah, it was poignant. That dog's got a sixth sense." Nick's outrage was abating.

"You two ventured to the gardens to cheer yourselves up after Edna went inside. First, you played hide and seek around the gnomes. Later, you accused Royo of licking your side of the ice cream you were splitting. I told Lilly, and she remarked you two behave like kindred brothers do."

Nick scrunched his face. "How were you aware of our silliness down there? Were you in cloak-and-dagger mode like today?"

Jules glanced around. "Yes, I'm ashamed to say. I spied on you from behind the Three Little Pigs House."

Nick wasn't sure whether to feel gooey-warm or alarmed. He stayed neutral. "Since the snowstorm postponed my last ostrich rodeo, I'm developing a new trick, a semi-handstand that will have Edna giggling. I've always heard that's potent medicine."

Jules looked up and exhaled. "Oh, Nick. Edna died that same night. Mrs. Bang requested the Busches subsidize the funeral. Her parents are destitute after the bills."

The news hit him like a sucker punch to the gut. He picked up a small branch, cracked it over his knee, and chucked it over the embankment. "Nobody told me. She was, gosh, the same age as my little helper, Reginald. It's not right."

"It's not. But, there's something else you should know. Mrs. Bang confided to me that Edna didn't tremble in bed her final night. Edna told her that when Royo set his paw on her, she saw in her mind a carnival full of everything she loved. Rides. Popcorn. Games. She was convinced that's where she was headed hours before she passed away."

For the first time, Nick saw Jules stricken with emotion. She wiped a tear and dropped her head. Mourning too, he fell backward onto the dirt, angry and sad. Royo went over to lick his face, and returned to lying between them.

"I need to leave," he said sitting up. "This was supposed to be a relaxing afternoon, and it's contorted into a very black one."

Nick expected her to bid him goodbye, but instead, she swung her own legs over the rampart. "My watch," she said in that strong, feminine voice, "says we still have an hour before the next train departs."

Nick puffed air out of his cheeks in the piney air. Somewhere above them was the shriek of a circling hawk, which he'd rather go away, and the delirious scream of a hiker over the hill.

"Strawberry. Anne Brontë. Beagles."

Nick, picturing Edna's sunken eyes, said: "Excuse me? Am I supposed to decipher that?"

"Only if you wish. I wanted you to know a few of my affinities, so I listed my favorite ice cream, author, and dog breed. Jules Cumbersmith, making your acquaintance."

Either she feels sorry for you or she's flirting. "Okeydoke," he said cautiously. "Chocolate swirl, Mark Twain—and peculiar half breeds."

"Prime relaxation?" Jules asked, unveiling those darling eyeteeth.

"Admiring the Colorado Street Bridge from Busch Gardens, what else?"

"You and that bridge. I prefer a late-night bubble bath and a lavender candle."

Jules's "favorite things game" cycled through several rounds. They proceeded to give abridged backgrounds of themselves next, omitting anything sensitive. Jules did describe a girlhood trip to the Chicago World's Fair, where she'd watched horses run on a pre-nickelodeon zoopraxiscope, imitating their galloping legs with her fingers. Nick enjoyed that: he was cannibalizing part of a nickelodeon for another of his gizmos.

As Jules pealed back more about herself, Nick wasn't sure if what he was sensing was chemistry or unilateral infatuation.

They returned in the gloaming to the Alpine Tavern, which was rowdier now that liquor flowed and a brass band played. One of Mount Lowe's open secrets was that it turned a blind eye to alcohol and extramarital hanky-panky discouraged in public in Pasadena proper. Whispers of religious cults performing forest ceremonies were another matter.

On the tram down, the sky arranged itself in pastel striations of orange, pink, and blue; the periwinkle light that glazed the Sierra Madre was already gone. The mountain breeze had stopped too, though the evening nip had passengers bundling up inside the Red Car. Royo sat between them on the backbench as the trolley rounded canyons and past spooky caves you wouldn't want to hang around at night. There wasn't much conversation.

Halfway back to the Lake Avenue depot, Nick mentioned how "starved" he was in a coy bid for an impromptu date. "I'd trade my kingdom for meatloaf and potatoes."

Quietly, Jules said: "I'm sorry. I need to attend to my other job."

She's retreating again. "A second job, besides committee work? Doing what?"

"It's confidential," she answered, gaze fixed on the back of a napping passenger's head. "But for a good cause."

Nick played her intrigue the way he now handled Chester's superstitions: by outwardly listening and inwardly questioning. Following a sharp turn, he asked her if she'd like a stick of Wrigley's. She waved no thanks, so he and Royo divided his last piece.

Jules said nothing until the cab abruptly jerked approaching the Echo Mountain promontory. "Did we strike something?" she asked, whites of her eyes protruding.

"Probably just a branch; nothing to worry about. The trams sport metal bumpers to sweep debris away. Mr. Lowe thought of everything." Impulsively, he reached his hand over Royo and briefly rested it on one of hers. Head still focused ahead, Jules withdrew it. "That was a comfort pat," he said lamely.

At every landmark the mountain Red Car passed—at Granite Gate, the vertigo turns at Circular Bridge and Horseshoe Curve—Nick tried thinking about anything *except* the living nesting doll beside him. Imagining an April Fool's Day trick on Fleet, something maybe involving his toothpaste, chewed minutes. It wasn't until they'd transitioned to the funicular that Jules initiated conversation. Nick's self-diversion by then was exploring the imbecility of a solar inventor like him almost flambéing an eyeball with a rickety telescope.

"I don't want you cultivating the wrong impression of me," she said. "I'm not like the other eligible girls in your town. Status—a husband, a full wardrobe, a gabled roof—is inconsequential to me. If I could afford it, I'd join the suffragette movement full time. Also, I've heard things about you."

"About me?" *Don't let it be the parrots.* "Such as?"

"Your reputation as a Romeo, and as a fair-haired sort able to get away with mischief. Lilly divulged a little about your previous employment. Parenthetically, you should avoid working retail. Please understand: what I'm aspiring to doesn't wear pants."

Descending Mount Lowe's Great Incline, on a glorified sleigh full of strangers, was an odd spot for her to open up. Then again, she *was* odd. "Hey," he said. "You don't need to justify anything. I'd scarcely heard you complete full sentences before today. And I'm aware my mouth can runneth over when I'm antsy or yammering about Pasadena. I will concede this at my own peril, Jules. When we were exchanging the things we adored up there, I experienced something unique, something I have yet to with anybody else. Like there was—helium in my veins."

In his head, it took her longer to respond to that than it took Mrs. Grover Cleveland to work a large orange down her skinny throat. By the time she spoke, they'd shifted from the funicular to the tram for the journey's final leg. "I cannot deny harboring a flame of interest in you, either, and you're certainly not my usual type," she said, lake-deep eyes beaming at him.

"You do," he said, trying to keep his fanny on the seat.

"Yes. Definitely. But *if* we pursue a courtship, you just must tread at a pace amenable to me. Should that be off-putting, let's just strive to be friends. You also must agree to not besiege me with questions that I'm currently unprepared to answer, notably about my schedule. I recognize that must sound bizarre."

"Am I allowed any levity about heifers?"

"I'll mull that," she said, smile lines twitching. "One last condition. Address that cowlick. It reminds me of a baby antler."

Nick ruffled Royo's ears. "You hear that, boy? Keep your teeth off my comb."

Jules brushed her pinkie over his for a thrilling second.

Minutes later, they stood on the Lake Street platform, in the dark of that revelatory Sunday evening, preparing to depart their separate ways.

"Before you go," Nick said, "I need to ask you something."

Jules sighed. "Remember, no incessant questions?"

"Not about you, about Edna. Do you believe," he said, modulating his voice, "honestly, that she glimpsed the beyond? It must've been a delusion, right, from a child terrified of her casket? Morphine, if she was on that, could've been responsible, too." He peered down at Royo, who was busy sniffing passengers' cuffs as they strode past. "Royo's no miracle worker. He doesn't turn water into wine. He turns furniture legs into kindling."

Jules deliberated before answering, as was her custom. "It well may have been an illusion, or medicine, or both. Our speculation isn't paramount, though. It's what Edna believed in her mind's eye."

Nick nodded. "Suppose so. By the way, and this isn't meant as a probing question: do you own Epsom salts?"

"No. Why?"

"Those red welts on your right hand are definitely poison oak."

DEVIL'S GATE DALLIANCES

THE NEXT MONTHS WERE the best of his life, one long, proverbial lick from a chocolate-swirl cone. Walking the trail toward the bridge every morning, Nick stopped to blow on dandelions to watch their fluff helicopter over the goldenrod. He grinned hearing trolley bells and whistled on the toilet. Everything he did, whether buying potato chips hot off the cart from E. L. Daughtery's Relish Factory on Union Street or mounting another solar lamp in the Arroyo, was zesty. It was as if he were the lead in his own happily-ever-after.

Their maiden date was a stroll down Colorado Street, where they lingered in Vroman's new fiction arrivals. The following weekend they took the Red Car to the Long Beach Pike, an amusement park on a pier, to munch saltwater taffy and slam bumper cars.

On the ride home, Jules, unprompted, peeled back another layer, saying, "You know, I really shouldn't be here."

"On this train, with me?" he asked deadpan.

"No, in Pasadena. This was never the destination where I intended to relocate. That was Seattle."

Jules revealed before that an "abysmal personal situation" precipitated her departure from Illinois, but she reminded him not to "interrogate" her about it. And he didn't. "So why aren't you up there now, living in the rain with the fishmongers?"

"Happenstance."

She said that it was somewhere between the point her locomotive crossed the Rocky Mountains in Colorado and its northwest bend toward Washington state that she realized her train was steaming in the *wrong* direction. "I was of the conviction to stage a one-woman protest against the incompetent railroad that issued me an incorrect ticket. It read Seattle when we departed, I promise you. When the conductor scrutinized it, it said Pasadena. Regardless, I planned to switch trains in San Francisco. But, a mental birdie spoke to me as I collected my bags."

"A birdie? What did it tweet?"

"That fate could be interceding, regardless of who bungled the ticket. I decided six months in your blue-sky city would be adequate to gauge if the birdie was right."

"I'm glad you did," Nick said, unwrapping a piece of strawberry taffy. "Though I believe fate is a product of what we design."

Sometime later, after letting what she disclosed settle, he said, "Incidentally, if Lilly tries foisting marzipan on you, decline. It tastes like armpit."

Their date after Jules's bombshell admission was dinner at the Japanese teriyaki house where Nick had banked a tofu cube off Fleet's forehead on the night Fleet met Hattie. Over green-tea ice cream now, Nick confessed to inadvertently releasing the parrots responsible for those Amazonian-jungle squawks over western Pasadena.

"You?" Jules said, chuckling. "*You?* You're the one responsible for the commotion Lilly's girlfriends grumble are robbing them of their beauty sleep. I cannot believe it: I'm being romanced by an outlaw" (not that Jules wasn't one herself).

"Only partially," Nick said. "Others have feathers on their hands, too."

After that, Nick opened up further. He told her about how the coot heaved his knife at him, likely as a warning shot, and how he met Royo that smoky day on Fair Oaks Avenue. He didn't tell her that Royo saved his life.

Strapped between paychecks, their next after-work rendezvous was what Nick termed a "cheapskate's picnic": Cokes, bread, salami, and cheddar at sunset in Busch Gardens. Smitten with each other in springtime Pasadena, peanut butter would've sufficed. They swung hands around a shady pond and passed the Three Little Pigs House. Nick, remembering that this was where she spied on him, dubbed himself "Big, Bad Nick" and chased her with a convincing snort. His Chicago girl produced an infectious laugh.

Walking her home to Delacey Street, Nick shared something else: his lunch at Buford's shack with Upton Sinclair, one of Jules's favorite male authors, and the subject of a slight celebrity crush. She blitzed him with questions, particularly about why he didn't mention this earlier. "What?" Nick asked. "I can't contain mysteries?"

Hanging out with Fleet that evening, Nick's goofy smile remained.

"Let that persist," Fleet said, "and your Zygomaticus Major (a crucial facial muscle) may snap off your cheekbone. I hope she's worth it." He hesitated next before continuing. "Speaking of injuries, my besotted chum, come clean. Tell Dr. Norwood whether you've experienced any lingering effects from that explosion? Regular headaches? Memory loss? Disorientation? Injuries to the neocortex don't always present immediately."

"None. Never felt better. Why are you bringing this up? You were studying toe warts and hemorrhoids last week."

"Because, I know you. You can be sneaky sometimes about acknowledging what's transpiring between your ears."

"Old man, you have textbook on the brain."

If Nick told him everything, Fleet would've been more than inquisitive. He would've marched Nick to a neurologist for an extensive look under his hood.

Nick wasn't divulging to Fleet, or anyone for that matter, anything about Royo's sporadic mindreading. It seemed too intimate to disclose, too special. Besides, he'd persuaded himself that the dog's powers were grounded in science, not mysticism. Royo's genetic wiring must've endowed him with an anomalous capacity for brainwave detection, if not the ability to comprehend English. Someday, Nick was certain, researchers would document the phenomenon specific to hyper-intelligent animals with statistical tables and photos of autopsied brains in highfalutin technical journals.

His other learning curve made this delusion simpler to rationalize.

Consider how well he described the Mercereau Company's formula to erect a hundred-year structure for potentially millions of automobile trips, in unpredictable soil, and in earthquake country no less. Asked by

Jules at their picnic for a general explanation, he compared it to "baking a layer cake—a structurally webbed layer cake that'd crack your teeth."

Every arch, he told her, hewed to the same recipe. Step One was pouring and then burying the footings, each the rough dimension of Cormoran's calves from "Jack and the Beanstalk," to support the tremendous weight coming above it. Step Two: harnessing those footings to the parabolic arches that suffused the bridge with its Romanesque majesty. Step Three: adding everything else—the blocky, arch-linking ribs, the open spandrel columns, the transverse girders, the mini beams and struts you barely noticed—into a superstructure that'd gird the deck for perpetuity. Expansion joints throughout let the concrete breathe.

Step Four in Nick's metaphor: slathering the frosting. Once the heavy construction was done, the company still needed to finish the deck, scallop the roadway curbs, mold the balusters, and chisel the "flying" pedestrian bays and benches. Lastly it'd install the grape-bunch lamps, which Nick predicted one day would be "upgraded" to his wireless models.

"Don't forget," he said, "that without lumber to mold every block of concrete, that cake wouldn't get out of the oven."

With each shift, Nick also appreciated what was hazy prior: folks wanted that webbed-together roadway opened something fierce.

Even with several arches to go, the bridge was shaping up to be the most tectonic public-works endeavor in the whole San Gabriel Valley. Every day on the eastern bank off Orange Grove, clusters of pedestrians assembled behind barricades to gape at the future. Merchants, retirees, aspiring engineers, high school kids, maids, aging Union soldiers; something about the job's immensity transcended people's class and past. You'd have to handcuff artists to keep them away, too. Braving thistles and insect nips, they planted their butts on the hillsides, painting and sketching those arches in creative strokes. Nick filled with pride noting their dedication.

But one day, on the bridge's western bank outside town, he discovered another clique of people seemingly less attuned to whimsy. Nobody here was scrawling charcoal lithographs or ogling as molded concrete defied gravity by engineering technique. Nick, who'd trod across the ravine to evaluate solar-lamp locations for this side of the structure, decided to postpone his work a few minutes. He was deputizing himself to spy.

He crouched himself behind a stand of oaks, extracted his telescope, and aimed it at the hills under the gopher-riddled Annandale County Club. A swarm of men in fedoras and heavy boots were walking around boulders and brush there with alacrity in their steps. Above them, a boss gripping what Nick assumed was a topographical map instructed them what to do. That mainly entailed squinting through transits and jabbing poles with measurements on them into the soil.

Pop: another light bulb went off. These men without identifying insignias *weren't* from these parts. They were from Los Angeles City Hall. And they weren't benign. The city and its real estate proxies already were exploiting the terminus of the Owens Valley Aqueduct in the San Fernando Valley as an excuse to snatch and annex wide swaths of property from private owners. If Nick's gut and scope were correct, Los Angeles's next conquest was in its battle-planning phase. It'd expand its northeast reach here.

The timing begged for it. Completion of the Colorado Street Bridge would turn the unincorporated hills of San Rafael Heights and Linda Vista into exceptionally valuable real estate—real estate too tantalizing not to try poaching. It'd lead to development that'd be worth *tens* of millions of dollars, and corresponding political clout, for the first city that nabbed the acreage.

Wealthy landowners and others with property here were split on this issue, some amenable to being swallowed up by Los Angeles, others vehemently opposed. A divide-and-conquer campaign would likely resolve that. Who then was going to repel the land sharks of Los Angeles? Henry Huntington would rake his profits whoever he answered to, and it wasn't like Hattie's vegetarian colony could rig Linda Vista with booby traps. With automobile traffic about to roll, this side of the Arroyo Seco was ripe for the taking.

And should Los Angeles acquire first dibs, Pasadena would have egg all over its face. Few organizations would be wiping off more yoke, either, than the city's Board of Trade, the hard-charging booster group responsible for convincing voters to approve a hundred-thousand-dollar bond issue for the bridge two years ago. To this day, it still gloated about what a bargain it struck, since Pasadena taxpayers were contributing just 47 percent of the total cost of a job that was 60 percent inside city limits. (The county and private deep pockets were ponying up the balance.) How sweet would that deal look in retrospect, Nick asked himself, if Los Angeles hoisted its flag across the canyon? If it snuck in at the last minute to reap the corollary benefits of Pasadena's sparkling bridge?

He collapsed his scope. Tried not to succumb to cynicism. Every day walking home from work with Royo, he bought the afternoon newspaper where, alongside stories about unrest in China, or fasting fads, or President Wilson's new Federal Trade Commission, were tucked-in articles about "the bridge effect." Longtime residents in white-shoe Prospect Park and elsewhere were selling off their own holdings to syndicates and individuals pining to build new neighborhoods. The *LA Times* was involved, too, lobbying for "a great public park" throughout the entire Arroyo.

This is what happens, he concluded, when you live in a "veritable paradise" about to get infinitely more reachable.

∦∦∦

"ARE YOU ABSOLUTELY CERTAIN that you desire to hear this?" Jules asked.

"Try me," Nick said, sandwich in hand. "I always find humor when people exaggerate, regardless of what they're representing."

They were enjoying the second sunset picnic of their budding courtship, this time on the grassy hammock in the Devil's Gate Dam area roughly a mile north of the bridge. Jules, who earned more as Lilly's Girl Friday than Nick did as Marcus's "lamp boy," organized a meal that put Nick's to shame. Onto a blanket she unpacked deli-bought roast-pork sandwiches, tins of applesauce, carrots, vanilla wafers, and sweet tea in mason jars.

"All right, here goes," said Jules, reading from an index card with some of her Pasadena Perfect research on it, which she'd toted as entertainment (with Nick's advanced permission). "After the real estate crash of the 1880s, your town fathers were so apprehensive about the declining population that they decided to nationally advertise the city's advantages. Or should I say embellish them. One pamphlet described Pasadena as 'a Mediterranean without the marshes and malaria.' Another declared the land so fertile that cash crops grew tall enough to pluck from horseback."

Nick looked at her cockeyed. "Maybe tall enough to grab from a Shetland pony," he said. "You ought to read some of Cawston's advertisements. You'd think feathers conferred eternal happiness. Truth and advertising: never shall they meet."

"You're taking this exceptionally well," Jules said, handing him a napkin. She wore a yellow dress and black sunglasses, suffragette chic. He was in black trousers that he trimmed at the knees for the warm season ahead. Though he scissored them raggedly and drew pejorative glances from seniors who deemed them slovenly, Nick prioritized comfort above decorum.

"I'm not a blind patriot," he said. "I consider myself more as a realist Pollyanna."

"Realist Pollyanna—isn't that incongruous?"

By him sat Royo, head twitching at Nick's every movement, because a distracted Nick was a Nick who spilled food he could snag. Jules lay sideways, cupping her chin in her hands, her head slanted at an angle that magnified the nuanced shades in her blonde hair; Nick drooled to kiss her. His own mental birdie suggested he wait.

Jules was reserved though smiley while hiking here from town. Nick, limping with a bruised lumbar from a fall at today's ostrich rodeo, was learning this was no accident. Her inner spark flared when afternoons became early evenings. She alerted him this might happen.

Nick went without lunch today and Royo's belly was a bottomless pit. Now they were ingesting every crumb.

"Slow down, you two," Jules said. "You're going to eat yourself to sleep. You need to hear what I uncovered in that moldy journal from the Alpine Tavern."

"Ah, yes, the day your allergies turned into our matchmaker," Nick replied. "I toast them with a wafer."

"Hey," she said. "Leave me a few."

Nick saw that Jules was so busy trying to amuse him with florid propaganda for a city that didn't require it, as well as setting out this feast, that her own food was untouched. "I propose a deal," he said. "I'll entertain you with a campfire tale so you can catch up eating and then you can reciprocate. Beware: the Bandit's Ghost is not for the faint of heart."

"Ready," she said. "I'm partial to spook stories. I even had a Northwestern professor who told us ghosts are the best teachers for the living."

"This one supposedly happened just over there." He pointed toward a craggy rock formation reputed by locals to resemble Satan's profile. A small lake formed by pale boulders shimmered ripples off of it. North a half-mile was the steel-and-wood Devil's Gate Bridge, circa 1893 which Nick already disparaged as a technological weakling.

He chomped his fourth wafer and began. Some years back, he explained, a notorious Mexican gang stashed gold, silver, and other booty from a robbery inside the walls of a cavern behind the Devil's Gate face. Lawmen on horseback pursued the thieves, eventually apprehending ringleader Juan Flores. But they gave him no trial. They gave him a tree, from which they hanged him. Flores's partner-in-crime, a bandito named Rodriguez, escaped, fleeing south of the border on a fast horse.

"You know crooks," Nick said. "Money is their religion."

Sure enough, Rodriguez snuck back to Devil's Gate with a two-pronged plan. He'd slither down into the pitch-black cave on a rope with a pickax while a lookout maintained watch outside. "He should've stayed in Mexico," Nick said. "Something was waiting for him in the dark."

"Something?" Jules asked.

"Yes, one very dead Juan Flores, according to legend. '*Leave!*' the ghost warned his friend, lest he, too, tumble into the entrance of hell. Rodriguez didn't believe it."

The lookout heard a spine-tingling scream next, and then the crackle of disintegrating rock. Rodriguez was gone. "Needless to say," Nick said, "the thief bailed out of there, never returning to Pasadena, whatever its advocates said about the magical climate."

"*Ooh*, not bad," said Jules. "Not Mary Shelley, but decent."

"Top it if you can," Nick said. "I expect gooseflesh." He wedged a blade of grass in his mouth and ordered Royo to chase squirrels, of which he was particularly adept.

Jules set down the remains of her sandwich and tucked her hair behind her ears. "Challenge accepted, though my story doesn't involve phantoms. It's about a spectacular dog."

She said she'd learned about him from an abstract mention in her Pasadena Perfect files. When she told Lilly that she wanted to visit the Alpine Tavern to assess the story's validity, her employer encouraged her to go. The Arroyo's humane legacy with animals needed fleshing out. Jules didn't inform Lilly that she already exhumed archives about early Pasadena showing things weren't always so humane.

"Enlighten me," Nick said, challenging her.

She obliged him. During last century's droughts, some farmers elected to lead their starving horses and cattle to quick deaths over the sides of the Arroyo to spare the animals suffering and themselves money. People later chloroformed feral cats and "skunked" canines. Teenagers themselves played a game where they attempted snatching chickens buried up to their necks as they galloped by on horseback.

"Appalling," Nick said, patting down his cowlick. "Though is it fair to judge what happened in history by today's standards? We did once burn supposed witches at the stake. They'd ship you to Timbuktu for replicating that behavior now. Tell me about this dog?"

"Gladly," Jules replied. "And sadly. Remy. Popular history forgot him."

Remy was a young, mixed-breed pooch owned by the Difford family, who were among the first to migrate to Pasadena from the Midwest's plains. To explore their new climes, they hiked up to Mount Wilson one shining afternoon. The parents wanted their daughter and younger son to stomp in fresh streams, observe wildlife, appreciate that America wasn't completely flat.

But amid the serenity of a mountain picnic, four-year-old Tommy wandered into an open field, unbeknownst to his folks. They assumed the brown-haired boy was still behind them, fashioning a miniature teepee out of sticks and leaves. "It proved a deadly assumption," Jules said. "Two lurking bald eagles with seven-foot wingspans spotted a child by himself."

"*Uh-oh*," whispered Nick, skin crawling.

For their surprise attack, the birds swooped down in the harsh glare of the sun. In seconds, two sets of black talons ripped into Tommy's bony shoulders to clutch him. Tommy's parents sprinted toward him once he cried out in pain. Thirty yards away, they pelted the shrieking, yellow-beaked hunters with stones. Yelled at them to fly off. But the animals bore no intention of retreat. He was food, and they lifted the writhing child several feet off the ground.

Enter land mammal on the job: Remy. The Difford family dog catapulted himself into the fray, clamping his fangs into one of the eagle's hideous claws. The bird squawked and counterattacked, pecking Remy's head bloody until the dog unclenched his teeth and fell. Bighearted Remy, though, leaped back up, this time grabbing one of Tommy's boots. A tug-of-war ensued, producing an unforgettable visual, in which the dog yanked down on the boy and the eagles pulled up.

The aerial killers—America's national emblem (and the Anheuser-Busch's corporate symbol)—relented after a few minutes in this intense fight for Tommy. Their talons released him and, in a riot of flapping black feathers, they winged off.

"Tommy's parents," Jules said, "hugged him tight, believing the sinister creatures gone. That was their second error."

With babies to feed a mountain away, the eagles returned. This time they dug their hooks into the canine, hefting him up by his mane.

"*Remmmmmmy!*" Tommy wailed. "Not my dog."

His death yelp ricocheted off the treetops. Three blips soon disappeared into the atmosphere.

"Is that not the creepiest story you've ever heard?" Jules asked. "It so shocked me that I needed to sit down in the tavern's rocking chair to gather myself. I kept imagining Remy's expression being dragged up; how he'd sacrificed himself for the boy he loved. Your city cares about animals, but the animals care right back. Nick, are you listening?"

He was, unfortunately, and now he had a vacant stare and a rapid pulse. Eagles and their ilk (hawks, osprey, vultures) always seemed monstrous to him, not awe-inspiring. He favored ostriches and peacocks, ornithology's village idiots. "So," he asked, after a second, "what became of the family?"

Jules said they recounted their story to a friend of Thaddeus Lowe, sold their house on Euclid Avenue, and relocated to San Francisco. They might've died in a house fire not long after that.

"Okay, okay," he said. "I concede. You out-petrified me at my own game."

"I did, didn't I?"

"Yeah, the question is whether the story is apocryphal. It feels rather dubious that your tale ended up in a journal, and not in a book or authenticated article."

"I've been thinking about it within the context of what else I've gleaned," Jules said. "Publicizing the existence of bloodthirsty eagles would've been detrimental to wooing new citizens to the foothills, wouldn't you think?"

She's quick. Nick poured himself more iced tea to rid his mind of those flesh-shredding talons. "Allow me to quote Napoleon Bonaparte, who, by the way, was an ardent believer in solar-powered steam engines."

"Is there no subject where you cannot insert your obsession?"

"Probably not. 'History,' Napoleon remarked, 'is a version of the past that people have agreed upon.'"

Jules smirked. "I'll see you one Napoleon and raise you a Ralph Waldo Emerson, if I may."

"You may, I think."

"Emerson said, 'History is a *fable* agreed upon,' but I choose to believe in Remy's heroism. The mystery is why his story disappeared."

"We'll have to agree to disagree on this," Nick said, badly needing a subject pivot. "Did I ever tell you about Upton Sinclair's junky teeth?"

Jules recognized what Nick was doing. "No," she answered. "Please expound." She didn't have the heart to relay another historical nugget that she discovered in her committee folders. At Pasadena's inception, there were more *Iowans* here than Indianans.

Later, Jules executed her own strike in the sun. She shoved Nick onto his back and rolled on top of him. There, she kissed him, acquainting him for a precious second with the tip of her vanilla-tinged tongue.

When she retracted, Nick revealed a ten-kilowatt smile. "Royo, where are you?" he hollered. "I'm being accosted by a gullible suffragette."

His mutt galloped over, pouncing onto Jules, who lay over Nick, licking both their faces in sloppy delight. Hoping Royo's telepathy was working, Nick thought, "She's a keeper. Now get off of us before you spoil the mood."

The dog heard that, for he woofed, and then trotted back to where he was cavorting before. While Nick and Jules tilted their faces to the fading light, Royo pursued a squirrel across the rocks and up into one of the nostrils of the Devil's Gate's rock face.

AIRBORNE CINEMA

A S A NATIVE IN a city with a foothold in the embryonic aviation business, Nick had seen his share of identifiable flying objects. He was in the whooping crowd when a Wright Brothers' EX biplane touched down at Tournament Park for its record-smashing, transcontinental flight. He watched with his father at an airfield near the Raymond Hotel for the climax of a hotly publicized race between a locally operated zeppelin and a motorcar.

The automobile won; it wasn't like it'd dueled Mrs. Grover Cleveland.

Now, as a new object streaked over the Arroyo in the early hours of this Friday, all Nick could think about was Reginald's question about flying vehicles. That day was here, accidentally. Horrifically. He saw it all: the spinning tires with no road to grip, the dark-painted truck about to be crumpled.

The five-ton vehicle was moving at high speed on Colorado Street when it barreled through Orange Grove Boulevard and onto the access road angling downward to the bridge's elevation. To avoid the barricades in front of the deck, the driver jerked to the right, and the truck sailed over the edge of the ravine with a head of steam.

It flew for twenty yards before its nose dipped and it slammed into the hillside. The truck jackknifed, rolling downslope like a kicked-in Campbell's Soup can. When it stopped, it lay on its side in the dry creek bed next to the Scoville property.

Black smoke was seeping out of the truck's grill by the time Nick ran there. Crushed-granite pebbles that were in the cargo bay now speckled the hillside's dirt and vegetation. Surely, there'd be a corpse behind the wheel.

The twenty-year-old driver was alive, however, sitting on the ground with his head between his knees. He was bleeding from the forehead and arms, talking in a shaky voice to Marcus and others who rushed over to help. He said he panicked when the bridge he assumed was open wasn't, and bailed out the side window before the truck's second rollover. Someone soon took him to Pasadena Hospital.

An hour later, after a flatbed hauled his vehicle away, Marcus buttonholed Nick by the administration tent. "He's lucky to be alive, that kid, even if his father may skin him for destroying his business's truck. We've got problems of our own. As this demonstrates, it'd be half-baked for us to erect a world-class bridge and then have drivers killing themselves because they couldn't see at night, or weren't certain where to turn."

Nick held up a finger. "My lamps should help illuminate the entrances, but—"

"But," Marcus said, hijacking Nick's sentence, "you were going to add we need a bigger batch of them. And you'd be prescient. I want thirty-six lamps on this side of the Arroyo, another twelve on the west."

"Thirty-six—great. Is that adequate, though, on the other side?"

"Probably not. You just get started. The more light the better. Stay in budget parts-wise and keep me apprised. Chop, chop."

For the rest of the morning, the image of the flying truck remained with Nick the way the story of Remy, wonder dog, remained with Jules. At noon, he took his lunch tray up to the deck. It was getting harder to find a seat in a mess tent crammed with so many new workers.

Fifteen others, including some of the Nellies, were already up top. How peaceful it was under the dumpcart's trestle track during break time when no smoky engines roared or foremen yelled. You couldn't beat the view, either.

Nick squatted down next to Darby, the rebar wire cutter. On his other flank was the temperamental Chester, who said "afternoon" and then resumed rolling his normal, post-meal cigarette. A short, animated Chinese American in a cowboy hat leaned against a post not far away, biting off the head of a dried fish he'd brought from home; the company was showing backbone hiring Lei Wong as some local firms advertised their policies against employing Asians. The two Colorado brothers, who mainly spoke in Spanish among themselves, sat cross-legged on the other side of Wong, fashioning stick figures out of wood scraps.

"Nick, I've been fixing to ask you what's it like riding an ostrich?" Darby said. "I was at Cawston's last year with my girl. When I saw those cowpokes bumping along low on them, I couldn't believe my eyes."

Nick grinded a cracker into his chili and smiled; Darby was welcoming him by raising a subject in his wheelhouse. "I can't lie," he said. "Horses are more regal, smarter, too. But there's something invigorating about mounting them."

"I don't know," Darby said. "Seems a bit to me like, well, dry humping a feather cushion. I'll stick with palominos."

Everybody busted up, even Chester. Lei Wong must've understood it, for he naughtily waved his dried fish at Darby. When Darby left, Nick lost his buffer from Chester, whose pitted face was four feet away.

If there ever was an opportune time to inform Chester what he suppressed before—that A. J. Pearson's machine shop debunked the superstitions about the bridge's rattling and groaning—it was now. What was Chester going to do: throw him over the side for being rational?

"Chester," Nick said. "I never told you about what I discovered a while ago."

Chester spit out a fleck of tobacco and match-lit his cigarette. "Jesus. What's that, college boy?" he asked with a scathing lilt. "Something new from your science book?"

The Colorado brothers and other blue collars nearby scowled; Chester's lunchtime-asshole routine must've been wearing thin. Why bother, Nick thought. Better to drop the subject for good. "A book? No," he said. "I was going to tell you about Buford's Meat Shack, the best sandwich in town."

🔊🔊🔊

THE NEXT EVENING, A Saturday, was his eighth date with the reliably logical Jules, and Nick scored them tickets to a sold-out lecture by a controversial explorer; he'd plotted a surprise for later. Dinner was a quick one—"commoner's steak and fritters" at Smilin' Dan's, a casual diner next to Pasadena's new Ford showroom.

Walking afterward under a starry sky, past shops advertising summer hats and sliced pumpernickel, they swapped job stories. Nick heard further about the good and bad of working for Lilly Busch, and Jules learned about the Mercereau Company's cast of memorable bridge rats.

Nick then said "enough of business," and suggested they play another round of the word-association game that Jules conceived on Mount Lowe. Tonight's theme for "Things I adore, what I abhor" contest: canine doppelgangers of famous humans.

"Woodrow Wilson," Nick said in front of Munger and Griffith's, the plumbing store that sounded like a law firm.

"Starting big. Let me cogitate on that," Jules said. "Okay. An erudite collie—a collie who's as fanatical for sliced ham as our president, Mr. Princeton."

"That's daffy," Nick scoffed. "Afghan hound: there's your comparison. Same bone structure."

"Nope," Jules said. "Round one to me."

"Debatable," Nick said, bouncy-stepping around one of Colorado Street's new pepper trees. "What about the Orville Wright of dogs?" Just as he asked this, an elderly neighbor of his wearing a small, tin "hearing trumpet" around his neck waved, and Nick waved back.

"Very tricky." Jules smiled, eyes rotating upward in that fetching manner. "A Doberman. No, check that. Airedale terrier. Those lanky legs could negotiate a plane rudder."

"Not a bad choice. How about something more your bailiwick: Susan B. Anthony?"

Jules pinched his arm as they stopped to let a carriage pass Cruickshank's Dry Goods. "Boundaries, Nick. Disparaging one of my suffragette icons puts you on dangerous ice."

"C'mon. She'd be a Bassett Hound; flat nose, soulful eyes."

Jules slipped her arm through his. "Two can play this game. Upton Sinclair, the best male author of his generation. Hunky, too."

"*Yow*; that stung. I need a breed with a big forehead and a rail frame. Chihuahua—a muckraking Chihuahua who enjoys the occasional greasy sandwich. Now let's switch it up. Who does *Royo* remind you of?"

Royo, Jules knew, was Nick's first dog. He didn't have one in his house growing up because of his mother's dander allergy. Missing that experience, Nick volunteered during high school at Pasadena's Humane Society, which was regarded as one of the best around. "Royo deserves his own category," Jules said. "With that big head and beige fur, we should call him the, uh, butterscotch wolf. Yes, the butterscotch wolf."

"I like it," Nick said immediately. "Suits him. Lord knows he attacks food like a wolf."

What a time for frisky banter. The warm May evening was a showcase of Pasadena's charms. Tipped bowlers, respectable cleavages, gum-free sidewalks. You wouldn't find any pituitary giants or painted ducks trolling the Crown City.

At Clune's, the white-bright marquee read, "Tonight: Dr. Frederick A. Cook, International Celebrity."

Inside, Pasadena's luminaries were out in force. As Nick and Jules walked to their seats, they passed rows of movers and shakers, some snacking on popcorn in white gloves. There was former Los Angeles mayor and water engineer Frederick Eaton; two guests from the Hotel Green hoedown (the tobacco heiress and a vacuum-cleaner scion); a son of Thaddeus Lowe; and numerous Pasadena politicians. There also was Edwin Sorver, amateur meteorologist and young chief of the Board of Trade, a go-getter to whom Nick was compared sometimes. These flashy names held the hottest ticket in town.

Nick saw further evidence upon reaching their row. Sitting in front of him, adjusting his tie, was none other than Charles Frederick Holder, Pasadena's original Renaissance man—author, museum curator, naturalist, paranormal archaeologist, even a Throop Institute trustee.

"You want history," Nick murmered to Jules, scooting in. "There he is."

"I'd rather have Jujubes," she said. "I'm up to my elbows in this stuff six days a week."

"He's a different breed. There's no canine analogy for him."

Holder, bushy-white at sixty-two, was among the first to market the city's climate as a sellable brand. A cofounder of the Tournament of Roses, he sold the sun. "In New York," Holder famously said, jabbing the East Coast cognoscenti that periodically debased Southern California as a repository of know-nothings and crazies, "people are buried in snow. Here our flowers are blooming and oranges about to bear. Let's hold a festival to tell the world..."

After Nick returned from the concession stand with teeth-sticking candy for Jules, he asked her impression of Pasadena's original movie palace. "Passable," she said teasingly. "But I haven't traveled to San Francisco yet."

"Pshaw."

Before them, Clune's stage was lit with bulbs studded like giant baby teeth. The paneled ceiling oozed European sensibility, the intricate wainscoting English royalty. Since its curtain first rose, Clune's performers included composer John Philip Sousa, actors in black face, and the "Dramatic Sopranos." D. W. Griffith screened his films here.

The overhead lights were cut and the middle-aged Dr. Cook, a surgeon by training, strode out to polite applause. Mustachioed and faraway-eyed, he began presenting a travelogue of his harrowing trip to the North Pole. In reaching it, he'd bested, by a year, fellow explorer/rival Rear Admiral Robert Peary to the top of the world. During the excursion, Cook said his crew endured blizzards and near-starvation, and absorbed Eskimo wisdom. Rumors of cannibalism and mutiny were false.

The crowd, whether in black tie or plain pants, listened intently to what was both adventure story and victory lap. Nick, having been up since dawn, conked out ten minutes in. Jules's nudge to his ribs soon brought him back. "Wake up," she whispered. "The North Pole is turning hot."

Nick did just as a banker named William McShane was hollering ten rows from the stage that Cook was a shameless fraud. Cook, who'd faced professional doubts before about his claim, did himself no favors now. He engaged the heckler, denouncing him as a liar. The audience stirred, organizers squirmed. Cook returned to his prepared remarks, but he and the banker went at it again. At one point, it appeared that Cook might leap from Clune's venerable stage to punch out his naysayer.

The crowd took sides with hissing and catcalls. Who knows how the machismo-fueled debacle would've culminated if city rules didn't stipulate the event conclude at ten. People exited the lobby in states of disbelief and titillation. Jules said it best: "What that lacked in dignity it made up for in fireworks."

"I'm starting to question if there's something in the air," Nick said, "considering all the other odd happenings of late. Now, if you're not too bushed, I have something to show you. And it's nowhere close to the North Pole."

ON THEIR TWENTY-MINUTE WALK there, Jules prodded Nick about something she was reluctant to earlier: why he was so preoccupied with the bridge. She, after all, originated from a city littered with them. Approaching from Colorado Street, the moonlight doused the arches with a creamy tint, and he tried enunciating his feelings.

"From the time I saw a rendering, Jules, it called to me. Busch Gardens and Mount Lowe are special. Don't get me wrong. But this gal here," he said, patting a bag of cement, "she's unmatched. She isn't here to impress us. She's here to give people in their motorcars, and I'll be acquiring one someday, the liberty to come and go as they please; to trust that this will stand as an exemplar of function and style."

"That was eloquent," Jules said, stifling a yawn. "I only wished I believed in something as material as you do this hulk."

"Believe?" he said with a grin. "We're staring at Euclidean genius here. It's the suppleness in her lines; the way she's curved and straight simultaneously. Have you taken her in from Ivy Wall? She jigsaws into the canyon as if nature willed it."

"All that poetry for a bridge? And you get to overlay your other passion: solar power. It must be a dream come true."

"Take my hand. You ain't seen nothin' yet."

They stepped toward the deck, where Nick hours earlier watched a gravel truck wing over the edge, and walked onto the boards. They stopped before reaching the tunnel under the dumpcart's trestle track. "Don't move," he said. "As someone warned me, it's a long ways down."

Nick dipped under a sawhorse barrier and momentarily disappeared under the track. There was little street noise this late, leaving an army of crickets to serenade them. He returned with his daypack, which contained the implements required to plop a cherry on the evening.

"Turn around and stargaze while I set up," he said, unpacking his things into an empty wheelbarrow. "I think Saturn's out."

"Coy distraction," Jules said.

While she searched for it, Nick placed a black, shoebox-shaped contraption on the temporary railing on the bridge's south side. Extending from the front of his metal device was an old nickelodeon lens. A ring of small, concave mirrors on top connected to a tube that dove into the machine's chassis. Behind the mirrors was a slot the width of a standard postcard or photograph. A hinge operated the lid. At the bottom of Nick's solar projector was its energy vault: three inches of crumby, dark glass and earthenware, which stored heat from sunbeams channeled into them by the reflecting mirrors.

The principle was identical to his solar lamps, except there the heat activated the phosphorous gel coated inside the globe when darkness fell. The difference here: at nightfall, the trapped heat didn't make a bulb glow. It illuminated and enlarged an image held inside the device by two treated magnifying glasses.

Into the slot he pressed a photo that A. C. Vroman, one of Pasadena's most notable merchants and its best roving shutterbug, snapped a year ago; Nick had met AC ten years earlier when AC presented him an award at Nick's high school graduation.

"Close your eyes," he said, twisting the activation knob. "Now, open them up."

Before Jules was airborne cinema: a grainy photograph that captured Mrs. Julius Caesar mid-step while ridden by a beanie-clad Nick. The twelve-foot-by-eight-foot photo radiated diagonally over the darkened canyon. For reasons still mystifying but welcome to Nick, the image shimmered with a slightly holographic effect. It did this when he tested it with Fleet behind his Green Street bungalow last month on a cloudy evening.

"Well, I'll be," said a gushy Jules, careful not to speak too loudly after Nick warned her he could get in trouble, even fired, being on the deck off-hours. "How can this be real? There's no screen, no electricity. It's breathtaking."

Nick saw the beamed photo reflected in her eyes. "You really like it?"

"Nick, you're on the cusp of, I don't know—a floating movie palace."

"Hardly. The pictures are stationary. But what do you think of Mrs. Julius Caesar? Wasn't she something?"

Jules yanked him in by the collar. "Yes," she said. "And so are you."

Nick smooched her quickly, and then felt the top of his machine to ensure it wasn't overheating. "Don't blink," he said. "It only lasts a minute before it fizzles. Guess I have kinks to iron out before I take it to D. W. Griffith. I was joshing about that last part."

"Don't josh. He'll be groveling to you."

Mrs. Julius Caesar, restored from death in floating pixels, actually lasted two minutes. Then, as predicted, the image wobbled and dissolved as Nick's solar-powered projector lost power. He toggled a knob, withdrew the photo, and started repacking it into his gunnysack.

Leaving the deck, back on firm ground, Jules was still enthralled, though not blind to their surroundings. They weren't alone. She pointed to the second floor of Mrs. Bang's boardinghouse for the sickly, where a lamp was on in the background of a room. In front of the window were three small faces hopping up and down in excitement. They, too, must've enjoyed the ostrich in Nick's floating movie palace.

"Looks as if you have your first fans," Jules said. "Next time, you ought to beam a picture of you and the butterscotch wolf."

TEDDY STUMPER

Nick squeezed Jules's hand, fearing he'd lose her in the scrum of other guests who entered the property exactly when they did. To access this bash, everyone needed to survive the human bottleneck on the pathway. When they finally made it inside the host's residence, Nick crossed himself in jest. "I think I cracked a rib," he said.

"A rib? I have someone's handprint on my spine," Jules added. "Though I hear wine is a curative."

Nick left, returning moments later with two goblets, and they dodged their way to the corner of the immense room to soak up the ambience. After two of the more uniquely garbed attendees brushed by, one in a raccoon hat, the other in a sort of fancy loincloth, they had their unofficial welcome to Charles Fletcher Lummis's orbit.

If there was an alternative universe to Millionaire's Row, this was it

They finished their wine, deciding to eat before socializing outside. The spread before them was fittingly exotic: arugula salad, cured meats, chicken paella, platters of maize and chorizo. In the center of a redwood table were artisanal cheeses stacked like an Aztec triangle, a tribute to Lummis's multicultural tastes.

Jules's head already was spinning knowing she'd be meeting Upton Sinclair tonight. She'd even boned up on their frizzy-haired host, who was outside just then greeting arrivals in a tan buckskin coat, which must've been sweltering on this warm June evening. Then again, the reigning master of oddball festivities could dress anyway he wished.

Every spring here, Lummis held an "Order of the Mad March Hares" for people born that month. Other times, he conducted "mock trials," where newcomers to California were grilled about their knowledge of the state. But tonight's wingding was his signature event: a "Noise." There'd be loud voices, liberal personalities, and anything goes.

Nick, spooning his paella, admitted feeling out of his league. Jules told him he shouldn't, and teased him that if a cow broke loose, he'd be their huckleberry.

They walked out into an enchanting backyard teeming with people. Chinese lanterns swung from sycamore branches. Beneath them, two flamenco guitarists played, some folks dancing barefoot to the music. The couple strode the grounds of the cliffside property situated in the Arroyo just south of Pasadena. Lummis's place, the "El Alisal," wasn't as capacious as Ivy Wall, though it was still mighty impressive: a stonewalled castle boasting a tower and exhibition hall. It'd taken Lummis thirteen full years to build it.

After their yard promenade, they sat down at a candlelit table, where Jules refreshed Nick's memory about the so-called "The Tramp."

Lummis came west from Cincinnati in his mid-twenties to work as a reporter for the *LA Times*. He refused to arrive by train. To educate himself about America, he walked, leaving Ohio in a wide-brimmed hat and setting here four months later with a sombrero on his head and a stuffed-coyote necklace around his neck. Three years of tireless journalism later, he was fried, and wandered off to New Mexico to recuperate. Upon his return, his eclectic interests forged him into a Renaissance man somewhat like Charles Holder, only more skewed toward the marginalized. Lummis advocated for Indian rights and the American Southwest; he headed a library and edited the *Land of Sunshine* magazine.

"Makes sense," Nick said, wishing he'd worn his adult knee pants. "His guests tilt to a certain artistic class. Now let's dance."

They kicked off their shoes and free-lanced moves when they weren't laughing or reverting to the basic foxtrot. They admired the guitarist's skill and rubbernecked Lummis's friend's—poets, ballerinas, writers, naturalists, socialists, and experimental painters—funky dancing. Jules, after twenty minutes of this, declared herself parched. Nick, light afoot, went into El Alisal to grab them more wine.

Once he returned, eager to tell Jules about his clever remark inside to the weirdo in the raccoon hat, Jules was under a lanterned tree talking to *him*.

"Upton," Nick said. "I so thank you for greasing us this invite. It was kind of you to remember me."

"My pleasure," Upton said, shaking hands. "You enjoying your immersion into the stranger side?" A teetotaler, he was nursing a cup of un-spiked punch.

"More than I can express," Nick said, glancing to check if Jules was batting her swimmable eyes at him.

"When I told Charles about you after our lunch, we agreed you were our type of Pasadenan."

"And that is?"

"The interesting type, the no toffee-nose, trust-fund type."

"The only toffee I like," said Nick, in a play to impress Jules, "have wrappers. It's humbling being surrounded by so many famous faces, nonetheless."

He wasn't exaggerating. Over Upton's shoulder was Clarence Darrow, the famed lawyer who'd defended the anarchists indicted for bombing the *LA Times* over its anti-union stance. He was jabbering with a pair of young actors, Mary Pickford and Douglas Fairbanks, who appeared wide-eyed in his midst.

"Your time is coming," Upton said. "And I must say how heartened I am encountering a Chicagoan on safe turf. That city and I have had a tempestuous relationship since my book."

"Speaking of Chicago," Jules cut in, "would it be too cloying of me to inquire about the inspiration for a few scenes? Chalk it up to being a history major at Northwestern."

Nick, who rarely got jealous, was experiencing gale-force insecurity. He needed to remove himself before he acted foolishly, and he had a ready-made excuse. A. C. Vroman was there by the edge of the property, so Nick excused himself from Jules's literary swoon.

AC, to him, was the best of Pasadena: accomplished, altruistic. A studious man, he glowed when Nick said he used his photograph of Mrs. Julius Caesar for the solar projector. "You give the word," AC said, "and I'll be back with my camera for more action shots. A fella can only snap so many portraits of trees and streams."

They gabbed until AC went to use the john. Nick stood alone then, listening to the party hullabaloo and whiffing the skunky smoke from three guests sharing a "wacky-tobacky" cigarette nearby. "You want a drag, mister?" one of them asked. "It's a chest-full of euphoria."

Nick, while tempted, declined. He circled Lummis's land again, thinking it could use better lighting, and went to unlatch Upton from Jules. But she wasn't talking to Mr. Decorated Author anymore. She was saying goodbye to Elizabeth Boynton Harbert, a graying feminist activist/writer whose works Jules held in high esteem.

When it was just the two of them, Jules's face was incandescent, Nick's zestless. "Are you all right?" she asked after he told her he didn't care to dance. "You behaved a smidge upset when you left."

"I needed to catch up with AC, that's all. How was meeting your idol? Intoxicating?"

Jules never saw Nick territorial before. "He's amiable in an inured manner," she said. "And he's taken with you. He called you a principled cookie."

"Oh, hooray," Nick said, kicking dirt.

"Don't waste this night. Most people would lop off an arm to be around these names."

"You're right. I don't know what's wrong with me. Shall we mingle or have more wine?"

"Both."

Jules laced her arm through his. For the next hour, they drank and met other attendees. Watched a juggler. They couldn't believe it either when larger-than-life Will Rogers blew past them.

They were tracking him when Lummis sashayed up, arms wide. The Tramp had a craggy face and an animated chi to go with shock-white, Brillo-pad-esque hair. "What's a Noise without fresh faces?" he said. "Someday, son, I hope to have a lively discussion with you about the lamps our mutual friend informed me you're developing. Not every town requires smokestacks for prestige."

"Just name the time," said Nick, deciding not to tell Lummis that Pasadena forbid grungy smokestacks.

"Now cavort," said Los Angeles's fifty-something man of letters. "We start howling soon."

At eleven, Lummis scaled an outdoor bench, tapping a knife against his chalice to get partygoers' attention. It took repeated clinking before the most garrulous in the bunch stopped yapping. Lummis spoke briefly about honoring California's native tribes and questioning "the onslaught of the motorcar," the latter a point Nick disagreed with. He plugged his museum, which was premiering next year, and thanked everyone for "being different." Finally, he hoisted his goblet, saying, "To a Noise we'll never forget. Friends, convene your inner-animal."

"*How-uuuuuu*," he caterwauled. "*How-how-howwuuuuuuuuu!*"

The yowl was contagious, for everybody soon was woofing and howling in a cacophony of pitchy keening. Nick, trying to wick away the jealousy he denied having, joined in with a Royo-esque "*Roh-Roy-Ro-uwhooooo.*" Jules added a schnauzer-influenced "*Yip-Yip-Yip-Yip.*"

The frenzy grew, with the wilder guests boozing it up more, flinging artisanal cheeses, smoking herb, and slurring ribald jokes. When the flamenco guitarists paused for a break, a small pack encircled Will Rogers, begging him for an anecdote. The rubbery-faced actor didn't require much cajoling: "Everything is funny," he said in that squeaky voice, "as long as it's happening to somebody else. To wit, one night in New York I finished a Ziegfeld Follies show with dried tar on my ass and lipstick on my neck."

Nick quizzed Jules about what she wanted to do after Rogers removed his hat and bowed. She stretched, whispering over the din that she was ready to leave. Nick didn't contest her. They made the rounds, saying goodbye to Upton and AC. They tried thanking Lummis for inviting them, but he, too, was storytelling—about an Albuquerque llama he swore could predict electrical storms.

On the Red Car home, Nick's resurgent smile faded. This time, it wasn't only residual insecurity. It was the creeping realization that'd struck him at El Alisal. To fall so completely for somebody like Jules was to cede them agency over your joy, your mood. Whether you regarded the common buttercup as evidence of divine flourish or ho-hum photosynthesis.

Jules, normally the opaque one, saw him brooding again, and tried vanquishing it by revealing something that she was plotting. Lowering her voice so no else on the trolley overheard her, she began telling Nick about her risky scheme in the name of equality. At the end of a future Pasadena Perfect Committee function or another event, she was planning to give an impassioned speech to Lilly's wealthy girlfriends and acquaintances, beseeching them for their money and support advocating for women's right to vote. The Prohibitionists who'd kept the town largely dry—one saloon, fiats against public drinking, no liquor stores—didn't own the franchise on social justice.

Suffragette petitions and pickets, she'd note, aren't free.

"That's industrious, if it doesn't get you pink-slipped from Ivy Wall," Nick said, drooping in his seat. "I can imagine husbands protective of their businesses getting vexed, if you catch me."

"Yes. I need to weigh that aspect more. What I cannot do is bypass the opportunity."

"Is Lilly on board?"

"Absolutely. Behind all her baubles, she's a progressive."

"Genuinely?"

"She has daughters, daughters she knows occupy a man's world that'd prefer them restricted to kitchens and bedrooms. She respects what our sisterhood in England is sacrificing for fair treatment."

"Good," he said. He rubbed his face: it'd felt prickled since he observed Upton schmoozing her. "Luck favors the bold."

"Switching gears: something you abhor? Vegetable, mineral, people named Chester?"

He didn't want to play but did. "Broccoli," he said as if he were chewing it.

"I guess that counts. My turn. I abhor cod-liver oil. And freezing rain."

She wasn't going to stop. "All right," Nick said. "I adore the crisp chill of a pillow after a grueling day. And stealing Fleet's toilet paper from his water closet."

"Shameless. I abhor men with snaggleteeth. Like a certain author's."

Nick's eyes narrowed. "You're just saying that because I turned covetous."

"Time to switch," she said, glossing over his admission. "What do *I* adore? How about humility?"

"Humility?" he asked. "What was the provenance of that?"

"Since *you* inquired," Jules said, "I'll answer. " She withdrew from her purse a sheet of sepia paper. She unfolded the 1903 *New York Times* article next and read aloud. Nick's chin hooked down after the first sentence.

On his recent, triumphant visit to Pasadena, California, to celebrate his negotiation of the Panama Canal, President Theodore Roosevelt was rendered speechless for one of the few occasions in his illustrious career. A high school student, awarded the occasion to pose a question to him after winning a science contest, pointed at a stuffed grizzly next to the podium, where Mr. Roosevelt had spoken to an exuberant audience.

"Mr. President, you once declared that 'all hunters should be nature lovers', and that the days of 'wasteful, boastful slaughter are past.' Yet, in the North Dakota badlands, you yourself shot dead an innocent mother bear and her cub. Logically, sir, if that's loving nature, what constitutes despising God's glorious creatures?"

The President, his lips convulsing beneath his auburn mustache and round spectacles, attempted, halted, and reattempted to articulate his evolving view on the subject while the restive crowd murmured. In the end, the man who led the Rough Riders up San Juan Hill and later confronted a railroad monopoly as a "trust buster" smiled self-consciously.

"As my children can attest," Mr. Roosevelt told the crowd, "I'm rarely stumped for words, but this young man managed the feat. Bully for him. From hereon, let young Mr. Chance be known as America's Teddy Stumper."

It was a moniker that inspired humor and dialogue for a week, until Mr. Roosevelt had to dissuade other adolescents from attempting to pretzel him into silence.

"Dilly," Nick said half-heartedly after Jules stopped reading the end of the story. "You found it. I'd spotted that it'd gotten lost in your research mountain."

"It was already in a folder about newsworthy youths when I accepted the job. I spotted it first last week. It's remarkable, even so."

"Or just old news."

"That's not what I meant. I doubt a single man at Mr. Lummis's would've desisted from tooting his horn about that. It was a pro-Roosevelt crowd."

"You got me. Cocky without the nostalgic conceit."

Jules didn't understand why he was behaving churlish. Two stops before theirs, he elaborated.

From childhood on, Nick said, he revered the man only slightly less than he did his own father. Roosevelt was Pasadena's sort of he-man progressive, and the town celebrated his visit with a "flower fantasia you probably could have glimpsed from outer space." Wreaths and palm branches were strung in abundance. An arch fashioned from lilies over Marengo Avenue was high enough for a locomotive to chug beneath it.

"And what did he do before I fired off my loaded question denigrating him as an animal murderer? He compared Pasadena's natural beauty to 'a garden of the lord,' and said its plains remind him of a blooming rose. Over his head was guess what: a floral banner reading 'Panama Canal.'"

"It sounds as if Queen Victoria would've received less accord."

"She would've. At first, it was flattering garnering all that notoriety. At school. At Boy Scouts. At the Tournament. Eventually, it became shackles defining me. Almost nobody even bothered to inquire how I won the science fair."

"How did you?" Jules asked.

"I made a miniature ballerina on a jewelry box twirl using a box of birthday candles."

"I wish I could've seen that. Not that I would've understood it."

"Neither did I," Nick said. "After a week, the ambient heat melted the ceramic."

They giggled for the first time since Will Rogers' showboating.

At the Santa Fe depot, Nick turned in the direction of Jules's place to walk her home. She wasn't ready. "There's more to the story, isn't there?" she said.

"I'm that transparent, huh?"

Even once Roosevelt left office, after a term in which he'd championed the Square Deal and was awarded the Nobel Prize, Nick told her he still longed to apologize. It mattered nothing to him that Roosevelt's 1912 presidential campaign as an independent in the "Bull-Moose Party" split the conservative vote, which enabled Woodrow Wilson to take the White House. He still felt rotten that he embarrassed somebody who handled his comment so magnanimously.

Two years ago, when the former president appeared before a packed house at Pasadena's Hotel Maryland, Nick said he was in the back, yearning to say his peace man to man. Roosevelt talked ebulliently for two hours about his travels through Africa, his disdain for Congress, and his fondness for the Throop Institute as the kind of technical school that made the "Germans the great race they are."

"During the middle of his speech, we locked eyes, and he recognized me all these years later. He never glanced my way again. And he's ahead of Thaddeus Lowe on my list of all-time heroes."

"Yes," Jules said. "But even great men aren't always good, and the hypocrisy you accentuated in your question was worthwhile."

"Especially if you're trying to spur a president to shoot you like a bear cub."

They got off the mostly empty trolley at the station under the Hotel's Green breezeway. The baking winds were dying down, though Pasadena Fire Chief Dewey Morgantheau must've been nipping from his flask, praying no embers drifted onto any fancy wood structures.

Outside, Jules wasn't finished with her game. "You know what else I abhor?" she asked. "Regrets."

"I get the message," Nick said. "I need to let my complex go."

"But do you get the message? Because I regret bidding goodnight— particularly to someone with whom I'm hopelessly in-love."

As in with me? Nick briefly vacated his body, witnessing the scene on a helium cloud. How could he have been so petty before? "You're not trying to jolt me out of my funk?"

She stepped back. "Nick: am I someone who throws around words loosely? I meant it. Every letter." Tears rolled down her smile lines. "You're why I'm not supposed to be in Seattle."

"I hear that place stinks of salmon. Jules, I love you back. Have from Mr. Mercereau's funeral service and will to, uh, my own."

"Teddy Stumper: why are we still here?"

◆◆◆

THEY DIDN'T SO MUCH as enter Nick's bungalow as execute a controlled stumble, kissing and groping like gravitationally intersecting planets. He somehow kicked the door closed as she tugged him toward his fast-idiously made bed.

Eager fingers peeled at clothes, flinging them with glee. Nick's trousers landed in the sink, her bodice under his desk. Unbuckled boots clunked onto hardwood.

Nick, who'd only had relations with one other woman, a pageant beauty who'd visited Cawston, kissed, tongued, and stroked every wet cleft available. Jules reciprocated with fearless hands and a fiery hunger.

He could barely unwrap his German-made condom before the mattress turned into a steam bed. He hoped all that wine he consumed helped him last with this wondrous girl peeling back more than her past. They were four thighs, one friction machine.

"Keep doing that," she said, purring. "Right there."

More quick-slow gyrations, a torrent of "oohs," and one "oh God" unfit for the pulpit.

Minutes later, Jules retracted from a kiss as they thundered toward climax. "You're making the Earth move," she said. "Just stop cramping my shin. Scoot inward."

"Huh? 'Kay," Nick said distractedly.

Thrust, parry, grind.

"Oww," she said not long after. "My leg. Get off of it."

"If I was any more inward," Nick said panting, "I'd be one of your organs. Your leg must be seeing things."

Jules drew him back in, until the pain in her calf surpassed the elation in her loins. She pushed him off toward where the bed met the wall. "I'm not kidding. Your toenails are sharp as claws."

"I propose we investigate later. It's not me."

"But, if it's not you, then who is it?"

Jules whipped the sheet off them. Now, this was a mood-killer. From his horny smirk to his still-grinding torso, paws clenched around her right shin, Royo was having himself a party to remember.

"You four-legged cad!" she hollered. "Release me. I'm not some lascivious poodle."

Jules shook her leg, trying to knock him off her; Royo kept pumping. "Do something, Nick. I'm not that type of girl. You didn't concoct this, right?"

"Of course not! You think I'd risk being murdered—on a night I didn't expect?"

He drove the heel of his foot into the top of Royo's white-patched chest, causing the mutt to flip backward off the bed with an *Arf*. Naked Nick flew after him, hooking Royo by collar to drag him and his resistant nails toward the opposite wall. There, he snatched him by the mane and hurled him into his closet, slamming the door. "Consider yourself lucky," he said, "I didn't castrate you with my old ostrich shears."

Covering his blue orbs in self-defense, he trudged toward Jules, assuming their coupling was over, and maybe more than that. "I cannot begin," he said, "to apologize profusely enough for that. I was so preoccupied when we burst in I forgot he existed. The lech crept in, I guess, while we were, um, busy."

Jules, moonbeams splashing her face through Nick's window, said nothing. She was now leaned up, examining her leg. That's when her eyes bugged out.

"For both of your sakes, that better *only* be slobber on my shin. I mean it."

Wasn't this romantic: an unscheduled, cross-species *ménage à trois*? What's a guy to do but pick up one of his discarded socks to mop away any offending fluid?

"You can relax. It's only drool," Nick said, bowling the sock under his bedsprings. "Let me reiterate by everything I hold holy, it's slobber. Pasadenans don't endorse this brand of carnality. Or much of any, to be honest."

Jules snagged him by the wrist. "I believe you," she said, her shock tapering. "Next time, if there is a next time, you're bunking him at Fleet. And giving him a saltpeter tablet."

"I'll make it two. Delayed justice." He bent over to kiss her.

Jules guided him back atop her. "Now, where were we?"

"You were mentioning a higher power."

"And you'll be calling for one if I so much as discover a single flea."

Back at it they went, with Royo sighing and periodically launching himself against the closet door.

🙣🙣🙣

BEFORE JULES AWOKE THE next morning, Nick freed Royo from his penitentiary and tapped on Fleet's window. Soon, his sleepy-headed chum agreed to house him for the morning, provided that Nick agree to a double date with him and Hattie, who didn't appreciate that Fleet was still conducting transactional coitus with the dowager.

Jules was up when he returned, smoothing out the wrinkles of her creased party dress. Both were mildly hungover, if not self-conscious after last night's gymnastics. Nick pecked her and said, "Good morning. How about some coffee and eggs?"

"Please," she said.

Nick, as a morning person, could talk the clay ears off a Busch Gardens gnome. So he prepared breakfast in his boxers, aflutter that Jules was stroking her hair with his comb, while rambling impressions of Lummis's Bohemian guests.

"Once we eat," Jules said when she could, "I must return home. I have tasks to complete. Do not read anything into it."

"Me? Never."

She didn't laugh, and after Nick set out scrambled eggs, blood oranges, and coffee, they chewed in silence. To hurry things along afterward, Jules rinsed the dishes as Nick searched for fresh clothes in his closet; Royo yanked down almost everything in there in rebellion.

"Jules," he said, after he dressed for another hot July day. "We need to talk."

"Must we?" she asked from the sink, hands sudsy. "I'm in a pensive state."

"This isn't about me trying to plumb the dark sides of your moons. It's about me."

"It is?"

"Yes. On our second date, you inquired why I punched my adversary at Cawston. This relates to that. Following last night, I'll explode if I don't explain."

Jules switched off the faucet to face him. Nick's chest got heavy.

"My father, Nathaniel, was a mechanical whiz—a whiz always in demand. Present him a busted machine, and he'd repair it. Any kind. He made good money doing that and took good care of us. When I was a sophomore at USC, he opened a shop on Fair Oaks to be his own boss—and everything fell apart. He began hearing voices."

"Oh, no."

"Unhappily, oh, yes. The doctors ran tests, but they were unable to formulate any conclusive diagnosis. My father hadn't struck his head; he was rarely sick. Even after my mother gave birth to a stillborn daughter before me, he recovered in his own reserved manner. I take after my extroverted mother. Obviously."

Jules wiped her hands on the dishtowel.

"The doctors suggested he spend a month 'relaxing his mind' in a Sierra Madre sanitarium. My mother disagreed. She believed, in the absence of any identifiable trigger, that Pasadena's atmosphere might be causing his distress because he toiled outside so frequently. She suspected the brown air that intermittently films over the valley. Needless to say, I thought that was poppycock and we quarreled. I wanted another medical opinion. She insisted my father be removed from lurking dangers."

Jules inched toward him. Nick held up a palm to keep her away.

"Let me continue or I'll crumble. They decided to return to Indiana, where they both had family, and purchased a home in Bloomington. My father got hired with a company assembling mechanical harvesters. But the voices resumed. It wasn't Pasadena's fault."

"How soon?"

"Two months. He told my mother that the voices promised to disappear if he listened for their message on, this is hard to say—the railroad tracks outside town."

"Lord, Nick."

"In desperation, he complied. After that locomotive clobbered him," Nick said, flicking water from his eyes, "it was like that train struck us, too. Mother and I grew estranged after the first wave of grief passed. I needed to leave USC for a semester to earn tuition money. Believe you me, I couldn't have survived that black tunnel without Fleet. Mother and I have reconciled since, and I send her back whatever I don't spend. *When we correspond, I avoid being a Pasadena Pollyanna and she omits her trepidation about the atmosphere. You might say we blot over our despair."

Jules mouth was now an O. "That's heartbreaking," she said. "Through and through. What I cannot fathom is why you're putting yourself through this anguish now?"

"Because, after our relations, you needed to appreciate I'm not always as blithe as I outwardly appear. My father's death taught me that I possess the capacity to seal hurt away in my psyche's lockbox, if you catch me. It was how I survived college and rose at Cawston. Then surprise. Otis's repulsive comments proved there was some TNT in there."

He bent over, hands on knees, and came back up red-eyed.

"Father's Day was only a few weeks ago," Jules said. "That ginned up the sorrow, didn't it?"

Nick sniffled. "You think the Busches have an in with Sigmund Freud so I can lie on his couch?"

"Probably not. He's Austrian, not German."

"Same continent."

Gloomy laughs ended Nick's confessional.

"Now can I embrace you?" Jules said.

"Definitely."

⑃⑃⑃

THIS BEING EARLY ON a church-mouse Sunday, nobody besides milkmen and gray hairs were out when they left Bungalow Heaven West. Jules lived four blocks away in a Busch rental property, a quaint, Scottish-style cottage with a rounded front door. Overhead, Pasadena's morning sky was another work of art. With that load off his chest, and Jules at his side, you could've tricked Nick that Michelangelo painted it.

A block from her place on Delacey, Jules stopped on her heels. "This is where I need to take my leave," she said, surprising him. "Those tasks."

Nick stuttered. This, to him, wasn't a walk of shame. Last night they'd exchanged I-love-yous. "I wanted to escort you all the way," he said. "Royo's no gentleman, but I want to be one."

That elicited a smile line. "Don't fret," she said. "You are."

"Brontë-sisters approved?" he asked kiddingly.

"Yes. Brontë's-approved." A shadow then crossed her face. "Furthermore, I owe *you* a quick revelation. I beg you to listen without follow-ups."

Nick's flywheels spun. Was she secretly engaged, sick, a cat person? "I will."

"The primary reason I departed Chicago was a man, Nick, and, no, it wasn't a romantic entanglement. Boys come and go, no offense. It was the odious realization that I could not spend another second around a father who'd rather control me than love me in all my idiosyncrasies. His cruelty was a form of barbarism. That's all I'll vocalize."

"Understood," Nick said without understanding much.

"Think of it as one of the dark sides of my moon best to explore in time. I'll see you at Ivy Wall Monday when you drop off your cad."

"Okeydoke," he replied.

"Perfect answer." They kissed and she walked away.

Nick went to grab a doughnut and more coffee from Smilin' Dan's to process everything. Outside the joint, a dozen parrots, a few as chunky as squirrels, monitored him from the branches of an aspen tree. Their population, some speculated, was double what it was since their mysterious arrival.

Two flatfoots were talking shop at the counter over pancakes while he waited for a fresh pot to brew. The officers had sleepy eyes, dense mustaches, and voices louder than they realized.

"In all my years, we've never had a spate like this," one said. "Fourteen burglaries in six months, all at fancy estates. He snatches valuables some days, and pinches nothing the next. He busts in late at night, and in the afternoon. If it's the same crook that targeted Cawston last year, he's trying to throw us off his scent. We'll get him. We always do."

Cawston? That's my yesterday. Nick exited ten minutes later with crumbs from a sugar doughnut on lips that couldn't stop smirking.

PHOSPHOROUS DAYS

THERE ARE THINGS YOU write your mother to assure her you're thriving—solar lamps glowing like magic; a girl who might be "the one"—and things you hold back. One of these days, Amelia "Amy" Chance would be receiving a bubbly letter from California. It just wouldn't be in July from a son living life with blazing wheels on his feet.

This year's Fourth was Nick's best ever, one that commenced with a morning Red Car to Santa Monica beach with Jules, Fleet, and Hattie, and climaxed ogling fireworks at a Pasadena park while eating strawberry ice cream. Two Busch Garden football games followed, as well as his best-attended ostrich rodeo yet. "Bravo, flying dog!" the sick children yelled out after Royo leapt onto Nick's shoulders as he rode Mrs. C. "Bravo, ostrich man!"

His stumbling into a job on the Colorado Street Bridge was responsible for these trappings. Soon, the roadway would be christened, and he'd springboard into his future.

The project only had two more arches to complete, both on the west side of the canyon, before the finishing work started. Bridge rats nicknamed the largest of them the "Big Whopper," for it'd be taller than any local building, vaulting twelve to fifteen stories above the valley floor.

Nick's contributions were already in place: thirty-six installed solar lamps salted around the eastern bank. A dozen new ones on the western slopes, not far from where he'd seen Los Angeles City Hall's scouts licking their chops about a potential annexation, were now trenched, too.

Marcus's pro-forma inspection this upcoming Monday was all that stood between him and his next meaningful step: pitching the city of Pasadena to buy his wireless, bargain-priced devices for its street-lighting program. With that legitimizer, he could sell anywhere.

On the Sunday before he was to meet Marcus, Nick introduced Jules to the grilled-meat wizardry prepared by his Cajun friend. Walking off their leaden sandwiches afterward, they passed the yellow-brick walls of Pacific Electric's fully rebuilt railcar-maintenance shop. Unlike other times, Nick didn't shiver with goose bumps or vague sensations of being airborne in proximity to it, just a flush of appreciation about being alive in an era where everything seemed possible.

Under eighty-degree skies, they promenaded south on Fair Oaks, and continued on until they were in South Pasadena at the bottom of the lush hill at Walter Raymond's resort. Jules admitted never being inside before, and Nick told her it was worth blowing thirty minutes. She agreed, vowing not to fall asleep this time to his narration.

They took the pedestrian tunnel to the hotel's ground floor where a chalkboard listed the amenities you'd need a week to sample. Shetland pony rides and bowling, golf and other outdoor sports, a house orchestra and private tours: the Raymond boasted it all. "Tally-Ho" coaches to ferry guests to the adjacent train depot, which first delivered sun-seeking Bostonians here in the late 1880s, remained in service.

"What do you think Mr. Lummis's left-wing friends would say about this, besides it manifesting the excesses of capitalism?" Jules asked, watching a sweating bellboy push a heavy luggage cart.

"Whether somebody had a match?"

Done in Second Empire architecture, the ornate, two-hundred-room building glamorized the Pasadena region before Adolphus and other tycoons discovered it. While, that is, the glamor lasted. On an Easter day nine years after it opened, a chimney ember fluttered onto the Raymond's wood roof and the entire hotel burned to a crisp while most of its guests attended Sunday church services. Seven years later, a less flammable Raymond Hotel was up and running.

They walked an elegant hallway, dipping into an enormous room with a crenellated ceiling. The only people in there were two stern-looking men reading *The Saturday Evening Post* in green wingback chairs. Nick and Jules spun around and left, sticking their heads in other public spaces in the citadel of paneled wealth many called the West Coast's Waldorf Astoria. In every corner were brass vases and potted ferns.

On their stroll out, they passed the main dining room crowded with guests being fussed over by tuxedoed waiters. The jasmine-entwined pergola beyond the open doors perfumed the air with a sweetness even a socialist would find intoxicating. Though full, Nick couldn't help salivating about today's chef special: turkey legs brushed with Bordelaise sauce.

Heading back to town, Jules was her typically quiet daytime self. She let her smile lines and expressive eyes do her talking, and Nick loved her even more.

"I think that completes your education of Pasadena and its surroundings," he said. "I'll request Lilly order you a cap and gown."

In that moment, his future tickled him again: after his first major payday, he'd treat her to an overnight stay at the Raymond, however indifferent they were to wealth and privilege, just to say they had.

֍ ֍ ֍

EARLY THE NEXT SUNRISE, Nick swayed on his heels in the middle of the deck, almost sugary with anticipation. His lamps were shining well, save for the two embedded in the ice plant directly under Mrs. Bangs's boardinghouse, which flickered every few minutes. He was unconcerned. Truly. Sometimes, the phosphorous gel inside the globes wasn't coated as evenly as they should've been, and the spots with too little of it caused the bulbs to sort of wink. He'd improved how he applied the stuff by using a denser paintbrush and would recoat the problematic ones later today. Marcus's haggard eyes probably would miss them.

Tonight, he'd write Amy Chance a long-delayed letter so celebratory, so uplifting she'd junk her worry beads. Perhaps, she'd move back to Pasadena.

Dear mother, I'm without doubt on my path to a solar future.

Waiting for Marcus, Nick had time to scan the newspaper he squished into his work gunnysack. The front page was your usual catalog of other people's pain. Winds of war gusting in the Balkans, an industrial fire killing fifty-five in New York.

Deeper in were stories of cultural change resonating more with him today. One, about a lady doctor in Chicago arrested for ditching a traditional "bathing skirt" for a more skin-tight suit model, would infuriate Jules. Another, about a St. Louis housewife who declared she was in contact, through her Ouija Board, with a woman dead for two hundred years, to him was sensationalistic bunk.

"*Ahem,*" Marcus said from behind, just as Nick finished the story about the Ouija Board woman. "I didn't want to make you jump out of your socks again. You ready?"

Marcus was toting his usual accessories: an unlit cigar, a mug of coffee, and his shopworn clipboard. The only difference today: he had a pair of binoculars and a face not as saggy as before.

"Let's have at it," Nick said.

"Let's." Marcus's inspection routine followed the previous ones. He tugged a stubby pencil from behind his hairy ear and got busy walking around scrawling checkmarks on the light site plan. With more lamps for him to inspect today, it took him double the time to ensure each one was still glowing through the night. Using binoculars was wise.

Nick could practically taste those Bordelaise-dipped turkey legs.

"You gave it your all, Chance," Marcus said twelve minutes later, blasé as someone saying good morning. "Sorry. You're out."

"Excuse me?" Nick said, intestines curling like a wisteria vine.

"Excuse what? You promised me every single lamp would be functioning, and I'm counting five that aren't cutting the mustard. Close doesn't win you anything with me."

"You're mistaken. Two were wavering a little before you arrived, which I should've mentioned, but they're simple fixes."

"Says you. I just counted five either blinking or dead, and I know my math. Care to look?"

Marcus held out the binoculars. Nick waved them off, digging into his gunnysack for the pocket telescope in a rush. Now, he was the one traipsing around in the dimness under the concrete dumpcart track tallying lights, instead of standing where he was waiting for Marcus's judgment. He was the one trudging back manufacturing explanations.

The man was right. Five *were* malfunctioning, meaning three more with shoddily applied phosphorous were now on the fritz since Marcus turned up.

"What'd I tell you?" Marcus said. "You got sloppy, didn't you? Sloppy or cocky: they bleed together."

"That's not so!" Nick said, cheeks flushing. "I worked my ass off. If my hunch is right, it's not the design. It's how I coated the globes with phosphorous. Or outright defective gel."

"Flies in your ointment aren't my concern. You know how many balls I have in the air."

Or mine in a vice? Nick exhaled, trying to stay professional. "I appreciate that, sir. But glitches notwithstanding, I have forty-three out of forty-eight working. That's a pretty nifty average for cutting-age devices. We're making history."

Marcus scoffed openly. "History? That's some hubris, son. Your metal petunias just aren't ready."

Nick wanted to slap his stubbled, grizzly face. "So you're going to throw it all away because of a minor issue? Let's meet tomorrow and you'll observe perfection."

Marcus's head vanished in a plume of smoke from the cigar he now lit. "Think of it from my perspective, Chance," he said after a puff. "The bean counters have me by the short and curlies after we hired a third shift. Your politicians want this done, like yesterday. You knew all along that your endeavor was a concession to the Busches. If you strike it big with these later, you'll thank us for field-testing them."

"No disrespect: I'd like to appeal to your superior. You're being rash. I grew up here, and this shadowy canyon is going to give people trouble. Remember the truck that flew over?"

"Going over my head," Marcus said. "That's cute. Decision's made. It's never fun being expendable."

Expendable? After all the miles he'd logged tramping the slopes, all the cuts and chemical burns he'd suffered, the rattlers he nearly stepped on, the bullshit he'd stomached? Pursed lips, eyes downcast: Nick was a poster boy of hangdog blues.

He turned to leave, for where he wasn't sure.

Behind him, Marcus blew a smoke ring and took pity. "Tell you what," he said, piping up. "Since you abstained from stirring the pot with the Nellies, I'll grant ya another week. We need utility men up here while we pour columns for (Arch) Number Nine. After our gal opens to traffic, you remove your lamps and walk. Deal?"

Nick deplored himself for his prudent reply: "Deal."

Striding off, Marcus whistled what used to be one of Nick's favorite childhood ditties: "She'll Be Coming 'Round the Mountain."

He decided to inform neither Jules nor Lilly of his predicament until he'd crafted a Plan B (with a meager seventy-three dollars in savings). Only Fleet heard the truth, the strands of which braided such a sad-sack tale of failure that he didn't try cheering Nick up with customary sarcasm. Two firings in less than a year: for someone convinced destiny is what you build, Nick had a knack for disassembly.

So, yes, there are things you never want to write your mother, like keeping a room handy for her wisecracking, self-torpedoing boy. If he couldn't persuade Aubrey Eneas to hire him in Arizona, where he was experimenting with a bigger solar motor, he'd have no choice but to relocate to Bloomington to hawk lamps to Luddite farmers. It'd be a living death, a psychic bludgeoning without the people he loved and the mountains he needed.

SNAP, CRACKLE, AND DROP

O N AUGUST 1, 1913, Nick awoke with chest pain—chest pain from having the better part of a fifty-two-pound dog lying sideways over him, panting musky morning breath into his face. How else to kick off his last day on the Colorado Street Bridge?

"The devil you looking at?" Nick asked, stretching. "My tonsils?"

Royo crooked his head sideways at him, scrunching his expressive brow into wavy shapes. It didn't take clairvoyance for him to recognize that he was staring at a Nick who'd lost some voltage, a Nick coming to grips with the enormity of his screw-up.

You can't pay bills with fickle prototypes. And you can't deny when a springboard to your future becomes a trapdoor to the cornfields.

"Least we're in it together, boy," Nick said, scratching Royo's whiskers. "Tell you what: I'll buy us scarecrow back there; first you chew it, then I'll drench it with gasoline and torch it."

Royo, boxy head still angled, panted closer. He was nervous, hating the pain he *sensed* was about to be inflicted for the greater good.

Forty minutes later, Nick patted him goodbye at Ivy Wall, where Jules, luckily, was away on committee business. When Nick spun to leave, Royo barraged him with pistol-sharp barks. The butterscotch wolf galloped toward him next, doing something even ordinary dogs do when they're jittery: he squatted on Nick's boots and whimpered.

Nick bent over, smooshing foreheads to console him. The salami and saltines they'd had for breakfast lurked hot on his mutt's breath now.

"What's unsettling you today? Go torment Maty while you can. We're probably short-timers here."

But the clingy animal wouldn't budge, and Nick lacked the energy to coddle him. So he let him read his mind. "Everything's okeydoke so long as we're breathing. Catch me?"

He unlatched the gate and turned toward the switchback, trying to bat away self-martyrdom as Royo's staccato *Ruf-ruf-ruffff-rohrrr* echoed over the bluff.

The zeitgeist at base camp that morning was one-hundred-eighty degrees different than his. People were spunky, even punch-drunk. Blue collars gobbled complimentary pastries and horsed around limbering up. The esprit de corps wasn't lost on the button-down executives. Two engineers, in fact, jousted with rolled up blueprints, pretending to be musketeers, not the brains of this operation.

Perfect. All that was missing were a laudatory cable from President Wilson and an organ-grinding chimp.

Nick didn't feel much better when a usually hard-nosed foreman approached him with a lively step, apprising him he wasn't "needed to pinch-hit up top pouring concrete. You're free to do, um, whatever it is you've been doing."

Just as well. He'd only worked light construction there about four hours this week. Hence, he reverted to his primary activity: dismantling the solar array that he'd hoped Pasadena would toast him for inventing.

There must be more to his firing, he bitched to Fleet last night. "How can there not be? On my worst day, I had almost ninety percent of my lamps working. I wonder if that Edison Electric fella is involved?"

"Two words," Fleet responded, influenced by a med-school urology class that kept him knee deep in the *male vas deferens* and *corpus spongiosum*. "Pecker-head politics."

"I hope not," Nick gruffed. "And wasn't that three words?"

"On the upside," a term he shelved this week, it was less arduous removing his inventions than installing them. Setting them up, he'd grappled with a round robin of backaches, lacerations, sunburns, and aching soles. This week was about ruptured pride; about putting his optimism through the ringer by breaking down each metal-and-glass lamp and heaping them on a tarp to drag across the hillsides or carry over the

Scoville footbridge. It was about staging a brave face inside the requisition tent, where a mousy clerk with a bowl haircut inventoried the parts.

On this Friday of cottony clouds, the two men from the Automobile Club of Southern California astride the eastern bank didn't have to fabricate any expressions. They were there, bursting their britches in the sunshine, whacking a road sign into the ground with a mallet. On their panel were two arrows fraught with symbolism. One pointed west, notifying motorists that downtown Los Angeles was twenty miles away. The other arrow faced east, telling them that New York City was twenty-eight hundred miles the opposite direction. Soon, *you* could get there from here.

The second the bridge's celebratory ribbons were snipped was the second dirt streets and old buggies were closer to obsolescence in the birth of a true, American road system. From now on, people would expect nothing less than modern concrete streets for their crank-started motorcars. No longer, either, would locals have to take circuitous routes, including Huntington Drive to the south, to travel any distance. The Red Cars would remain the backbone of the working class's transportation, but a pathway zipping you in and out of town via a short crossing would be seductive.

Just not for Nick. At his final mess-tent lunch, he picked at his mac-and-cheese at a table overrun by fresh hires. Afterward, he slung that grimy tarp, which he started to think was inscribed with a Scarlet Letter, over his shoulder. For the next five hours, he'd continue decommissioning what a mere four days ago was his million-dollar idea.

"Chance," Marcus shouted at him emerging from the outhouse. "Glad I saw you. McClaren went home an hour ago—stomach virus. Suspect I have it, too. We need you to sub in on the hopper. The fellas will show you what to do. Try not to bumble it."

"Sure," Nick said. "I wouldn't want to taint the glory."

"Don't be brash. I'll be sorry seeing you go. I was hoping you'd teach me to ride an ostrich for the inaugural party. Scoot."

On the plank immediately below the deck, Nick was part of a six-man "pour team." Another dozen or so bridge rats were underneath them preparing new falsework or prying off the forms from beams and columns whose concrete was dry. They'd already finished Arch Number Nine's most daunting features: its buried footings, two parabolic spans, and open-spandrel columns. The job ahead was webbing the "smaller" pieces—the span-tying ribs, the transverse beams—into the superstructure. Though still latticed in scaffolding and metal framing, the arch was supposed to be done in weeks.

Maybe it was his crustiness, but Nick doubted what the suits were estimating: that the entire project would be ready for christening by Labor Day. He'd seen the finishing punch list. It ran five single-spaced pages. Then again, what did he know?

Today, he was just another set of arms in a place where dawdling equaled failure. As soon as the robotically operated dumpcart idled above them with its load, the clock began ticking to deliver the concrete where it needed to go before it hardened.

Over and over, the process repeated. The team tilted the cart, feverishly raking its pre-mixed batch through its attached hopper into a movable steel funnel, something, it seemed to Nick, *The Wonderful Wizard of Oz*'s Tin Man could've donned as a party hat. The funnel was then swiveled over the open end of a falsework mold awaiting the pebbly goop. A swivel of a handle later and it poured in there with slushy force. A rebar man next snaked reinforcing poles into the mush before it set.

This was how you erected a roadway in the sky.

The grunt work and concentration required made the afternoon blur by. Everything here was specialized, be it the know-how operating the machines and tools, or the whistles and slashing hand gestures that blue collars relied on to communicate. Every shift was a ragtag fraternity whose members hailed from all over, with splattered trousers and fat paychecks the common denominator.

In between pours that afternoon, Nick snapped mental photographs from his vantage, believing he'd regret it if he didn't. To the north, he eyeballed the milk-white funicular creeping up Mount Lowe, and the scrubby land across from Linda Vista the city hoped to grade into a verdant park. (Park? Ten years later, the Rose Bowl stadium was there.) On the other side, he squinted at the shiny greens of Busch Gardens, thick today with sun-worshippers and parasol twirlers.

Twenty minutes later, still thrashing inside, he lamented allowing himself time for any nostalgia, any maudlin farewell. His personal connection to the bridge was about kaput, and, going forward, the harshness of his disappointment over his lamps wasn't going to be easily quarantined in the lockbox of his mind.

So, when no one was watching, Nick scrabbled onto the deck and vanished under the dumpcart's track. If he couldn't visit Echo Mountain to air out his spleen, this was a decent alternative. *"God damn my luck,"* he hollered beneath the construction racket. *"I'm in a river of shit over five bad lights. How's that fair? I'm an inventor, for Chrissakes."* He felt lighter after venting some of his black singe of resentment.

Around four forty-five, he and the rest of the pour team listened to the foreman's closing speech. "Nearly quitting time, boys. Let's make this pour our best one yet."

They'd already funneled an impressive one hundred cubic yards today.

"You heard the man," head-Nellie/carpenter Chester added, pumping his fist. "Good, tight seal, no mud left in the cart."

Nick didn't know Chester was here until now, and what did it matter if he was working on a lower plank before? He wasn't wasting his last minutes here stewing in bitterness, not when he *still* loved this beautiful bridge that he was proud his city commissioned. *Stop bellyaching. You've led a charmed existence compared to most of these men.*

Dwelling on that rather than self-pity, he was the first to snatch the hopper on the final pour. Afterward, he wiped gunk from his ungloved hands onto his trousers while the shift commenced their daily mop-up duties.

At about five, comic relief arrived for this bittersweet afternoon. It was fluky, really—fluky that Nick saw the ends of his shoelaces jitterbugging around the tops of his boots. He wanted to giggle, for they reminded him of centipedes twitching on a scorching sidewalk.

But then he pondered it deeper: if the dumpcart over them wasn't rumbling anymore, and the other equipment was just switched off for economy, what was stoking the trembling, the one now vibrating both ankles?

Before he could ask the foreman about it, or question if A. J. Pearson's machine shop was revving up, came a bloodcurdling crack. Everyone in Nick's group heard it.

Something under the deck just snapped. Something ominous.

A second, sharper jolt shook the planks and then *wham-bam*, a rapid-fire chain of unwelcome noises: the creak of splintering wood and a mushy roar. The next sound was the most petrifying yet: the violent crash of wreckage hammering into the earth. Besides filling the terrified ears of the afternoon shift, the reverberation ping-ponged from base camp, off the Arroyo's hillsides, into Millionaire's Row, and points beyond.

Scarier still, three men on the lower scaffolds were swept away so abruptly that you might've wondered if they'd shown up to work at all. C. J. Johnson (concrete raker), Harry Collins (rebar clipper), and John Visco (carpenter) had vanished. Snatched from the heights in an avalanche of wet concrete and jagged debris, they were now embedded in the canyon floor.

Those remaining on the bridge found themselves stranded on a quivering house of cards roughly one hundred thirty feet above the ground. When everything is hemmed together, one small failure can provoke ungodly damage.

Nick peered down at his feet again and then lifted his head with goldfish eyes. Some of the planks on the levels directly below him were flipping on edge and dropping like toothpicks; their metal supports had bowed. "Help," he cried out. "What do we do?"

Nobody answered. But it was far from quiet.

"Oh, Mother of God. She's going. *Jump!*" someone yelled.

You could appreciate the logic, what with nails and fasteners in the falsework popping out and rakes and shovels pitching over the side. Every board, including Nick's, was oscillating and swaying. A second collapse seemed to be building.

Workers' salty exclamations acknowledged they were in a full-blown disaster: "Christ!" they said; "Shit-shit-shit;" "*Ahhhhhh*, motherfucker!"

A jelly chinned bridge rat down the scaffold from Nick shrieked, "Get off the boards or you're *dead*." He heeded his own advice, leaping diagonally into one of the rounded nooks of the adjacent—and finished —Arch Number Eight to the left.

In forty seconds, *three hundred* tons of man and material had already plummeted.

Hopper-operator Angus Freeman, a redheaded Scotsman, as well as a second cousin to Adolphus Busch's head landscaper, went airborne next. He threw himself four feet toward the crown of one the Big Whopper's main arches. He struck it chest high, and nearly fell, but was able to drag himself up onto his stomach.

"Go," Angus shouted at Nick once he turned around.

"*Where?*" Nick shouted back, spreading his boots to keep from tumbling. Angus's position was too far for him to jump.

"Anywhere," Angus yelled. "Do it or you're *dust*."

Anywhere? Nick bent his knees, searching across the deck for any reachable cranny or ledge. Blanks. His plank shook hard again, and he knew he needed to leap soon or it was death guaranteed.

"*Go!*" Angus said, clapping his hands.

Here goes everything. Nick flung himself at the only object within view: an eighteen-inch-long leather strap bolted into the underside of a pedestrian viewing bay jutting over the deck. Midair for what seemed forever, a chilling thought occurred to him: what if the strap sheared off from his weight?

But it held firm as Nick snatched the grainy length with both palms and clutched it firmly, swaying two feet from the rim of the deck.

"Well done, lad!" Angus exclaimed. "Well done. Someone will get to you. Stay calm."

"I'll try," Nick said.

Angus waved, gyrated around on his belly, and crawled into the depths of the arch to seek help. He wasn't doing any good there; if nothing else, he could play the bagpipe at a funeral.

Nick took a deep a breath and tightened his grip. He then swiveled his head in his new surroundings and couldn't believe his company. At least seven other men were hanging along the deck's edge or deeper underneath it; seven men hanging like cuts of meat gripping concrete ledges, un-snipped rebar, and leather straps. There were no nets, no safety harnesses. Only upper body muscle and sheer will was preventing them from splattering.

An eerie silence pervaded initially, one condemned man taking stock of the other. That didn't last. The danglers reacted as anybody would: they screamed for rescue by colleagues or their creator—a discordant chorus of voices piggybacking on the other.

"*Help!*" they bawled. "*Get me out of here,*" they sobbed. "*Down here,*" they screeched.

Nobody in the mad scramble at base camp, though, could do anything immediately to save them. Suits, whose tents rattled with earthquake force when the collapse struck, were ordering everyone under the deck to run for their lives. It took them a few minutes to point up and gasp at the carnage: the hanging men, the slanted debris threatening to drop.

Nick clenched his hands in a death grip around a strap, whose intended function was lost on him. *Dig deep. Slow breaths.* He drew himself up a couple inches in case his perspiring hands slipped. On his last thrust, he rammed the top of his head into the bottom of the structure. Any harder and he would've knocked himself out. That would've been it.

Darby dangled to his left, arms around a wedge of concrete bulging from the side. The wirepuller's signature tweed beanie was history; it'd flown off when he'd jumped. "If I go," he said, staring at Nick with semi-catatonic eyes, "have them put me in my best blue shirt."

"I will, but we're getting out of this," Nick said. "They'll mount a rescue." This he said for his own sake as much as for the Nellie.

The Colorado brothers were on the other side of Darby. They, too, were hanging from the leather bands, which they knew were there to secure construction ropes or hold tools. Unlike the others, they weren't pale or caterwauling for "Help!" every other breath. Uh-uh. They were speaking calmly in Spanish, reminiscing about the hairy moments they'd survived as kids in Mexico around drunken thieves and natural disasters. Their next topic was how to rescue themselves.

Nick couldn't rip his eyes away from their do-or-die acrobatics for one second.

The brothers first twisted around on their straps to face outward. They began swinging to and fro next in a pendulum motion. Once they had good momentum, they started kicking their legs up high over their heads like audacious kids on a swing set. It wasn't long before they'd scissor-clamped their calves around a pair of two-by-fours on the deck bracing the dumpcart's track. No longer clutching their straps, they now were hanging *upside down.*

For their trapeze-esque finale, they embarked on what were effectively zero gravity sit-ups. Their objective: to heave themselves upward enough to wrap their arms around the same wooden supports where their legs were hitched. Their faces were beet red, and Nick wasn't certain if he could bear to watch anymore. But he did. On their eleventh attempt, the siblings exchanged kindred smiles, grunted loudly, and stretched, reaching their fingertips as far as they could go. To make it, they needed to un-hook their legs from the support, meaning, for a second, they were attached to nothing except the belief this wasn't how they'd perish.

They did it, and did it with uncanny synchronicity. The brothers popped to their feet, hugged, and kissed their crucifixes. Within a minute, Jesus Colorado was bending his entire wingspan downward to lift Darby up.

"You're an angel," he said, choking tears. "I'll grab the ladder."

Ladder? Nick plum forgot that workers stationed a few of them to move around the scaffolding levels when they weren't in a ballsy mood to lash ropes around their waists to arrive there quicker. Then he heard footfalls running the opposite direction of him. "Don't forget me. I'll take a ladder," he screeched. His hands were cramping badly.

"Me, neither," added another dangler in a clearer sightline than Nick. "Throw me a rope. Anything."

Six minutes: that's how long they'd been swinging.

Nick doubted how much longer he could hold on; five minutes max. When a plume of dust from the debris bilged up, he shut his eyes and re-clenched his moist strap.

But fresh terror circulated as the deck vibrated again, as if any of the survivors needed that excitement. Was the entire structure about to crumble? Was this the inevitable encore of a job with a whistle-clean safety record? Perhaps. That, however, wasn't the cause now. The dumpcart operator was bringing the vehicle back to the bank, lest it plunge over the side to crush workers below.

To avoid feeling hopeless in the most lethal moment of his twenty-seven years, Nick distracted himself with memory tricks. He cycled through every relative he could picture, every girl he'd been sweet on, and every big Pasadena event he'd attended. He ran through everything Royo filched from his pantry or possessions he'd annihilated, and that was a healthy list. By the time another man was hoisted to safety, Nick was running low on diversionary material. Almost.

As a child, "perseverance" was only a word on a vocabulary sheet until his father took him hiking one summer day in Rubio Canyon. Nathaniel Chance challenged his nine-year-old to push himself to the brink. How long, he'd asked Nick, could he hold his breath under water in a pond? "When you're frantic for oxygen, imagine lying in a cool meadow under a jacaranda. Transport yourself there when the pressure ratchets. The grit's in you, boy: I swear it." Seventy-eight seconds was how long he'd remained submerged, and his father rewarded him with a Smilin' Dan's sarsaparilla. *Thank you.*

Still, his shoulders then weren't about to tear out of their sockets like now. His desperation wasn't as raw as now. A meadow wasn't beckoning him; a grave was. "*Help!* I'm about to drop," shouted Nick—the last man hanging. By the lack of ruckus, no one realized he was still there.

He said his goodbyes. *Royo, Jules, Mom, Fleet, Mrs. Grover Cleveland: remember me when you see a solar machine, or a cowlick. Lord, make it quick."*

Then, miraculously, he detected movement above, movement that brushed euphoria through every nerve ending. He stared up, anxious to see an extended arm. Yet it wasn't a limb. It was an absurdity you couldn't invent.

A wild green parrot with a scarlet head and opinionated beak was perched on the lip of the pedestrian bay. *Ye-yonk, yonk, ye-yonk-yonk,* it cawed.

"Why are you jerks always following me?" Nick said, with a scowl. "Beat it!"

Ye-ye-ye-yonk. Eeeh, ehhhhhhheh.

Nick's moist palms were constricting so acutely he was taking turns gripping the strap one-handed to shake pain out of the other.

Ye-yonk, yonk.

"You know, if it weren't for me, you'd be inside some millionaire's cage instead of winging around the Arroyo."

When the bird flapped away, Nick resigned himself to the fact that this was the end. He'd exhausted his near misses: that coot's knife toss, the fireball on Fair Oaks. Pasadena always smelled flowery to him. In his last seconds it reeked of wet concrete. He'd count to seventy-eight in homage to—"

"Hey, college boy. Loop your armpits under this. Don't got all day."

What? He recognized that voice, that abrasive voice.

Chester Hockney was flat on his gut, lowering his brown belt over the side of the deck. He'd pre-clasped the buckle into a makeshift harness.

"Oh, bless you," said a spacey Nick. "Are you real?"

"Well, I ain't a physics book. After you get that around you, cross your arms over your chest so you don't slip when I lurch you up."

"Okay." Nick clenched his teeth and clinched himself, knowing the danger hadn't passed.

Chester, who'd double-wrapped the belt's end around his fists, still needed to shift from lying flat into a sitting position to lever Nick to safety. But when he rolled onto his side in the awkward transition, he couldn't maintain his grip, and Nick dropped a foot to a jerky stop, twirling sideways.

"Hey!" Nick yelled.

"Hey, yourself. I'm trying." And Chester was, breathing so hard that rubbery scar near his jugular pulsed. He leaned backward, grunting "*ooof*" and tugged. This reeled Nick up only eighteen inches.

"Christ," Chester remarked. "What'd you eat for breakfast? Horseshoes?"

If Darby didn't tear over just then, who knows what would've happened. Quickly, he squatted behind Chester, bear-hugged his chest, and tilted him backward with every muscle he had. The two-man action turned the rim of the deck into a more effective fulcrum.

The two Nellies yanked and hefted, pulled and strained, winching Nick up an agonizing inch at a time. After three minutes of this struggle, Nick was able to stretch his tiring arms out once they were parallel with the deck. Somehow, Chester grabbed him, rolling him over top of his sweaty body.

Absurdity Number Two: Nick spent his first seconds of salvation sprawled sideways over the man with whom he'd bickered with about science versus the paranormal. Chester himself lay back over Darby as if they were practicing a clumsy two-man luge.

"You saved my life, you pair," Nick said, tapping Chester's shin.

Everybody caught their breath and pressed onto their feet. Under all of their shirts were moon stains. Nick unclasped the belt and handed it to Chester.

"If either of you are beer men, the Budweiser is on me. I know a guy."

Chester lit a Camel and said, "Count me in. You don't owe us nothin', though. Up here, we're brothers."

"Thank God you heard me." Nick said, trying to windmill his tender shoulders.

"That was the queerness of it," Chester said, after a long drag. "I didn't hear you. I was about to rush off to the mess below when I saw one of those parrots everybody is always raving about making a commotion. After it flew away, I looked down and there were you, all by your lonesome."

Hearing that, Nick leaned over and puked the remains of his saltines-and-salami breakfast. He sleeved his mouth afterward, and hugged the pock-skinned carpenter. "Don't sell yourself short," he whispered. "*You* came through in the clutch."

"Yeah," Chester said after Nick released him. "Remember that when the suits tell you that everything is hunky-dory."

Nick dug out a stick of Wrigley's from his back pocket and chewed it on the now-deserted deck. Everyone else had trudged off in stupors, hustled to the bottom, or been swept away in the concrete avalanche.

"I'm going down there," Nick said, kneading his hands.

"So are we," Chester added. "Could be any of us smashed up."

RUBBLE SOLDIERS

THEY SPLIT UP AS soon as they hit base camp, or what was formerly base camp. Where there'd been military-caliber precision fifteen minutes earlier was a mothership of horror now. People were running in circles, running while hollering at colleagues to "*get back*," or running just because everybody else was. One suit crouched outside the administrative tent with the traumatized daze of a general watching his troops lanced by surprise arrows.

Nick hadn't been here for more than ninety seconds before Wink Prescott stood on a chair and shouted, "We need lookouts. *More's going to plummet!*"

Plenty, Nick realized, already had at ground zero. The area under and around Arch Number Nine was a jumble of broken concrete, splintered wood, bent metal, and barrels worth of little parts. The dust cloud whipped up by the fallen wreckage was rendering the air a gauzy, dirt brown whose particles quickly lodged in your throat.

When he squinted upward, he appreciated why scouts were needed. Beneath the tattered arch were rows of scaffolding and framing skewed at cockamamie angles. A number of the arch's sub-beams and columns, some still encased in wooden forms, tilted or teetered precariously, appearing as if the meekest vibration would rain them down.

If they went, would the monster parabolic arches be so compromised they'd follow?

Beat up as he was, Nick still felt adrenaline gushing through him. He was in the grip of an unfurling tragedy, and survivors have responsibilities. He only wished someone detailed what they were.

"*Run, people!*" Wink shouted again from his chair. "Get away." The medley of jarred wood and steel that boomed with a hollow thump proved he was no Chicken Little.

Since others were dashing for cover, Nick did, as well. He sprinted diagonally under the buckled arch, toward the bridge's northern side, and stopped by the Scoville footbridge. He waited for another crash, hearing only agitated voices. *Go back. You're doing jack here.*

He wheeled around to cut directly under the arch this time when he came upon four blue collars knelt around a person lying in the open. They'd encircled one of men thrown off the deck in the collapse's earliest moments. Nick never saw anything so gruesome before.

The spill didn't merely kill John Visco. It dismantled him. Caved his skull in. Bent his limbs at angles physiology never intended. Pummeled his spine. Nick only knew the carpenter/concrete man, a soft-spoken Italian immigrant, from chin nods and cap tips. He kneeled, too.

A long-necked woodcutter from Alabama closed John's marbly, dark eyes, for even a dead man shouldn't have to witness what'd become of him. The woodcutter removed his cap and bowed his head, and the others followed. "Ask Saint Peter to carry him through the pearly gates after this. Now git. Nothing more to be done here."

Nick crossed himself and rose, trying to shed the image, and sensed something behind him. It was a crowd, a crowd gathering between the Scoville property and the hill winding down into the Arroyo from Orange Grove Boulevard; a crowd that must've heard the deafening blast and rushed here to offer help or rubberneck calamity.

He hustled back toward base camp. The first person he encountered was the requisition clerk. He was scurrying around with shovels, pickaxes, and spades cradled in his arms. "Where should I go?" Nick asked.

"There," the clerk said, aiming his elbow at a cluster of men encircling a pile of rubble. "They need all the diggers they can muster. Just watch your head."

Nick took a trenching shovel from the clerk's bundle and approached. From what he could tell, it was one of two ongoing excavation efforts under the Big Whopper.

At the mound, he listened to the *shurrup, shurrup* of metal-tipped instruments tunneling into debris. He wedged his way into a gap to add his shovel, going at it with inflamed palms. Every scoop ached.

James "C. J." Johnson, concrete-raker, was trapped in a waist-high mishmash of broken timbers, concrete (both drying mush and semi-hardened stuff), and miscellaneous detritus. If that wasn't enough of a befuddling sight, a pair of wood beams crisscrossed over the Missouri native. Nick asked a fellow digger about them, and he said they'd landed around CJ *after* he'd fallen. They resembled the frame of a steeple.

Nick, remembering John Visco, tried to avoid staring directly at CJ but he couldn't help but catch glimpses when he leaned in to scoop. He'd been carried off the deck, too, and the results were stomach curling. One of CJ's eyes was a destroyed, along with bloody gashes around it and an ear, and an arm was misshapen. He'd undoubtedly suffered other injuries, inside and out, that'd only be revealed once he was untangled from the pointy heap.

After about twenty minutes of life-saving shoveling, with hands and shoulders burning in pain from gripping that strap, Nick needed to step away to refortify himself. He looked north again and was astounded to see the throng of onlookers was double what it'd been, now with seventy or more people. In there were haberdashers, grocers, and chimney sweeps, off-duty Red Car conductors and clock factory employees. You couldn't fault them. What'd happened here, on a civic showcase across a rugged canyon, was legacy being written.

In the front of the pack, a round-faced Episcopalian minister preached to those watching the all-out effort to spare CJ's life. "Believers: focus on the miracle within the misfortune," he said at a sermon pitch. "Psalms 91: 'he will cover you in feathers, and under his wings you will find refuge.' It's not unreasonable to believe the wood trussed over our brother there is protecting him, so he may attend to other Earthly business." People listened respectfully to his homily, some muttering "amen" afterward. Others lifted up on tiptoes, craning for a better view of the triage.

Back on shovel duty, Nick resumed scooping. A couple of the men now were speaking softly to CJ, reassuring him he'd be all right, that he was fortunate, that they'd free him soon, even though he veered in and out of consciousness. One man clambered onto the pile to trench a path directly in front of him, so it'd be quicker to pluck him out once they'd reduced the debris.

Twenty minutes later, the diggers hefted him out of it. Bystanders applauded as CJ was lain on a stretcher and deposited into an ambulance idling on the dirt road normally traversed by company trucks. He'd be rush-ed to Marengo Hospital, on a pepper-tree-lined avenue, in grave condition.

Nick by then was a pincushion of conflicting emotions: determination to keep going, frustration he wasn't able to scoop better, not to mention astonishment at what he'd been through on what was supposedly an indestructible hulk.

He'd need, though, to dissect that later because Marcus was now standing on the same chair Wink was before hollering into his bullhorn for people to evacuate again. Maybe thirty seconds later, a transverse beam that probably weighed more than a Model T tumbled down end over end, slamming into a stack of neatly arranged lumber earmarked for the job's last arch. The impact scattered the wood, as if it were nothing, and rocked the earth. The aftermath was more group panic; more pointing upward at what else might drop, more spectators covering their mouths.

Nick ran toward the tent area south of the bridge to get separation, eyes craned backward in case a bigger section toppled. Then *boom*. After twenty strides he collided head-on with somebody else not looking where they were going. The force knocked the shovel from his hands and sent him rearward onto his keister. But even with the crud in the air, Nick had no trouble identifying who flattened him.

"Otis?" Nick said, getting up. "What are *you* doing here?"

Otis got to his feet, too, tamping his chin to see if it was bleeding. It wasn't. "They hired me a week ago to saw falsework. I knew I'd run into you eventually, just not like this."

Nick kneaded his left shoulder. "And you decided not to seek me out first?"

"We didn't part on a high note at Cawston, did we? I needed the money."

"'Kay. Whatever."

"Where were you when it happened?"

"I don't want to talk about it. And I need to get back to lend a hand. See ya."

Otis flipped Nick a quick salute, and Nick wouldn't see him for a while.

Jesus: Otis, of all people. Soon he was back at the spot he'd run from, listening to Marcus seethe into his bullhorn

"*Goddamn it,*" he bellowed. "I need lookouts stationed right this instant. Three down here, one on the deck. I don't care if they wear a tie or clean the shitters. We don't know if she's a levee about to break. While we're at it, push those onlookers back. This isn't a Vaudeville show."

As Marcus took charge of the scene, Nick watched Lei Wong, the lone Asian on the job, dart up to him. He volunteered to watch a sub-column that rescuers were eyeing anxiously. He also saw the crowd had swelled, whatever Marcus's irritation. Percy Fixx and two other members of the Board of Trade were now there, as well as some Busch Gardens' landscapers eager to pitch in. Police in their Bowery-esque uniforms were working crowd control, stretching a rope to steer folks back. The cops looked thunderstruck themselves.

Still, the chaos eased after that transverse beam hit the lumber. Nick waited behind a ring of men working furiously to extricate the last man still buried. Between his body aches and dehydration, he knew his shovel would be contributing diminishing returns once it was his turn. When those diggers filthed in sweat and dirt stepped back to get their wind, he heard them predicting it'd be hours before they could leave. After Nick got close to Harry Collins, he appreciated why. Harry was engulfed up to his neck, mainly in soupy, wet concrete, along with gnarled metal and snapped two-by-fours in a pile that appeared impregnable.

Increasingly out of it, Nick was oblivious that inside the horde of lookie-loos were faces worried that *he* was dead.

Jules waited until a police officer was distracted mollifying a retired engineer, who was rankled that nobody was taking his advice about structural shoring-up, to skirt under the barrier rope. She walked toward the sound of working pickaxes, crowbars, and spades, calling out, "Nick. Is there a Nick Chance present?"

He turned in the direction of her voice, unsure if he was imagining it. As he did, the first set of diggers, the acrobatic Colorado brothers among them, recommended whacking away at the debris just about mummifying poor Harry Collins.

Jules was squinting, looking for him as he trudged around the side of unscathed Arch Number Eight. "Jules," he said. "Here!"

She rushed up and looped her arms around him. "Thank heavens," she said, eyes big. "We had no idea where you were."

Nick melted into her and kissed her neck. "I was up there, when it struck, when it came down," he said still hugging her. "A bunch of us dangled for our lives. I feared I'd never see you again."

"That's over now."

"You won't believe it. Chester. He was the one who saved me. He and a parrot."

She pulled back, caressing his cheek. "That's incredible. Are you injured?"

He displayed his red-welted palms, which made her cringe. "Don't suppose you have any water on you?" he asked.

"No, but I saw a man passing out canteens a second ago. Stay here."

People keep telling me that. Jules was aces, back soon with a half-full canteen. He drank it dry. "Thanks. I was wilting."

"How long have you been here?"

"Since the morning shift. I, um, I'm not thinking lucidly." He might've dropped if she didn't catch him by the waist.

"If I may, you're *not* fine," she said. "You're in shock. We should whisk you home."

But the accident soundtrack—Marcus yelling instructions, nickering horses, the constant *shurrup, shurrup* of tools clawing at the muck around Harry—wouldn't relent. "I can't," he said in a raspy voice. "Not yet. And what's with the we?"

He got his answer as Royo raced up and immediately slapped his front paws onto Nick's hips. Nick tilted down, petting him and touching foreheads. *You knew, didn't you?* Nick thought. Royo didn't nod. He licked Nick's nose.

Lilly, in a light summer sweater and pearls, waddled over next to join the Nick's-alive party.

"I couldn't restrain him; he's your guardian," she said in an accent soothing to Nick ears. "None of us could stand the prospect of losing you. Dear boy, won't you come back?"

"You two reading off the same script?" he said, hearing the *shurrup, shurrup* again. "Just a little more time. My city, catch me?" *Yeah, and if they knew I'd been fired, they'd drag me away.*

Against their wishes, Nick returned for a last round of shoveling. By seven, with sunset looming and weak oil lamps set up to watch for other wreckage threatening to plunge, Harry only was dug halfway out. He was groaning something awful now, complaining of excruciating pain in places nobody could reach. The hardening concrete was squeezing him to death. "I can't last," he kept repeating. *"I can't."*

"Never mind, old man," one of his rescuers said. "We'll have you out soon."

Marcus, overhearing this, left the area to confer with Wink, an engineer, and R. H. Newcomb, a well-respected Pasadena doctor who'd hurried down here with his black medical bag. With the three others observing him, Marcus scribbled a design on his clipboard and presented it to the doctor. "That," RH said, "should get the job done."

Marcus called out orders, and in no time there was a burst of sparks from the sawmill, followed by the pounding of multiple hammers. Marcus and others soon dragged over a hastily cobbled, C-shaped winch approximately eight-feet high. The excavation paused while it was hauled to the edge of the mound. Wink then strung a rope through a set of pulleys on its top and knotted it around the doctor's waist. A couple diggers stood on the winch's base to stabilize it, and Wink levered the physician up over Harry.

Levitating above him, the physician extracted a pre-cocked hypodermic needle filled with a yellow liquid. While one hand snatched Harry by the hair in a steadying maneuver, his other jabbed the needle directly into Harry's temple area. "There," RH said. "That should dull the pain afflicting you."

After the doctor and the winch were removed, the men resumed shoveling by lamplight to unfetter now-passed-out Harry. There still were *hundreds* of pounds of construction wreckage encasing him.

Standing there, Nick was too fatigued to do anything more. So, he walked his jelly self over to his support unit, which had returned behind the crowd-control rope. Half the crowd had dissipated.

"If you can make it to Ivy Wall, I'll have my chauffeur take you home," Lilly said.

"Aww, thanks, Lilly" Nick said. "At this point, you can just strap me to the hood."

The three of them plus Royo set out for the trailhead leading to the Busches's estate. None of them expected Marcus to gently grip Nick's elbow from behind, asking to talk.

Neither exhibited any emotion during their brief conversation. Both were too whipsawed. When Marcus tried shaking hands at the end, Nick showed him his palms and Marcus patted Nick's shoulder. He then left to supervise the rest of Harry's untangling.

"What did he want?" Jules asked snidely. "Another ounce of blood?"

"Sort of," Nick answered, leaning on her. "In a good way."

֍ ֍ ֍

He stood at his kitchen window, captivated by the moon in the inky, night sky. Dust still was in his throat from yesterday's drama, so Nick bent over his sink to slurp water directly from the faucet. When he returned to the window and gazed out, something celestially disturbing was occurring. The moon was gone.

He blinked twice, thinking it was exhaustion, and checked again. The moon remained missing, but there was something in his courtyard even harder to comprehend: a scaled-down and completed Colorado Street Bridge. This is what happens when you have bridge on the brain: uninvited hallucinations.

Nick fisted his eye sockets to make it skedaddle, yet all that did was incite it to shape-shift. A predatory insect, with spiny legs for arches and onyx eyes for lamps, was its first incarnation. A flash of bright light later, it was a black sun outlined in flickering orange. Nick gripped his counter, hoping this would end. There was a second flash, and the bridge was restored to its Beaux Arts Luster, kind of. Instead of automobiles puttering across it, people were *leaping* from its sides—leaping by the dozens—each one silhouetted in luminescent purple the exact shade as the light misting off the Sierra Madre range at sunset.

The last mirage from his window wasn't a concrete Zelig. It was a Colorado Street he'd *never* seen before: a street with a wide-glassed store advertising an unintelligible product.

Nick shot up in bed the moment his night terror scattered into black dots. It was six in the morning and his now-bandaged palms smelled of tincture. Slumped next to him, on his hardback desk chair, was a snoring Fleet. Royo was asleep, too, on the wall side of Nick's bed. He was experiencing his own nightmare based on his *arf, arfs* and twitching paws. On the nightstand were a damp washcloth and the remains of Fleet's midnight snack, a half-eaten bag of Fig Newton's.

He crept out of bed and edged toward the kitchen window. *Hallelujah*: there were rose bushes in his courtyard and a Pasadena peach-tangerine sunrise above it. The sinister bridge from his nightmare was vapor. A creaking floorboard, though, stirred Royo, who jumped off the bed for a wake-up shake. It jarred Fleet so, now, no one was sleeping.

"Sorry," Nick said. "Were you on vigil all night?"

"More or less," he said, arching his back.

"Last thing I remember you were tugging off my boots. Jules, I think, was warming a can of pork and beans for me."

"She was. You ate half of it, gave me a condensed version of events, and proclaimed your desire to pass out. How are you faring? Achy? Beffudled?"

Nick flexed his fingertips and tried rotating his arms, which made him wince. "I won't be executing any ostrich tricks today, but I'll recover. I do appreciate you taking care of my hands. From now on, I'm going to quit comparing your bedside manner to Dr. Jekyll."

"You should. I also must note *your* latest mishap is costing me study time. Did I mention how much I detest organic chemistry?"

"Would coffee help?"

"It couldn't hurt."

Nick switched the stove on with his wrists. "Tell me: how did you get enlisted into nursemaiding me again?"

Fleet shifted from Nick's desk chair onto his bed and leaned back, folding his hands behind him. "Jules. After she shepherded you in here, she knocked on my door asking me to examine you. She stayed for a few hours while you slept. Later, she checked her watch, and said she had a business appointment she needed to attend."

Nick set out two mugs. "That's curious. Who has an appointment late Saturday night?"

"I doubt she's two-timing you, if that's what you're intimating. She's bananas for you, galling taste notwithstanding. But I will contend she's odd. She reminds me of a Busch Gardens duck: calm at the surface, kinetic legs below. As opposed to Hattie: that woman conceals nothing. Don't tie yourself in knots. Jules probably needs the extra dough."

"Suppose you're right," Nick said. After a pause, he continued: "Speaking of odd, I just had the most extraordinary nightmare, and it all transpired outside my kitchen window. Most of it was about the bridge."

"Unsurprising, everything considered. What did it entail?"

"That's the rub. The details are fraying every second I'm awake. What's glued in my brain was the last scene."

"Do tell."

"This will sound loony, but have you ever heard of a store, in Pasadena or anywhere, called Banana Republic. Or a product pronounced, I think, as chinos, like rhinos."

Fleet scrunched his face. A banana republic, as he understood it, was a derogatory term for a tropical backwater governed by a tin-pot dictator. And "Chinos" might've been a strain of dermatitis. "I unequivocally can say no, Nick, I haven't. That was quite some dream. Be honest: you didn't conk your head in yesterday's bustle, did you?"

Nick assured him he didn't, and elaborated further about what'd unfolded, including running into Otis and how R. H. Newcomb injected morphine directly into Harry Collins's forehead, which Fleet said he didn't know was possible. After they sipped coffee, he rechecked Nick's hands, and Nick said he needed more shuteye. Fleet dubbed that a good idea and walked toward the door.

At the entryway, he turned. "Nick, as your oldest friend, I suggest that you consider visiting a neurologist. Just out of precaution. You've been roughed up over these last months; the explosion, this. Your skull isn't made of iron."

From bed, with Royo's chin on his chest, Nick said: "Pass. My acuity is tiptop. Plus, I have *you*."

Fleet smiled saying goodbye. Outside Nick's bungalow, that expression shriveled into a frown. Nick's dream wasn't the only alarming neurological symptom. Fleet had twice spied Nick nuzzling foreheads with Royo, as if he were trying to convey something psychically.

WILDE STREET BLUES

IF THERE WERE ANY cosmic justice, August 1 wouldn't have killed
John Visco. And Nick certainly wouldn't be here, listening to Marcus
Stonebreaker rattle off a construction war story about a barnacle-strewn
harbor of which he gave not a fraction of one scintilla. He'd still be dozing
off in bed, recovering from a humdinger of a shift.

Sometimes, though, the cosmos have you cornered.

"I ever tell ya about building Mercereau's first wharf, at Hermosa
Beach?" Marcus asked, an unlit cigar between his teeth. They were sitting
in his jazzy Cadillac Roadster, idling at the Carmelita fairgrounds that
overlooked the shellacked-but-still-standing Colorado Street Bridge.

"No, I don't believe so," Nick said, yearning for his sweet pillow.

"It was a doozy."

So, too, were the last twenty-fours. It was Marcus, after all, who'd
rehired Nick just before he slogged home last night. In elaborating why,
Marcus had described himself as "genuinely impressed" by how Nick
joined the rescue party, particularly after he'd "nearly bought the farm
earlier." This, too: his supervisors were "mighty displeased" that there
weren't more lights illuminating the banks of a flagship project just socked
in the mouth.

The upshot: Nick would be adding *more* solar lamps around the bridge
and would remain employed on the project until it was finished, whenever
that was. Marcus, never much of an apologizing sort, even apologized for

firing Nick in the first place, conceding that he "can be too much of a bear casting judgment on other people's promising ideas."

Nick was touched by that concession, if not amused by the company grizzly acknowledging his own genus. He also knew that Marcus was a man of many motives. Why else would he have unexpectedly tapped on Nick's door an hour after Fleet departed, insisting he required Nick's "immediate assistance on a delicate piece of business?"

"You think a canyon is a devilish place to work in, try the ocean," he said now. "We dealt with high tides that were supposed to be low, kelp beds wide as baseball diamonds. When our crew waded into the surf, to drive pilings, there were blue sharks all over, some six footers, snapping at legs."

"Did anyone die?" Nick asked, eyes on the kinked metal framing and missing scaffolding pegged around the semi-buckled arch. A mini-asteroid could've brushed it.

"Not that I know," Marcus said. "Point is construction is a hazardous way to earn a buck. You start digging somewhere, there's no telling what forces you'll unleash."

There was no way, Nick realized, he'd write his mother anything about the collapse. He prayed the Indiana papers didn't carry a national story about it.

"Here's what I'm getting at," Marcus continued. "That busted arch ain't gonna stay down for long. If San Francisco can rebuild after its Leviathan quake, this will be a cakewalk. Debris clearance starts tomorrow."

"Wow. That fast? Any word on Harry Collins?"

"Last I heard, he and the other fella are still alive." Marcus then lit his stogie and notched the Roadster into gear.

From Pasadena, they took Verdugo Road, weaving around Elysian Park and the dry Los Angeles River, to Alameda Street in downtown LA. On the drive, Marcus addressed what Nick still was mulling: why he picked a neophyte like him for this assignment. Marcus said it was because "all the suits are in emergency meetings and a construction roughneck isn't the right man for this. Nuance is required."

Whether that was whole truth—and nothing but—was murky. At least with his job back, and a chance to peddle his lamps to Pasadena City Hall, Nick wouldn't be shuffling off to Bloomington, and that was no small relief.

Forty-two minutes after leaving, the Roadster stopped on a dirt road in front of a rickety house on Wilde Street. It made Nick's Green Street cottage a Swiss chalet by comparison. Under the sagging porch, Marcus repeated the game plan. "Condolences and handholding," he said. "Steel yourself. We're trudging into somebody's hellhole."

His warning resonated at the front door.

"I suppose you're from the builder," said the hawk-nosed man with black bangs who flung it open.

"That we are," Marcus replied. "Mercereau Construction Company. Is Mrs. Visco in?"

"Yeah," their greeter said. "What took you so damn long?" He tramped into the house without bothering to invite them in.

The main room had no lights on, only fluttering candles. A crucifix hung crookedly on the wall, and the air inside wasn't only muggy but pungent. In the corner, an olive-skinned woman with swollen eyes cradled a baby in a rocking chair. Marcus removed his bowler and Nick his cap approaching her.

"Ma'am," Marcus said solemnly. "We apologize for disturbing you unannounced like this. We're representatives from your husband's employer. Unfortunately, we bear tragic news. John was killed yesterday afternoon."

The woman looked at them blankly, or through them.

"Juana already knows," said the door-answerer. "A neighbor who read the morning paper was here at first light. You ought to have seen her flail. It'd rip the heart out of your chest."

"It took us a while to identity his next of kin," Marcus said. "And you are?"

"Ernest Scuzzi, John's friend. We met mortaring brick on a theater up the street. He'd been letting me live here after some hard-luck times. I'm speaking for the family. Or what's left of it."

"All right," Marcus said.

"Juana can understand English," Ernest said. "She don't speak it so good. She had a premonition that John was dead when he didn't come home." He strode to the side of the room, where he loitered his fingers over a candle. Nick watched him, thinking he was a human Molotov cocktail primed to detonate. They were roughly the same age.

"This is a tough situation," said Marcus.

"Situation?" Ernest said, sauntering back toward Marcus, who was far bigger than him. "That's what you think this is?"

Marcus held up his palms in a peacemaking gesture. "We need to introduce ourselves. I'm Marcus Stonebreaker, construction chief for the Colorado Street Bridge. Nick Chance here is my colleague."

Marcus extended his hand, which Scuzzi disregarded. He glared at Nick, whose eyes were gravitating onto Juana's cherubic baby.

"Nick Chance, huh? You used to work at Cawston, didn't ya?"

"That's me," Nick said.

"Isn't that a kick?" Ernest said.

"Why's that?" Marcus asked.

"None of your fucking business."

Wordlessly, Juana rose, handed the child to Ernest, and motioned that he take the baby out the back door so they could have some privacy. Ernest, looking demoted, obliged. Juana then pointed them to sit on a Craftsman-style bench.

"John make," she said just above a whisper. "From spare wood."

"Handsome," Marcus said.

"Please," Juana said once she sat down. "Tell truth. Did mi esposo suffer? Were his insides spilled? Was he fear muerte?"

Marcus clasped her hands in his. "No. Mrs. Visco, not at all. Now, I can't lie. He might've been scared, but that only lasted a few seconds. Being the good Christian I see you are, rest assured the Good Lord was there to lift him up. No pain. Comprendo?"

Juana smiled (all lips, no teeth) and exhaled. "Oh, gracias, señor. Gracias." She looked sideways toward Nick and his bandaged fingers on the opposite end of the bench.

"Tus manos? Your hands?"

"Just scratches, ma'am; nothing that won't heal," Nick said, trying to erase the image of her husband's body from yesterday. "What can we do for you?"

"That's right," Marcus added. "We're here extending sympathies."

At his comment, Juana began weeping in that gloomy room. Its reek—a blend of tortillas; turpentine, which blue-collars used to clean grease off their skin; soiled diapers; and mustiness—was its own fragrance of despair.

Marcus passed Juana his handkerchief. She blew snot into it hesitantly, as if she didn't want to soil its quality fabric. "Breathe, Mrs. Visco," he said. "The darkness won't last."

Even had she understood his message, she would have probably doubted its veracity today. But she heaved and sighed, trying to steady herself. In mutilated syntax, she itemized her star-crossed past to these strangers. The premature death of her first husband in San Diego: consigned her to work sweatshop hours for money. A second spouse left her cold. Now John was dead for the sake of a roadway she'd never use.

"Shame. A damn shame," Marcus said, air-washing his hands. He inquired where her older children were. With a neighbor, she mumbled.

Ernest returned from outdoors, done with his temporary banishment, and laid Juana's baby in its Sears-bought cradle, which was the only store-bought furniture there.

"How old is the cute, little tyke?" Nick asked. "Three months?"

"No. Tiene tres semanas de edad. Tres semanas y nunca volverá a ver a su padre. ¿Donde está las justicia en eso?"

"Come again, Mrs. Visco?" Nick said.

She didn't answer, but Ernest did, leaning against a termite-chewed column.

"She said he's three weeks old and will never see his father again. Where's the justice in that?"

After that soul-crusher, Marcus took interest in his boots; Nick flexed his left palm.

Then Juana tilted up on the bench. She needed to put her grief on ice to learn the practical facts while she could. For the next few minutes, Ernest translated her questions and Marcus responded: Where was John's body (at a Pasadena mortuary); when would it be released (after an official inquest into his cause of death); how could she afford to bury him, let alone subsist? (the company would furnish a posthumous severance)? Lastly, why was she so cursed: "Because," Marcus said, "I suppose you're a little like Job."

"I want you to know," he added, "that John was a superb carpenter, the best of the bunch. Kept his nose to the grindstone. Said concrete was his future, if memory serves."

Juana, again through Ernest, said she valued hearing that, and wanted them to know about *her* John: the John who'd been brought to America from Italy as a child; the John who enrolled in English classes so he could better his family's standard of living.

"A fine man, Mrs. Visco. Eternal peace to him."

Nobody said anything, not even smoldering Ernest.

When the stillness broke, it was Juana doing the breaking. Without warning, she pushed off the bench and threw Marcus's damp handkerchief at his lap. She didn't say goodbye. She hustled out the front door in her sandals, calling her dead husband's name as she jogged down Wilde Street. "John, *my John*?" she cried. "You come home now. No more pretend you're gone. World lying about you."

Marcus and Nick went to the open door, observing her lose it in her black mourner's dress. Every ten feet she pivoted her head, shrieking for her beloved.

"She's berserk," Ernest said, walking up behind them. "She teeter-totters between expecting him to breeze in and saying she's returning to Mexico. John never should've taken that job. He would've been safer operating a hot-air balloon."

Nick spun Ernest's direction so aggressively that Marcus half stepped between them. But with his bandaged palms, and a career on the line, Nick wasn't going to swing on him. He was going to defend what he still believed in.

"The Mercereau Company is no fly-by-night operation, I'll have you know. It's a respected company trying to do right after an atrocious mishap. Thousands have died building the Panama Canal. Are you going to condemn it, too?"

Ernest rolled his eyes. "Apples and oranges. How much is your *respected* company willing to spare? I want specifics, not cheap sympathy."

"We were thinking a hundred and twenty dollars," Marcus said in a perfectly reasonable voice.

Juana's cooing infant interrupted the doorstep confrontation. Ernest walked over to the white cradle, stroking the child's bald, brown skull. Its innocence seemed to pacify him; well, that or hearing about the money. His scowl was gone when he rejoined them. "A hundred and twenty?" he said. "The family would mightily appreciate that."

Marcus stepped onto the porch, putting his derby on. "We'll expedite it," he said. "Please reiterate our condolences to Juana. We're all hurting today." He then walked back to his Roadster.

"And forgive my outburst," Nick said from the stoop. "I've never done this before."

"Fair enough," Ernest said with a penetrating look. "Just promise me this. If there's someone responsible for what happened, don't let any fixers sweep it under the rug. John shouldn't be construction fodder."

"Will do," Nick said. "Pasadena's an honest town."

"Incidentally," Ernest said, tugging on his collar in the broiling heat. "I've been working at Cawston the last few months. Mr. Jenks told us rookies we could do a lot worse than emulate you, far as being industrious. He misses you."

"And I him," Nick said. "Best of luck to you and everyone there, feathered and otherwise. And God bless the Viscos." He bobbed his chin in goodbye.

By then, Juana was nowhere around.

◆◆◆

NICK UNWRAPPED HIS BANDAGES after Marcus dropped him off at the bungalow. Jules brought dinner later: takeout from Smilin' Dan's. He abstained from questioning her about her whereabouts last night, knowing she divulged things at her own clip. After dinner, Nick strummed his guitar to a folksy tune to exercise his sore fingers and lift his spirits after his time in Juana Visco's sorrow.

Royo, as usual, teetered up on his hind legs and walked to the acoustic melody. This time, though, he introduced a wrinkle, clapping his front-paws together, diviner-like, during his steps. His audience chuckled at the circus-dog spectacle of it, assuming he was hamming it up for them. And yet neither Nick nor Jules seized on the real crux of the stunt: Royo's paws were aimed at the bridge.

THE ARROYO SECCO'S FAULTY TOWER

D OWN IN THE ARROYO the next morning, Nick's new mission was to reverse the past. Or rather, his previous week there, when he'd begun removing the solar lamps that Marcus now instructed him to reinstall, along with a bevy of new ones. "If we need eighty of your little metal petunias to address the shadows," he'd said driving back from Los Angeles yesterday, "so be it."

Who was Nick to argue with a so-be-it? He'd be toiling backbreaking hours again to get it done, but that wasn't too steep a price to pay. It just needed to wait, at least today. When he saw Wink at seven a.m., he asked him what he could do. The area under the Big Whopper remained a vast wasteland of rubble, with sawhorses up prohibiting anyone from going beneath it without permission.

"Nothing. Just tend to your lamps," Wink said confidently, his eye twitching less than it was on Friday. "This crew's resilient. It'll have the debris gone in a jiff. You'll probably see new falsework up in weeks."

Wink's bravado juxtaposed with the somber aura as the morning shift straggled in like the walking wounded. Workers hugged and shook hands with pronounced heaviness. There was no macho bantering anymore, no one sword fighting with rolled-up blueprints, no gleeful donut eating. They'd lost friends, suffered close calls themselves.

Nick noticed this all, as well as something else distinct. The bridge rats were warmer to him, some even calling him by name. Jesus Colorado grasped his hand when passing by to collect his hammer. One of the fellas he'd dug with to free C. J. Johnson poured him a cup of mess-tent coffee before he poured his own. "I wish I didn't have to grip a shovel for a year," the man said.

"Me, too," replied Nick.

Elsewhere in the bridge ecosystem, it was a walking-on-eggshells atmosphere. From Pasadena's official corridors of powers to its Board of Trade, this marked the darkest August weekend in collective memory. Project engineers and chief inspectors, for their part, barely experienced any weekend. They'd been at the jobsite nonstop since the collapse, probing the battered arch from its flanks in order to rush out a damage assessment.

On Sunday, preachers citywide grieved the dead and injured, leading parishioners in a moment of silence. Several Los Angeles County Supervisors, representing taxpayers on the hook for about half the project's tab, weren't able to attend their own services. They'd spent part of the day in Pasadena for a firsthand look at the roadway everyone was depending on. They'd departed without comment, probably none too happy.

City Public Works Commissioner T. D. Allin attempted erasing some of the apprehension in an update to reporters. Don't let the bridge's disemboweled visage fool you, he said. There was no obvious harm to either of the arch's two primary spans, or their spandrel columns. In fact, only one portion of Arch Number Nine's falsework, a thirty-foot-by-sixty-foot-section, would need rebuilding. Total replacement cost: fifteen hundred dollars (less than the tab for a handful of luxury bathrooms at the Myron-Hunt-renovated Huntington Hotel).

Better yet, Allin emphasized, the setback only would tack a month or so onto the project. The other bullet dodged: the disaster hour. If the shaking occurred fifteen minutes earlier, instead of at quitting time, another dozen men on the shift would've been up there, meaning it could've been a mass-casualty event.

As a whole, Allin said, Pasadena's gemstone structure passed its "severe test" with flying colors. He'd be "satisfied" if there was traffic over it by Thanksgiving.

How that timeline squared with a supposed Labor Day premiere, the latest in a spool of delays, was taboo that no journalist broached openly. Neither were there explanations about the maze of contradictory information, such as which concrete members were destroyed. Same for the three-hundred-ton gorilla in the room: what specifically precipitated this mishap? Allin's working theory: the concrete dumpcart must've rammed into something.

The narrative city hall wanted emphasized—the narrative superseding the whats and whys of calamity—was the story of the courage exemplified by the workers rescuing their colleagues amid danger that could've killed any one of them anytime. Just one eight-foot-by-eight-foot timber or ruptured beam dropping on them would've orphaned their children.

Pasadena had enjoyed noteworthy moments in its illustrious, if short history, but this ranked up there. The *LA Times*, in its write-up, described blue collars that'd valiantly "burrowed into the heap like prairie dogs, sawing their way as they went."

The newspapers highlighted those who'd jeopardized themselves for others, particularly the men who'd scooped by dim oil lamps. Nick's name was missing in the coverage, and Fleet could see the slight chafed his pal. He urged him to register a correction. Nick, after chewing it over, said that struck him as vain. What mattered was that *he* knew what he'd done, as did the Mercereau Company. It was his solar inventions, anyway, that'd engrave his legacy, though he did store copies of the bridge-rescue accounts in his desk drawer.

On the back page in one of those papers was something everyone missed in the frenzy over the precious bridge: an article about police searching for a man they suspected was continuing to snatch and kill stray dogs near Devil's Gate Dam with a chloroform rag.

♦♦♦

JULES, WHO'D MISTAKENLY ENTERED Pasadena eight months ago and was delighted she had, inserted herself into all this that Monday. It's why she was sitting where she was: in a building that purchased formaldehyde by the truckload.

She'd heard over the weekend that a "coroner's jury" assigned to determine John Visco's cause of death would be convening at the Turner & Stevens mortuary on North Raymond Street. Could she attend "for general perspective," she'd requested of Lilly.

"By all means," said the wife of America's ailing beer king. "You've spent months researching the history around the gardens. A day learning about its present would be *aufschlussreich*, insightful."

The inquest was being conducted in a small room down the hall from the autopsy tables and body saws, and Jules snagged one of the few public seats. The men bidden to testify assembled in another area, looking alternately stone-faced or emotionally sledgehammered.

A bureaucrat in wrinkled trousers called the proceeding to order. Before any witnesses spoke, the clerk reported on the wounded. C. J. Johnson, despite a fractured skull, severe cuts, and broken ribs, might recover. Harry Collins was in direr shape with internal injuries, two compound fractures, and a decimated eye. R. H. Newcomb, who'd administered him that painkiller from a winch, spent the weekend with the nurses scraping and chiseling dried concrete off his body.

A cross section of people involved with the project took the stand next, all of them trying to explain (or rationalize) whether those men were victimized by Murphy's Law, institutional overconfidence, or the unforeseeable. What stuck out most to Jules was the collective anguish: the fidgeting, the admissions of puzzlement—the obliquely pointed fingers. For these witnesses, she reported to Lilly, the pain was existential, not clinical.

"Something gave way—nobody knows what," testified F. W. Proctor, a Mercereau Company vice president and civil engineer. "It's one of those things that makes a man wonder how much he knows after all." Proctor didn't blame the concrete dumpcart. He suggested an alternative scenario: that a length of defective timber used to mold concrete midway up the arch "gave way." When it did, it ruptured other attached falsework, inciting a domino effect. All that heavy material must've crashed onto the scaffolding where Visco, Collins, and Johnson were. After it took them out, the vibration rippled upward, flipping over planks and forcing men to scramble for their lives.

Under questioning, Proctor dropped some of his earlier humility. "Our falsework was the same (on this part of the job) as on the others," he said. "If we hadn't known our business we would have been (stopped) on the first arch." Pasadena, he noted for the record, assigned its own engineer to the jobsite. Where was he on Friday? Now it wasn't the only the bridge that'd fissured.

Four carpenters who routinely scoured for structural fatigue disagreed with the substandard-lumber theory. They'd seen no sign of any "strains and shocks" that day.

C. K. Allen, head project civil engineer for the bridge's celebrated design firm, Waddell and Harrington, expressed an opinion no obsessive detective or victim's family would've cared to hear. Barring any new evidence—and how many smoking guns are isolatable in a debris field—he doubted that "anyone can tell" what piece of wood was guilty.

Citizen juror F. F. Berry was disgruntled by the testimony—disgruntled and curious. What about safety precautions, he asked John Galloway, the foreman-carpenter who'd inspected the timbers twenty-five minutes before the incident? Galloway answered something about "ropes" but appeared confused. Could he have meant the straps, from which Nick and others dangled?

Before the jury could grill anyone further about the specifics, City Coroner Calvin Hartwell effectively pulled the curtain on the hearing. As inquest czar, he was up against jurisdiction. Of the hundreds of tons that'd fallen, the bulk of it dropped from Arch Number Nine. And the Big Whopper, technically, rested *outside* Pasadena's western border, in the unincorporated San Rafael Heights' side of the Arroyo. He wasn't the coroner there. With that, Hartwell ordered the audience to vacate so the jurors could deliberate. Even mortality required a paper trail.

Later the jurors issued a verdict assigning responsibility to shoddy lumber. John Visco's death, they concluded, was the result of a fractured skull "caused by faulty construction of the falsework of the Colorado Street Bridge." There'd be no further investigation, no referral for prosecution, no fine levied, despite the word "faulty" being typed on their report.

Jules was scribbling notes as the jurors filed out of the mortuary. She then departed for Ivy Wall to brief Lilly on the baffling testimony, walking along a high shrubbery planted to block Turner & Stevens's corpse-loaded property from its neighbors: a bell-tower church and parcels razed for development.

It was there, on the opposite side of the hedge, where she overheard an unfamiliar man's voice speak harshly to the coroner, who'd trod outside himself. "Mr. Hartwell, you're using an imaginary border to look the other way. Color me disgusted."

Jules never caught his face.

꙳꙳꙳

Four days later, Nick was in town on a buying spree, glad to be here instead of at Tilly's Emporium in downtown Los Angeles for a few dollars' savings. As much as he cherished his Saturday adventures with Royo, he was wearying of the city's boorish capitalism and freaks. How many times can you watch a preacher holding a drugged Copperhead to entice sinners into a crackpot church? Three: that's how many.

By staying in orderly Pasadena, Nick also avoided running into the Spring Street graybeard, the twinkle-eyed charlatan who'd guessed his name and talked codswallop about how he was "selected" to expose a pervasive myth.

On Colorado Street, Nick had everything he required to start fashioning dozens of new solar lamps: an apothecary that sold passable phosphorous gel, a hardware store that stocked gaskets and filaments, and a convenient trolley to Buford's should he need rejuvenation by greasy sandwich. Bruised, not bowed. That was him: a realist Pollyanna always searching for the upside. Not every tragedy needs villains.

Jules, who'd once mulled writing a book about the spectacular Ashtabula train disaster, which had killed ninety-two people on a badly designed and inspected Ohio bridge, agreed. And, from what she discerned from the coroner's inquest, nothing shady was being covered up here, "just men grappling with carnage they never anticipated."

Nick was thinking about her en route to the hardware store when he noticed something past Warner's Photoplay Theater that he never anticipated. A five-deep crowd was mobbed around the Union National Bank at Colorado and Raymond Avenue. Was it free ice-cream day, the return of Teddy Roosevelt (not that he'd be doing backflips seeing his Stumper)? Whatever this attraction was, people were packing themselves in, or rubbernecking the action with dreamy expressions from building windows.

Nick's eternal fear of missing out switched on, to heck for now with his errands. He walked up for a view, soon realizing he could've used a ladder. There was no seeing over the forest of undulating hats and kids atop their fathers' shoulders. Behind them on Colorado Street, a chubby street cop was directing traffic by flashing hand signals rather than using his whistle. This was no ordinary happening.

He meandered for a few minutes along the perimeter, hunting for an opening. There was none to be had. Spectators were squished in cheek-to-jowl in U-formation at whatever this can't-miss event was. Salesmen were loitering around, waiting for the horde to break up so they could pass out fliers for digestive tonics, mini hot dogs, and William Thum's amazing Tanglefoot Flypaper.

Then, finally, he spotted a bystander hovering about whom he could quiz: a freckle-faced bystander who knew his way around a mangy ostrich. "RG," Nick said, striding up to him. "Fill me in. Is it a fire-eater from a traveling carnival causing all the fuss?"

RG, holding a bag of Daughtery's potato chips, which Nick could've binged on until the end of time, smirked. "Not even close," he said. "They're filming a moving picture, about what I can't fathom. But it's got a razzmatazz feel. Maybe you can find out. I can't stick around any longer. I don't fancy the boss man on my case."

Nick promised he'd tell RG the subject at their next night of Budweiser and football in Busch Gardens. "Provided," he said, "I can steal some of your chips." RG shrugged okay, and began to walk away when he flipped around.

"I neglected to mention," he said, "I saw your dog loping along Orange Grove Boulevard the other day. You might want to corral him better."

"Wrong hound," Nick said. "Royo's penned up during my work hours."

"If you say so. Sure looked like the same rascal to me."

Waldo headed out, and Nick carried out his scheme to learn the film's plot. He cut up to Union Street and then south into the alley, where he knew he could get within twenty feet of the movie production without having to battle the crowd. Once there, he regretted downing any of those salty chips. The backstreet wafted a nauseous bouquet of wet garbage, horse apples, and tossed-out fish from a café. It was more vile than Juana's place.

Nick, consequently, watched the cinema-in-the-making pinching his nostrils.

"*Stop, stop!*" yelled the director, a short, weak-jawed man who pretentiously tucked his knickers into his boots. "You call those lovebird eyes after declaring your undying affection for each other? I've seen department store mannequins evoking more passion."

Len Siegel—his name was written in cursive on his folding chair— threw his script onto the sidewalk in a melodramatic fit. "While we break to reload film, you two go practice your chemistry if you intend to make acting your profession. Broadway veterans are relocating to Los Angeles every day."

His browbeaten thespians stared at each while Siegel marched off, turning right into the fetid alley. He and Nick were alone.

"Must make you want to pull your hair out when people waste their opportunities," Nick said, trying to flatter the showboat director into recounting the storyline.

Siegel picked his nose and examined the contents. "Brother, ain't that the truth?" he said looking up. "I wrote this. Blocked it. Fundraised for it. I can't do everything." Then he paused, giving Nick the once-over. "Don't tell me you're spying for D. W. Griffin—or trying to steal my idea."

"Me? Heavens no. I work for Mercereau Bridge and Construction Company."

Siegel's face relaxed. "The Mercereau Company. Are you here about tomorrow, because we're definitely going to require assistance with the lighting and camera set-ups down there? Audiences crave realism nowadays."

Nick's cheeks flushed. Nobody mentioned anything to him about a film shoot at a bridge limping post-tragedy. "Consider me a point man," Nick said, doing his own acting. "It'd be beneficial for our preparations, though, if you went over the plotline. You know, so we can be ready."

After Nick heard what *The Bridge of Sighs* was about, he promptly thanked the director and speed-walked west on Colorado Street before he did something rash—like kicking over one of Siegel's pricey cameras. Despicable fiction was being filmed close to where the carnage that inspired it occured, and city hall, located in a Mission Revival building not far from here at Fair Oaks Avenue and Union Street, condoned it? And his employer was assisting? *Sonofabitch.*

A morality tale wrapped around a love story: that's how Siegel phrased it. In his story, a talented architect, designing a bridge similar to Pasadena's, swoons for the daughter of a bank president. Stunner: the structure falls, compelling the guilt-wracked banker to make painful choices.

The more Nick fumed at the heartless insensitivity of it, the faster his legs moved. Pretty soon, he was trotting past storefronts he knew like the trails of the Arroyo: Nash Bros. Grocery, whose jingle was "Rich and poor treated alike," and a horseshoe-maker; Vroman's and Arnold's Jewelry; Juddah and Seaman's Art Store; and Wetherby and Kayser's Fine Shoes.

Would any of the respectable merchants in there, many of whom once revered his father, endorse this insult? Not on their lives.

It was another scorching August day, and Nick was lathered in sweat as he reached base camp; he'd neglected to buy a single part he needed. He stormed toward Marcus's tent, as livid as he'd been since Otis uttered those unspeakable things in the Cawston gift shop.

Yet when he lifted up the flap, he knew he wouldn't be lodging any moral objections about *The Bridge of Sighs*. How could he? Marcus was behind his messy desk getting his hat handed to him. The same suits critical of Marcus's decision to fire Nick were now lambasting their task-mastering construction chief for his priorities, however ably he'd managed the post-collapse triage and the Visco condolence visit. "Stop worrying about the rumor mill," one said, "and recommit to production that avoids us another fiasco. This city is depending on us."

See, there's accountability. Nick released the tent flap and tried persuading himself that he'd overreacted about the film. A little piece of his compartmentalizing soul even sympathized with Marcus.

The next day Nick's trust was further restored. When Siegel and the Lubin Company crew unpacked their gear for the movie shoot, scant accommodation was provided. No machinery was idled, no debris cleanup slowed. They were just little maggots fooling themselves that they were serious artists.

Besides, real life took precedence. Harry Collins died the following day from his extensive injuries, leaving behind a wife and five-year-old son. Seventy-two hours later, C. J. Johnson, who'd previously shown signs of improvement, joined him and John Visco in the concrete-free afterlife.

AUF WEIDERSEHN

THERE WERE AIREDALES TO the left of her, greyhounds to the right.

On her last, full day in the "paradise" her husband blabbed to his tycoon pals about, Lilly Busch was surrounded by a kennel's worth of lolling tongues and wagging tails. To Nick, her goodbye party, thrown in Ivy Wall's bluff-perched backyard, was classic Lilly: as in *not* about Lilly.

She'd insisted that her Millionaire's Row girlfriends bring along their cosseted pooches so they could romp with the two-dozen children, ages eight to ten, she'd invited from the orphanages her family supported. *Noblesse oblige* didn't always mean cash, though greenbacks were always welcome. Serving up the magic of dogs, for kids usually bereft of them, was her latest shrewd philanthropy.

This is what she hopes to remember crossing the Atlantic: the giggling, the woofing, anything except the idea of Adolphus with coins over his eyes. Nick, waiting in a line to bid farewell, felt a hollow pit in his gut, his joy of the canines notwithstanding.

By this time tomorrow, she'd be on Adolphus's luxury railcar speeding toward New York City. From there it'd be an ocean liner to Lindschied, a German hamlet west of Frankfurt, where her blustery, brilliant spouse of fifty-two years was shuffling closer to a deathbed his assorted doctors were unable to keep at bay.

Somehow, Nick knew he'd never see his accidental godmother again.

Even as a middle-class kid who'd received his early education in a one-room schoolhouse, he recognized many of the elite here as FOL (friends of Lilly). There were Rockefellers and Huntingtons, a Wrigley and that tobacco doyenne, as well as others from the Hotel Green hoedown. It wasn't, however, aristocratic airs most palpable today. It was how the guests' full-breed dogs embraced the orphans, licking hands, playing tug-of-war, and chasing anything without a whiff of snobbery. Even Maty, Lilly's ne'er-do-well schnauzer, was fetching sticks for a waifish boy in scruffy trousers.

Nick, who'd trod here straight from an ostrich rodeo, observed the column of expensively attired women tear up and clutch Lilly, who sat on a regal chair padded with a pumpkin-colored cushion. Something grander than blue-blood status was about to be ripped away from them on this Indian summer September day: an original spirit. Lilly dabbed her bloated eyes, periodically glancing at the kids between well-wishers.

Where Jules was, Nick could not say. To his delight, he *did* know that her employment at Ivy Wall would extend beyond completion of the "Pasadena Perfect" award application; she was that irreplaceable as a Girl Friday. Pity she was absent now, for she was missing heartwarming scenes of high-legged dogs and ribbon-wearing poodles gamboling among kids fed too much gruel; kids who watched Rose Parades through the slats in the grandstands, not in them. This day was also especially worth treasuring given the other lurking development.

Only he, Jules, and select insiders were aware that Busch Gardens, the supposed "Eighth Wonder of the World," could well fold if Adolphus died soon. Lilly was mortally opposed, adamant the grounds remain open at least for disenfranchised children and traumatized war veterans. Still, the park was costly to run, and the logistics of maintaining acres of exotic plants, animals, and serpentine paths without its goateed champion would be daunting. "You might as well amputate one of Pasadena's limbs if that happens," Nick told Jules when she'd confided this. "It's our special green."

But he bottled up his angst in his preparation to say goodbye to Lilly, an un-wundebar prospect, indeed. He also wished he were mildly deaf.

Directly in front of him, two of her peripheral acquaintances were dishing out vile commentary in casual clucks. He'd already overheard one woman—the still-ham-faced Constance Prunell—snipe that she planned to give her Pomeranian a flea dip tonight. "I don't mean to sound heartless.

Adolphus is going to pass on knowing the Prohibition movement he battled could prevail, and that his wife will be in charge of his empire when she'd rather be coddling this rabble."

"You're wicked, you know that?" her knock-kneed friend replied. "Wickedly entertaining. Don't you breathe a word of negativity to her; they say Adolphus needs assistance just to stand up."

"Well, that's what butlers are for—and for lighting those heinous cigars he'll be puffing until the Grim Reaper snuffs them out," Constance said. "For someone who preached moderation, he assuredly didn't practice it."

That's it. After Lilly bid another woman adieu, Nick zipped ahead of them to butt in. "Unpardonable manners," Constance said at him, not recognizing Nick from their tiff on the Red Car, when Royo saved the day for that Chinese dry-cleaner lady.

The way Lilly looked at Nick was the way his father looked at him boarding a train out of Pasadena for Indiana: with a melancholy smile surrendering to circumstance. "Oh, dear boy, bold to the end," she said after Nick kissed her on the cheek. "I'm going to miss your antics terribly."

Nick swayed on his heels, trying to pack everything he needed to say into three minutes, each invitee's allotted time. His words sprayed out in a geyser of appreciation. She was *the* reason he'd gotten hired on a historic job utilizing his gadgetry. She was *the* reason he'd met an enigmatic girl who loved social justice, dogs, and him.

Lilly, her gray-blue eyes full of caring for him (and dejection for this moment), returned serve, praising him for his ostrich shows, for his chivalry the night Harry Collins and C. J. Johnson were buried in wreckage. She encouraged him to start a company to "give Mr. Edison a challenge," and said that *when* he wed Jules, Ivy Wall would host the ceremony, whether she'd returned from Germany or not.

Nick craved to hear her every last syllable, one last sweetly misstated aphorism. He didn't anticipate philosophy. "Never forget," the First Lady of Budweiser counseled him, "an endeavor is only as worthy as the intent built into it."

"I don't understand," he said, close to tears, while Constance stink-eyed him for taking too long.

"All *das Glitzern ist nicht Gold*," she said. "Auf Wiedersehen, dear boy. Take these."

Nick then hurried away from another searing goodbye, turning his back on the festivities. As he did, Royo loped in a wide circle around Lilly, with half the dogs and seven children trotting behind him in an impromptu game of the follow-the-mutt.

He entered Ivy Wall through a side door and unclenched his hand. Into it Lilly had placed a small bag of, yep, marzipan, which Nick suspected some anti-sugar crusader concocted to punish sweet tooths like him. In the foyer were five steamer trunks and associated cases. Lilly's chief butler, Gilbert Olmstead, a sprightly seventy-five-year-old, pantomimed an aching spine to try to pry a laugh out of Nick. It pried nothing.

A frazzled-looking Jules opened the front door a moment later, saying, "I know I'm late. How is she?"

"Stiff upper lip. Grace. The usual. So, where were you?" he asked, still raw.

Without responding, Jules went to the ground-floor bathroom. Nick, to her consternation, was outside it when she exited.

"Really?" he said, hands on hips. "You couldn't have picked another day to be gone?"

Jules said nothing, striding toward the parlor with Nick on her heels. But she stopped abruptly in front of a cleaning-supplies closet. In brisk movements, she whipped open the door, flicked on the light, and yanked him in, shutting a door she acted like she wanted to slam.

"Need I remind you again," she said in an acid whisper, "I have a second job that necessitates erratic hours. Lilly has supported it wholeheartedly without once cross-examining me. Do you know why? Though I may speak infrequently during daylight, my work production speaks for itself. And she trusts me. Provide me space."

Nick, surrounded by enough mops, dustpans, and floor wax to beautify Buckingham Palace, wasn't in the space-giving mood. "Eventually, you're going to have to fill in the pieces of your puzzle. Furthermore, *she* needs you today."

Jules's tightening features made her sharp chin sharper. "This self-righteous side of you is unbecoming, Nick. And curb lecturing me what Lilly requires. I've spent hundreds, no, thousands more hours with her than you."

"Nobody would dispute that," he said. "Nor would anyone begrudge me for inquiring about your disappearances. I love you. Plus, I devised this idea for your benefit I'm keen to bounce off you."

Jules brushed past him out of the closet. "Next time," she said "try loving me in a less obnoxious manner."

She closed the door, leaving Nick to ruminate with the whiskbrooms.

❁❁❁

TWO DAYS AFTER PASADENA'S pearls-swishing bleeding heart embarked for Europe, the couple still wasn't speaking. This was their first meaty tiff, and Nick found himself pining for Jules, neither able to sleep nor focus, knowing that he'd misread the situation. Retrieving his dog from Ivy Wall Wednesday, he opted to take the temperature on her anger. Happily, Royo's doggy-care was continuing here out of Lilly's generosity—and because Maty still needed company; the pampered schnauzer, whose constitution was too fragile for a choppy voyage, was staying in California.

Yet when Nick waved at Jules outside the parlor window, not only wouldn't she reciprocate, she reverted to one of her old tricks: sinking low to camouflage herself behind committee documents teetering on Lilly's Queen Anne desk. Around her, Nick viewed a space already being transformed from gilded manner to museum, as with everything at Ivy Wall. A dust cover now swallowed a coach. Valuable bric-a-brac was being transferred to the Busches's fireproof vault.

Nick didn't relent attempting to make amends, tapping a fingernail against the window; Jules's blonde tresses remained hidden. So he thwacked his forehead against the glass to a *doo-do-doo-do-doo-do-do* cadence. Ignored. This was one tough parlor. Hoping she was furtively watching him, he pressed his nose against the window, smearing it as he slid face-first onto the patio.

"Go away," she finally yelled. "I'm busy."

Nick held up a finger, and returned minutes later with Royo, who'd been mind reading him all day. By brainwave, he messaged his win-her-back plan; Royo's head jerk signaled assent.

Back in front of the window again, Nick and Royo bowed their necks in unison. When they lifted them, they were both mashing Wrigley Spearmint in Nick's exact, side-check chewing style. Nick then began strumming an air guitar as Royo bopped up on hind legs. Soon the butterscotch wolf was dancing, not just walking, in what you might call a pre-Hokey Pokey. As

Royo shimmied toward Nick, jaws working that gum, Nick backpedaled to give him space—and then tripped backward over a bucket.

The racket—a tinny, rolling sound and the smack of Nick's torso hitting the patio deck—drew Jules from her lair. He was on the ground, massaging his knee, when she cracked open the French door. "You're hopeless," she said, trying not to snicker. "Are you injured?"

"I don't know. Does the apothecary sell liniment for idiocy?"

Nick picked himself up, as he'd been doing repeatedly the last year and self-consciously patted his cowlick. "Can we *please* pretend I never said what I did? You cautioned me about being nosey, and I trespassed. I was beside myself about Lilly's departure. Let's make up."

Jules folded her arms. A canyon breeze ruffled her daffodil sundress. "I suppose," she said. "It pains me being away from you and your miscreant. But Nick, you mustn't push me to disclose that to which I am not ready. It only shoves the answers you seek deeper."

"I won't. Lord knows I've stuffed things down about me." *Like having a semi-clairvoyant dog. Or why Chester provoked me before I elbowed him that day.* "We all guard secret maps of ourselves."

"That we do," she said.

"At the risk of re-infuriating you after you've completely forgiven me—"

"Who said anything about completely?" she said, smile lines rippling.

"All right, mostly forgiven me. I had another rationale for inquiring about your whereabouts that day." Jules's chin aimed its tip at him; he was tap-dancing in a minefield here. "I hatched this scheme for your cause that I was dying to share."

"My cause?"

"Yes, the woman's right to vote. What better occasion, I figured, to round up all those moneyed women so you could pitch them about joining a suffragette drive? Your eloquence would've had them lining up, checkbooks in hand. Anyone displeased couldn't exactly grouse to Lilly, either, not with her about to leave town to reach a sick husband. If the ladies of Los Angeles are marching, they should be marching in Pasadena, too!"

"Wait. That's why you were flustered I was tardy? To rally Lilly's girlfriends before she set off?"

"That was one reason. Dumb idea, huh?"

Jules's tone betrayed no emotion as she said, "I need to show you something. Go stick Royo back in his pen."

Nick did, and Jules took charge. Grabbing him by the hand, she led him down the hill into upper Busch Gardens. Was she going there to break up with him? Wag her finger in his face about intruding on her suffragette-ism? He jabbered when he was nervous, and all he could think to jabber about was something far afield of romantic complexities.

"Here's something you probably don't know," he said, as she dragged him deeper in. "Leonardo da Vinci and Sir Isaac Newton were fixated by the sun's potential in their eras. The French were later, too, but you know about their flamboyance. They'd blow up obsolete ships using mirrors and solar beams in front of audiences to demonstrate its potential."

"I don't suppose they ever used them to disrupt vocal cords going a mile a minute?" she said. They now were in front of the Gingerbread Hut, whose door handle contributed to Nick's firing at Cawston when he entangled his trousers on it.

He thought this was where she'd guillotine their courtship. "Go ahead," Nick said. "Put me out of my misery."

"Misery?" she said with a wry expression. "Why would I commit such an action to somebody with such klutzy fealty to me? Not one other person in my life has *ever* appreciated what equality of the sexes means in my depths."

Nick felt a helium bubble arising. "Honestly?"

"Honestly. I'm touched, profoundly so, that you were thinking about how to secure me a captive audience for what I hold so dear."

"You are?"

"Yes. And don't despair. Lilly slipped me a copy of her guest list, with phone numbers, before she left. Just worry about getting in there."

"Does this indicate you've completely forgiven me?"

He'd find out. Under the Gingerbread Hut's thatched roof, Nick and Jules enjoyed relations for the fourth time. This sex was different than before, devoid of *Royo-interruptus* or backstory intrigue. This was animal-lust on, against, and around a miniature table, whose bolted legs would waver forever after. For twenty-three minutes, it was the fulfillment of the limericks that Nick and Fleet were reprimanded for when a teacher discovered they carved them, graffiti-like, on the underside of a desk.

The Pasadenan and Chicagoan grounded the corn. Danced the Barnaby. Joined the giblets. The Brothers Grimm, in their wildest pornographic dreams, never could've have imagined such make-up sex transpiring in anything their books inspired.

She was outside the fairy-tale hut afterward while Nick stood inside buttoning his shirt on a dopamine high. To the north, the late afternoon sun glinted off the majestic, gray curve of the mostly done bridge.

"I should've blindfolded her," Jules said, referring to the kindly ceramic grandmother bearing cookies by the door when Nick emerged. "A Victorian like her never would've approved of a liberated woman's carnal initiative."

"Is it my elation," Nick said, "or is she blushing?"

"Both."

MYSTERIES OF THE GINGERBREEAD HUT

HIS FEET SCARCELY TOUCHED the sidewalk passing Colorado Street newsboys weeks later. One October day: two monumental events. He floated. They shouted themselves hoarse.

Extra! President Woodrow Wilson, foreshadowing the new push-button generation, earlier tapped a telegraph key in the White House. Then *kablooey*. Forty-two hundred miles away, dynamite blew up the last formidable barrier between the Atlantic and Pacific oceans. The Panama Canal would open next summer.

Extra! Adolphus Busch was gone at seventy-four. The creator of "everyman champagne," who'd loved being outdoors, died an invalid as one of the planet's wealthiest men, worth tens of millions of dollars. Fluid in his lungs killed him, though, truth be told, the anti-booze Woman's Christian Temperance Union could've been listed on his death certificate.

Nick had met the city's first "wintering mogul" once by sheer accident, capering in his gardens as a high schooler. By the time he befriended his wife, Adolphus was in failing health at his "Villa Lilly" compound in Germany.

Gliding down the sidewalk, Nick didn't stop for a paper now. He'd already purchased one that afternoon from the newsstand in front of Vroman's, where he'd gone to collect the photograph that AC snapped for this special moment. Jules and everybody else at Ivy Wall, he presumed, already received word about their patriarch.

And not to be callous toward Lilly, whom Nick could picture swampy in grief, comforted by family, tranquilizers, and, he hoped, a backup schnauzer, but he had a glittery future to chart tonight.

Everything was ready. He'd booked reservations with the balloon operator next to the Raymond Hotel and dropped off his solar projector and AC's photo with the pilot. He'd filled his flask with Budweiser to toast this milestone (and, now, wish the original King of the Beers Godspeed). In Nick's pocket was the silver ring that'd creamed most of his savings. Its filigreed style reminded him of the accents of the bridge, which, after all, had paired them months back through Lilly.

Swaying outside Jules's Delacey Street cottage in his best collarless shirt, he visualized her saying "yes" from eight hundred, tethered-feet up. Saying yes after he beamed the image of him on Mrs. Grover Cleveland's mane holding a sign asking her to marry him.

Jules roommate, Stella Webster, a mousy secretary at the city's gasworks, answered the door. Typically peppy, her features drooped.

"Evening, Stella," Nick said. "Balmy night. You should amble out. Jules back there, putting on her face?"

Stella looked surprised by the question. "No, Nick," she answered in her squeaky voice. "She's not. I thought you would've known by now."

"Know what: she running late from work again? Or," he said with a self-laugh, "her second job? That woman needs a watch."

"I wish that was it." Stella thrust her hands into her dress pockets. As if it wasn't balmy out at all. "The police. They showed up this morning and arrested her. Jules is in the hoosegow."

Nick could hear himself say, "For what?"

"Burglary charges," Stella said.

꩜꩜꩜

HE WALKED INTO THE Pasadena Police Department's drab headquarters convinced his fiancée-to-be was wrongly implicated. He'd spring Jules from this cut-slab carryover from last century, and they'd have a farcical anecdote for their future children. Jail was no place for a woman so honest she'd return a lost penny to a Rockefeller.

A young, acne-splotched cop named Jep escorted Nick down a flight of steps, where six cellblocks lined a wall opposite a scuffed desk and wooden file cabinets. All the cells were vacant save for the two on the far ends. He nearly choked on his spit passing the cubicle nearest the stairs.

In there was a man that Nick hadn't seen for months, a man he'd hoped never to eyeball again. The grizzled coot that'd flung his Bowie knife at him, after Mrs. Grover Cleveland unintentionally freed his black-market parrots, was passed out drunk on the bench, drool running into his scruffy beard. The last thing Nick needed was for him to wake up and start raving.

Jules was in the basement jail's other side, pacing in a blue, taffeta dress. Seeing him, she rushed up to the iron bars, squishing her cheeks between them. "Nick, Nick," she blurted. "They wouldn't let me contact anyone, the Neanderthals."

He kissed her and clutched her hands. Her lake-deep eyes were coiled with worry. "We can still make our date," he said. "Tell me this is a mistake. A mix-up."

Jules looked around to ensure the pimpled cop was gone. He was. "I can't," she said, sniffling. "Just know that I'm not the serial bandit they contend. They may be trying to scapegoat me."

Nick longed to be inside her cell, to be her Sir Galahad. His brain reeled him back. "I can't believe I'm saying this, but what class of bandit are you?"

Jules moved back from the bars to stand under a bulb hanging forlornly from the ceiling. "I deserved that, but I'll explain everything," she said. "For now, I need a favor."

"Don't ask me to smuggle a hacksaw in a cake."

"Save the levity for later."

"I'm joking to assuage myself."

"Stop assuaging then. I need you to go to Western Telegram and wire my father. Tell him I'm embroiled in a landlord dispute that has me predisposed, and that I require a fifty-dollar loan. That's my bail amount."

"*Whoa*. You're living a double life and expect me to be complicit?" he whispered, so as not to rouse the coot. That ring in his pocket could've been on the moon.

Jules returned to the cell door. Unlike before, Nick didn't grip her fingers. "Precisely," she said. "I'm in here for a noble purpose: for *your* city."

Always a sucker for idealism, that got to him. "Okeydoke. I'll do whatever you request. Provided you give me the whole skinny, including your—"

Nick halted when Jep reentered the room. The pizza-faced jail cop sat down behind the desk and picked up the newspaper to mask his inmate eavesdropping. Taking up the entire back page was Adolphus's tome-length obituary.

"And that includes your disappearances," Nick murmured. "No more 'When I'm ready.'"

"Promise," Jules said.

✤✤✤

NOT LONG AFTER, NICK was on bended knee, and it wasn't inside the wicker basket of a balloon on what was supposed to be a night of exultation. It was under the desk in his bungalow, loosening the floorboard where he stashed his rainy-day-only cash. He'd be dining on saltines and salami for weeks.

Breakfasts would be tricky, as well, courtesy of the genius dog that never missed a chance to avail himself of human delicacies. In the time he'd been gone, Royo looted his pantry again, despite the eye-hook latch Nick bolted to repel his incursions, and emptied his cornflakes; last week he gashed half a loaf of pumpernickel. If Nick didn't know better, he'd posit that the Royo learned to scoot his desk chair over and back so he could unclasp the hook by his snout without tipping off how he'd achieved it.

Now he had two thieves in his world. Royo, habitual food felon, was coming with him.

At police headquarters, Nick leashed his hound around a fire hydrant, imploring him to be good. This included not snarling at uppity people, or doing his Oliver-Twist-esque street hustle, where he begged gullible passersby with food to break off some for him after he lifted up a trembling paw he faked was deformed.

Nick had to wait a couple minutes before Jules walked up from her cellblock, and a few minutes more while she signed paperwork agreeing to appear in court Monday to hear the preliminary charges against her. After she slashed her signature across the forms, she asked the mustached, heard-it-all desk sergeant whether detectives were "pursuing other subjects, as I am not the prolific burglar you are after. Search my house. You will not locate a single object of anyone's property. Not so much as a souvenir glass rose."

"We do have the bead on a suspect, miss," the sergeant said. "I'd worry about atoning for your own behavior, though. Orange Grove's mansions aren't your playgrounds."

Nick, thinking a guy on his engagement evening has his limits, handed Jules the fifty dollars for her bail and then burst out the station doors ahead of her. He zipped down the steps, untied Royo, and gestured Jules over to him. "So," he said, "how many houses did you creep into?"

"Seven," Jules answered without hesitation. "That sounds like an awful lot, doesn't it?"

Nick stared at her. Even one sounded like too many.

Under the streetlight, Jules's pretty face seesawed between contrition and defiance. "If you come with me," she said, "I'll show why you I hazarded doing it."

They walked east in stony silence until they passed a hot-dog vendor where Jules slowed, licking her lips. "I'll faint if I don't eat," she said. "It's been twenty hours. You want anything?"

"No," Nick said. "I've suddenly lost my appetite."

She bought three hot dogs with spare change at the bottom of her purse: two for her and one for Royo.

Fifteen minutes later, they were winding along the path by Ivy Wall, where they'd stolen kisses before, and descended into Busch Gardens. The Arroyo's vivid autumn colors were in nocturnal repose as the three of them went past the splashy water wheel and replica Snow White dwarfs. They were at the Gingerbread Hut before long.

There, disheveled Jules was eager to spill her story; Nick's body language, conversely, was taut as a crossbow. "Don't," he said, "expect me to be a pushover because we have history here."

"I don't expect anything," Jules said in her wrinkled dress. "I hope you'll listen with an open heart—and a flexible imagination."

They entered the hut that they'd sexually desecrated and squeezed themselves onto wooden chairs sized for munchkins. Nick turned on the oil lamp stored there for kiddy scavenger hunts; Royo curled under the table.

"You've begged to learn my past," Jules said. "Now you'll hear it."

She told it swiftly, like a toxin she needed flushed from her veins. Daughter of an autocratic businessman dismissive of her adolescent independence and fascination with world movements; a girl whose mother prized her but lacked the fortitude to defend her; a teen diagnosed with anxiety and mild kleptomania. "Yes, Nick, I shoplifted merchandise when I was younger, I'm ashamed to say."

Nick's eyebrows ridged. "What sort of merchandise?"

"Anything that fit into my purse: cheap bracelets, pens, key chains. I didn't covet any of it. The subversive in me took them, and my Catholic guilt was repulsed. A tug-of-war raged inside of me at seventeen."

Royo, hearing the words "tug-of-war," his favorite game, raised his head. Nick shoved it down.

"Father," Jules continued, "insisted I was a brat trying to discredit him after I was arrested for *returning* a snow globe to the Sears store on Michigan Avenue where I stole it. While we didn't get along, I wasn't attempting to smear him. I was a straight-A student. I worked at soup kitchens in the summers and could best any neighborhood boy at marbles. I just happened to suffer a nervous disorder through no fault of my own. But to teach me a lesson over the snow globe, even though the police dropped charges, he made humiliation my punishment."

"How?"

"He compelled me to parade in front of Sears with a sign around my neck with the word 'Criminal' on it—in the middle of the day."

Nick glowered. "Am I supposed to pity you now, say that accounts for your reluctance to speak during the day?" He was twisting a piece of straw, which earlier fluttered down from the hut's thatched roof, around a purpling finger.

"No. What claim do I have for pity in a world of deprivation? I want to be understood. Anyway, when we arrived home, it was still light out and I was too rattled to say a peep. Father then accused me of staging an act." Jules paused so as not to melt. "And you know what that beast did? He snatched the beagle puppy that I'd beseeched my mother for to rectify my loneliness after my brother left for college and tossed my Lizzy out the door. I watched from my upstairs windows when she darted onto the busy street and a funeral carriage, if you can believe it, squashed her. He indirectly murdered the one creature that loved me as much as Royo worships you. It was then I had real difficultly expressing myself during the day. Soon, I began plotting my escape from his stranglehold. I won a scholarship to Northwestern and haven't stepped foot home since."

It was now Nick reaching for Jules's hand and Jules denying him contact. "Horrid," he said quietly. "His vindictiveness crushed you into silence. And here you later fall for me, an inventor focused on the sun. That squares the circle. I'm still confused, though. Did something in Pasadena incite a relapse of your kleptomania?"

"Yes, but it wasn't kleptomania. I'm over that. It was—" The stress of Nick's question, of everything, overloaded her. *Ick, ick,* she hiccupped. "Damn it. First time I've had a flare-up of these in California," she said. *Ick.* "And I've had reasons for anxiety here. Just wait." *Ick.*

"I am."

Jules held her breath trying to extinguish her hiccups; it failed. *Ick.* She'd have to convey the story of how she became a jailbird over her spasm-ing diaphragm.

"The Svengali, or whatever he is," she said, sat down uninvited next to her on a park bench not far from here. It was a peaceful Sunday after her first week working for Lilly. She was rereading *Wuthering Heights*, trying to acclimate to a new town.

Jules then recited the Svengali's introductory lines. "Ms. Cumbersmith, I most urgently need to speak with you. You have been deigned for a mission, by forces above me, that only you can complete. We know everything about you, from your favorite color (burgundy), and first kiss (Joseph Palmer, on that rainy field trip to Lake Michigan), to your diary entry lamenting your mother's choice in men, to your train seat (row seven, seat two) traveling west. Your favorite candle is honey-lavender. However, you are graced with free will, so you may accept our challenge or disregard it."

Her first instinct, she said, was to scream or flee from the quack, preying on her for money, sex, or other nefarious intent. As he continued speaking, a premonition blossomed inside her that he was pursuing none of those. "Before you ask, knowing your penchant for details, he refused to disclose his name, and I cannot for the life of me recall his face. Believe me, I've tried reconstructing it a thousand times." *Ick, ick.* "I only remember the basso inflection in his voice, its sterling confidence. He said, 'our solicitation will necessitate bravery, faith—and your willingness to pick locks. Your objective is to recover a valuable object inscribed with words of wisdom.'"

"My sympathies were with you before," Nick said, now drumming his fingers on the table, "but a Svengali? Asking you to commit crimes in his name? This stretches credulity."

"I agree. It does." *Ick, ick.* "And I reproached him for speaking evangelical jibber-jabber. I even threatened to knife him in the gonads with the letter opener in my purse if he weren't more forthright. 'Be my guest, Ms. Cumbersmith,' he said. 'You'll merely snap the tip into the bench, wasting the dime you paid for it at the Merz Apothecary in Chicago when you were twelve years, two months, and fourteen days old. My genitalia, like me, are vapory."

"This is nonsensical," Nick said in a huffy tone. "What was the object? A goblin's tie clip?"

"No, smart-aleck, a plaque, a gold-embossed plaque he said he'd created and mounted near Colorado Street and Orange Grove." *Ick.* "He said it was an admonition that in the coming world of machines, everyone needs to be vigilant how quickly pride disguises itself as advancement."

Nick smacked his palm on the table. "Either he's manipulating you or *you're* manipulating me. Hattie told me about the same missing plaque months ago. It restated what Roosevelt said on his presidential trip here when I became the Teddy Stumper. He feared the Arroyo would be torn up for development."

"I know, Nick, I know." *Ick.* "He said, 'what a splendid natural park you have right here! Oh, Mr. Mayor, don't let them spoil that.' The mystic forced me to memorize it."

"Yeah, sure he did." Nick whacked his hand onto the little table again, this time followed by Royo's guttural growl of disapproval. "What game are you playing?"

"None," she said, with an *ick, ick* kicker. "If I were deceiving you, it'd be less lurid than this. I may be impenetrable sometimes, but I'm not a liar. And there's that I-love-you matter. Remember?"

"Course I do, Jules. But wouldn't you be skeptical if you heard this from me?"

"Yes. Though you'd expect me to listen to everything. The Svengali, or whoever he was, stated if I declined the assignment, I'd never fulfill my potential, just as my father desired. He said I wouldn't live to see the women's right to vote come true, either, because I'd die in the throes of depression."

"That's it," Nick said. "I can't take another word. It's too dark. Too implausible." He rocketed up from the munchkin chair, poised to leave.

"Stop! If I'm so conniving, why would I have imperiled so much on this cursed metal?" She rose up, too, wiggling her fingers into the underside of the straw roof's crunchy matting. In seconds, they extracted the plaque emblazoned with Roosevelt's cautionary pearl. "See? I stashed it here until I formulated how to tell you."

She sat down. Nick, frothing and befuddled, did, too. "Finish your story," he said.

From her time around Millionaire's Row, Jules said she'd whittled down a list of suspected plaque-stealers. The lock picking came elementarily after she'd read some Sherlock Holmes' mysteries; learning when to break into those luxury properties was more nuanced. She needed to burglarize them when the women of the house were attending committee meetings— and Pasadena was a town with more committees than causes—their servants were out, and the children in school. Dogs always trusted her, so they never barked as she tiptoed about the premises.

Just the same, she claimed she was ready to quit, whatever the consequences. She'd second-guessed herself endlessly. Questioned if she were experiencing a nervous breakdown. Six times she'd snuck into houses, one late at night the morning *before* Nick played the docent on her Pasadena-history tour, and each time skulked out empty-handed.

"I tried deluding myself that the Svengali was a private detective that my father hired to scare me into returning to Chicago." *Ick.* "But, Nick, he knew details about me no person possibly could."

"Since he's so omnipotent, why didn't he snap his magic fingers to recover his stolen property?"

"You don't think I asked him that in our single encounter?"

"And?" Nick said, fingers drumming an impatient beat.

"He said he'd chosen me because of my capacity to help 'bring the world into the light from every bend in the road.' I memorized that, as well."

"Jesus Christ, this guy speaks absurdly, assuming he's not imaginary."

"He's not. He's real. Real as vapor can be, anyway."

Two days before the bridge collapsed, Jules said she met an affluent contractor at an Ivy Wall social event that Adolphus earlier requested Lilly host. Burl Ingram sold the Mercereau Company some of its locally sourced cement. The uncouth man with bad breath asked her, after two glasses of champagne, with his homely wife ten feet away, if she was "as blonde below as she was above?" Jules said as tempted as she was to splash her drink on him, she felt a "bristling in my blood" that he was the culprit.

On the night the arch fell, she twisted in a Gordian knot. "I could obey my intuition, after learning Ingram had taken his family to San Francisco, or tend to you after your ordeal." *Ick.* "You were in Fleet's capable hands, so I left, feeling rotten about it." She changed into her burglary get-up, a pair of black, baggy men's clothes, and picked Ingram's rear-door lock. *Jackpot.* She exhumed the plaque in a steamer trunk in the basement, underneath risqué photos of women wearing ostrich feathers over their erogenous zones. Ingram, the concrete monger, didn't want people reading Roosevelt's admonition about preserving nature.

"How convenient you found the thing beneath ostrich feathers," Nick said tartly. "Is that also supposed to affect me?"

"No, it was intended to clue me in. I grilled the Svengali how I was supposed to contact him if I prevailed at his wild goose chase, and he informed me that we wouldn't be meeting again. He said that I'd simply know in my heart to whom to give the plaque."

"Don't tell me: Upton Sinclair?"

"No, you, Nick. When we made love here before, the plaque was over our heads and I felt a different bristling in my blood. The Svengali was using *me* to reach you."

"Oh, I get it now. You were his middleman. What horse crap."

"If I may, I prefer middlewoman. This is 1913," she said, trying to cut the tension.

"Who cares *what* you may!" This time Nick left, walking outside for a lungful of Busch Gardens.

Jules chased him, snatching him by the hips. "Look into my eyes," she said. *Ick.* "You'll know I'm telling the truth, as outlandish as it sounds."

But he wouldn't look. He stomped a lap around the hut and repositioned himself in its doorframe. Royo himself was now outside, padding back and forth between him and Jules like a conflicted referee.

Nick sputtered air from his cheeks. "Final question: What was this Svengali's name? Was it MZ, that Spring Street bastard I told you was attempting to hoodwink me? Sparkly eyes, a shiny suit? *Think*, Jules!"

"I, I don't know," she said, as she began crying while continuing to *ick, ick*. "Maybe. All those details, they just flittered away. He might've erased them to test my faith. No matter what I do to reassemble him," *ick*, "I fall short."

"You're falling short—short on the credibility scale. I don't believe there is any Svengali. You and Hattie aren't conspiring to fleece me out of my inventions, are you? "

You could see Jules recoiling before she exploded. "*Go to hell, Nick!*" she yelled. "How could you utter such an abomination? And what about the secrets you're harboring? When I inquired about how you met Royo, you omitted telling me he saved your life. Fleet confided that. What else are you withholding, Mr. Honest?"

"Don't make my dog a red herring," he yelled back. "Was your dead-puppy story even true?"

Jules slapped him across the face so quickly that Nick barely registered her approaching hand. "Says the man who guzzles appropriated Budweiser; the man who never publicly confessed his role in releasing those noisy parrots."

Nick now was inches from his ragged-breath beauty. "They were peccadilloes compared to willful burglary," he said softer. "What should I do with you, Jules? Go to the police? Alert Lilly? I was intending to ask you to marry me. Tonight."

Jules dropped her voice, too. "And I was going to say yes, before this ended so appallingly. Follow any course of action that suits your conscience. Before they arrested me yesterday, I completed Lilly's portion of the committee application. Here's my belief: the Svengali recruited *both* of us, and others, for something beyond our comprehension. At any rate, I've fulfilled my duty to him. Do with the plaque as you will!"

"And?"

"And this is where we part."

"Part?"

Jules and Royo had been exchanging subtle glances since she walked out of police headquarters, glances that weren't telepathic but darn close.

From under the table, he was gazing at her in a manner that communicated that he'd assist her to do what she must. And that he was contrite, mostly, for the leg-humping indiscretion.

In the darkness, Nick wasn't aware that Royo was flying at him until the dog was inbound for his solar plexus. The two tumbled backward into the hut, striking the floor inches shy of the miniature table. "Hey, dunce," Nick said with Royo splayed over him. "You're supposed to be siding with me."

Jules immediately slammed the door shut and, with a vigorous kick, whacked its brass handle out of alignment. Nick pushed his seditious mammal off him and tried twsiting the knob. It was broken. "Let me out," he said. "You want false imprisonment added to your charges?"

Jules, without saying a word, dragged the ceramic grandma over and tilted the smiling old lady against the door.

"Jules," Nick called out. "This is oppression."

He heard an *ick* and fading steps next. Terrific. The Gingerbread hut was too well-constructed for Nick to bash his way out. After shouting for rescue for twenty minutes, he gave up, lying down next to Royo for warmth. "How could you?" he asked him before a restless sleep.

Easy, Royo could've told him—if Nick could've sliced through his membranes of self-absorption to recognize that mind reading worked *both* ways. Royo, you see, served two masters: Nick and the graybeard. He was also comfortable in the hut; it's where he frequently slept as a canyon dog.

At morning light, a Busch Gardens groundskeeper who noticed the leaning ceramic grandma jimmied open the door with his German-produced Boker pocketknife, which Adolphus gave his gardeners for Christmas years back. As soon as they were out, a bleary-eyed Nick ran home to Green Street, dropping off the plaque and Royo. He then went to Jules's cottage on Delacey with a fatalistic sense.

"Where is she?" he asked Stella, once she answered the door.

"Long gone," she said. "She packed a bag last night, embraced me, and took off."

"To where? Seattle?"

"Your guess is as good as mine. She asked me to give to you this, if it's any consolation."

Nick read the letter at the tail end of sunrise, the Sierra Madre range brooding in shadows.

Nick: I am composing this farewell note tonight in haste. Please know I abhorred trapping you and the butterscotch wolf in our special hut, which was never my intention. But I will always adore you for saving me from that berserk cow at the Hotel Green, and, more importantly, saving me from an existence previously bereft of joy and laughter. Unhappily, I must depart Pasadena. I cannot head to jail knowing my sisters are picketing without me. Nor will I tarnish the Busches's good name by association. I beg you to refrain from searching for me, for I do not wish to be found. As Charlotte Brontë once wrote: "if you are cast in a different mold to the majority, it is no merit of yours. Nature did it." So I must obey my mold. Everything I confessed last night was the truth, and I am confident that you will eventually unlock the mystery of the plaque. In the meantime, I will forever adore the bountiful error that relocated me to Pasadena. Had I not met you, my love, I would've skidded off the edge of the Earth.

Goodbye, solar boy. Eternally yours. J.

A DAMNABLE CURVE

T HE BEST SALVE FOR Nick's broken heart wasn't any rebound fling or drunken escapade in Busch Gardens. It was his belief in his solar lamps and his attachment to the Colorado Street Bridge. You want to squelch the painful past? Renew yourself in your present. It sounded pithy, anyway.

By early November, seventy-eight of his eighty planned lights glowed nightly around the bridges' banks. His days of stomping about the hillsides, fly-specking where to house each unit, were over; so was his time as a one-man assembly line manufacturing them. Soon, he'd be assisting electricians wiring the deck's grape-bunch lamps, eye-catching fixtures, even if they required bulky, black wires.

He didn't even have to speed through mess-tent lunches anymore and could listen to the Nellies' fizzy scuttlebutt without worrying whether they mistrusted him.

In a way, their tales symbolized how Pasadena was steamrolling its own past. Like how one of them overheard a son of the deceased J. W. Scoville arguing with a bureaucrat about "the insulting price" the city was offering for the family land it seized for the bridge's right-of-way. Like one of them reading a story about how a masked man with a revolver robbed one of the Arroyo's last gold prospectors of two of his mules near Devil's Gate, and the ensuing police gunfight with the criminal two days later on an Oxnard beach; while the robber wasn't apprehended, authorities did return "Bossy" and "Missy" to their grateful owner.

For all the Nellies' colorful yarns, for all their gossip du jour, Nick found Jules Cumbersmith's story the most compelling. After hours trying to untangle it, he reached a pair of mutually reconcilable conclusions. She was being honest about the stolen plaque, and that the graybeard and Svengali were the *same* man: a masterful PI hired by her domineering father. One way or another, he pledged himself, he'd be seeing her again, even if he had to employ his own detective.

Staying busy until he did was his drug, this canyon his therapist. And he'd need to keep sharp, for 1913's wild weather wasn't relenting. The slopes bracketing the roadway were sodden after the constant rainstorms; property owners were gnawing their cuticles about erosion. Their apprehensions soon infected him, because if more topsoil slid in a deluge, it could undermine the pits where his lamps were trenched and send them sliding, too.

Nick was on his haunches, spading the earth around one of his lights to gauge how loose it was when he noticed men swarming around the base of the arch closest to him, the arch next to the rebuilt Big Whopper. He couldn't ignore the hullaballoo. The Nellies called the bridge "a drama queen," and they weren't half-wrong.

Workers were lowering a body down from the bottommost scaffolding onto a plywood board as he got there. The corpse, which was draped in a tarp, was then carried behind the company administrative tent. Fourteen men, most of them blue collars, removed their hats as it passed. Turner & Stevens mortuary probably got itself more business.

Marcus, back to being his sardonic, whip-cracking self, was acting the grief counselor, going up to everyone to console, back pat, and point to where the death occurred. Faces were grim, but not shocked. Not anymore.

Nick waited until Marcus was alone to inquire about the particulars. The unfortunate man, he said, was foreman Normal Clark, whom Nick didn't know. A screwy accident killed him. He'd tripped on one of the bottom-level planks and fallen headfirst onto the one below. Snap went his neck. "I'll spare you any homilies about construction being a rough trade," Marcus said. "You've learned that firsthand."

The next morning, Nick arrived at base camp before most everybody else, including Marcus, who must've slept in his own bed for a change after losing another employee. He was in the supply tent checking out bags of decomposed granite, thinking he might salt some of the material around his lamps to stabilize them. When he heard someone else enter the tent, he spun around anxiously.

"So," said Chester. "We sacrificed another one yesterday."

"Terrible. I hope Mr. Clark didn't have a big family counting on him."

"Between you, me, and the tent, that's five men we've buried to date."

"Five?"

"No one told you? Another fella, a new one, died last week, if my sources on the late shift are right. I guess he was up top, alone, scooping cement into the concrete mixer while it was spinning. That greenhorn must've dropped something in there, a tool or glove, and climbed in to fetch it, and couldn't climb out of the mush. You know how powerful that mixer is. It'd chew steel. If he yelled, nobody could've heard him over the earsplitting racket."

Nick already doubted this was true and was about to doubt it even more.

"Grisliest thing of all: after it ripped him to smithereens, his shift-mates didn't know, and when they poured the next batch, *he* was in there."

What was Nick supposed to say to the man who saved his ass August 1: that he now was adding kook to a résumé that already included the jobsite's preeminent crank and rumormonger? Playing dumb was the most courteous tactic to make him go away. "Excuse me if this sounds naive. Wouldn't somebody, though, have spotted part of a leg, or skull bone, or blood in the hopper?"

"Good question, college boy, but no, not when everybody's racing willy-nilly to finish on time. Not unless they were looking. This job's a hot potato. Let's suppose the suits did know something. You think they'd halt operations to chisel open a beam to investigate? There'd be scandal like you couldn't believe."

And because Nick *didn't* believe Chester, he didn't bother posing the obvious follow-up: that colleagues and loved ones of this unnamed victim, this man supposedly hacked to ribbons and embedded in concrete, would've been raising holy hell about his whereabouts. Instead, he said, "That is disturbing. I'll keep my ears open." Jules's eagle-fighting-dog myth was more credible than this.

"Good," said Chester, giving him a chummy thumbs up. "Let's stick together."

◆◆◆

THEY SAY YOU NEVER get a second chance to make a first impression, but Nick had his opening to flip that proverb on its head, with one proviso. That William Thum would *still* be in the mood to hear Nick advocate for his solar lamps, and apologize for previously wrecking his slacks, after bridge architect John Alexander Low Waddell was done tearing him asunder.

Thum's house off Orange Grove Boulevard, where miniature palm trees and spritzing fountains were *der-rigueur* landscaping, was pure Craftsmen panache. The sconces and wainscoting inside accented the varnished beams, and the Tiffany-style mosaic lamps bathed the living room in tasteful radiance. Still, for all that refinement, you'd suspect that Thum's recliner was fashioned from itchy horsehair, not fine leather, by how he squirmed on it listening to Waddell hand it to him.

"Never," he said from Thum's sofa, "have I had plans bastardized to this extreme. I realize that you're out of office, but I thought it only proper to air my grievances to somebody with whom I've developed a professional relationship. This isn't personal, William. I admire you."

"And I you, John, immensely," said Thum. "No one wants to disillusion someone with your credentials. Any alteration to your firm's blueprints, as I've tried assuring you, was done strictly out of our familiarity with the Arroyo's fickle terrain."

Waddell blotted his forehead with his handkerchief. "For the record," he said, "there were multiple revisions."

Nick witnessed the fight parked on a maple-wood chair in the corner of the room. He was an unintended observer here, having knocked ten minutes after Waddell showed up for an unscheduled meeting with the former mayor. When he wasn't keeping his head down, simulating interest in the papers that Marcus asked him to deliver, he stole peeks at the erudite combatants glaring at each other.

Thum, an efficiency zealot and consensus builder, had smooth, light features under his spectacles that reminded Nick of a slice of sourdough. Over his tenure, he'd ably guided a city putting its upstart, Indiana-Colony roots behind it as it flexed into a self-sustaining force. The bridge, a municipal water system, garbage collection, bronze streetlamps, an updated charter; Thum had advanced it all with a measured disposition.

And now he was being eviscerated in his own sanctuary, one partially bankrolled by the sales of his Tanglefoot Flypaper.

Waddell was fifty-nine, eight years older and incontrovertibly more famous than the man opposite him. A shaggy mustache swept over his small nose into an upside-down "V." If he slicked his gray, curlicue hair back and squinted more, he could've been Teddy Roosevelt's grumpy older brother.

Neither gentleman, Nick noticed, had the slightest interest in the wafers or hastily prepared tea that Thum set out on a silver tray. Not that he was offered any.

"Again," Thum said, "we never intended to insult you. Our people, in conjunction with the contractor, believed the alterations were necessary to address the precarious soil around the footings. I cannot tell you on how many occasions city engineers complained about how the earth there changes from bedrock to sand to loose granite in a matter of feet. We had to curve it."

"Be that as it may, William, you were obligated to confer with me before your men redrew anything. None of my clients, neither foreign nor domestic, would've taken such liberties."

With every cross word, any hope this flashpoint would metamorphose into rapprochement diminished, and that pained Nick, who respected both men. He also, though, hungered to pounce on his opportunity after Waddell departed. By making him his errand boy today, Marcus was granting Nick access to a VIP: a Very Important Pasadenan.

"This is my gift to you, Chance, a door opening to present your case for your metal petunias," Marcus said. "It's on your shoulders what you do with it."

"I don't intend to waste it," Nick said. "I'll plant a lamp in his flowerbed if need be or next to an outhouse."

He'd have to bide his time as Waddell rounded third on his scolding. Before taking on Pasadena's ravine, his firm had engineered a futuristic bridge over the Mississippi River. Its showstopper feature was a movable deck that lifted vertically, enabling ships and barges to pass underneath it.

"We simply differ," Thum said, "about whether liberties were taken in the name of a joint effort. We retained the vast majority of your ideas. The concept is uniquely yours."

"Immaterial. It's the principle," Waddell responded. "Accordingly, I've committed my objections to paper. I'd like to read you the first stanza in the event I make my letter public."

"Please do," Thum said with the expression of a man determined to maintain dignity during a lengthy proctologic checkup.

Waddell unfolded his two-page letter and began.

"Mr. Mayor, it is all very well for you to state that the people of your city understand the reason for building the structure on a curve; but in the future when intelligent people view the bridge they will exclaim, 'what kind of city engineer did they have.'"

Waddell ran his finger down the page, skipping ahead a few lines.

"Unfortunately, the real reason for this peculiar layout is hidden from sight."

"Hidden?" Thum said, stifling his pique. "Please elaborate?"

"Gladly. As you recall, I objected when I learned that your team implemented such an unorthodox contour instead of seeking a meager six thousand dollars more to construct what I designed: a straighter, marginally longer bridge. You insisted that your hands were tied. I questioned by whom, and never received a satisfactory response. To this day, I am hazy about who navigated this ship: your political brethren, the contractor, private parties guarding their interests, or some inestimable combination."

Thum answered with a soft-spoken defense of city decision-making. Nothing unseemly occurred. Bending the bridge, as Marcus continually reminded Nick, guaranteed that most of the footings were sunk into firmer substrate.

The sparring between the two gentlemen with pocket squares ended not in melodrama but in dialectical stalemate. Thum walked the globally-in-demand bridge architect to his wide front door and clasped hands.

"Thank you for your time, William," Waddell said. "I must now inform you that, in good conscience, I've opted *not* to attend the ribbon cutting. I appreciate that's a disappointment. I, nonetheless, wish your town well and the bridge a long life."

Blindsided by this latest piece of bad news, after just hearing part of Waddell's incendiary letter, Thum remained a model of restraint. He told him he understood, considered the job "an overall success," and wished his guest an uneventful trip home to Kansas City.

Nick stood up, too, waiting for Thum to collect himself. When he pivoted, he looked like a man who could've used more than a Budweiser.

"Mr. Chance, I'm afraid we'll have to discuss your business at a future date so I may relay what's transpired to my former colleagues. Leave the papers with you on the credenza. Between this and your scuffle at Cawston, we never seem to have our timing aligned."

"No, sir, we don't."

"Do not be discouraged, though. The city remains supremely intrigued by your solar lamps, and I will remind the appropriate personnel to schedule an exclusive meeting with you about them early in the New Year, if that's satisfactory?"

"Quite satisfactory. And, before I go, please accept my belated apology for ruining your trousers that embarassing day. I lost my cool."

"All's forgiven," Thum said. He paused for a moment, watching from his lead-glass window as Waddell drove off. "When you ponder what you saw today, I encourage you to take the thousand-foot view. To build something this complex is to invite, well, a schism between pride and thorny reality."

֍ ֍ ֍

IT WAS A WEEK before Thanksgiving and Nick was alone on the deck, trying to preserve his "upside" spirit after this latest bewildering turn. Buoyed as he was by Thum's promise, he now understood, maybe better than anyone without access to Pasadena's smoke-filled backrooms, that the Colorado Street Bridge was like a virtuoso child conceived in a secretly adversarial household.

A rare quarrel with Fleet over dinner at Smilin' Dan's did his outlook little good, and it was Nick's fault. Unwisely, he recounted the scene at Thum's house, because he needed to tell somebody. Fleet's response: that he'd rather hear Nick describe his fanciful dream about banana republic and chinos than listen to "another word about a bridge that nearly killed you. I'm sick of it as much as your willful gullibility."

Nick set down a forkful of steaming chicken to glower at his best friend. "Tired as you are, I'd rather believe in something than scoff at everything. For the sake of our bond, let's avoid this subject for the time being."

"We better," said Fleet, who'd recently taken another side job, mopping the floors at the Marengo Hospital, where he aimed one day to be a doctor.

He'd severed ties with his dowager, saying the sex-for-tuition-assistance arrangement was "too unsavory to continue."

Nick's spat with him was a week ago, and it wasn't dancing days being on the outs with your lifelong chum.

Leaning sideways on a pedestrian-bay bench, he had to think professionally now. He certainly was in familiar territory waiting for nightfall with his pocket telescope to certify that none of his eighty lamps flickered or were dark. Audition time was over.

The bridge *was* opening December 13, and she was just about primped for her coming-out party. From tie beams to transverse girders, every concrete member was inspected and ready. The dumpcart and its trestle track: gone. The sidewalk curbs: chiseled. The scrabbly balustrades, urn-shaped supports, and other embellishments now only needed sandblasting and cleaning. Old wood was being sawed up and given away.

Nick would head to Ivy Wall from here to collect Royo, and that was a whole other pickle. His animal was more distracted and less clairvoyant of late, which Nick ascribed to him missing Jules and the fact he was spending less time with him; since she left, there'd only been two Saturday afternoon excursions. But credit the butterscotch wolf. At the ostrich rodeos, he performed as energetically as ever to jostle laughs out of those little, emaciated faces—still flew just as high on his finale jump—even when Nick, in his modish, side-shield sunglasses, rode with desultory showmanship.

Near sunset, the deck's lamps switched on, and Nick fished out his moleskin journal. Time to review his personal punch list before he conducted a lamp bulb-count.

Incorporation forms for "N. Chance Solar Industries" were mailed in. Train tickets for his mother to visit in February he purchased last week.

But he still owed Lilly Busch a second condolence after America gave Adolphus a send-off for the ages. Nearly a hundred thousand fans observed his funeral cortege, and a hundred eighty people, including Joseph Pabst, served as honorary pallbearers. Thirty-five cities, Pasadena included, hosted memorials. Hotels went dark, streetcars stopped rolling.

In his PS, he'd prod Lilly, begging her if he must, for any tidbit about Jules she had. He needed her new address to tell her it was safe to return; that police nailed Pasadena's serial cat burglar trying to break into the house of lumber kingpin (and Roosevelt pal) Arthur Fleming; that he'd help exonerate her by alerting prosecutors how her research was a linchpin in the city's application to be crowned America's marquee small town.

Let her go for now. He shut his journal and inhaled the Arroyo, sniffing fireplace smoke from homes on the bank and the minty eucalyptus trees that poled up next to the bridge like grazing giraffes. After motorcars began gunning about, it'd unlikely be this tranquil here again.

Actually, it wasn't even tranquil for thirty seconds.

Somebody mumbling was approaching from the other side, and Nick stood up. "*Hey!*" he called out. "You have to leave. The bridge isn't open yet."

But whoever dodged around the sawhorse barricades didn't abide him. Indeed, the self-muttering grew louder. When a grape-bunch lamppost illuminated who it was—and where he was standing—Nick went rigid. The trespasser was walking one foot at a time, à la trapeze artist, on *top* of a balustrade, arms outstretched. The limb over the north side of the bridge clenched a Jack Daniels bottle too.

"*Otis!*" Nick hollered. "Get down. That's a fourteen-story drop."

Otis glanced at Nick and continued on. He might've been dumbfounded to see Nick if he weren't sloshed.

"C'mon," Nick said, moving toward him, palms up. "Whatever is eating you isn't worth it."

Otis waved his bottle at Nick, and the gesture so unbalanced him that he almost plunged into the nothingness. Only by flapping his opposite arm did he regain any equilibrium. "What's eating me?" Otis said with a slur. "You're a riot." He kept going.

Coyly, Nick dipped behind him and when Otis's right arm dipped, he snatched his wrist and yanked him off the balustrade. He came down directly on Nick, causing them to roll in a heap onto the sidewalk. The whiskey bottle that slipped from Otis's mitt exploded in the center of the deck.

"What the hell's wrong with you?" Nick said, getting up. "You trying to off yourself?"

Five men had already died around the bridge if you counted not Chester's conspiracy-theory-death but a recent suicide. Last week, a Busch Gardens' worker found a superior court judge lying by the water-spouting elephant statue. The judge, inconsolable after his wife's death, killed himself by overdosing on laudanum, an opium tincture favored by Victorian-era writers. Nick couldn't let Otis become number six.

He tried hoisting him up, but Otis pushed Nick's hands away and staggered onto his feet unaided. "You might say," he said, "I was on the fence, if there was one."

Nick scowled. "That's not funny."

"Once upon a time, I believed it was that unholy ostrich stink that made my sinuses pound night and day. Now I assume it's my destiny."

"Is it this desperate?"

Otis ignored him and started walking east in the middle of the road, past where his spilled whiskey was now a brown, amoeba-shaped blotch that somebody would have to mop up. "You owe me a bottle," he said.

Nick went up and blocked his path. Otis shouldered past, leaving Nick no resort but to walk next to him.

"If fair was fair," Otis said, stinking of Kentucky mash, "I never would've had to work at the farm. I could've gone to an Ivy League school. But those slick talkers who duped my father out of selling his lots on Oak Knoll with their champagne promises bankrupted him. They put him in the ground and stranded me on my own."

"That was, what, twenty years back, during the land speculation?" Nick said. "Wounds heal."

"I have some fresher ones," he said. "*You* should know."

Even a few sheets to the wind, Otis had a way with words.

Eighteen months ago, after Nick was promoted at Cawston, he was also on an entrepreneurial roll. For two weeks, he toiled into the wee hours in a shed behind the feather dye house, obsessing over an idea. He wanted to try adapting the business's solar-powered water pump into a miniature-lamp prototype. So, he gobbled articles on the subject. Overcame snags. Learned to shape mirrors. Dodged a fiery chemical blast.

And then *eureka*: one night at three o'clock a test lamp glowed silvery outside an ostrich pen by Cawston's fake mini pyramids, which wasn't too shabby for someone who bombed high school chemistry. But his prototype had an Achilles Heel: anemic staying power. The crumbled glass and earthenware that stored heat from the sun during the day activated the filament and phosphorous gel only for a crummy few hours at night.

No company or city would buy something that didn't shine from dusk to dawn.

After another all-nighter trying to crack the problem, Nick griped about it to Otis—the pre-sullen Otis that Cawston also harbored big plans for because of his science aptitude. It took him a single afternoon of reverse engineering to diagnose the glitch. "Try thicker, black glass to boost the charge," he said. "It'll absorb wavelengths better than lighter elements."

A mentally fried Nick said why not. And when he substituted opaque glass for black shards, his world lit up. The prototype blazed for eight hours! A promising bust was now a toehold to wireless energy.

Cecil Jenks, Nick's milquetoast boss, was wholly impressed, complimenting his protégé's tenacity, his ingenuity. Exhorted him to plug it at the next world's fair in London, and to patent it first. This could rate up there with Marconi and Pasteur. Months removed from his father's funeral, Nick believed he'd done his family proud.

Amid all the attaboys, though, he neglected to credit Otis for the breakthrough. Once Otis requested Nick correct the oversight to advance him up Cawston's management chain too, Nick did mention it—at the tail end of an exhausting meeting, where he and Cecil debated marketing pink and baby-blue feathers for newborns.

Nick, appreciating he'd wronged a friend, this just as Otis's sinus affliction reared up, eventually took Otis behind an ostrich paddock to announce he'd dish him three percent of future profits from his lamps. Otis erupted, slamming the retroactive offer as "chickenfeed reparations" by someone who "camouflaged raw ambition behind sunny enthusiasm." Nick called him ungracious, and they were never close again.

"I betrayed you, all right," Nick said, standing again in front of Otis and creasing his brow as Royo did when distraught. "It was petty. And I don't have a time machine to undo it. You're too bright to be at a sawmill. I want you to be the old Otis—the one who howled with me when Mrs. Julius Caesar stole one of those Shriner's hats and galloped off."

"That Otis is dead and gone. Like Mrs. Caesar."

"Stop being fatalistic. You're young. Go apply to Throop Institute or USC."

"Too late."

"Despise me as you may, I'm giving you twenty percent of profits, in perpetuity. There's going to be money next year, too. I'm founding a company."

"Twenty?" Otis said, eyes wider now. He wiped his unshaven face with his shirt sleeve; the man was out in fifty-degree weather with no jacket.

"Yes. And if it makes you feel any better, my jaw still aches from where your elbow said hello during our scrape. I'm trying to be civil."

"Or your guilty conscience is killing you."

Nick bit his lip before responding. "My guilty conscience also could've just let you fall. Don't forget what *you* said about me being the fruit of my father's deranged tree."

Otis, who could've had it all with his film-star-worthy face and crackerjack mind, appeared to sober up some being reminded of this. "That's the challenge, isn't it, Nick? Not allowing life's haymakers to rearrange one's molecular composition to unleash the ogre." He paused. "I'll forgive you if you forgive me?"

Nick didn't hesitate. "Done!"

"You know what'd boost your offer from good to great?"

"Don't mention Jack Daniels. Or anything about feathers."

"I wasn't. How about if I take ten percent but become your first employee? I know my way around wavelengths, and you have a grasp on the sun. What do you say?"

"I say we should explore the idea further on January second. Hopefully, I'll have recovered from my own hangover by then. Swing by my bungalow"

They shook hands, and Otis walked away not staggering as much.

THE DOWNSIDE OF PAGEANTRY

ON THE SATURDAY THAT Pasadenans fretted might never arrive, Nick was alarmed. Something was demonstrably wrong with the wonder mutt.

For two days, Royo barely touched his food, be it dog chow, saltines smeared with Crisco or, as a last resort, cornflakes with beef-jerky topping. And it wasn't only a weak appetite that was so concerning. His jet-black muzzle was graying, almost overnight. The expressive tail that poked straight out when he was engaged, or wagged propeller-esque when joyous hung limp—or curled between his legs.

By eight in the morning, his mutt was circling the bungalow, whining and panting more than he did August 1. Nick bent down to touch foreheads, trying impatiently to arouse his clairvoyance. "You can't be sick," he thought. "Understand? I have too much to do."

The animal didn't nod, couldn't nod, despite hearing every syllable of Nick's brainwave. Between his furry ears was a premonition—a premonition that if Nick failed to wake up, they'd finish this day with dirt on their backs. And there wasn't anything the bravest of rascals could do to forestall it.

Nick snatched his guitar and strummed some angry chords. No circus-dog walking, just room circling and sniveling, lamenting what might be.

"What am I supposed to do with you?" Nick said. "Pour you Budweiser so you pass out until I return home?

He put Royo's distress on his back burner and got dressed. He was bobby-pinning a yellow carnation to his lapel, which identified him as an event guide, as another hassle cropped up. Someone rapped on his front door. Nick stabbed his finger in surprise.

The knock was too restrained to be Marcus. And it couldn't be Fleet, who Nick knew was gone all day at USC medical school. Thankfully, they'd reconciled since their quarrel, and were planning to spend Christmas together. On New Year's Day afternoon, after the Tournament, they'd even attend the fun-filled "Karnival of Komikal Knights," a lampooning, counter parade of clowns and fringe acts with an acronym somebody really should've thought through.

As he sucked blood from his fingertip, Nick peeked out the side window. *No!* "Whoever it is, give me a minute," he yelled to his waiting landlord, the starchy B. F. Noble. "I need to locate my trousers."

Doing his best burlesque dancer routine, Nick ripped off his clothes and launched into artifice. He seized Royo by the mane and bowled him under his bed. He took dirty laundry from his hamper next, stuffing them in front of him. Then he scooped up Royo's water and food bowls and concealed them behind potato chips in the pantry.

"Mr. Noble, what a pleasant surprise," Nick said at the door, out of breath and in his boxers. "What can I do for you?"

"Nothing," Noble said with a grunt, blowing past Nick. Even in the weakest of morning light the bungalow exhibited a startling complement of canine criminality: divots, nail scratches, gnarled furniture legs, to say nothing of the tufts of tan fur that'd gathered in the corners like incriminating tumbleweeds.

"Shelve the malarkey," said BF, a mirthless sixty-three-year-old with an aquiline nose and a gait suggestive of someone grinding a carrot between his butt cheeks. "You're boarding a dog in here in direct violation of our lease. Don't bother dissembling. The evidence is marring my property. I've also heard barks emanate."

"Mr. Noble," Nick said with contrived indignation. "I resent your insinuation. And I must go. We're christening the Colorado Street Bridge at two, and I'm going to be busier than a one-armed paper hanger."

"By all means leave, then," BF said. "I'll show myself out."

"Suit yourself," Nick said, faking calm and re-dressing in a cold sweat.

While he did, BF became a man possessed, scouring for the destructive critter he knew his tenant was hiding. He whipped open the closet door and checked the water closet. He peeked under Nick's desk, where Royo's leash lay out in the open. Then he lowered onto his knees in front of Nick's bed. Every garment that his tenant packed under there BF rototilled out.

His stretched his arms underneath the bedframe until they felt a warm body. "I gotcha, you stowaway," BF said. "Present yourself!"

Royo belly-crawled out, bleating *Roooooh* in shame.

BF stood up, clapping fur from his hands. "Mr. Chance, you're one insolent individual. Your vandal has chewed and scratched the renovated cottage I rented you at an affordable rate, partly on account of your family name. I cannot overlook such a willful offense."

"Consider me admonished," Nick said, buttoning his shirt. "I'll reimburse the damages."

"No, consider yourself evicted! You two rule-breakers are to be gone in ten days. I'll bill you for the repairs."

"But can't we forge a compromise?" Nick asked, trying to wriggle his way out of another mess. "I'll pay extra rent. Fashion you a free solar lamp."

"I don't care if Teddy Roosevelt and his Rough Riders storm in to your defense," BF said, arms crossed.

Teddy. It's always Teddy. "Where am I, or we, supposed to live? You can hardly find a room. Pasadena's thriving again."

The landlord marched toward the door, butt protruding behind. "That isn't my problem. Buy a tent. There'll be a slew of new homes in the western Arroyo soon. I may invest there myself."

"Come again?"

"The San Rafael Heights and Linda Vista: the city is planning to annex them early next year. And it couldn't have happened without the bridge; I heard they're contemplating running water lines beneath it."

Nick went over to him, shaking his cowlick-haired head. "You're mistaken. I've been on those hills. It's Los Angeles scheming to acquire them. The bridge is just a road, not a real estate deal."

BF's expression shifted from aggravated to smug. "Before you started with the Mercereau Company, you were at Cawston, correct?"

"As everybody reminds me, yes."

"Well, if you deluded yourself that the bridge wouldn't redraw Pasadena's map, you dug your head into the sand like those repellent birds."

Nick dabbed perspiration from his neck. "That's an old wives' tale. Ostriches have small heads. They'd suffocate if they burrowed them."

"Mr. Chance, you're mistaking me for someone who gives a toot. Ten days."

Before Nick could fire any more questions at him, BF closed the door.

꘎꘎꘎

FROM THE CARMELITA FAIRGROUNDS, the staging grounds for today's festivities, Nick gazed west at a sea of starstruck people. The bunting and streamers adorning the oyster-skinned bridge gave it the aura of a World Series game. The collective energy crackled.

"Cleans up real well, doesn't she?"

Nick recognized Marcus's voice before he clamped a meat hook on his shoulder. "That she does, Mr. Stonebreaker. Congratulations."

"You, too, Chance."

Nick turned to face him. "Where do you want me? Crowd control, registration, tours?"

"All of the above. Hope you had your cornflakes. Gonna be a long day."

Gonna be? "Okeydoke."

"Don't forget," he said, lightly pinching Nick's arm. "I'm still expecting ostrich-riding lessons from you someday."

"I've already notified the farm," Nick said.

"Always the cutup. But I do hope to see your metal petunias win customers. You made a believer out of me, and that's not easy."

Nick then watched him move toward the dais with that grizzly stride of his. In the sun, his scalp really showed through his curly locks. This was a hair-losing profession.

Pomp and hyperbole commenced midafternoon with speeches high over the canyon. Five thousand people, roughly one-sixth the city's population, listened, many crammed onto the deck. In the lead-up to today, some newspapers hyped the bridge and its environs as "splendid," "great," and "lovely;" others applied adjectives bordering on preemptive idolatry.

Mayor Richard L. Metcalf, the retired dry-goods merchant who succeeded Thum, was first up at the platform. The chairman of the county

Board of Supervisors spoke next, drawing gasps from the crowd with a prediction: that *every* one of the region's forty thousand motorcars and trucks would at sometime utilize this roadway. A Pasadena commissioner followed, invoking the record book: "We know of no concrete bridge (in America), he said, "combining as great a length and height as does this." Finally came the formal handoff from Mercereau executive W. M. Ledbetter. "We built this structure honestly," he said. "This is your bridge."

Nick, listening in a cluttered mind, was glad engineers didn't measure load tolerances by glossy embellishments. Having led tours before, he regurgitated trivia to any interested citizen: 9 major arches, 1,458 feet long, 10,000 barrels of concrete. When not spewing facts, he fixed rose boutonnieres on dignitaries' lapels. Hung garlands from motorcar doors. Brown-nosed efficiently.

Midafternoon, whistles blew and tinny horns and trumpets sounded to herald the start of the procession. Several high-school bands paraded across the deck, playing sentimental classics majorly off-key; the clarinets alone were sonic violence. Behind them rolled VIPs in a slow-speed caravan of puttering, waxed automobiles. In their back seats were the speech-givers, members of the Board of Trade, county officials, Mercereau Company suits, and associated cronies. Many waved with crinkly smiles.

In the convoy's rear were honchos from the Southern California Auto Club all beaming wide. Next year, the organization was sponsoring a film starring a vaudevillian at Warner's Photoplay Theater, *Trixie Joins the Auto Club*. Don't laugh. With all the new gas stations, repair shops, and motorcar dealerships popping up, it'd probably rake in the dough.

Nick, who still adored the bridge but abhorred the monkey business around it, stood on the sidewalk while the motorcade rolled, dwelling not so much on who was here as who wasn't. The two most conspicuous ones were John Alexander Low Waddell, who was boycotting the event because rational cities don't curve their bridges, and John Drake Mercereau, who died in that rollover automobile wreck fourteen months earlier. The bridge's godfather, who'd kept the project alive when it appeared doomed by infighting, was another one MIA. Harry Geohegan, former Board of Trade president, was in northern Los Angeles County today, investigating the possibility of a new road into Pasadena through the Antelope Valley. As a bigwig, he'd driven the deck—yesterday.

If there was any mention of dead blue collars Nick missed it.

After the cavalcade, people flooded behind in a block of humanity, many dressed up for the coronation. There were ties under heavy coats and mufflers around necks, ostentatious hats and more than a few ascots. They'd probably reuse the same clothes in a couple weeks at the 1914 Tournament of Roses, where a bridge float was being entered.

Intermixed in the mob were dozens of people Nick knew. Sometimes it smacked of a life reunion. He shook quick hands and pecked the cheeks of ex-neighbors, former classmates, the doddering Gilda Figgleberry, and friends of his parents from the Indiana Colony. He hugged old Cawston workmates (RG, Waldo, Cecil) and greeted a few pasty millionaires he met through Lilly, whom he so sorely missed. When an ex-girlfriend, the one who worked at George Hale's observatory, ran up to him, saying they should have dinner sometime, Nick wondered what Jules's smile lines were doing.

Yet he was still on the clock, and after he spied a young boy leaning over the balustrade in a loogie-hawking contest with his older sister, he forgot about her. "Get back, kid," he hollered. "That's dangerous." The boy skipped away.

Nick trailed the spectators plodding in waves, some lingering to admire the fluted lampposts, romantic sitting bays, and other accents from Waddell's imagination. When he wasn't on the lookout for others tilting over the sides, he picked up Wrigley gum wrappers and cigarette butts, trying to stay present in the moment and not backslide into this morning's bleakness. A man in a black trench coat and tweed cap tapped him as he balled a dry-cleaner's flier in his hand.

"So, this is what everybody is doing cartwheels over?" Upton Sinclair said, playing tourist with anonymity from autograph hounds and political ear-benders. "You must be in nirvana. She is spellbinding, Nick."

"If not nirvana, a reasonable facsimile," he said, shaking hands. "You getting much rest between Annandale tennis matches?"

Upton showed him an elbow too creaky to bend. "I had to retire my racket. My backhand was killing me more than my opponent."

"There's always Buford's to build muscle," Nick said monotone.

Stragglers wove around them, oblivious to the biggest name on the concrete. For the last half hour, they'd ogled at landmarks inspiring from these heights: the snow-peaked Sierra Madre, local bell towers, and distant whitecaps off the coast. Mostly, they fawned over how Busch Gardens still shimmered in winter—while Nick wondered whether Lilly was already feeling heat to sell it, and whether any new owner would maintain the park as it was or divvy it up for greed.

A tubby woman in a mink coat squinting to see a fairy-tale hut bumped directly into Upton's back. She kept walking with only a curt "pardon me."

Upton gave it little attention, for he was focusing on Nick. "Say, what's wrong? You have a decidedly gray complexion on this momentous day. Are you indisposed?"

"No. Just harried. Interested in any trivia? Weight loads. Tedious trigonometry?"

"No. I'm curious what could be troubling somebody normally so keen."

"Personal matters, to be honest."

"I'm sorry," Upton said, seizing on the dull light in Nick's eyes.

But Nick's mind wasn't flat. It was now awhirl about whether to divulge everything he knew, minus anything Chester said, about this place: Waddell's accusations, the planned land grab, that hideous movie if local millionaires had influenced the bridge's height. *Who better to wrestle out the truth than the world's top muckraker? There's material galore.* "Since I'm running around, perhaps I could elaborate further, man-to-man. Are you available Monday? Anyplace?"

"Rats. I am not," Upton said. "I depart for New York first thing tomorrow. I've procrastinated too long here on my book, about Standard Oil. One cannot lounge outside in one's bathrobe forever."

Nick barely heard the last part of Upton's eloquence as he calculated the pros and cons of how to handle this serendipitous encounter. If he tattled the wrong thing out of context, Upton's typewriter would shred Pasadena. Should he be exposed as his source, the city would never buy a single solar lamp. They'd bind him on a one-way train to Bloomington. Then again, if he swallowed his tongue, how could he call himself a stand-up citizen who espoused sunlight as antiseptic?

"Do you have a headache?" Upton asked. "You're grimacing."

"Indigestion. Question: would you be amenable to me knocking on your door later tonight? I'll be concise."

"Sure," Upton said. "I'm a last-minute packer, anyway. Some matters can infect the spirit, as I've learned firsthand."

"Thanks," Nick said, handing Upton his moleskin notepad and pen to write down his address. He knew Upton appreciated his drift.

"Until this evening," Upton said, swishing his tongue over his snaggleteeth. "I hope your indigestion wanes." He tugged his cap down over his matted, side-parted hair and then blended into the mob.

◖◗◖◗◖◗

NICK WAS BACK AT Bungalow Heaven West around seven as rainclouds swirled in from the coast. One of the largest recorded events in city annals was in the books. The bridge now belonged to anyone with a gearshift, be it a Chalmers, Buick, Cadillac, Ford, or Stutz.

To whom *he* belonged was a trickier matter.

Since talking to Upton hours ago, he was having second thoughts about spilling the beans to him later tonight. He wasn't certain if he believed what his landlord intimated: that Pasadena was plotting to lunge at those western hills, using the bridge as pretext. Frankly, Nick wasn't certain he believed what lunged out of his own mouth these days.

On the walkway in, he wished he could've diverted to Fleet's to ask his advice. But he was attending a night lecture on the bile catcher of the human body: the gallbladder.

That thought didn't persist, anyway. Not when Nick realized his door was ajar. "Crap," he muttered. "Is there a bull's-eye on my back?"

He poked his head through the gap and stepped in, grabbing the solar lamp he kept on his desk and raising it to strike. "I have a weapon you don't want to get clubbed with. Anybody there?" Silence.

He toggled on the overhead light, and saw he was alone. How flummoxing, too. Nothing appeared missing or ransacked. He circled back to his door and leaned down to investigate. Yep. Someone picked his lock, as illustrated by the scuffmarks around the keyhole. Nick lumbered inside, on the brink of screaming why now? The only burglar he knew was Jules, and she wouldn't do this to her solar boy. Could it have been someone from Edison; the coot; a double-crossing Otis?

But he stopped evaluating suspects after a thunderbolt clapped him.

Royo was missing!

Missing after Nick chastised him, before leaving on a day he didn't bother taking him to Ivy Wall, that he was "a destructive pain in the ass."

He immediately began searching and yelling for him everywhere he could imagine: up and down Green Street, north to Colorado Street, by the grassy lot where he rolled on his back making yummy noises. Nick pounded on neighbors' doors, quizzing them if they'd seen him or anything hinky. No one had; they were celebrating the bridge, too. He even jogged behind a Delacey Street boardinghouse whose trashcans the imp rifled through for soup bones.

Back on his front step, he shouted, "*Ro-yoooooo. Get your butt home!*"

The empty echo was a dagger, so he left his door cracked and walked to his cabinet. He uncorked the schnapps that Lilly gifted him and guzzled a few fingers of it. Seeing no reason to be upright, he went to his bed and fell backward, feeling sorry for himself.

My bungalow gets broken into and he exploits it for a night romp.

Even if he neglected the fur-ball a bit, took his kinship for granted, he was still being kicked out of here thanks to his dog's indefatigable chompers. Wrung out from everything, Nick tucked into bed and shut his eyes. Seventeen minutes later, a nagging hand wiggled his arm.

"Nick, wake up!"

His sleep center tightened its vault.

"You've been drinking—I can smell it. Get out of bed. It's an emergency."

When Nick's breathing changed to snoring, Reginald whisked the blanket out from under his chin. He flipped onto his side, facing the wall. Reginald countered that by filling a mason jar with water and throwing its contents at the back of his head.

Nick turned over, looking at Reginald like a breaching whale. "Scram, pipsqueak. No ostrich rides today," he said. He closed his eyes in adjournment.

Reginald's little fingers pried them open. "This isn't about Mrs. Cleveland. It's about Royo," he said in a fraught voice.

Nick yawned. "What about that ingrate? I'm sick of him."

"You don't mean that," said Reginald, who evidently wasn't leaving. "You're best pals."

Nick hauled himself up in bed. "Yeah, well, pals are overrated. Someone busted into my place tonight, and he's out suckering people for food again by faking he has a limp."

"No, he isn't. An evil man took him. Get up."

Nick did—to go to the kitchen. He tore off some stale pumpernickel, mashing it into his mouth. "How do you know, anyway?"

"Because I was in the fairgrounds after mother and I walked that boring bridge with a million other people. She let me stay behind to buy cotton candy."

"For the love of God, kid, shut up about the sweets and finish before I boot you."

"I'm trying to tell you I saw a man there dragging Royo down the hill. He'd wrapped something around his mouth so he wouldn't bark. Do something! He was suffering."

"Wrong pooch," Nick said, thinking back on the day of the movie shoot, when Waldo contended that he glimpsed Royo loose on Orange Grove. They both needed their eyes checked.

"*It* was Royo. He's got a bigger head than other half-breeds, and a darker tail."

"And who is this supposed dognapper?" Nick asked derisively. "The bogeyman?"

"I don't know. He has black hair. Don't let him kill Royo."

"You're seeing things that don't exist."

"Let's go find out," Reginald said, stomping his foot. "Our friend deserves that."

"You do it," Nick said, returning to bed. "I've done plenty for the kids and animals of Pasadena. I'll hunt for him tomorrow. He's a survivor."

Reginald stormed toward the transom, looking bigger than his years. "You know who the real ingrate is? It's *you*. I'm going to find him, and when I do, I'm keeping him."

Soon he was out on the pathway in Nick's flower-filled front yard.

Keeping him? A wrath Nick didn't want to acknowledge had been smoldering inside him shot through him with volcanic force. He bolted from bed, ran up behind the boy, and spun him around. He then lifted Reginald up by his armpits as his legs scissored air trying to escape. "Who made you judge and jury, huh?" he said.

"Nobody," Reginald said, getting teary. "But even a pipsqueak like me know there's something wrong with you. You tried acting happy during our shows. You pretended to be okay when you and Jules bought me a sarsa-parilla. But you haven't been the same Nick, not since the bridge accident."

Words, for once, failed him, as he hoisted his grade-school accuser three feet off the ground. Also failing him: any awareness that a wild parrot was flapping its wings ten feet above in preparation to release a goopy, white shit-bomb on the side of his livid neck.

When Nick looked up after it did, Reginald capitalized. He jammed his right thumb into Nick's squishy left eyeball while simultaneously kicking him in his right gonad. *Poke. Whack.*

Nick dropped Reginald onto the brick walkway and fell to his knees, hurting so badly he didn't know what to clutch first. Reginald's foot to his nut-sack knocked the breath out of him; had the eyeball in white-hot pain been shoved any deeper into his skull, he would've have forgotten his times-tables, if not most of 1912.

He attempted getting up without success. Reginald observed it from ten yards away at the low picket fence, where he scampered for protection.

When Nick spoke again, he spoke one-eyed in a higher register, like a Cyclops entering puberty might. "What you said before, about me being a different Nick, you were on the money."

"I was?" Reginald said, with a look of wonder and a dash of pride.

"Somebody once warned me that not everything that glistens is gold, but I wouldn't listen. Just because the bridge was stunning; just because she was daring."

"What does that have to do with Royo?" Reginald asked, edging nearer.

"Everything. And he's tried telling me. Him, the Spring Street graybeard."

"You're talking gobbledygook, but your heart's back, I can tell."

Then a second epiphany clocked him: Royo didn't tuck tail to gambol off amid a burglary. He was the *reason* for the break-in—the only reason. Taken by someone who loathed his "owner."

"You're right about something else, kid," Nick said, voice less falsetto. "Somebody did swipe him. Now help this dingbat inside before I pee blood. We have a plan to craft."

It was simple: Nick would dash to Busch Gardens to save Royo, if he was savable. Reginald, meantime, would run home and then to the police should he not hear from Nick within twenty-four hours.

"But I want to go with you," Reginald pleaded. "To help. I can fight."

"You proved that. It's too risky for you."

"But."

"'But' and 'why' are your two favorite words. Thank God for that."

"You know what: you're still my hero."

"Pick better heroes next time," Nick said, as his gouged eye started to open.

Before they left, Nick gave Reginald two items, one for bravery, the other for safekeeping. Upton would just have to wait.

SCREWING THE POOCH

*H*OW-RU. HOW-RUUU. HOW-ROO-A-ROO.

Royo's distressed wail sounded less Labrador-boxer in pitch and more beagle-ish, just not like any belonging to Valley Hunt Club members in the Pasadena of yore. This hound-ish baying was a canine SOS for *"Get me out of here!"*

He listened to it from the threadbare patch outside of Mrs. Bang's, close to where Reginald claimed witnessing that "evil man" dragging their muzzled friend away.

How-roooo, How-rooooooo.

It was killing Nick hearing this; killing him not knowing where the yowling was originating because of how sound pachinko-ed maddeningly off the hills. If he had any advantages here, it was his familiarity with the terrain, and the almost spooky incandescence produced by the white rainclouds, the bridge's grape-bunch lamps, and his own silvery lights.

How-ra-u-eeeerrrrr. Arrrrrrr-huh.

Oh, no. The previous yelping signaled desperation. This last one was the muffled garble of a windpipe being crushed. Accomplishing zero where he was, he hustled down the trail toward base camp. There, he jogged parallel to the arches, looking out with an inflamed eye (and ignoring a bruised testicle).

Arrrrr-urrrrrrrr. Uhhhh.

Then the howling ceased, and Nick's heart practically did, in concert.

"*Royo,*" he yelled, staring up at the moon gauzed by the clouds. "*Tell me where you are.*"

He ran back and forth, searching for a shallow grave around the bridge's mammoth footings. Panting, in his second cold sweat of the day, he thought about breaking into Marcus's tent to grab his bullhorn to demand Royo answer him. A minute passed, and hopelessness spiked.

"I'm on the bridge," a disembodied voice whispered when all seemed lost. "Find me before I drift off."

Oh my God. He can mind-talk, too. How could I not know that?

Nick rushed back the direction he came. Up on the deck, everything was so illuminated that someone with cataracts could've spotted the rope knotted around a baluster in a place he now officially despised: the pedestrian bay over the Big Whopper arch.

He raced along the curve, past the ceremonial bunting, hurtling onto the inlaid bench on the deck's south flank. Scanning downward was the most horrific sight he'd ever seen, and he'd seen some horror in his time. Royo was swinging by his neck on a makeshift noose, tongue protruding.

"Don't *you* dare die on me," Nick hollered. "You battle!"

His hands worked frantically tugging Royo up by the five-foot lariat. His dog was twitching as Nick brought him over the rampart and laid him sideways on the bench. He undid the noose, unbuckled Royo's collar, and, on a flier, began pushing on Royo's distended stomach to billow air into him. He'd shadowbox his past later.

When the spasms ended and the dog went completely still, Nick hurried out a crumpled stick of Wrigley's, waving it under Royo's dry nose. The only sounds were a gramophone from a nearby house playing "Silent Night" and Nick's voice. "Return," he said chokingly. "You hear me? Anything you want. Just *return.*"

He curled over him, squishing foreheads. "You can't go, boy," he thought. "Tell the graybeard to keep his vapory mitts off."

But it was too late: those mitts had an agenda. The only motion was the artificial movement of Royo's stomach from Nick compressing it. He lifted the dog's head into his lap, his tears dripping onto the animal's grayed muzzle.

This was premeditated murder—a homicide—nothing like leading starving farm animals over the cliffs in drought-time mercy killings. This was abomination from which no optimist could recover. This needed avenging. A minute passed and the stars weren't interceding

Or were they? Royo's nostrils puffed, and his tail jerked. Nick stroked his snout, goading him to breathe, praying for him to live. Then came a sputter and rasp. "Amen," Nick said, snot trickling down. "Welcome back, rascal."

Unless he received medical attention, however, this was going to be a short homecoming. Royo regained consciousness laboring to swallow. Watching him struggle for breath, seeing the blood coating his tongue, Nick knew he needed a veterinarian—and that the Pasadena Humane Society was mere blocks away. He'd smash its doors down if need be. "You hold on," he thought. "You have triple the grit I do."

◉◉◉

At last, Ernest Scuzzi was seeing the worm turn his way. He wouldn't be observing this tender scene from the leafy shadows of the bridge's western entrance otherwise.

Until now, the pattern always repeated for the sharp-nosed, high-school dropout from Des Moines. A construction site would hire him and, within a few months of getting acquainted, sack him. He needed a do-over, so when John Visco agreed to let him stay in his tiny guest room, Ernest resolved to try sidelining his blackest impulses.

John's death, just below where he was now, proved an ironic test, for it deprived Ernest of the *one* person who still believed he was redeemable. In attending the hearing at the mortuary housing John's corpse, Ernest expected justice but only heard about "faulty" lumber. He wanted someone to be prosecuted, not coroner Calvin Hartwell citing jurisdictional technicality for handcuffing him. Ernest stalked him outside to denounce the whitewash, which Jules overheard, but words only get you so far.

Even so, he might've forgotten Nick's broken promise that the guilty would pay—if he didn't happen to see Nick again. And he did, by pure luck, or fate, on a Santa Monica Ferris wheel one Saturday evening in September. The Goody Two Shoes was yucking it up with a blonde and his idiotic dog, which smirked and sat upright in the seat exactly like his owner. Such rage encased Ernest's throat.

Everything, as always, soon unraveled. Two weeks ago, he showed up to Cawston drunk; the next day, he made a rough play for the sexual favors of a gift shop cashier, and Cecil Jenks fired him. Juana, alarmed by Ernest's shifty eyes, ordered him to move out that night. Ernest decamped to a Los Angeles flophouse, where shaving the next morning, his razor encountered a gumball-sized lump along the base of his neck. There was one under an armpit, too.

At least that brought clarity. Reckoning he had a death sentence, he planned to hop a train to Denver to live out his final days in a Rocky Mountain haze of booze and brothels. First, he'd get justice for John. And he'd make it poetic. Two days back, he returned to Cawston to ask for his last paycheck rather than having it mailed. When the secretary left the room to speak with the payroll czar about it, he swiped Nick's Green Street address from a file drawer.

Ernest knew Nick would be gone all today at the bridge, so he broke into his bungalow in the late afternoon. Royo growled and sprang at him, but it wasn't anything Otis couldn't subdue. After he looped a rag around the dog's mouth, he used one of the ropes with him to yank him into the canyon; they'd then hid under oaks until the deck was vacant. Up there, Ernest converted his other rope into a noose, untied the dog's mouth, and hung him from the lamppost. In loitering around to enjoy the torment, he was ecstatic dwelling on how Nick was losing something that believed in him.

Just imagine Ernest's sadistic joy when Nick himself materialized, trying to rescue a pal closer to death than resuscitation. Two murders for the price of one: *yessiree*, that worm had turned.

❧ ❧ ❧

PFSSSSHHHHHHH: NICK'S HANDS WERE sliding under his dog's chest as that rustling noise from the bottom of the arch perked up his ears. *Ten seconds*: that was all he'd need to identify the monster that did this. He'd hotfoot Royo to the humane society.

In stepping onto the bench and leaning over, not once did Nick weigh the possibility he was being lured into a vulnerable position. For he was: the rustling was the sound of a boot crashing into the vegetation below— the boot Ernest removed and chucked there over Nick's head.

Royo understood this scenario was possible, for the graybeard had been whispering to him in his dreams that Nick was only allotted so many chances to wake up—to swat away the inanities and vanities of everyday life to be the real him. Accept that as he must, Royo couldn't watch the human he loved get a face-full of karma. When Ernest ran up from behind with a wicked smile and shoved Nick over the edge, Royo kept his eyes sealed.

Aaaaaaaaaah," Nick shrieked somersaulting downward at thirty-two-feet per second, "Royo. Oh, God! *Aaaaaaag.*"

He bounced into the hardpack, missing any cushioning brush or oaks. The blunt force impact did to him what it did to others: it rearranged an intact anatomy into splintered remnants. Blood spilled everywhere it shouldn't, including from a perforated intestine bulging from his abdomen like pink sausage.

His fall wasn't entirely negative, morbidly droll as that may sound. Because of the shock and paralysis, Nick wasn't in crippling pain like Harry Collins was during his rubble imprisonment. Nor was his brain without electricity, for how else could he watch a neural nickelodeon of himself heaved into the sky by the Pacific Electric rail-barn fireball, and then a tail-singed Royo tug him to safety down smoky Fair Oaks Avenue? How else could he watch himself dangle by a leather strap from this very bridge?"

In his real time of dying, a sonnet next filled Nick's head. It must've been a passage from Henry David Thoreau, his father's favorite writer, or a prophecy of where he was headed.

> *Fly away leave today,*
> *Way up high in the night*

◆◆◆

FIFTEEN STORIES ABOVE, ERNEST took Royo's un-clasped collar as his trophy, and trotted off with one boot missing. Happy enough to squeal, he'd be in Denver in two days and dead himself inside a month.

After he left, Royo raised his mangled neck in that pedestrian bay carved for romance and panoramas and jumped down off the bench. He forced his wheezing self along the trail to where he intuited Nick lay. The graybeard—wrongly besmirched as a Svengali, huckster, hypnotist, puppeteer, and private dick—still guided him, though Royo wished brutality wasn't the medium by which this story unfurled.

By the time his face loomed over Nick, the butterscotch wolf no longer aspired to be human. He was too jaded a creature for that now. You think a husky would shove a Doberman Pincher to his death because he was too timid to rat out the city he loved? The jury was in: those highest up the food chain were the Earth's most diabolical. That's why *his* human was imprinted into the dirt—with oozing brain matter and a leg angling forty-five degrees—as the Colorado Street Bridge's inaugural murder victim.

"I knew you'd come, boy," Nick thought seeing Royo, unable to talk. "What a mess of things I've made."

Royo collapsed next to him. "What can I say? Man struggles, we snuggle," he responded clairvoyantly. "Admit it: you were too caught up in your own hurly burly to realize that, on some days, I could speak."

"*You're* the voice I was supposed to tail. And here I wanted to punch that graybeard."

"Regrettable, though I'm not permitted to confide much more."

"At least confess you broke into my pantry again. I can smell your breath."

"Daugherty's potato chips. If it crunches, I need it in my mouth: cereal, wood, tennis rackets." The dog let out a scraping cough and continued. "I must show you something."

Royo lifted a shaky paw onto Nick's dislocated shoulder, just as he lifted it onto Edna Hollister's before leukemia took her. Nick, though, didn't view the afterlife; he viewed an earlier life, one on a mountaintop pasture on a brilliant day before Thaddeus Lowe and Adolphus Busch arrived. He *was* Tommy, the little boy attacked by carnivorous eagles, and Royo was Remy, the land mammal who saved him.

"So that's why birds of prey mortified me. You've rescued me twice now, and I've returned the favor once. I failed you." A tear rolled from Nick's bloody eyeball.

"No, you failed yourself and your town. But I'm not crucifying you. How often is a canyon dog permitted to slurp Budweiser, or make sick children giggle, let alone watch someone decapitate a clay elf?"

"If we're tied together, why couldn't I have remembered our lives before? I'm not a bad egg. I'm the history buff—the Teddy Stumper."

Royo's own tears splashed onto Nick's face. Yes, dogs can cry, among other surprises.

"It brings me no pleasure informing you of this as you fade out. Your actions haven't merited rewarding you with memories of who've you been."

"Why?"

"You never risked enough when it mattered."

"*Aw*, not much longer, boy. Something's barreling at me. Listen. When I go, you live to the fullest. You find somebody who appreciates your rapscallion spirit."

Royo licked Nick's face for the last time. "Why? I already found that in your Green Street bungalow. If only—"

"Sap, are my lights glowing?"

Royo whimpered. "Still incorrigible, Nick. But yes, brighter than ever."

"Bravo, flying dog!"

"Bravo, ostrich man!"

That was a wrap. Nicolas Augustus Chance died still believing the sun rose in his Pasadena.

◈◈◈

ON THIS DAY OF civic accomplishment, many living near the bridge heard the plaintive howling that next rang out; one homeowner cracked wry about Baskerville hounds.

A couple of entrepreneurs resembling the future Laurel & Hardy comedy team chalked the sound up to a manic coyote closing in on somebody's pussycat. Last month, Nick himself chased the pair off after they snuck onto the deck to test launch a parachute they hoped to sell to local aviation startups. "You may have interrupted us tonight, but you can't forever," the fatty of the two shouted at Nick.

Two minutes ago, they made good on their promise, returning in a jalopy while clueless about what just happened here. Like Ernest, neither bungler appreciated that they, too, were bit players in the celestially orchestrated Nick Chance Awakening Project. That's why their prototype parachute, the one created with too little chute for their experimental payload (fifty pounds of bricks in a wicker basket), was destined to fail.

Royo, draped over Nick's body, sensed this was how he'd pack it in. *Arrruggghhhhhhhh,* he yelped when the weight clobbered him. And then there was no pain as a wheel of purple light spun toward them.

Both he and Nick were gone, but we're nowhere near an end.

Overnight on December 13, 1913, the storm clouds helping to radiate that eerie light uncorked a downpour that gobsmacked even old-timers like A. C. Vroman. Citrus trees snapped. Red-tile ranchos you could get for a bargain leaked. Upton Sinclair believed that's why Nick didn't knock: Mother Nature waylaid him.

The normally gurgling stream under the bridge within hours transformed intself into a churning river of destruction. The muddy tide sucked away everything not lashed down: deflated balloons, construction nails, a parachute, much of the Scoville footbridge, as well as the bodies of a twenty-eight-year-old man and his frisky Lab-boxer. The already sodden banks around the roadway contributed to this fast-moving flotsam. When the top layer slid away, it carried down tons of dirt as well as *every one* of Nick's eighty solar lamps; they didn't even survive one official night. The ruins cascaded into the Los Angeles River, before bobbing or sinking in the Pacific Ocean.

After the storm, Fleet's search efforts to locate Nick and Royo went nowhere, despite his canvassing the town and presurring reporters to write about their disappearances. When the two never returned, he supposed they'd bailed on Pasadena to begin anew somewhere else and had their reasons for not communicating. Fleet didn't know whether to be furious at them or mystified about them. Nick's mother, Amy, was caught in that same ambivalence, once she bawled her eyeballs out and told God to take her, too.

Oddly, those emotions proved ephemeral. Six months later, Amy Chance and Fleet began forgetting details about Nick—his smile, his catchwords, his favorite sandwich—as if he were sun-bleaching figure in an aging photograph. This same specific forgetting also befell Jules, the lonely Portland suffragette, widow Lilly Busch, chef Buford, young Reginald, and Nick's closest Cawston friends. After the initial panic and dread over the pair's whereabouts, everybody went about their lives, always loving and missing Nick and Royo, but not able to fully grasp them in their mind's eye anymore. Once Fleet died, following a long career as a joke-cracking doctor, traces of him then faded, too. Indeed, somebody rummaging through vintage yearbooks or government records would've found nothing about him, Nick, and some of the others. As if they never existed.

Presented these facts, 'ol Chester would've reminded you that Pasadena's blindingly beautiful bridge wasn't inert by any means; that it must've been visiting amnesia on folks for reasons beyond their pointy heads (and certainly any Mercereau Company suit). Not an entirely bad guess for somebody making a living with a hammer and a sneer.

In any other news, completion of the Colorado Street Bridge thrust Pasadena over the top to win the blue-ribbon prize early in 1914 for "America's Best Small Town." In doing so, Nick's Crown City beat out Annapolis, Reno, Greenville, and Cape Cod; nothing in Indiana made the cut. In August, citizens, in a low turnout election, voted to annex Linda Vista and the San Rafael Heights. This time, nobody gave any lofty speeches.

FAILING MAC

"THIS FLANNEL WILL POP over your Levi's. Pair it with some Timberlands and *cowabunga*; you'll be a grunge god fighting off the ladies. Hey, mister, are you okay?"

Jorge Silva's customer, alive but not living by most New Age standards, didn't answer. He was too distracted by something outside the plate-glass window of Colorado Boulevard's Banana Republic.

The effeminate sales clerk in Beatles' bangs and a paisley shirt jiggled the man's shoulder with one hand, while his other extended the red-and-black, long-sleeve shirt he was peddling. "I can buzz my manager if you need medical attention. My cousin is an epileptic. He gets this way sometimes."

A head twitch, then scrunch of the eyes: "Sorry 'bout that. Wandering mind. Must be that Muzak version of 'Stairway to Heaven.'"

Jorge stood there, balancing compassion with his sales quota. Behind him, an associate reorganized chinos beneath a blown-up photo of a dewy, Peruvian rainforest.

"Now that you're back, should I fetch a different shirt, something more Bill Gates, less Eddie Vedder?"

Nick, who people often said resembled the Dr. Pepper ad-man, except with a slightly crooked nose and a perennial cowlick, stared again at the street banner promoting the eightieth birthday of "Pasadena's Original Dame." Now Jorge locked onto it.

"I've never seen a town so addicted to its own history," he said. "Sure not like that in Sherman Oaks, where I live. Culture there is Galleria deep. Here you have the museums, a Cheesecake Factory, JPL, Julia Child's childhood home."

Nick barely heard him. "Off the wall question: you wouldn't happen to know when Colorado Street became a boulevard?"

"No idea. But I do know everything up front is twenty percent off."

Nick, the southpaw, patted his jeans' left back pocket. "Dang. I'm sorry, uh, Jorge," he said, after zeroing in on the salesman's plastic nametag. "I forgot my wallet."

In his driveway, Nick wondered why he bothered browsing amid that politically correct capitalism. He already owned seven shirts (and a pair of chinos). The lengths the underachieving will do to forget what doesn't matter. Like waking hours.

The young, floppy-eared dog, which he adopted a year ago after it followed him during a jog around the Rose Bowl, bounded off the tan leather couch to greet him. Technically, he wasn't supposed to be on there after his puppy incisors earlier reduced one armrest into a carcass of tattered foam, but Nick let it slide. He named him Royo in homage to the Arroyo Seco. Fleet Burdett, Nick's best friend, argued "Luffy" was more apt, as the destruction he inflicted on Nick's place was in scale to what Hitler's Luftwaffe exacted on London's architecture.

Hattie, Nick's wife of two years, had her own tag for him: Royo Asswipe. Did he forget, she once asked, that he wed "a non-animal person?" Even as a child, she never liked TV's Snoopy and Scooby-Doo, and thought Old Yeller had it coming. After Royo mauled her stiletto heels, old Girl Scout sash, and box of tampons in one chew-fest week, she didn't hesitate exiling him outside—in the rain—if Nick were away.

His affection for the dog and Hattie's revulsion of Royo Asswipe, coupled with her disgust over Nick's general indifference on other matters, became a metaphor for an un-gratifying union between two ill-suited people. Post-honeymoon, there weren't any "for better." There were only Hattie's mutterings of "for what?"

In a phone conversation with her mother that Nick overheard, she compared him to "a light switch set permanently on dim." Harsh as that assessment was, Nick knew she was right. So, he drove to the Santa Anita mall in Arcadia to prove he could still make her smile, buying her an eighty-dollar "sun" necklace festooned with teensy diamonds. After she opened it, there was perfunctory sex and tepid vows to be more attentive. By dinner, though, they weren't speaking. Royo had filched the necklace from the coffee table, bolted outside with it through the doggy door, and buried it in the same hole in which he buried Hattie's best yoga pants.

To punish Nick, Hattie weaponized her absences. She began working long hours as the assistant to a cable company CFO notorious for fetishizing women's elbows. And Hattie's, he remarked to her over a spreadsheet, "are the sexiest this side of Paris."

Then again, Nick was less devoted to his profession than his curly haired vegan spouse was to hers. Life at Wham-O Corporation nowadays wasn't scintillating. His favorite time of day was coming home to his small, English Tudor home, in the San Rafael hills on Pasadena's western quarters, to cavort with the most idiosyncratic personality under his roof.

Almost telepathically, the dog grabbed his own leash the second Nick's brain decided on a walk; he found Nick's misplaced car keys simultaneously with Nick's realization he lost them. Royo whizzed on stucco, barked at BMWs, and rolled on dry grass like it was seeded with dead-cat fur. When Nick played Led Zeppelin tunes on his sunburst Les Paul guitar, the scamp often danced on hind legs. Every morning, the mutt licked Nick's face three times.

"Sounds like you have a special bond," Fleet said during a backyard BBQ at his Euclid Street cottage. "I hear in Arkansas, you two could make it official." Nick laughed. Then he beaned Fleet, an aspiring alternative medicine doctor, in the chin with a half corncob.

Royo's larcenous streak eventually changed everything. During a weekend visit from Maude, Hattie's college roommate, and Maude's three-year-old daughter, Royo cunningly waited for them to depart the living room. Unsupervised, he snagged the little girl's Crump 'N Curl Cabbage Patch Kid doll and carried it outside to behead in his backyard killing fields.

Hattie phoned Nick that night at his hotel in San Francisco, where he was attending a business conference. "Sit down," she said with bogus concern. "*Your* dog is missing. He must've wiggled out through the backyard gate. Don't blame me. You were supposed to tighten the bolt months ago."

Nick cut his trip short, rushing home on Southwest Airlines. Paranoid about Royo's safety, he imagined the worst outcome first. Eaten by foothill coyotes. Abducted by medical researchers. When the Pasadena Humane Society phoned the next morning, Nick almost moonwalked. His pal was there, unharmed.

"So, where did you find him?" he asked. "In the trash cans of the restaurant up the street?"

"No," the rep said. "The guy in a Nissan who brought him in here said he watched some woman shove him out of her car in front of the federal appeals building; you know, the pink tower where you'd expect to see Philip Marlowe loitering. He thought she was trying to get him run over by traffic on Orange Grove Boulevard."

"Let me guess," Nick said. "The woman was driving a green Saab."

"How did you know?"

"It's my wife's car."

Bombs flew afterward. Nick accused Hattie of "attempted dogacide," of cheating on him with her perverted boss, of serving him tofu, quinoa, and other vegan horrors she knew he disliked. She upbraided him as "a sleepwalking loser" more protective of Royo, with his obsessive, two-page list of instructions for his care, than about her bliss.

"How can I try making you happy," Nick said, "when you're happiest being miserable?"

"For starters," she answered, "give a shit about something."

To get away from her, he stamped into the garage, where the snow skis, tennis racket, telescope, and other hobbies he once enjoyed lay on a shelf in cobwebbed repose. That's when he noticed something new in there: the folded U-Haul packing boxes and bubble wrap that Hattie pre-positioned to leave him. In a rare burst of emotion, Nick wrenched open the aluminum garage door, hoping it'd snap.

Hattie was soon in the space where they resumed their woolly fight in view of neighbors doing weekend chores. Some of them lingered outside, trimming hedges or painting chipped columns, just to watch the sparks fly where there were none before.

"You need a shrink," she yelled. "Tell him the dog you allow to lick you on the mouth spends hours a day tongue-bathing his privates."

"I will. But it's the closest I come to genitalia these days."

Hattie flared her lips and swiveled her head looking to redress that insult. Target located, she marched toward Nick's workbench and took the box cutter from it. She then crisscrossed the garage to where Nick kept his junior-high-era beanbag chair and slashed a two-foot laceration across its vinyl membrane. So ferociously did she do this that the white pellets inside burst out, showering the pair in a Styrofoam-ash storm on their last day together.

A month later, their cozy home on that shady block was a desolate bachelor pad. Among its winnowed contents were a king-size bed, an Ikea dresser, Nick's leather furniture set, plus his classic rock CDs and USC diploma. Peculiar, Nick thought, after Hattie moved out. Royo mainly wrecked her possessions.

◈◈◈

FROM HIS JUNIOR YEAR at the Lord-of-Flies-Esque Stone Canyon Prep High to this rudderless moment of his late-twenties, Nick was often wide awake at two a.m. Awake staring at the ceiling, or drenched in sweat following a recurring nightmare about dying. With Hattie gone, he could exploit his insomnia to enjoy a tranquil Pasadena where the luxury cars and latte drinkers were replaced by streetlamps burning intriguingly.

It was only a nine-minute drive to his office on Green Street, whose bushy trees formed an arboreal tunnel over the asphalt. This road, one block south of Colorado Boulevard, was unrelated to Pasadena's celebrated Greene brothers, a pair of sibling architects who, at century's turn, elevated the boxy bungalow design into a fusion of style and function. Darlings of the Arts & Crafts movement, they created the gracefully trussed Gamble House on Orange Grove, which no respectable tourist map would exclude. Yet even that masterpiece of dark wood didn't get a street named after them, something irreverent Nick and Fleet found endlessly hilarious. There was no third "e" in this Green.

Nick, with Royo in tow, keyed the creaky door and switched on the fluorescent lights that whirred like summer cicadas. Wham-O rented this dumpy, industrial annex to house poor-selling merchandise and product engineers deluding themselves that toiling for a former retail juggernaut was wise career trajectory. Nick realized he should've quit to focus on an invention he'd been fine-tuning for years. Still, he lacked what self-help guru Tony Robbins claimed was essential for success: "either inspiration or desperation."

Wham-O's founding partners, Richard Knerr and Arthur "Spud" Melin, never were psychically crippled. Can-do sorts, they generated millions from mirthful ideas in a Cold War world. Just surveying the vintage posters on the metal-sided walls reminded Nick of that. Hula Hoops, Frisbees, Super Balls, Slip 'N Slides, Hacky Sacks, Wham-Os molded plastics and polymers *were* retail Americana. Busts along the way, like the Mr. Hootie Egg Rake, and lawsuits didn't faze the headmen. It was the knock-off competitors and ascent of electronic games foreshadowing the company's obituary that did.

Wham-O, nonetheless, left its mark. Unlike Nick, who'd yet to leave a scratch.

Now he swayed on his heels, questioning where he was headed. Across the annex, Royo was up on his hindquarters sniffing a teetering stack of boxes containing one of Nick's products. "Get down!" he said, noticing this. When Royo obeyed, the highest carton fell smack into a puddle of brackish water from a leaking, underground condensate line—the one Nick's muddling boss had promised to have fixed.

Royo grinned and trotted off, as if his mischief was intentional. Nick went over to the waterlogged box and pulled it onto dry floor. "Way to screw me," he said. "Those were meant to go to QVC next week for a tryout. That was one Royo Asswipe move."

He cracked the box to inspect the merchandise, and though it was dry, it remained depressing. The Di-Crapper, that's what was in there: disposable diapers embossed with cultural lightning rods that folks loved to hate so much babies could defecate on their facial likenesses, pending trademark approval. In this particular box, Saddam Hussein and Yoko Ono starred on the composite-fiber lining.

Nobody in the novelty product business would ever mistake them for genre classics: the Ronco Pocket Fisherman and the Cha-Cha-Cha Chia. Should QVC reject the Di-Crapper, he'd be fortunate to sell his gimmickry at Costco, or the bargain bin at Piggly Wiggly markets. Nick's previous concept didn't knock anyone dead, selling a pathetic three thousand units. The Finger was another kitschy, lowbrow item he hatched for the smart-ass demographic. Every gift-wrapper who ever wrestled with an uncooperative present, he thought, could use an extra digit to tie fluffy bows or tape festive paper. Imagine the jungle, Nick told Wham-O management. "Give your mother the finger. She deserves it."

Crunch. Nick punched his hand through his crate of joke diapers. He could hear what his mentor would've said about the crass junk: "You want *this* on your tombstone?"

Of all the people from Nick's childhood, in the hills west of the Rose Bowl known as Linda Vista, Buford McKenzie was a soul without equal. "Mac," as everyone called him, was an easygoing carpenter from New Orleans, a man with a receding hairline, beer belly, and not un-sexy wife. For many of the elementary-school-age boys on Nick's street, he was their surrogate pop. They must've logged a hundred hours in Mac's garage listening to him wax on about his favorite subject: "history's doers," which Mac described in thrilling ways no teachers could. During his pep talks, he swigged Michelob, the boys Fresca. Sometimes he grilled them Cajun sausages.

What most tickled Mac's fancy were solar-power dreamers, and Nick caught the bug. Da Vinci, Newton, and Galileo, he said, all tried mining the sun to light the world. "With dumb luck, they could've. But kings and emperors feared those sunrays could be turned into weapons of war, the ultimate laser, and stuffed the genie back in the bottle. Think of that next time you pass a Shell station."

The cross-legged boys in his garage stirred in amazement.

"Did anyone around here invent anything like that?" a young Nick asked excitedly.

"Aubrey Eneas did."

"Aubrey? What a dorky name."

"Would you prefer Thomas Edison?"

Aubrey, Mac explained, perfected "a bitchin' solar engine" that channeled heat used to run massive water pumps. He introduced it in 1901 "down the road from here at a place called Cawston Ostrich Farm. Yes, once upon a time women would sell their firstborns to buy their feathers for hats and clothes. But Aubrey's machine mattered more than silly fashion, and you, young grasshoppers, all need to matter yourselves someday."

It was Mac's last garage bull session. In winter 1973, heavy rains shellacked Southern California. Few places took the brunt more than the

Devil's Gate reservoir, which paralleled the Foothill Freeway's western spur then under construction. Mac and two dozen or so blue collars were there on an early Sunday morning pouring concrete for a flyover bridge. Wrong place, wrong time; water gushing over the dam from the northern Arroyo Seco flooded the work zone, creating a torrent of steel, concrete, and lumber that carried away Mac and others. Some of their corpses needed to be jackhammered from the muck. Stories later circulated about neighborhood dogs barking crazily minutes before the disaster.

Nick wept for days, moped for a week—and stayed fascinated by the sun's inexhaustible magic on a fossil fuel planet. These many years later, The Finger and Di-Crapper was all he'd accumulated for his tombstone.

╪ ╪ ╪

ON THE SUNDAY FOLLOWING his insomniac visit to the Wham-O annex, an absentminded Nick went to fetch the paper. That's when he nearly somersaulted over a duct-taped cardboard box left on his doormat. *Hattie.* She must've returned some of his things that she inadvertently packed in her hurry to move out. She probably wanted Nick's canned chili con carne and bacon-infused beans out of her non-meat life as much as him.

He lugged the thing into his sparse living room, and sliced the tape sealing it with a car key, a trick that Mac taught him. Inside it, however, wasn't a carnivore's delight. It was a black, metal device that appeared, on first glance, to be either an antiquated slide projector or nickelodeon. On top of the doohickey were mirrors, a slot the width of a photograph, and a retractable lid. When Nick opened it, he saw a bed of crumbled dark glass and earthenware.

If Hattie didn't drop this here, possibly in some kind of divorcing, gas-lighting stunt, Fleet was Nick's other suspect. Perhaps he did it as a cheer-me-up, even though Nick last April Fool's Day snuck wasabi into Fleet's toothpaste. He probably bought it at the Rose Bowl Swap Meet. "You wonderful clown," Nick said aloud, patting the box.

Royo trundled over to investigate. He cocked his head, and the vertical lines on his forehead, the ones normally frizzed in the shape of the Atari logo, straightened. *Roooooh*, he said.

THE VROMAN'S GIRL

A CUSHY PERK OF a listless existence is never feeling guilty about a
ninety-minute lunch. And, by the looks of the crowd this Thursday
at Pie 'N Burger, Nick would be fortunate to get back to his crummy metal
desk at his crummy Wham-O job before two.

The San Gabriel Valley's best burger joint had twenty-plus customers
brushing up between its faux-wood walls. Most were waiting for that
heavenly patty, sautéed onions, and tangy goop, which Mother Teresa
would've stopped blessing the poor to chow down. Sure there were French
bistros and scrumptious ethnic joints in trendy new Old Pasadena. Yeah,
there were steak-and-bourbon grills on their last heart-clogging legs and
stalwarts like Mijares, whose zesty margaritas Paul McCartney was known
to swill when in town.

But, as Nick told everyone, your salivary glands hadn't lived until they
visited here.

Today's patrons included a former ace Dodger pitcher and an aging,
bouffant-haired political consultant, whose views skewed just to the left
of the nearby John Birch Society. Also waiting for a table were a Spandex-
clad soccer mom scribbling notes in her day calendar, and three Caltech
astrophysicists, whose sleepy, universe-exploring campus was just down
the block.

One of the brainiacs in that group was a visiting professor from Indiana
University. Rather than continuing to debate string theory with his fellow
eggheads, he extolled his coordinates. "Pasadena," he said, "is even more

magnificent in person than it comes off on TV during the Rose Parade. Now I know why Einstein loved it. It radiates peace at a quark level."

God, what a rube. Nick had seen "the Pasadena swoon" before. Sometimes, just informing people you're from here induced a semi-hypnotic state characterized by dilated pupils and cooing voices. "Oh," they'd gush, "I love Pasadena." Mount Wilson trails, Warhol at the Norton Simon, those manicured neighborhoods, the playhouse: many would relocate here in a Burbank minute if they had the cash. Nick turned away from the fawning Hoosier. To him, civic pride was for blue-hairs, history for preppy preservationists. All that mattered was the present. And, speaking of which, someone just vacated a counter seat at the back of restaurant, the one opposite the mirrored pie cabinet reflecting seafoam-meringue frostings.

He rushed off for it, passing the first set of bolted, red vinyl chairs and the blackboard-size menu above the soda-syrup pumps. Halfway to the open seat, realizing who was next to it, his amperage rose. A woman he had a crush on was sitting alone, nose deep into a chunky book. Man does not live by the Di Crapper alone.

Naturally, his right foot tried making a chump of him. Mid-step, it caught the bendy strap of a purse that a customer didn't know was on the floor. Nick, perennial klutz, stumbled over it, fated, it seemed, to smash his face into the ground racing up to meet it. But deliverance spared him, the deliverance of a lightning-fast hand grabbing him by the belt from behind. There'd be no public humiliation, no Bronx clap.

Hoisted up by the Good Samaritan, Nick spun around expecting to eyeball Orel Hershiser, star of the '88 World Series. It wasn't Orel. It was a tan, middle-aged Chinese-American in his signature rawhide vest and cowboy hat. Nick recognized him from a recent story in an alternative weekly. Lei "Giddy Up" Wong, it said, was "Pasadena's Marlboro Man," though he didn't smoke and only rode his palomino to the lucrative Kinko's franchise he owned on Lake Avenue bi-annually.

"*Whoa*, pardner. You okay?" Wong said, playing to idiom.

"Yeah. Think so," Nick said. "Thanks to you."

"Shucks. Was nothing," said Wong, who smelled of Wrigley's Spearmint, which Nick himself adored, going back to the days when his buddies tore through Bazooka. "Never much liked seeing falling objects."

Nick soon folded into the vinyl seat next to the woman he thought of as "the Vroman's girl," having spotted her numerous times recommending non-fiction titles to customers in Vroman's, Pasadena's oldest and most esteemed bookstore. Hattie was cute. The Vroman's girl was mesmeric. Everything about her—her intelligent hazel eyes; candy-dish cheekbones; pointy chin; shoulder-length, dirty-blonde hair—made Nick oscillate.

He stole glances at her in the pie mirror, but the curt smile she flashed at him sitting down broadcast she had all she needed: her tuna plate and Adolphus Busch biography.

"Hey, Nick," said the waitress, an effervescent, brunette burger-slinger, to whom old-men regulars told off-color jokes in hopeless flirtations. "We've missed you. Your buddy Fleet came in last week; said you've been going through some stuff."

"Not anymore," Nick said with a dismissive chuckle. "I'll have my usual. Fries extra crispy."

He was halfway through eating when he caught the Vroman's girl giving him a side-eyed checkout, which nearly made him drop a fry. Then *no*. Two minutes later, she was fishing cash out of her wallet to pay her tab. Nick's mind scrounged for an icebreaker—a PETA joke, something about the high prices—when he looked again in the pie-cabinet mirror and found his second deliverance. "Excuse me, miss," he said. "I think you've got ketchup in your hair, the right side."

"Really?" The Vroman's girl felt around until her fingers brushed the slushy condiment. "Oh, geez. Thank you. It would've been embarrassing to walk around with that." She uncrumpled her napkin and blotted it.

Steady, boy. "You work at Vroman's, don't you?"

"Part time. Hey, weren't you in last week?"

"That's me. Blowing my paycheck, one inventor at a time. So, you an alcohol enthusiast?" Nick said, nodding at her book.

"Only weekend chardonnay. But I'm sort of fixated on Busch Gardens. On hectic days, I dream of transporting myself there. You ever heard about it?"

"I grew up here, so yeah. I'm a recovering homer."

"Besides all the trails, and ponds, and animals, I guess there were fairy-tale huts and figurines from the Brothers Grimm. So quixotic."

"That rings a bell from school. Closest I ever came to the Busches was gulping too many free samples with the aforementioned Fleet at their Van Nuys brewery." *Smart, she thinks you're a lush.*

"Well, who doesn't enjoy complimentary Budweiser? Anyway, I find Adolphus engrossing. Complicated person."

"Didn't he rock a goatee?"

They introduced themselves, and their chemistry drummed off that pie rack.

"Everybody told me this place was a must," Julie Cumbersmith said. "I'm already berating myself for not ordering the burger. Rookie mistake. I'm still learning the Pasadena ropes."

Nick pounced on that like Royo once did on an unwatched Bundt cake. "If you're interested, I'll be your humble guide to show you around. A goopy burger does not a town make."

"*Hmmm,*" she said, putting her finger to her chin, adorably so. "I'm not accustomed to getting hit on over Formica."

"Better than a noisy bar, especially one playing disco."

"For the sake of my education, I'll agree. You're not married, right?"

"Only to my dog. But it's not weird."

╫╫╫

FOR THEIR FIRST DATE, Nick took her to landlocked Pasadena's marine institution. Cameron's Seafood—faded, fish-shaped sign, sawdust floors, barn-ish building—would've blended in organically along San Francisco's Fisherman's Wharf. Instead, it was struck on Colorado Boulevard's tragically passé eastern sector. Senior citizens fond of its affordable wines and denture-friendly white fish kept its cash registers sentient.

Second impressions were forged over steaming sourdough. This was oppositional attraction. Julie was a together, former magazine editor from Chicago who relocated west to consider a local master's program in Progressive Age history. A Northwestern graduate, she was spunky and upbeat, the anti-Hattie. Long term, she aspired to be an author specializing in forgotten personalities.

"You came to the right place," Nick said. "We have a boatload of them here. From what I foggily remember."

"And current Hollywood people," Julie said. "Kevin Costner sometimes comes into the store. Sally Field, too. Voracious readers."

She continued the dime tour of herself. *Wuthering Heights* and *The Jungle* were favorite novels; as a teenager, an Eleanor Roosevelt poster hung above her bed. She liked oversize sweaters, candle-lit baths, and, counter-intuitively, Clint Eastwood westerns. Someday, she wanted a yard full of beagles.

Screw it. Nick told her the unvarnished truth about himself. He was a classic underachiever: high IQ, lackluster GPA. Every Sunday, knowing he should be doing better, gloom set in about his Wham-O Mondays. Once a month, he rendezvoused with Fleet, as they pledged they would at eighteen, to split a Shakey's pepperoni pizza, party, and gab. His passion: solar power; his guilty pleasure: B-grade sci-fi flicks.

Julie ate her butter-drowned shrimp scampi, staying quiet as Nick segued into why his young marriage to Hattie grew old. "Lying is no way to start off with someone else," he said, nipping his food. "About a year ago, I lost all my steam. My soon-to-be-ex told me I needed therapy for depression—and electric shock for smart-ass syndrome."

"That's rough, Nick," Julie said with a quick stroke of the hand (and a smidge of butter on her chin). "I say leave her in your past. Where she belongs."

Nick, after dinner, suggested a landmark visit. She anticipated a cruise past the iconic Huntington Library, Art Collection, and Botanical Gardens, which many Pasadenans claimed as their civic treasures despite being in San Marino, or a drive by city hall's capitol dome. *Ehhhh.* He whisked her to outer space: a steel-bar rocket ship at Victory Park in east Pasadena, where he hung out as a boy.

"Okay, Ms. Writer-To-Be," he said after they climbed to the top of the capsule. "You ever play word association?"

"Who doesn't? Fire away."

"Hillary Clinton?" he asked.

"Better off divorced," she answered.

"Snappy. Jack Parsons?"

"Oh, I just read up on Devil's Gate. Wasn't he a Satan worshiper *and* rocketeer? He must've driven his high school guidance counselor nuts."

Nick laughed, and when he heard her infectious chuckle, it made butterflies dipsy-do over the swordfish kabob and au gratin potatoes in his belly.

"My turn to ask one," she said. "Jurassic Park?"

Nick paused to be witty. "Um, fat guys always get eaten first."

On their second date, Nick acquainted her with another slice of OG Pasadena. The corporations could build their featureless multiplexes, drizzle their imitation butter. Nick preferred the dilapidated majesty of the Pacific Theater on upper Rosemead Boulevard, where he once was a pubescent ticket-ripper in a rank company blazer.

They saw "Groundhog Day" holding hands sticky from Starbursts. Nick thought Bill Murray was hilarious but was unable to identify, as a lapsed Presbyterian, with the premise that souls must pass tests before advancing. Their twenty-second goodnight kiss outside Julie's Marengo Avenue apartment was more tangible, proof positive his dimmer could be rebooted.

On the drive home in his burnt-orange Toyota, Nick popped in Zep's *Houses of the Holy* CD. Now that they were opening up, he told Julie the group's songs spoke to him the way the burning bush must've spoken to Moses; that its mysticism-dappled lyrics and thunderous guitar "was what it would've sounded like if J. R. R. Tolkien ever flew a stereofled F-16." She said their hard rock tunes were okay, though Squeeze and Elvis Costello were more her cup of tea.

Exiting the freeway now, Nick floated to the resonant outro of "Over the Hills and Far Away." Then it bled into the unsyncopated funkiness of the next song, and he hastily changed the track to "The Ocean" for sanity's sake. Robert Plant's spoken coda at the end of "The Crunge" used to be the party-cranking slogan for he and his fellow prep-school hooligans. But something scarring happened to Nick one night down at "that confounded bridge," and from then on he refused to drive or discuss it.

Pasadena's historic Colorado Street Bridge—or, as it was popularly and pitilessly known, "Suicide Bridge"—was currently barricaded while a twenty-seven-million-dollar seismic upgrade and face-lift wrapped up. When he spaced out inside Banana Republic noticing the banner advertising the bridge's December rechristening, it only reaffirmed the structure's dark grip on him. He abhorred any association between his favorite band and most dreaded spot on Earth. Best to keep that lodged away. In Julie Cumbersmith he had a reason to smile, and a hope that his pain bore, as the man once crooned, some "silver linings."

DON'T FEAR THE HOJACK

Mark Stonebreaker, Nick's boss, was a Dilbert-esque character if there ever were one: a meek, inept middle manager who'd stumbled up the promotion ladder that no MBA yearned to climb. Built like an upright buffalo, he acted more like a swarthy, sugar-craving Cowardly Lion. Nobody at Wham-O's backwater annex respected him.

Today, Nick sat in the chair facing his desk, watching him hoover up the last of his Winchell's apple fritter. You'd need an oracle to predict what Mark was going to say, because he smiled just as awkwardly disciplining someone for insulting a distribution rep as he did when informing them of a dental-plan change.

Nick, whom he'd asked to see this morning, expected to hear retailer feedback about his latest prototype, and it wasn't the Di-Crapper.

"I'll be candid," Mark said, struggling to complete the sentence as he sucked glaze from his fingertips. "And that's not easy for me. I dislike confrontation."

And vegetables. "Confrontation? What are you talking about?"

"Nobody is looking for the next Frisbee or gag gift anymore. The next time somebody swaps their Game Boy for one of those will be the day, um—the day the Earth's axis reverses polarity."

Mark leaned forward in a desk chair whose hinges squealed for WD-40. He started at Wham-O seven years ago as a product engineer hawking an inflatable isolation tank. Promising as it sounded, it either leaked or trapped stressed-out customers in their homes. The gremlin: "faulty" zippers. What did management do? They promoted him.

Before the Nintendo Corporation cherry-picked him, Nick's closest workmate, Otis Norwood, once described Mark as "the Peter Principle incarnate in the worst of J. C. Penney's spring lineup." Nick missed Otis, a man as talented as he was incisive.

"That's not exactly news," Nick said, cringing about where this was leading. "Everybody knows kids don't play outside like they once did. In fact, if we were smart, we'd partner with a vitamin D company to pitch a Bart Simpson chewable."

"I should that write that down," Mark said.

"But funny never goes out of style in the adult demo. Now spill. What did QVC say? It pre-ordering ten-thousand units?"

Mark smiled toothily. "The executives there thought your idea was witty and would do well. Let me check my notes," he said, flipping pages on a food-stained yellow pad. "Here it is, do well in flyover states hospitable to trailer parks and bowling alleys, places where folks are more plainspoken."

Oh, no. Here it comes.

"But they were anxious your product could backfire on the coasts, where consumers are more quickly offended, and in evangelical districts. Holy Rollers aren't known to be the jokesters that rednecks are."

"What are you saying?"

"I'm saying headquarters has decided against going into production."

"So the HoJack is dead?" Nick asked, mouth a rictus. "We're not even focus-grouping it?"

"No. The bosses are concerned if word got out, we could have the National Organization for Women picketing us."

Nick wasn't proud he invented The HoJack, a mash-up of the popular LoJack car alarm and the antediluvian chastity belt. He simply thought it was his Wham-O winner. He envisioned people fighting over it, not against it, at Secret Santa parties or bachelorette nights out. To boost its crass pizzazz, he created a fake "transmitter" that simulated a locking noise. The settings ranged from "Hands Off" to "Horizontal Hootenanny."

"Then they're being myopic. I've been reading up on this World Wide Web thing coming. We'll have access to all types of fresh audiences."

Mark's three chins jiggled agreement. "I'll mention that webbing at the next meeting. But you won't be attending because I've been ordered to fire you."

"Fire me?" Nick said, bolting up out of his chair. "What the fuck, Mark? I know my last performance review concluded I wasn't living up to my potential, but, to quote a friend, 'I've been going through some stuff.'"

"Then let me quote what my supervisor said. 'We're bleeding money. Wham-O needs slam-dunks, not a national shaming on Maury Povich.'"

◖◖◖

REVERSE POLARITY? *HE* NEEDED a reverse in fortunes as a guy with three thousand dollars in savings, legal bills, a mortgage, never mind a ravenous dog prone to staring at him. At least his mother didn't charge for her unsolicited psychological evaluation.

"You've always been an enigma, darling: fast learner, late bloomer," she said after he broke the news over the phone. She was speaking from a small house in Indianapolis, where she relocated four years ago from Pasadena. She still missed its mountains and culture, just not its pricey, gentrifying-fueled cost of living. "Can I give you some guidance?"

"Please, no," he said, puckering at the idea he might have to move into her guest room should his options dry up. "I'm reminding myself it's not as hard as it seems."

"Is that from a sermon? It wouldn't kill you to go to church, incidentally."

"No, it's from the gospel of Robert and Jimmy. It's okay. I have some things cooking. I'm viewing this as a blessing in disguise."

"Listen to you," she said. "Thinking like an optimist."

A week after his firing, Nick decided to walk in a circle: a therapeutic circle around the Rose Bowl. Without Wham-O's three-month severance, he'd be in deep yogurt, and not the trendy kind they sold at Colorado Boulevard's 21 Choices. So, he leashed Royo and snagged his Walkman. Pulling into a lot near Brookside Golf Club, however, he realized he forgot to load a CD. His distracted head strikes again. He'd have to listen to AM talk-radio; FM reception was spotty in the canyon.

A screechy host was doing a segment about how Pasadena was "finally getting its comeuppance." Topical subject. If Nick figured he was having a year to forget, a city whose glossy history was its own self-perpetuating PR agent couldn't wait for the calendar to flip. In October, a brush fire tore through the eastern foothills, devouring homes like a five-hundred-degree Pac-Man. Days later, three teenagers leaving a Halloween party in the city's violent northwest, a once-proud African American stronghold across the Arroyo from billion-dollar JPL, were gunned down in cold blood. They'd done nothing wrong.

Nineteen ninety-three, the liberal host clucked, was "Pasadena's year of blood and color." The WASPy Tournament of Roses Association, headquartered in the colonial-white Wrigley Mansion, was in the crosshairs of activists demanding minority inclusion. They threatened to block the unimaginable: the parade that was the town's stock-and-trade and never-ending cash cow. At city hall, the usual patrician civility was on sabbatical, too. Mercurial Councilman Isaac Richard, who saw bias and Uncle Tom sellouts everywhere, battled misconduct charges; colleagues were aghast at what his outbursts were doing to Pasadena's good name.

The commentator wouldn't let it go either, squawking about the Foothill Freeway's "carcinogenic-smog footprint," and the sale of the elegant Huntington Hotel just outside city borders. "Where's that little old lady from the Beach Boys song?" he said. "Dead! She was a speed demon. Ladies and gentlemen: always peek behind the curtain. This town of a hundred twenty thousand plus has the same issues as any place. Drive Orange Grove Boulevard, not just Millionaire's Row. All of it. You'll appreciate that not all Pasadenas are created equally."

Not that he much bought into his hometown's myth as a citadel of virtue, but the loudmouth's shtick revolved around hyperbole. Nick stripped off his headphones to enjoy the people watching, instead. It didn't get any better than the three-mile loop on the area's community treadmill. Out on the pathway today were serious-minded, amateur bicyclists, who pedaled in intimidating swarms; fanny-packed speed walkers; arthritic grandmothers; and chatty domestics pushing other people's children (in high-end strollers). A robed Buddhist monk passed Nick with an excellent stride, prayer beads bobbing. Nick loved it here.

Walking in to see his answering machine blinking, he hoped it wasn't his divorce lawyer. Wish granted.

Mr. Chance, David Loomer here from Silicon Valley. We met at the Hollywood inventors conference about three months ago. You may remember that my investors were hunting for something in the alternative energy field. Boy, did we pick the wrong horse. We analyzed the urine battery showcased at the event and it flat didn't work. It also stunk like a fraternity bathroom. But your idea, based on the specs, could be a difference-changer. That's what my experts report. Nobody ever thought to engineer a removable solar panel on a car roof as a backup generator. Not until you. Genius. Call me as soon as you can.

Nick replayed the message eight times and followed up with an encouraging phone call to Loomer. His investors, he learned, were willing to pay him a *six-figure* advance if his device tested out. Hearing the best news of his career, Nick bubble-wrapped one of his prototypes for Loomer and messengered it to him via UPS that day. His ship may have just come in, HoJack free.

That evening, on his fourth date with Julie at the soon-to-be-closing Moonlight Roller Rink, he divulged his "big break" while they skated the Hokey Pokey. She was excited for him, even as they both silently contemplated what that meant for *their* future.

Julie insisted on arranging their next date by taking Nick into the past. She'd read up about the centennial anniversary of the Mount Lowe Railway and thought a trek into the San Gabriel Mountains to observe it sounded intriguing. "I don't know if you learned about this at school," she said on the drive there, "but it was literally a high-class train into the clouds. I can't get enough of the Parasol Era, except for that whole inequality thing."

They joined a crowd of about two hundred history buffs singing "Nearer My God to Thee," the same ditty sung when Thaddeus Lowe baptized his endeavor. There were nostalgic speeches, including about the former "White City in the Sky," refreshments, and, after twenty minutes, Nick's boredom. They left the pack to stroll over to the crumbling remains of the Alpine Tavern at the end of the railway's terminus. Someone there had sprayed purple graffiti over a rampart with a message they both endorsed: "Dogs are the best fucking humans."

"Finally," Nick said, "some lasting wisdom."

Royo, registering his displeasure about being excluded, also left Nick a message: cooping him up came with consequences. As evidence, there was shredded lettuce on the kitchen floor, from the leftover sub Royo stole from the fridge by negotiating his snout into the door, and tin foil wrappers from the Wrigley's gum he poached from the counter. Nick sniffed the dog's breath for confirmation: definitely minty fresh. In his bedroom were wood shavings he'd apparently spit out after taking Nick's laminated college diploma from a cinderblock shelf to chomp like a Tootsie Pop. For his *coup de grace*, Royo's paws switched on the TV. *Heaven Can Wait*, the Saturday afternoon movie of the week, was airing when he strode in.

Nick, falling for Julie and about to get rich in the San Francisco Bay Area, refrained from any discipline. Soon the two of them were watching the movie, on the couch Royo previously thrashed, and sharing pretzels. "Yeah," Nick commented to him. "Like a second-string quarterback could waltz in like that."

⤙⤙⤙

JULIE FLEW HOME TO Chicago for Thanksgiving weekend while Nick and Fleet stayed in town, promising relatives a Christmastime visit. Nick spent the morning analyzing schematics for his solar generator, trying to hike the energy output. At two in the afternoon, Fleet knocked on Nick's door carrying a Vons grocery bag and a Manila envelope.

Padding in first was Fleet's dog, Sarge, a sweetheart German shepherd who'd flunked out of the US Drug Enforcement Administration for erratic professionalism. At airports, Sarge spent as much time wagging his fluffy tail at little kids and folks in wheelchairs as he did double barking at professional cocaine smugglers. Fleet adopted him because of their connection, and Sarge rewarded Fleet by using his taxpayer-trained snout to alert him to friendly neighborhood Indica dealers. The one who'd sold Fleet his current ganja lived on a leafy, Linda Vista block not far from Mac's old place. Across the street from dealer Roy was an immense, walled-in estate named "Pegfair," where horror-movie director John Carpenter and actress/Playmate Barbi Benton once resided. Scientologists, reportedly, were flirting with buying it.

In the entryway, Fleet showed Nick a forearm bristling with fourteen upright needles. "Go easy on the comedy," he said. "I'm making myself a guinea pig to test if my needles' locations alleviate my sciatica. I'm removing them in ten minutes. They hurt."

"Just goes to prove," Nick said deadpan, "one prick deserves another."

"I'll allow that, only because you're looking and sounding better than you did a month ago. By the way, this was on your doormat. And *no*, it's not from me. Neither was that other funny gizmo."

Fleet handed the Manila envelope and the food to Nick, who took them into the kitchen. On their "Bro-Giving" menu were Cornish game hens, instant stuffing, canned string beans, and a Pie 'N Burger pumpkin-cream confection. Fleet sat down in the living room, where the Thanksgiving football game was on. The Dolphins and Cowboys were tied in an unusual Dallas snowstorm. Sarge and Royo, good buddies themselves, played tug-of-war at his feet.

"Grab me a Bud and we'll spark this twister after I pluck these needles," Fleet called out.

"Perfect," Nick said from the kitchen. "Give me a few minutes while I get dinner started."

Into the oven he slipped the game hens, which he'd rather eat frozen than Hattie's horrifying Tofurkey. Before he got the stuffing and green beans going, he slit the unmarked envelope with a key and fanned the contents across his counter.

Holy time warp. Black-and-white postcards from Pasadena 1913—Clune's Theater, Cawston Ostrich Farm, the bridge, and others—stared back at him in grainy relief. Somebody abolsutely was toying with him, and his leading suspect remained his ex. In thinking about that, Nick neglected to see the jarring photograph tucked under the postcards.

But why sleuth when you're rediscovering yourself?

TRICKS OF THE TONGUE

A S HE DID MOST every morning now, Nick began his day with Egg McMuffins: one for him and one for the dog he nicknamed his "muttenheimer." They tooled around afterward in his '88 Celica, Royo in the passenger seat with his eyes either glued on Nick or his wolfish head out the side window. Fastened onto the roof rack was Nick's prototype, which stored photovoltaic energy from a solar panel in a soda-can-size lithium battery.

Boats used cells like it for emergency power. Nick was using it to reach his potential.

David Loomer deemed his idea "revolutionary." But Nick still considered it experimental, and knew he better identify any flaws before Loomer's experts did. Were the battery and inverter dependable? How much wattage could his panels generate? Another pressing question: would the components blow up over somebody's car on a blazing day?

The only way to know was to drive around testing it on his mirror-topped Toyota, which Nick did an average of forty miles per day. Sometimes he'd take surface streets into surrounding cities—homey Monrovia, gritty El Monte, company-town Burbank—or the bottlenecked Harbor Freeway to downtown LA's Spring Street.

The planet was going to require alternative energy for the masses if you believed in the abstract menace Al Gore continually talked about; Nick certainly did after studying up on global warming.

Week's worth of data collection persuaded him that his detachable generator might just be of benefit. For once, he was proud of himself, and got a kick out of how he'd converted his economy car into a mobile lab. His Lab-boxer had some grievances just the same. The Petco safety harness Nick purchased to strap Royo into the front seat couldn't secure a tubby ferret. The teeth on the buckle were too misaligned to restrain the dog's forward momentum whenever Nick stopped abruptly. A dozen times now, Royo crashed muzzle-first into the plastic-molded glove compartment and every time Royo side-eyed him. Nick might need to jerry-rig the seatbelt.

"Sorry, muttenheimer," Nick said after it happened in front of Pasadena's Central Library, a stolid Renaissance building designed by the prolific Myron Hunt. "That wasn't payback for you mauling my diploma. Honest."

"Just don't get me killed before you wake up. You're not as astute as last time, and that's already a low bar."

Nick did a double take and snorted hearing that impeccably timed line from the radio he forgot he had on, to a classic rock station, a second after lifting Royo back into his seat. Dogs don't sass humans. Deejays do.

Julie almost spit out her angel-hair pasta when Nick told her about it that evening over dinner at the Holly Street Bar and Grill, an expensive, brick-sided restaurant near city hall that might've been a Scottish church in a previous life. Nick, while counting his pennies, was glad to splurge on his Vroman's girl, who gave him a helium buzz whenever they were together. At the valet, she remarked that the leafage drooping from the sides reminded her of something she'd read about how Adolphus and Lillian Busch titled their Pasadena manor "Ivy Wall."

"You're kidding," he said. "They used to name houses back then?"

"More imaginatively than their own children," Julie answered.

Eighteen minutes later, back at Nick's little house in the San Rafael hills, the two were in a Chinese fire drill disrobing each other. One of Julie's dress buttons ripped off. Nick's Topsider thwacked his guitar case.

"You did it," he whispered as he unzipped her skirt and they tumbled onto his painstakingly made bed. "You saw in me what I couldn't see in myself anymore."

Three minutes in, Julie purred, "There, definitely there. X marks the spot."

"Hopefully more G than X," he murmured.

"*Mmmm*," she said a moment later. "Just shift off my leg?"

More grinding, more first-timers' zeal, and on full stomachs no less.

"I'm tingling," Julie said halfway through. "But my right calf's numb. Center yourself."

"I'll try," he said, moving his legs together like a cliff diver.

There was passion and sloppy kisses, all building to a crescendo.

"I need to stop," she said, halting again before their oxytocin payoff. "My leg, it's killing me."

"It's a just cramp," Nick said. "Shake it off."

"I'll try, Mr. Romantic."

They went back at it for another thirty seconds until Julie shoved him over to the side. In the darkness, she leaned up and flung back the sheet to massage a shin still oddly vibrating. When she reached down, her hands encountered long toenails, which they then traced upward to the hot-breathing dog thrusting away on her appendage.

"*Jesus H. Christ, Nick*—I'm not that type of girl," she screeched. "This is disgusting."

"Type?" he said from a blood-diverted brain. Groggily, he stretched across her to turn on his nightstand lamp. Now he saw what she screamed at: the muttenheimer was in bed with them with eyes rolled up in lecherous delirium.

Royo had just cost him carnal juju absent from his life for years.

"*You horndog!*" Nick said. "We share junk food, not women."

He sat up, twisted one of Royo's ears, which made him release Julie's shin, and kicked him backward off the mattress. The fifty-pound animal thudded onto the floor, and before he could shake it off, naked Nick had him by his thick neck. In one motion, he tossed him across the hardwood and out into the living room like an unwanted bag of flour.

He locked the door, trudging back to Julie with blue stones and red checks. "I swear," he said, "I had no idea he'd pull those shenanigans. He must've skulked in when our attentions were elsewhere." Over the next two minutes, Nick repeated "I'm sorry" four times, and added two extra proclamations of disbelief.

Once she cooled down, Julie said she believed his plea he wouldn't condone such depravity. Later she even giggled. "I guess," she said, examining her knee for anything besides light claw marks, "I should be flattered in a super-gross way." Next, she directed Nick from his standing position back on top of her.

"Would it help further," he said after pecking her, "if I mentioned my difficult childhood?"

"Don't press your luck," she said, smile lines curling. Weirdly, her expression flattened for a second. "Question: Would it affect the rest of our night if I admitted just having the strangest sensation?"

"If you're concerned about him, I'll buy you fishing waders for next time."

"No. Not about him. I felt like I've been in this situation before. A déjà vu situation."

"*Déjà vu*?" Nick said with a scoff. "Be logical—though I would like to experience my past from five minutes ago."

They walked out of the bedroom the next morning, goofy smiling after going at it again, discovering Royo sitting in front of the couch, unashamed about his bestial incursion. Nick wagged his finger at him, ready apparently to head to the kitchen to brew coffee when Julie hooked him by the arm.

"His forehead," she said, pointing. "Check out his forehead. The wrinkles, they changed. You compared them to the Atari logo before. But now they're an 'E.' He's not sick, is he?

Nick squinted. "Perfectly health, and obviously frisky. Maybe the E's for egregious. Let's get breakfast. I'm starving."

"You sure? We might miss doggy Wheel of Fortune."

They did. Once the pair drove off, Royo hopped onto the window seat watching them. The lines on his forehead now formed a series of letters that Royo himself just was beginning to understand. Strung together they former an acronym: E-I-T-D-I.

Not that Nick was "awake" enough yet to decode it.

◆◆◆

Western Colorado Boulevard's Egg-Cellent Café in Old Pasadena typified a retail district that'd done a trendy one-eighty. Last decade, portions of it resembled seedy Hollywood with rows of sticky-floored dive bars, pool halls, and T-shirt shops. Today it was resuscitated for yuppies. There was a Sunglass Hut, Victoria's Secret, spas, and Z. Gallerie. Instead of dodging riffraff, people prowled for parking spots, eager to throw their money around.

Egg-Cellent, which described itself as a "cozy breakfast eatery," fit the bill: a stuccoed storefront serving tasty food at highway-robbery prices. The proprietors must've heard the truism that in Pasadena you needed two lifetimes of money for one existence. The only things Egg-Cellent served for free were tasteless jicama as garnishes and vintage photographs of Pasadena from its "Indiana Colony" roots.

But Nick wasn't bellyaching after last night, digging into his fluffy Denver omelet with gusto. Julie cut precise forkfuls of her eggs Florentine while reading a weekly paper whose entire issue was devoted to the upcoming rechristening of the bridge. He took one gander at the cover picture—at the edifice he preferred to remain nameless—and shook his head. Julie was so captivated she couldn't stop reading.

There were sentimental features about the Board of Trade's "motorcars-not-horses" campaign to get it built, its singular curve, and how it loaded the starter pistol for Southern California's automobile industrial complex. Another delved into how its timeless romance still propelled a sub-economy: the oil paintings and lithographs that sold briskly at local art galleries, the charities and businesses that co-opted its arches in promotional literature when Pasadena's rose felt too cliché as a greatest-hits talisman. Hollywood, of course, over-exposed it the most as a backdrop in films, TV shows, and especially ads. Then, too, even the Ford Taurus looked sporty whipping past a grape-bunch lamppost. For location scouts, the bridge was their immortal workhorse.

What Julie, however, found most riveting wasn't the money or the car culture implications. It was the bridge's ghoulish alter ego. More than a hundred people had leapt to their deaths from a structure nearly razed several times to make room for a modern roadway. Folks from all walks of life had committed suicide from its panoramic deck, many during the Great Depression. Bankers and bond traders had jumped. So had housewives and the terminally ill, bible students and distraught mothers.

Over the years, some wondered whether city hall's efforts to stop or at least deter the hopeless from killing themselves rose to the challenge. Initially, with no fencing atop the balustrades, uniformed police were stationed. After further deaths, undercover officers disguised themselves as ice-cream salesman to prevent anyone else from thudding onto the bottom of the ravine. Other methods were attempted, with varying success.

"I can't believe there's been so much bloodshed," Julie said. "It's tragic."

"No kidding," Nick said, trying to focus on his nine-dollar omelet.

"They printed a poem that a cobbler wrote to a judge decades ago after he tried doing himself in. Can I read it to you?"

"I'd rather hear a movie review."

"It's short. He wrote, 'I will not jump off the Colorado bridge to escape from being in the ditch. With California sunshine, mountain views, wine, and beer, the temptation is too great for me to live right here—'"

"Okay, okay. I get it." Nick said, stopping eating. "What *you* might not understand, as an outsider, Julie, is what a spectacularly sore subject that bridge is around town. For many, it's their Bermuda Triangle—where someone they loved disappeared midair forever." He jabbed at his gourmet home fries, wishing they were hash browns. "People who've come across bodies down there suffer their own nightmares."

"You're right. That was insensitive of me."

They didn't speak for five minutes, the first awkward silence of an otherwise blooming romance. Julie, hence, was surprised when Nick cleared his throat.

"Remember at Cameron's when I said I didn't want to hide anything from you? You should know I have my own history there. And to borrow another metaphor, it's my Chernobyl."

"The nuclear reactor?"

"Yeah: where some of my joy melted down. I hate even mentioning it."

"I can see that," Julie said. "Your hands are shaking." She napkined her mouth and pushed her eggs Florentine to the side. Calmly, she added, "If I may, you are aware—"

"Did you just say, 'If I may?' That's so Victorian of you."

"I know. It just slipped out. Anyway, you know that San Francisco is a city of bridges? And that you're going to need to cross the Golden Gate if you relocate there."

"I've been thinking about that. Let me tell you what I have to overcome."

By the time he was a high school senior, Nick explained, he and his associated rowdies had transformed the lightly patrolled area below the bridge into their party central. Many a weekend evening they climbed into the arches of the Foothill Freeway's "Pioneers Bridge," which state engineers designed as a flavorless replication of the nationally famous/locally notorious Colorado Street Bridge due south of it. Their tomfooleries—shotgunned Budweisers, the truth-or-dares with coquettish private-school girls, the reckless tiptoeing around the ledges—all fell within the standard deviation of normal adolescent misbehavior.

As the mood-setter, Nick usually cued up on his boom box the coda to "The Crunge," where Robert Plant asked with funk whether anyone had seen an unspecified—and perplexing—bridge. Nick then would switch the music off, and everybody together would hoot, mantra-like: "That confounded bridge is *here!*"

Soon there was something really confounding. One summer night, amped up on intoxicants and testosterone, he decided he was going to clamber into the Colorado Street Bridge, prove *he* wasn't afraid of the ghosts and supernatural occurrences rumored to occupy it. Impulsively, he squirrel-climbed over the fence and searched for a place to hoist up into its underbelly, which nobody else ever attempted.

"This doesn't end well, does it?" Julie asked.

"Not particularly. When I touched the concrete, I fainted for first time in my life. It blew up from there. Fleet ran to call the paramedics, and they needed to cut through the fencing to reach me. Another buddy, RG, got everybody out of there and hid the contraband. My parents wigged out too. They forced me to visit a therapist after my blood tests came back normal."

"What did he think?"

"That I'd suffered a traumatic flashback to when Mac, my old mentor, was killed at his own bridge accident at Devil's Gate Dam. My father didn't accept that though. Called it a lazy, psychobabble diagnosis. My mother sided with the therapist. They were already on shaky ground, and they argued for days. A month later Dad left, and they divorced. I only speak to him three times a year now."

"That's awful," Julie said. "Though it answers quite a bit."

"Now you know why I'm off the Pasadena-mystique train. And why I'm acrophobic. I don't remember the last time I drove across the bridge. But you're also right. I better face my fears, high as they may be."

Julie dog-eared an article and slid the paper over. "You may have your start," she said. "Read this while I pay the check."

NICK ADJUSTED HIS RAY-BANS in the chilly November sunshine, waiting for the start of the "Arroyo-101 Tour" to begin. In signing up at Julie's urging, he didn't realize the outing was starting near the place he hadn't been back to since the Reagan Administration. Revisiting his decision as he already was, yearning for a rainout as he did, he knew inside this was where his demons needed to be conquered.

There were worse things to be doing on this Sunday afternoon than tolerating three hours of worthless trivia about the bridge and other Upper Arroyo Seco landmarks. He could be stuck with Mark "Donut Man" Stonebreaker inventorying returned merchandise, or still moping after watching his bumbling Trojans lose a heartbreaker to their crosstown rivals yesterday at the LA Memorial Coliseum.

Think ahead, he told himself. David Loomer might be extending him an offer sheet next week. *Just grit your teeth for now.*

Nick's manufactured calm had no sedative effects on Royo. While there were no alleged letters on his forehead anymore, there were clear jitters in his bones since they arrived. Whether it was tugging on his leash or wrapping himself around Nick's Levi-clad legs, he was acting like a high-strung Chihuahua sniffing poison down here.

"Relax, muttenheimer," Nick said. "I'm the one with the issues."

Other attendees dribbled in from the dirt parking lot bracketed between the two hulking structures. The lot itself was east of a new, Mediterranean-style condo complex, part of which nestled under the southern edge of the Colorado Street Bridge. Pasadena's uber-organized preservationists and NIMBY groups tried blocking the project. They were enraged the city would permit a "stucco monstrosity" beneath a historic site. But real estate trumped history and local ecology. Tenants were moving in soon.

Nick eyeballed his fellow attendees. Among them was a pair of slim, middle-aged women in designer jeans and hair bows, and a gawky, Art Garfunkel look-alike reading the tour brochure close to his eyes. Standing beside him was an elderly lady with bird-watching binoculars looped around her saggy neck, and a dark-haired man roughly Nick's age. He wore a personalized Dodgers jersey with his last name embroidered on the back: Scuzzi. He gave off a Mark David Chapman vibe; Nick kept away.

The most fascinating person was a twinkle-eyed, older gent in a classic Led Zeppelin jacket with that winged angel on it. Nick smiled whimsically, knowing it was from the same late-seventies concert tour that he and Fleet sweet-talked their parents into letting them see at the Fabulous Forum, a highlight of their rambunctious youth. The gent approached Nick, all friendly, and Royo's anxiety vanished.

"Love your dog," the man with the clipped gray beard said. "Seems attuned."

"Well, I love your jacket," Nick said. "Let's hope they reunite, only without Phil Collins on drums."

He and Mike Zachriel shook hands. Nick wanted to speak further with him, but a candy-apple-red Porsche 911 came gunning down the winding access road toward the bridge, and skidded to a grandstanding stop. Another five feet and he would've hit the saggy-necked lady.

Before getting out, the driver checked his feathery, chestnut hair in the mirror. Nick, seeing the forty-ish man with wide shoulders and a duplicitous smile, was certain they'd met before. The tour guide curled a finger at the participants to walk toward his Porsche so he didn't have to walk to them. Percy Fixx, in an orange Princeton sweatshirt, introduced himself, and then exclaimed, "Now who's ready for a trip into yesteryear?"

The hands that people were blowing on waiting for him in the cold temperatures rose. Percy was ten minutes late.

"We'd need a three-day weekend to fit everything in, but we'll give it a whirl," he began. He said he volunteered for this assignment out of "sheer passion for Pasadena's unparalleled history." What he didn't disclose? Doing this was part of his community service obligation for a pled-down stock-trading misdemeanor.

Percy passed around nametags and a Sharpie. While people wrote, he announced, "We'll start with this beaut above our heads, move on to the federal courthouse up the bank, where the old hotel Arroyo del Vista and a boardinghouse for sick children was before that. Next, we'll walk the trail to the Rose Bowl, and, time permitting, get to Devil's Gate. Shame Busch Gardens isn't around anymore. But you can't build subdivisions on unicorns, can you?"

"Good thing Joni Mitchell isn't here to respond," Mike said in his smooth, basso voice.

Percy appeared ready with a zinger; he didn't say anything, though, after viewing who needled him.

"Ordinarily, we'd talk on the deck. As you must've noticed from all the scaffolds and such, the city is still readying her for the grand reopening. Yours truly, I'm honored to say, will be speaking that day. We have some *other* illustrious guests lined up, too. Any comments?"

A split second after Percy asked that, Royo let rip a pretty extended dog fart; Egg McMuffins will do that. A collective snickering that excluded Percy followed. Trying to regain command, he looked down at his note card and said, "Call the bridge Pasadena's Panama Canal. Just don't call her average."

Three hours of this joker? Nick shuffled his feet, feeling his legs mildly quivering.

"Citizens approved a hundred thousand dollars for her in spring 1912," Percy said. "The job came in on time and under budget, as well choreographed as Operation Desert Storm."

An ectomorph Asian woman in a JPL hat lofted her hand. "Can you address the ghost stories and suicides? What has the city done to—?"

"Sure," Percy said, cutting her off. "When I finish my remarks. She's fifteen hundred feet long, built from ten thousand tons of concrete. Nobody had ever constructed such a handsome structure over such a dangerous gorge before. The two men in charge, John Mercereau and John Waddell, collaborated to change that. What a masterpiece."

Something, however, about Percy's last words jolted Nick out of the peculiar headspace, neither agitated nor distracted, from which he tried biding his time. It was as though he'd stuck his pinkie in a live socket, or gotten shocked by full-body static electricity. While Percy droned on about weight loads and spandrel columns, Nick popped in a stick of Wrigley's to center himself. Royo jumped up on him for his own piece; Nick jerked his head no.

"One last factoid. Visitors frequently inquire why she curves like a lazy S, if it's for the aesthetics. The answer is that a straight bridge would've sunk footings into unpredictable soil, and increased the length and costs. Together, Messrs Waddell and Mercereau outfoxed the terrain."

"Yeah, and who needs facts when you can spew misstatements and myths?" Nick said—if he'd said it. He marveled at whether the words springboarded from his own mouth or an alternative him.

Everyone stared his direction. Royo, in his finest Scooby-Doo, said *Ruh-Roooooo.*

"Excuse me. Are you accusing me of lying, or merely getting my facts wrong?" Percy said, glaring at his questioner's nametag. "In any event, enlighten us, *Ni-ck.*"

Again, as though it was emanating from another organism, he answered. "There's a lot more to that curve than what fits on your note card, *Per-cy*. Like how the early millionaires with homes on the cliffs applied pressure so the bridge didn't impede their mountain views. While we're at it, citizens voted in 1911, not 1912.

"Is that so?" Percy said.

"Yes. And Waddell was anything but gratified in his dealings with the city. After it altered his plans, he boycotted the opening." *Where's this coming from?*

Percy knifed through the startled group, striding up to Nick, whose unsolicited corrections had drenched Tabasco over a stock tour. "Okay, I'll play along," the beady-eyed tour guide said; the man wore enough Polo aftershave to trigger a smog alert. "Makes for robust debate. What's your source? A secret book, a dissertation, a fortune cookie?" Percy finally extracted a group laugh with that one.

"I grew up here, so I must've recalled the facts from somewhere."

Nobody on the Arroyo-101 outing was visualizing the next stops anymore. The Rose Bowl's inaugural game: who cared? Tales of how Jack Parsons & Company tried summoning Lucifer's moon child could wait. Everyone squeezed in around Nick and Percy like they were about to trade punches in a grade-school brawl.

"Here's two facts for you," Percy said. "If the minorities have their druthers, Jesse Jackson will be the next Tournament of Roses grand marshal—and your dog has a fat ass."

"Better," Nick said a foot away, "a chunky dog than a smarmy know-nothing."

Percy nodded and retreated a step-in outward de-escalation. "Okay, Nick. I'll cede the floor so you can school us."

Alternative Nick emerged further. "Thanks. I will. On August first, 1913, bad framing caused part of one of the arches to collapse. Three men fell to their deaths, and eight more hung for their lives. After the tragedy, no one went to jail or paid a fine. *Ooh*, and I just remembered how the city exploited that to acquire its westside."

"And to think I wasted two lunch breaks boning up," Percy said, getting the designer-jean women to smirk.

"Did you read then about construction workers who claimed the bridge creaked and shook for no reason, or animals petrified to get near it?" Nick said. "Or that the project actually wasn't on deadline. It was delayed multiple times, the last by a bloodbath." *Am I channeling an encyclopedia?*

Percy now shook his head as if he were hearing about an apocryphal Yeti. "What I'm reciting is from the books," he said, eyes veering between Nick and Royo, who growled whenever he spoke.

"I'm not doubting that," Alternative Nick said. "I'm suggesting those books were written in revisionist ink. Lastly, not to nitpick, the job consumed eleven thousand cubic yards of concrete."

Percy was tiring of this exchange. "Unless we have a history PhD among us," he said, "let's push on. I'm just a simple volunteer with an Ivy League education."

The confused bunch started walking away, believing détente was reached. But when it was only the two of them, Percy leaned toward Nick.

"How dare you humiliate me like that? Where do you think you are? West Covina?" He then looked up at the bridge and winked, saying in a normal tone for the benefit of any lingering ears, "When you get down to it, it's only molded concrete. Now, on to the Rose Bowl, granddaddy of 'em all."

Percy jogged past Nick and his snarling dog, trotting to get in the front of the others on his new Nike Air Trainers. Nick watched the entourage wind toward a trail, though he didn't notice the Zep-loving gent among them.

"Okay, boy," Nick said, tousling his ears. "Let's go home and split a grilled cheese. If I stay down here any longer, I'll be speaking in tongues."

THE ROCK STAR OF SUNNY SLOPE MANOR

Nick needed to lean in to hear Fleet speak over the juggernaut of campy iconoclasm rumbling past. Like Santa Claus, the Doo Dah Parade had come to town. After it departed, the world felt colorless again.

"You have no explanation?" Fleet said in a quarter shout. "You just opened your mouth and out pours dusty trivia, about a bridge that still gives you the willies?"

Nick and Fleet, here for their third year running, stood in front of a mishmash of fellow spectators, which ranged from families hungry for free weekend entertainment to hung-over Generation-Xers to aging hippies in denim jackets, one with an "Impeach Everyone" patch on it. A calm Royo surveyed the mobile carnival from Nick's kneecap.

"Yeah, pretty much," Nick said over the piped-in music and group incantations. "I'm trying not to get too worked up about it."

The performers in outlandish getups juxtaposed against the ashen skies and fizzy drizzle on the mid-city street. Some cheapskates donned black trash bags as raincoats.

"I detest saying this as an Eastern medicine man," Fleet said as a performer in a squirrel costume breezed by, "but you could use an MRI and a good neurologist."

"Really?" Nick said, tensing up.

A kinetic clown, wearing a sash reading "Komikal Knight: Pasadena Delight" over a traditional holiday nutcracker jacket, skipped past next.

"Relax," Fleet said after acknowledging the clown. "I'm kidding. You said it yourself: you probably learned everything you blurted in a civics class and catacombed it. When you returned to where you had your, um, incident, it pierced a neural network. Revenge of the hippocampus, I'd say. You're fine. That'll be two hundred dollars."

Past them now wheeled a Ford Pinto float, whose sign read, "The afterlife's a fender bender away." Satirizing the wholesome, and highly corporate Rose Parade, as the Doo Dah Parade did, was never dull. It was bawdy, tactless, and amazing.

"Why am I asking someone who practices biofeedback on unsuspecting shoppers at Bullocks?"

"Because you know I'm right."

"And it pains me when you are."

The next act was one for their suds-loving hearts: a top-heavy woman twirling a baton in a spray-on Budweiser label. Marching behind her were fan favorites: members of the Church of the Ornamental Lawn Decorations, the drag queens of The West Hollywood Cheerleaders, and The Synchronized Precision Marching Briefcase Drill Team.

You wouldn't find this grade-A establishment-skewering at Pasadena's best comedy club, the Icehouse, nor certainly at the blue-blood Valley Hunt Club, whose parking lot no Hyundai would dare enter. Fleet's shit-eating grin said it all. Even more cynical than Nick, he likened Pasadena to a starlet who read so many of her own press clippings she refused to purchase Glade for her powder room.

When Snotty Scotty and the Hankies, a popular, local party band, rolled up on a flatbed, jamming out a live rendition of "96 Tears," Nick was so relieved he didn't require a slide into an MRI tube that he hollered, "Scotty: we want Zep!"

"At least Stairway to Freebird," Fleet chimed in.

A few acts later came a special float timed for this particular year. Assembled from papier-mâché and covered in Reynolds Wrap to mimic its gray exterior, the scale-model Colorado Street Bridge rested on top of a roofless golf cart. A man in a chauffeur's get-up and gas mask steered it. A banner duct-taped to the side lampooned its role with the city's murky reputation: "Pasadena: the finest air you can chew: 1913–1993."

Nick and Fleet grinned at each other, trying to think of something glib to bellow, when their expressions deviated from jolly to dazed. Unexpectedly, Royo had charged into the street, ripping his leash out of Nick's forgetful hand, and toward the float. In one bound, he leapt onto the back of the cart and began shredding one of the "arches" with his teeth. The crowd mistook it for staged mayhem, clapping and cheering as raucously as they had for the Briefcase Drill Team. The float driver wasn't amused. He pivoted around and screamed, "Get down, you vandal!"

Next thing anybody knew, Royo had a slash of tin foil in his chops while two peeved cops dragged him off, possibly to Mirandize him.

◆◆◆

FOR DECADES, HUNTINGTON MEMORIAL Hospital was Pasadena's own Bedford Falls: a place where generations of locals did their "living and dying." In an extension behind its statehouse-esque building on California Boulevard was a nursery that pulsated with the wails of new arrivals, many bound for privileged childhoods. The basement morgue below held long-timers, a number of whom personified a civic ethos dedicated to social justice, the arts, and clustering liquor stores in the "distressed neighborhoods."

But the new millennium would usher in major changes at the venerable Old World Huntington. A post-overhaul rendering depicting a boxy, multi-tower configuration had drawn comparisons, particularly by wiseasses named Nick and Fleet, to a supersized Embassy Suites daubed in a shade of crepe-pink unfound in nature.

Where time remained frozen was the dated, tumbledown world behind the hospital. There, off Fair Oaks Avenue, set back from the smoked-glass medical buildings and dialysis centers, was a tangle of assisted-living "facilities." If you were a mortician, this was a lucrative quadrant to troll.

Today, Nick was at the end of a cul-de-sac on one of these blocks, inside the ironically named Sunny Slope Manor. His goal: keeping his criminal record clean on the cusp of leaving town. It might not have been, either, had a particular judge not been at the Doo Dah Parade—a judge who convinced the officers who detained Royo to spare Nick from being charged with disorderly conduct and destruction of private property. The judge, Cecil "Charles" Jenks, offered an altruistic compromise.

The Pasadena Humane Society, fresh off a four-million-dollar-plus remodel/expansion that added microclimate misting systems, walk-in showers, and towel-padded cages for its animals, was partnering with city hall on a new initiative. It dispatched dogs from there and elsewhere to nursing homes and assisted-living complexes to comfort the lonely and depressed. The research was incontrovertible about this sort of dog-for-the-day program. People receiving it, be it seniors or hardened prison inmates, exhibited improved health and better attitudes afterward.

On the mushroom-colored, industrial carpeting outside Room 118, Nick exhaled before he plunged in. "Don't go rogue on me again," he said without looking at Royo. He might've listened, too, had he not been lapping up a slab of uneaten Salisbury steak on a tray outside an adjoining room. Nick jerked his leash to stop him. Down the hall in the recreation room, you could hear the commotion from eleven other dogs, including an Airedale Terrier and Basset Hound barking in excitement about all these wrinkly people that smelled of Xanax and BenGay.

Before he knocked, Nick recalled his briefing from the orderly about the man he'd be visiting—the man known as Sunny Slope's "crankosaurus." "He's not a happy camper," attendant Wally Northcutt said. "I'd tread carefully."

Nick rapped on the door and waited.

"Come in," a reedy voice finally answered. "Let's get this over with."

"Great minds think alike," Nick muttered to Royo, cracking the wheelchair-accessible door.

A lanky old man in a burgundy tracksuit was gripping a walker at the far side of the room. He was staring out the window at the entrance of a nearby, subterranean garage, which swallowed cars like a concrete mouth at two bucks an hour.

"Sir, I'm Nick Chance. I have my dog, Royo, with me. He's a rascal but generally charming. We're glad to meet you."

"Whoop-de-do," he said as Grandpa Simpson might've. "Everybody's glad."

"Should we sit down to chat?"

"Whatever the rigmarole calls for."

It took the old man a full minute to hobble over on his walker to a worn, green Barcalounger. He crash-landed into the deteriorating leather, grunting "*oomph.*"

Nick went to fetch a visitor's chair. When he turned, Royo rushed toward the geezer, wiggling between his legs and pleading for attention.

"Hey," the crankosaurus. "Control your pest or I'll swat him."

Nick twirled around, reeling Royo in by his leash. "Apologies. I'll keep a tighter rein."

He sat down while his host fiddled with the volume buttons on his hearing aids. From there his brittle fingers dipped into the crevices of his chair to pluck out his eyeglasses. Watching him fumble made Nick not want to live to eighty-nine. He wondered whether the man's prickliness was innate, or the byproduct of his Medicare-funded purgatory? In his prime, though, he must've been something—six foot two, piercing baby-blues, square jaw. He still had most of his hair, snowy as it was.

"Can I help you with anything?"

"*No,*" he said gruffly. "Just because I wear a diaper doesn't mean I'm an infant. What do we do now, Dick? Twiddle our thumbs?"

"It's Nick, sir. Nick and Royo." The codger must've misheard his name before he toggled his hearing aids. "Wally mentioned you owned a hat store for thirty-five years, and that you had famous clientele. He also said you traveled the globe: South Pole, Africa, India. You must have stories about that."

"I did, when I could remember who I was. Old age is real a chuckle-fest, young fella."

"Do you have family nearby?"

"They're spread out. Now, cut the questions! I thought today was about dogs. Let him over."

Nick slackened the leash, and Royo, again, burst toward the space between the man's emaciated, track-suited legs.

"A million years ago, I used to have a pooch. That I do know. He was a mutt like yours. Called him Verne. You know, for Jules Verne. What an operator. Buddied up to every butcher in town for scraps."

For whatever reason, Royo tugged forward, resting his chin on the man's right leg. He whimpered *mmm-mmmm* and the man slowly kneaded his ears.

"Hey, whatever your name is. Clean my glasses with a tissue over there so I can see you too."

Yes, my lord. Nick took his black Where's-Waldo glasses smudged with dandruff and ear crust and wiped them with a Kleenex from the bedside table. He then put them back in the old man's blotchy hands.

"Much better," he said after snugging them on. "What kind of dog is he?"

"Boxer-Lab, I think. Has the appetite of Arnold the Pig and the libido of a Kennedy. He tried jumping a schnauzer in your lobby when we came in."

Royo could handle the mockery. He understood *who* was petting him.

"What do you do for work, when you're not stalking fossils like me?"

"I used to be a product engineer at Wham-O. You know, the Hula Hoop-Frisbee people. I'm a solar-energy inventor now."

"Solar, eh, that pipe dream? I thought Ronny R. killed that."

Thank you, Doo Dah Parade. "Were you born here?"

He scowled as if he were in a hostile deposition. "You're relentless with the questions. But, yep, I was. Back when cars were first entering the picture. They say I'm the oldest living native, if you call this living."

Nick, again, ignored the elder rage. "Born and bred here myself, too, though I'm probably moving to the San Francisco area for work."

"What, Pasadena not good enough for ya? Best small city in America, warts and all, I say."

Nick fidgeted in his chair. He'd been here seven minutes.

"Calm down. Just grinding your beans. So what's our game here? Do I keep stroking him until the nurses browbeat me into movie night with the other stiffs?"

"If you want entertainment, Royo chews gum," Nick said. "Got any Wrigley's?"

"How should I know? Check my dresser."

Nick dropped the leash, trusting Royo would behave, and walked toward the wall, where a beautiful mahogany cabinet from the old man's bygone life sat. On top were prescription pill bottles, hearing aid batteries, an ivory shoehorn, a chipped Rose Parade pin, and a nickel-plated pocketknife with the word "Cawston" on the side; just no gum.

There were, nonetheless, artifacts to explore. Nick's eyes gravitated toward the corkboard above the dresser, where someone tacked up a collection of photographs. One was of a woman with auburn hair, loving eyes, and a tender smile: must've been his wife. Another, Nick assumed, was of their son and daughter splashing at the beach, and one, in black and white, of the sourpuss in knee pants gripping an ice-cream cone. There he was again as an Army clerk and then, years later, in a sharp tuxedo accepting a proclamation from Pasadena's Brylcreemed mayor as "1978's Businessman of the Year."

Nick's eyes loop-de-looped the corkboard, seeing other photos of him in his haberdashery posing with Dudley Moore, Richard Branson, even a youngish, jug-eared Prince Charles. He was about to return to his torture chair when a less staged shot popped out at him. In this one, his host was a vigorous sixty-something with his arm slung around the neck of a smiling longhair with a bronzed chest opened at the second paisley button.

Misty mountain wow! The codger knew the front man of the world's greatest band.

"Excuse me," Nick said. "Was Robert Plant a customer? I'm thinking throwback fedora for the 'In Through the Out Door' album cover."

"Naw," he said. "My nephew didn't go much for hats, or any formalwear."

"But, but—you're his uncle?" Nick sputtered. "Honest? And he's been to Pasadena? I'm speechless. I'm a lifelong Zep-head. Their music's in my blood."

The old man retracted his fangs. Slightly. "Sweet lad, that Robert. Bookworm, too, He visited in disguise. You know how it gets with women and fans. Somebody always wanting something."

"How could *you* be his uncle when you're from here and he grew up in the middle of England? That's where Zep's bio said he's from. 'Hammer of the Gods' is my bible."

"My kid sister moved back to the UK in the twenties. Loved the cold weather. Said rain was her song. Personally, I never much liked the racket Robert and the other three fellas made. Except for, what was it called? 'Going to Scandinavia'?"

"'Going to California.' Geez, I have so many questions. What does it mean finding a bustle in your hedgerow? Is Jimmy Page's house really haunted because of the Aleister Crowley nonsense?" He took a breath and reloaded. "Most importantly, are they gonna tour again? I can write these down so you can phone him."

Nick had forgotten all about Royo's gum trick. The old man was enraptured, too, but it had nothing to do with his rock star nephew. Glasses clean, he now had an unhindered view of Nick from the reflection in his dresser mirror. His jaw was now bouncing like a creaky marionette.

"Sonny. If I can interrupt your hero worship, my watch slipped into the cushion; mind retrieving it?"

Nick glided close, dying to tack on another question: why his nephew had to ruin a song by asking about "that confounded bridge?" He bent over the geezer, sinking his hand into the side of the dingy Barcalounger.

And that's when the old man's bony hands made their move, snatching Nick by the collar. He tugged him near enough for Nick to whiff the bran muffin on his breath. "I know you," he said inches away. "You're Nick Chance!"

Nick couldn't pull away from the suprisingly strong grip. "I know. Can you let me go?"

He wouldn't: he'd been energized. Restored. "You're not getting it. This isn't *our* first meeting. No siree, bub. I'd bet every Homburg still in existence on that. Don't you remember me? Look past the liver spots. The name Reginald Plant doesn't sound familiar?"

Wally never mentioned his dementia was this advanced. Nick broke loose while Royo remained where he was. The old man was beaming, as Nick would've been had Robert Plant's uncle dialed his nephew in England stopped imagining ghosts in Pasadena.

"Mr. Plant. Not to disappoint you, but you're confusing me for someone else."

"Call me Reginald. You did before. Oh, more's flooding back. We met the day you were on top of Mrs. Grover Cleveland in the Arroyo. Nineteen twelve, I think."

If I ever get senile, I'm outta here. "This is lunacy. You think I had sex with a dead first lady. Your medication is making you hallucinate."

"No, my medication is making me constipated. Nick and Royo, back together again," he said. "Ain't that a kick in the pants! Mrs. Cleveland was an ostrich, Nick. I spooked her when I raced down the hill so you'd let me ride her. Yeah, yeah, that's it. She took off like a bat out of hell, and you almost ate crap. The bridge was being built then, and you were watching it through a little telescope. Jesus, were *you* were enamored with that bridge. I was your little buddy. You even have the same cowlick."

"Please. I'm not Dorian Gray," Nick said, backpedaling toward the dresser that instigated all this. "I'm from Generation X. Born in '66. What day is today?"

"You can't fool me. It's Salisbury steak day. You've returned so I can die and know I will return, too. God, you trickster, you."

Nick felt queasy listening to this, and even more so watching Royo attempt to jump up onto Reginald's lap to lick his craggy face.

Then it was salvation by smoke alarm. A blaring, jarring series of *beep-beep-beeps* erupted from Sunny Slope's Manor hallway speaker. The fire alarm bell was going off. In seconds, there were footfalls in the hallway while Wally and the other orderlies followed emergency protocol in case this wasn't a drill. And with all those weak bodies and flammable oxygen canisters around, it better not be.

From the speaker, someone announced, "All guests: please exit through the front doors. Don't bother cleaning up if your pets have had accidents. We buy disinfectant in bulk. To our residents, remain calm. We know what we're doing."

Beep-beep-beep. Flickers from the strobe lights flashing in the hallway spilled under Reginald's door.

"You heard the announcement, Mr. Plant," Nick said, so grateful for the fire alarm he wished he'd set it off himself. "Have a doctor check you out. Let's boogie, boy."

Nick yanked hard on Royo's leash to go, only to have the dog bristle against it before relenting.

"Until we met again, old friend," Reginald said with a jaunty wave. "Or should I say, ostrich man."

HUMAN THERMOSTATS

A T THEIR ROMANTIC TABLE set with a breadbasket wafting rosemary and pumpernickel, Julie had a rudimentary question. "Is everything all right?"

"Never better," Nick said. "Let's order the pork bellies. They're killer here."

It was days before the Colorado Street Bridge's relaunching, and Nick was tired of its weirdness glomming onto him like flypaper. As such, he still hadn't told her or Fleet much about the old man at the Sunny Slope Manor; only that he'd fulfilled his unofficial community service and met Robert Plant's addled uncle in the process.

"Sure," she said of the pork bellies. "But what was so fascinating about that decrepit, yellow building back there? If it weren't for the guy in the Nissan truck blaring his horn at you at the stoplight, you'd still be staring at it."

"Beats me," Nick said with a shrug. "I never paid the dump much attention before." (Said "dump" was the long-vacant, twice-built Pacific Electric Red Car maintenance barn in the shadow of Pasadena's power plant; it rested a block north.) "The preservationists must've kept on the warpath about it, whatever the thing was."

"Your city does treasure its past. But that wasn't much of an explanation."

"Can't a fella be distracted from time to time?"

In their corner booth of the Craftsman-y Raymond Restaurant on south Fair Oaks Avenue, they were talking history in a piece of it. The bistro was once the caretaker's cottage on the grounds of the original Raymond Hotel, which folded during the Depression. With its quaint ambience, wood décor, and vintage photos, including one snapped by A. C. Vroman, the turn-of-the-century breathed here.

"Speaking of history, Nick, I have something to discuss. You know I've been spending hours at the Huntington Library when I'm not at work, or with you, rooting through archives about that gruesome Ohio train wreck of 1876."

"Course. You called it a Greek tragedy begging to be written," Nick said, breaking off some pumpernickel. "Then you fell in love with Busch Gardens. And me. See? I'm not that spaced out."

"The gardens weren't just a paradise. They were a morality tale. I literally cringed reading about what befell Lillian Busch on her way back to Pasadena from Germany after World War I. Here's this aging baroness, who'd opened her park to orphans and veterans, donated money all over, and what did US customs agents do? They conducted a full-body cavity search of her. Asked her if she was spying for the Kaiser. Then, Busch Gardens later gets blacktopped over."

"There's your story. Smell dem roses, chamber of commerce."

"Well, right city, different location. The better morality tale is about the bridge. That's what I need to write about."

Nick's pallor blanched. "Need? Tell me I misheard you. Or that you're joking."

"I can't. And I'm not."

Nick slugged off his Budweiser. "Have you forgotten my Chernobyl analogy? How that bridge is radioactive for me?"

"Hear me out," Julie said. "If you leave Pasadena, it won't be a problem. If you stay, which I dearly hope you will, I'll help you confront your phobia. You're following your heart with your idea. I'm following mine."

The waitress approached, interrupting Julie's bid to grab Nick's hand and Nick leaning away. They ordered pork bellies, entrees, and more alcohol. Julie got a second chardonnay. Nick switched from beer to Tanqueray-rocks.

Because he'd swooned for Julie, he compelled himself to listen to her, already knowing he'd never bless any book on that confounded bridge. Anyway, she ran through what she'd excavated; how the stylish pathway was the city's greatest feat—a concrete foyer that elicited investment, skyrocketed car sales, and inspired engineers. She teased its dicey politics and dramatic collapse, some of which had flown out of Alternative Nick on the Arroyo 101 tour. She talked about the paranormal connections, including the tawdriest rumor of them all: that the ghost of a construction worker, who'd been inadvertently cut to shreds and poured into in a concrete beam, still haunted the deck in his suspenders.

"Captivating," Nick said when she took a breath. "Now, for God's sake, reconsider. Please."

"Couldn't I ask the same of you?"

Their decibel level gradually went up, at one point almost extinguishing the candle.

"I suppose you'll include the darkest stuff, too," Nick said.

"What choice do I have? Everyone in Los Angeles refers to it as Suicide Bridge."

Their drinks and pork bellies arrived, and then their entrees, all of which gave Nick time to reframe his argument to make her drop this. "Julie, you do have a choice, a good one. You can write about Busch Gardens instead of Pasadena's death zone."

She took a bite of salmon and responded. "I'm not planning to sensationalize anything, and that's assuming I can land a publishing deal. But this bridge *is* a worthy subject, and the people who died off of it warrant more than a paragraph in a coffee-table book. Did you know the city once explored installing nets along the sides? Or that sticks of dynamite were found below an arch?"

"No," Nick said, getting a piece of roast duck into a nervous stomach. "And I don't care. I have news to share with you too."

"And I can't want to hear it. Just five more minutes."

"This is our tenth date. You're spoiling it."

"What should I say? 'You're right. Now let's go do it at the top of your playground rocket ship'?"

"And they accuse me of being flippant. But yes, and yes." He rolled his hand in a get-on-with-it gesture next.

"You want to know one reason I feel so strongly about the subject? Let me introduce you to Myrtle Ward."

Myrtle, Julie said, was a young mother and wife crestfallen about losing her cafeteria job and about the shape of the world circa 1937. Deciding to leave the latter behind, she put her three-year-old daughter in the car and drove to Pasadena. After parking, she and Jean walked out to one of the bridge's pedestrian alcoves. When Myrtle lifted her daughter over the balustrade, two people watching them hollered, "No!" But disturbed Myrtle went through with the unthinkable, dropping the child one hundred forty-three feet. Seconds later, Myrtle jumped in the attempted murder-suicide to alleviate her pain.

Only Jean didn't die. She pinballed into the brambles of a tree and survived the normally lethal fall. Bruised, still wearing the name tag that her mother pinned on her dress for identification purposes, she crawled toward a corpse, crying, "Mommy, Mommy."

Pasadena, afterward, was mortified, and soon there was wire-mesh fencing that rose up about eight feet along the rim to prevent any repeats. City hall wanted reporters, who it blamed for embellishing the macabre, to now write about something other than Suicide Bridge. On the one-year anniversary of the tragedy, Pasadena highlighted its response while indirectly ridiculing critics accusing it of moving too slowly. Actors were hired to reenact Myrtle attempting to throw her daughter to her death, but this time her unspeakable crime was averted by that life-saving fence.

Whether or not that recreation sparked more bad karma, the suicides continued, though not as frequently. Newspaper magnate William Randolph Hearst supposedly offered to pony up the money for a stronger barrier. The city rebuffed him.

"I'm sure of all it, minus the Hearst story," Julie said. "Pasadena by then had a reputation for sophistication and Millionaire's Row, and also as the best locale in Southern California to die. Now I'm finished."

Nick was no longer interested in any of this fine cuisine. In the flattest of tones, he said, "David Loomer, my Silicon Valley investor, presented me an offer sheet."

"Oh, Nick," Julie said with appropriate zeal, "That's wonderful. You did it!"

"He's paying me one hundred fifty thousand dollars just to allow his engineers to improve my prototype. They're renting me an apartment near their office. If we go into production, a Japanese automaker might subsidize it."

"I should've let you talk first. Nothing I said was urgent. What are you going to do?"

"Leave. What else? I was intending to ask you to come with me. I still will, if you—"

Julie's eyes widened; her smiles lines retreated. "If I what? Abandon a book about the bridge? That smells like an ultimatum?"

"I may be burned out on Pasadena hype, but I'd never dream of picking at people's deepest scabs. The ambition isn't worth it."

"I suppose you avoid true crime books, then; even ones that try fostering debate."

Nick slapped his hand on the table, bouncing Julie's salmon. Diners swiveled their heads; hostesses stood guard. "You know, I think I'll fly to your hometown for a few weekends to write about Chicago's murder rate, or the old meatpacking factories that killed people. Worked for Upton Sinclair."

Julie snatched her purse, got up, and loomed over the table with half the restaurant eavesdropping. How often does a couple, where the woman resembles a pointy-chinned Jodie Foster and the man a cowlicked Dr. Pepper guy, squabble louder than the wild green parrots that'd returned to Pasadena after decades?

Noticing they'd created a ruckus, she lowered her voice. "When we met, I felt such a charge. Now I realize that it was infatuation. Hattie was wrong. It's not that your dimmer is set too low. It came out of the factory defective. Don't come into Vroman's when I'm in. And *I'm* writing that damn book."

She hustled out, regretting she hadn't ground a pork belly into Nick's face.

🙢🙢🙢

WHETHER IT WAS HIS angst around the moving boxes, or the dusty Hot Pocket he ate after extracting it from under the couch, Royo wasn't acting himself. Over three days' time, he lost interest in the food bowl he'd normally push around the kitchen floor trying to dab every crumb. Flecks of gray also were cropping up in his black muzzle. Then there was the change in peculiarities. On walks, he no longer stopped to smack his lips on exotic flowers. Nor did he fake a limp anymore to trick passerby into coddling him.

Nick took him to the Foothill Veterinary Hospital the day after his breakup with Julie—a severing, he deluded himself, made splitting town that much easier. The vet diagnosed nothing wrong. He speculated the intelligent dog must've sensed change brewing and recommended Nick continue monitoring him and unpack his favorite toy. When Nick pulled out the tug-of-war rope, Royo disregarded it.

Still alarmed, he summoned his muttenheimer up on the sofa for a heart-to-heart. He assured him that *they'd* never split. The Bay Area's green spaces exceeded Brookside Park's, he added, and the junk food was just as plentiful, as were the promiscuous lady schnauzers. Royo listened. Then he bounded down to pant in the corner.

When Fleet drove over, Nick had to think more human. Fleet was helping him tie up loose ends from his pell-mell relocation (utility shut-offs, mail-forwarding, etc.) and agreed to sell his furniture and other leftover possessions at the next Rose Bowl flea market. Nick wanted the house on the market and his Toyota unloaded ASAP.

"You have my eternal thanks for doing this," he said. "You're getting a solar generator."

"I'd rather have cold cash and Robert Plant's autograph," Fleet replied with a smirk. "But if you promise to visit for the next Doo Dah Parade, that'll suffice."

"As long as Royo's not on a wanted poster, I'll consider that."

After sipping goodbye Budweisers and splitting a farewell joint, they walked into the cleaned-out kitchen. Nick then microwaved the Sara Lee Butter Streusel Coffee Cake that he'd been reserving in his freezer's tundra for this bittersweet occasion. Reenacting what they did at two in the morning after their junior-year prom, Nick sliced the pie in two and they scarfed it, bowing again to the tyranny of the munchies.

Laidback Fleet turned serious after his last buttery mouthful. "Dude," he said, "are you sure, really sure about doing this? Your imagination is humming now. There must be a local investor you could snag. People don't usually leave Pasadena. Not unless they go feet first."

"I am. This is what Mac would've wanted want me to do."

Fleet, even with that Viking blood of his, wiped a tear. "Mac. I haven't thought of him in years. What was that broken-record saying of his?"

"To have something meaningful for your tombstone. Mine can't be the HoJack."

"Yeah, that'd be a waste. Though, I thought the HoJack had potential."

"Don't get mad at me for being a broken record myself, okay? Reassure me again it wasn't you who dropped that gadget and Manila envelope on my doorstep to screw with me?"

Fleet shook his head. "I swear on my acupuncture needles—and our friendship. It must've been you-know-who. There's no scorn like an angry vegan's."

"*Phew*. Don't forget. Southwest has forty-nine-dollar flights to SFO. Now get over here."

They embraced in a protracted bro hug, and Nick walked Fleet to his car. As he did, Royo scampered out the doggy door and whimpered, head upturned to the stars.

WHEN A DECK BECKONS

THE WINDOW-SHAKING COMMOTION JUDDERING him awake was reminiscent of his college years, when whirling Los Angeles police helicopters and car alarms stole shut-eye from him before a big test. This was like that, except that it was TV-news aircraft over the bridge and a virtual Elks Lodge gathering of parrots in his backyard lemon tree doing it.

Nick yawned from his sleeping bag, cotton-mouthed from last night's revelry with Fleet. Up next to him popped Royo, whose slate muzzle and lengthening whiskers gave him a kind of doggy Fu Manchu mustache.

"What did the man say about today being the first day of the rest of our lives?" Nick said, tousling Royo's ears and yawning again. "Apt for us."

Royo got to his feet on a day he'd been trembling about, a day the graybeard from the Arroyo 101 tour told him, via brainwave, would make history without telling him how. Nick had no inkling what awaited them, or that he'd just quoted a cult demagogue who'd ordered a rattlesnake snuck into an adversary's mailbox. He watched Royo perform a full-body shake, and listened to its sound ricochet through the soon-to-be deserted house.

It was only about five hours ago he finished packing his three suitcases and bubble wrapping the vintage projector. The machine was ingenious. You just positioned it so the mirrors reflected the sun's heat into the glass and earthenware base and it'd project images against the evening sky. After experimenting with it last week in his backyard, he decided he'd bring it with him up north. It might be scalable for environmentalists, or as a collector's item.

Breakfast would be instant coffee and a Pop-Tart for him, and yesterday's leftover burrito, from Lucky Boy on Arroyo Seco Parkway, for Royo, provided his appetite resurfaced. The dog needed something in his belly before Nick sedated him with a Snausage-wrapped Benadryl and put him into a cage bound for the plane's cargo hold.

Only piddling chores remained until his airport limo rolled up this afternoon. Nick had saved one task for its symbolism too: sweeping up the last of the Styrofoam pellets sent flying when Hattie slashed his bean bag. He had a broom and dustbin in his hands when the phone set to disconnect at midnight jangled. Nick hoped it was David Loomer, calling to announce he was throwing him a welcome party. Or that it was Fleet, home early from his class on ionic detoxification footbaths. It was neither.

"Mr. Chance: Captain Rick Crum here, Pasadena PD. You have a moment?"

"If this is about the light I shined over my house, that was a one-time deal," Nick said, just as those squealing parrots, the subject of a recent *New Yorker* article, flapped away en masse.

"This isn't about any light," Crum said. "It's about, uh, the most oddball predicament we've run into in a while. Your name came up."

Grudgingly, wishing he'd ripped the phone cord out of its jack, he set down the broom.

Roughly fifteen minutes and four blocks, later, he climbed the eastern steps onto the deck of the garishly decorated Colorado Street Bridge. Nick, in Levi's, a Barbara Bush Chia Pet T-shirt, and his "USC Inventors Club" sweatshirt, found Crum at the top.

According to urban legend, they were standing on the deck's spookiest point—the point where visitors most often claimed encountering ghosts of that construction worker as well as a despondent banker and other floating beings. Nick thought the supernatural was hooey. His ghouls were molecular.

After shaking hands with Crum, they got down to it. "Here's the thing," said the captain, a freckled, forty-something with a casual smile and a widow's peak. "We don't need this type of publicity today. Capiche?"

"I understand, the big party," Nick said. "And you have a nutcase holding your sergeant hostage with, if I heard you correctly, a walker and an acetylene torch."

"Precisely. And he's doing it dressed like Alfred."

"As in E. Neuman?"

"As in Batman's butler. But this prima donna's crafty. Knows we can't afford the PR black eye of sending in the SWAT team around all those balloons and banners. We're communicating with him on the sergeant's walkie-talkie, how he got it, I don't know. He won't divulge his name, either. Asks us to call him Mr. Incidental. From his voice we know he's old."

"Captain, I have a plane to catch this afternoon, a plane to a new life. You were vague on the phone about how I got dragged into this. Level with me."

"I will. Mr. Incidental says he met you and your dog recently at his nursing home. He promises to release our officer if you'll walk over to hear him out."

Nick threw his head back in disgust, which made him feel dizzier than he already did; saliva was pooling in his mouth. "His name's Reginald Plant, and he's off his friggin' rocker. He's from Sunny Slope Manor on Fair Oaks."

Crum grinned, jotting the information in his notepad. "That helps a bunch. Again, don't underestimate him. Not only is he pinning down a former LAPD gang-detective, he's sliced through part of the anti-suicide fence to get our attention. Convince him to surrender before this slides from embarrassing to FUBAR."

"FUBAR?"

"Fucked up beyond all repair."

"And there's no one else for you to call? No grown children, friends?"

"How could we? We didn't have a name until you just told us."

Nick was starting to feel green. "I still don't know if I'm your man. Words can't express how much I revile this bridge. I'm acrophobic here."

"Hey, you think we're walking on sunshine asking a civilian for intercession? Don't make me play hardball, Nick. If you wuss out and this goes further sideways, I'll have no option but to tell the papers you turned your back on the city."

Just what I need: my investors thinking I'm a candy ass. "Behind that smile, captain, you're an assasin. Tell me what to do."

"Outstanding. Lieutenant Figgle here will help you rehearse. This senior, as the kids would say, is being a buzzkill."

Nick looked at the crew-cut lieutenant, a three-generation Pasadena native whose parents shortened their last name by removing the "Berry" from the "Figgle." The way he cocked his head forward was pigeon-esque.

◆◆◆

NICK PLODDED EAST ON trembly legs, straddling the centerline of the pressure-washed deck. He lobbed a stick of Wrigley's into his mouth, trying to settle an acid stomach on Pasadena's Progressive Age darling. Refurbished or not, she remained a paradox: simultaneously regal and noir-ish, a Beaux-Arts tribute to imagination, and also the glummest place in these-there foothills. Practically speaking, she was even less: little more than a forty-second traffic shortcut in a freeway-bisected town.

Forget that: one foot in front of the other. You'll be gone by tonight. Nick's self-actualization was amateurish, for the only thing he put in front of him was his mouth over the side of the bridge, where he rushed to projectile vomit his breakfast. Still, he found a replacement stick of Wrigley's, pushed aside a déjà vu feeling of barfing here before, and plowed on.

Thirty yards ahead, up around the next congratulatory banner, was Captain Crum's potential FUBAR. Reginald—the tuxedoed provocateur— sat on an inlaid bench in an alcove over the bridge's highest span. His legs were stretched out in front, lying on top of a walker immobilizing the sergeant, who'd probably never live this down.

"*Nick!*" Reginald yelled out in the same jaunty, croaky voice. "You're a sight for these rheumy eyes." In one hand was the acetylene torch.

"Mr. Plant," Nick asked from ten feet away, "why are you doing this?"

"It's Reginald. And I had to." *Hu.* "I saw the shock on your face when you left my room. Even if I wrangled your number, you would've hung up on me." *Hu.*

"You have me there," Nick said.

"This was the only way, the only place."

The geezer looked like Nick felt: death warmed over. He was sweating, panting *hu* between some sentences, with the complexion of low-fat milk and blue-ish lips. He did, however, act more lucid than before.

"And you couldn't have worn anything nicer than the sloppy ensemble you have on, not a navy blazer? Dress for success. A Bowler would hide that cowlick." *Hu.*

339

Nick noticed the top hat in the street. "Hats are for bald guys," he said. "And crazy old men."

"*Yo*, show some respect," said the bald and still supine Donald Grubb. "You don't know who you're dealing with."

"Neither, sergeant, do you. He has dementia—and says he knows me from my previous life."

"Actually, I told him," Reginald interrupted. "He started out doubting me, too." *Hu, hu.*

"The only true things about him," Nick said, looking at Grubb, "are his quick hands. And that he's Robert Plant's uncle."

"Roger that on the quick hands," Grubb said. "I'm more of a Steven Tyler guy myself."

Nick wasn't bilious anymore; it was nervousness about being in this particular spot. "I thought cops were skeptical hearing mumbo jumbo," he said, exasperated. "C'mon, he claims we met when I was riding an ostrich. Not the Budweiser Clydesdale they ride at the Rose Parade. An ostrich. It's bullshit"

"I told you," Grubb said. "Show some respect."

"You're a stand-up fella, sergeant," Reginald said, blotting his forehead with a hankie using his free hand. "Even on your back." *Hu.* "At glacial speed, he removed his legs from the arms of the walker in this theater of the absurd.

Grubb gathered his fallen sunglasses and blue cap and stood up. Nick expected he'd be slapping the cuffs on before frog marching Reginald off on his walker. Grubb, instead, bent down, picked up the top hat, and dusted it off. Onto the sidewalk he stepped, where he kissed his abductor on the forehead and set the hat over his silvery hair.

"Sergeant, I pray whatever inconvenience I caused you will be surpassed by what our young friend accomplishes." *Hu.* "Though I don't know what that is. Thank you."

Grubb's eyes welled up. "No. I should be thanking you, sir. And you're anything but incidental. Listening to your story, I realize I need to stop burning through the Rolaids, dwelling on the situations I can't unsee. I'm going to start working more on my soul than my—my self-martyrdom. If the Dalai Lama comes to Vroman's, I'll be in the front row."

"Brilliantly put, as my English mother would say." *Hu.* "I hope to see you above a long time from now."

Grubb snagged his walkie-talkie and jogged off, whistling Aerosmith's "Dream On."

Reginald, spry of spirit, weak of flesh, motioned for Nick to join him on the bench. The gent did fill out a tux better than he did a mangy tracksuit.

"I think I'll stand," Nick said. "But congratulations for getting your way. Are you going to accuse me of riding Grover Cleveland's wife again?"

"She was a bird, Nick. She lived at Cawston Ostrich Farm. You used to work there."

"Yes, yes," he said. "The fog's lifting. Teddy Roosevelt and Booker T. Washington rode sidesaddle with me."

"Joke now," *hu*. "You told me back then you met Mr. Roosevelt. Go look it up." *Hu*. "Even after you left Cawston, you were happy as a clam. You devised some kind of lamps for around the bridge. On Saturdays we'd perform shows for the ill kids. Royo and me were part of the act. I'd hold up a hoop that he'd jump through onto your back while you were riding Mrs. Cleveland." *Hu hu hu hu*. "It was something."

"Yeah, something that never happened. You need to go the Huntington ER."

"You were such a bright light. But you lost it after the collapse. And you still don't have it back." *Hu*. "The day the bridge opened, someone dognapped Royo and we had a big fight. See how much I've remembered?" *Hu*. "You and Royo vanished." *Hu, hu*. "Everybody forgot you."

"You can barely catch your breath. You need oxygen."

"Oh, balderdash! You need to understand why this old gal meant so much to me over my life." *Hu*. "Why I used to visit here so often to think. It was you. You loved this bridge so much before that I loved it to keep you alive." *Hu*. "In my heart."

Nick checked his watch and looked back at Reginald. "If we were friends like you say, your friend is begging you to now hand over the torch and give up."

"No can do." *Hu*. "Though you may not be the Nick I remember, I'm finally the Reginald I wanted to be. I'm doing handsprings into the next life for Sally. Hubba hubba."

"You know what. Maybe you were right. Cawston sold knives then, didn't they?"

"You're lying—to me, to yourself." *Hu.* "You saw the knife on my dresser. You're a soufflé that hasn't risen. So I'm upping the temperature."

"What's with all the metaphors about my settings?" Nick mumbled.

Reginald tugged his antique, side-shade sunglasses down over his eyes. "I suppose you don't recognize these? You gave them to me."

"What can I say? I'm generous. Sir, let's go. Please."

Reginald pursed his mouth and flicked on that hissing, yellow-blue torch. "Don't you understand? It was no more an accident that you came to my room at Sunny Slope than it was a co-hinky-dink that I met Sally at the dentist's office when I bungled the date of my appointment." *Hu.* "Or that she was diagnosed with breast cancer on her seventy-fifth birthday." *Hu, hu, hu.* "The fight I got into with the juvenile delinquent who tried shoplifting cufflinks to feed his drug habit was the cosmos' way of sending me toward this." *Hu.* "It cost me my store and booted me into that nursing home just so—"

"What?" asked a flustered Nick.

"Just so this moment could happen." *Hu, hu, hu, hu.* "Reginald pulled at his tuxedo collar. "We're all connected strings, I tell you, strings plucking each other in a trillion directions."

Nick thought back to those Caltech astrophysicists at Pie 'N Burger talking about a different string theory. "Whatever you say, Carl Sagan. Put down the torch."

"Only if you put down your cynicism first." With one mottled hand keeping that welder's torch burning, his other groped around in the plastic Orchard Supply Hardware store bag next to him on the bench. With a grunt, he extracted a gold plaque and held it up for Nick to read. "I suppose you don't recall this, either?"

"How could I? I've never seen it before."

"Okeydoke," he said, borrowing one of Nick's old lines. He then gyrated around and methodically carved through the bottom, four iron bars of the anti-suicide fence; he'd cut the upper sections before Sergeant Grubb's appearance. Reginald gazed up afterward. "Lookie there!" *Hu.* "Greener than Busch Gardens."

The massive coronary that killed him seconds later produced a memorable daisy chain. After Reginald clutched his chest, his gangly upper body fell back hard against the compromised section of fence, which was about the dimension of a standard bedroom window. His weight caused the portion to snap clean of the bars above and below it, and it spiraled downward. The forty-pound section crashed like a bomb through the atrium skylight of the unoccupied condo project partly beneath the bridge's southern flank. After it shattered, Reginald's top hat and gold plaque, the one inscribed with Teddy Roosevelt's words admonishing Pasadena not to pave over the Arroyo, plunged, too.

Reginald's body might've followed if Nick hadn't rushed to grab his legs.

❖❖❖

THREE HOURS AFTER HE left, Nick keyed his door. At least he didn't faint.

Soon, a black Mercedes-Benz Town Car with tinted windows turned into his driveway. The limo driver, a quiet little German with a light bulb-shaped head and goatee, hefted Nick's bags into the trunk with ease.

By the time the Benz was gliding through Eagle Rock en route to Los Angeles International Airport, city authorities were nearly done with damage control. Reginald was in the morgue, a public works team was patching the fence, and workers had covered the condo skylight with plywood. Not a single TV news chopper or police-radio groupie knew FUBAR was averted. They were covering a freeway chase near Pomona.

Nick snaked his Walkman out of his backpack as the limo ascended the Harbor Freeway onramp by Dodger Stadium. *Click.* He teed up Zep's "In the Light" to get his headspace adjusted. The trippy, introductory synthesizer segued to his new creed about entrusting himself to find his road.

Even the headache that unmasked itself entering downtown couldn't dampen his spirit. He slurped water from the limo's complimentary water bottle, assuming he was dehydrated after vomiting, and would grab a snack at LAX. That "confounded bridge" could turn to salt.

And yet, the headache gave no quarter. Indeed, it clenched his skull like the first migraine of his life. Nick took deep breaths and applied reason. This was from stress, accumulated stress. In the last two weeks, his dog had assaulted a float, a girlfriend labeled him a defective product, and he speed-packed his house; earlier today, a codger spinning a ridiculous story died with melodrama. That'd fry anybody's circuit board.

343

He worked his jaw and put his Ray-Bans on because the migraine was making even the shaded interior of the limo intolerable. He shut his eyes, but there was no relief there. Under his eyelids little yellow dots whizzed in electron orbits. Every bump, every turn, every second cranked the turnbuckle on his frontal lobe.

Nick slouched low into the leather of the back seat, and peeked over at Royo, who was strapped next to him in that chintzy Petco harness. Typically, he could smell Nick's distress from a mile away, and would lick his face or nuzzle his snout under his arm to comfort him. Not now. He stared straight, appearing like he wouldn't need any Benadryl because he'd tranquilized himself.

The Benz took the Sepulveda Boulevard exit, and street traffic was gridlocked. The migraine had Nick digging his fingers into the bubble wrap around the mysterious solar projector squished between him and the door. Forget any LAX food. In the terminal, he'd be sprinting to a kiosk to pound five Tylenol with a Budweiser chaser.

Out of nowhere, the quiet in the Benz exploded with a gunshot-ish *pop*, *pop*. Two of the bubble-wrap capsules had burst from Nick's fingernails pressing into them, and the abruptness of it made his heart skip. Al, the German limo driver, lowered the partition to check if Nick was okay, and *tsk-tsk-ed* something.

Nick then swiveled his head inward toward Royo and noticed the detonating bubble wrap shook him out his daze. No longer was he gazing blankly ahead. No, he was pressing his wolfish noggin sideways into the seat next to Nick, so close Nick could practically taste the Lucky Boy burrito on which he'd nibbled. But that wasn't the headline here. The fact his forehead was shaping letters again was. *Shit.*

In front of Nick's glassy eyes, his brow formed an "E" and then an "I." They letters repeated as clearly as the letters on the airport billboards advertising foreign-currency exchanges and "gentlemen clubs" around. In as much as a scoff as a question, Nick asked: "You're not trying to tell me something, are you?"

The Benz approached the white curb, on top of which stood a toothy Southwest Airlines skycap; limo passengers generally tipped well. Nick, meantime, rubbed Royo's forehead to erase those annoying letters. His own brain throbbed so fiercely he wasn't sure he could recite the alphabet. The forehead letters had to be a nervous spasm, just as they'd been the morning after Royo grinded Julie's calf. The Atari-like symbol would reappear.

The Benz braked in front of the terminal, and Al got out to retrieve the luggage from the trunk. Nick puffed air trying to convince himself he'd get through this. He then turned back to Royo. His forehead still was forming "E" and "I." In moments, the dog would receive his drugging Snausage and be thrust into a claustrophobic travel cage.

"I can't believe I asked you if were communicating. You're just anxious."

"And *I'm* stupefied you still haven't gotten the message."

Al knocked on the tinted glass to indicate the skycap was waiting. Nick ignored it.

"I must be off my own rocker," he said. "I'm booking that MRI if this continues."

Al banged on the window again. This time, Nick rolled it down an inch and curtly said, "Give me a sec. I'm having an episode here."

Al smiled, as if not bothered a bit. And here Germans were disparaged for being efficiency freaks.

"Relax," Nick murmured to himself. "It's been a nerve-racking day."

"And it's going to have a disastrous ending unless you start putting things together."

If Nick opened his eyes any wider, they would've plopped onto his Levis. "Jesus, I can hear you, and you're not moving your lips. Are you a psychic?"

"No, only sometimes telepathic. And I am only permitted to disclose this: Reginald was right. Dig, Nick: there's no guarantees we'll be together again."

He frantically began searching the Benz—in the side compartment, between the seat cushions, around the overhead light—for a hidden microphone.

But Royo continued staring. "Stop asking *how* this is happening and start asking *why* it's happening. I may be a rascal, but I'm as honest as a border collie."

Nick slunk back down onto the seat. "So you were talking to me like this that day in the car when you bashed your head into the glove compartment?"

"Guilty. And it didn't feel wunderbar, either."

"And the movie 'Heaven Can Wait:' you flipped that on, too, deliberately?"

"Double guilty. Though I didn't cause your headache. My boss did. We're all trying to nudge something that's being stubborn. You!"

Nick gazed into the dog's saucer-y brown eyes while a motorcycle cop and driver Al bickered about why the limo still was idling in the white zone. "Let's say I believe you—if I'm not in a coma or in purgatory. What the fuck am I supposed to do?"

Royo slapped his paw onto Nick's shoulder. "You're supposed to solve my forehead."

TRUTH IN FAKERY

T HE SPEAKER IN A blue blazer and Banana Republic chinos was hamming it up for an audience that couldn't wait for the gasbag to sit down. With dinner nearly over, the guests were pining to dig into Federico Bakery's bridge-shaped "celebration cake." Afterward, they'd ride in decorated cars to recreate the procession across the Colorado Street Bridge for its unveiling eighty years ago this day.

Also, *Murphy Brown* came on at nine.

"They tried bulldozing her into rubble not long after she went up. America's car society demanded state-of-the-art infrastructure. But we showed them. Our gal here head-faked death more often than Keith Richards."

Percy Shine blinked, waiting for laughs. He'd been mulling doing stand-up comedy if his stock-trading career never recovered from his insider-trading conviction, of which no one at this soiree knew. There was a smattering of chuckles.

"Any-who, she had the fervent devotion of a community who appreciated that some old objects remind us who we are. Heritage matters in the Arroyo, so help me Thaddeus Lowe. Let's give it up for our preservationists. They kept the bridge standing long enough to be the royalty of Route Sixty-six."

Hands clapped, mouths watered. The invitees already endured a litany of speakers, from solemn council members to soporific state engineers, effectively repeating the same themes on this cloudless, sixty-degree afternoon. Everyone got it: the past is our parent, and prologue, and, Mr. Miyagi, *blah*-cubed.

"Before I turn this over to the mayor, who may be announcing a surprise guest that should wow us all, I want to pay homage again to John Mercereau and John Waddell for spanning this gorge with such durable élan. You think they could've managed that in LA, when jugglers and jezebels roamed Spring Street?"

Percy took a small step back from the dais, peacocking his head at his alliterative jewel, waiting for others to savor it. None were. They were pointing and muttering at an eccentric figure strutting toward them from the east side of the deck. When Percy twirled and saw it, he was irked, figuring a numbskull bureaucrat forgot to tell him about this impersonation.

"Hail to the chief," said the aspirational comic, winging it. "Nobody start any railroad monopolies, 'kay?"

Teddy Roosevelt had returned to life in a rubber mask exaggerating his squinty eyes and shaggy mustache, and a green, hunting-type jacket poofed up around the collar as if there were shoulder pads beneath it. On his way to the podium, he dropped off a carton at the same bench where Reginald died, though only select officials were briefed on his misfortune.

Fake Teddy clasped Percy's smallish hand and stroked his neoprene mustache. "How extraordinary it is to be at your rededication," he said into the mic with a fake, gravelly bluster, "and not just because I've been dead for seventy-four years."

The crowd roared louder than at any of Percy's rehearsed punch lines.

"Long ago, I look out from here, awestruck at the grandeur of the natural lands below. It was heaven on Earth before the Busches created a world wonder. Yet because modernization was accelerating, I fretted this valley would tantalize those who valued the dirtiest shade of green. I cautioned your mayor: 'what a splendid natural park you have right here! Don't let them spoil that.' Lo and behold, they mostly did."

The audience hummed. There were baffled expressions and wry grins, people suddenly forgetting about Federico's butter-cream frosting. One council member, a former Vietnam protester turned Brooks-Brothers-wearing, urban-planning junkie, clinked his salad fork against his plate in support. "Here, here!" he said.

"Now where Indians once worshipped and the Indiana Colony later settled, you have luxury homes, asphalt streets, as well as the total eradication of Adolphus's gardens. How, good people, is that fair trade?"

Through his narrow eye slits, Fake Teddy zoomed in on three side tables that could've starred on Pasadena's "Sgt. Pepper" album cover. The people there, either natives or city-associated, represented a town with talent in spades. TV show-runner Stephen J. Cannell sat next to guitar virtuoso Eddie Van Halen, who was beside band-mate David Lee Roth (a transplant from Bloomington, Indiana); paired by them were science-fiction writer Octavia Butler and Caltech physicist Kip Thorne; Vroman's regular (and Oscar-winner) Sally Field and a grandson of General George S. Patton anchored another special table. *L.A. Law* actor Harry Hamlin was there, too, blocking Fake Teddy's view of another costumed guest. The bogus ex-president really couldn't stumble now.

All this was chafing the ego of the speaker he interrupted, craving as Percy did to impress the VIPs with the glitzy morsels he dug up. How pilot Al Goebels flew a biplane with girls strapped to its wings under a bridge arch in a 1926 Flag Day stunt; that, six years later, actor Eddie Cantor drove a chariot beneath the colossus in "Roman Scandals"; or future leading man William Holden, as a local hellion, tiptoing outside a bridge column on a juvenile dare. Now a charlatan was upstaging him via righteous indignation

"A pox upon you if you haven't toasted the four construction workers who perished so his gal could rise," Fake Teddy said. "When we neglect others' sacrifice, we debase ourselves. John Visco, Harry Collins, C. J. Johnson, Normal Clark: this city is indebted."

Fake Teddy, much like Alternative Nick during the Arroyo-101 tour, couldn't believe the passionate language sailing out of his mouth. Nor that he was watching Sally Field ask someone, "Who's John Visco?"

He wasn't alone in crashing this December 13, 1993, party, just the most cartoonish. South of the ceremony, on the embankment below the orange-ish federal appeal's courthouse, twenty middle-aged and older women were arrayed in two choir-like rows. Each of the black-dressed ladies had lost spouses, siblings, children, and others from the deck, inducting them into a club they never sought to join: a club of people with missing pieces, in a city where the bridge was revered as its concrete *grand dame, its touchstone*.

During breaks in the earlier speeches, the ladies quietly chanted nondenominational prayers and sang verses from James Taylor's elegiac "Fire and Rain." Their leader was a fleshy-faced woman whose clinically depressed son leapt the same day the space shuttle Challenger exploded in 1986. Her name was Connie Prunell.

"We must distinguish fable from myth," Fake Teddy continued after steadying himself. "We must remember that when we gawk at man-made beauty, we blind ourselves to smaller wonders. Don't—"

"Take a hike, clown," yelled someone from the rear. "Who are you to scold us?"

Percy, energized by that catcall, sidestepped toward the podium with Pasadena's city's symbol, a key-crossed crown, on it. He tapped on Fake Teddy's jacketed arm to pressure him to yield. When he wouldn't, Percy, cheeks reddening, hovered.

"Don't misunderstand me," said Fake Teddy. "America could do worse than imitating the best of Pasadena in its ardor for the sciences and arts, in its stand against the unjust, in its opposition to spectators hurling marshmallows at those guys in white suits riding scooters during the Rose Parade. But you've closed your eyes for too long about an uncomfortable reality, or dis-reality: certain objects absorb the energy of man's lesser instincts."

Percy glowered at the police chief at one of the tables, making a throat-slashing gesture. Fake Teddy needed the hook. No one, though, expected canine surprise.

"Look, Daddy," yipped an attendee's young daughter. "A cute puppy crawled out of the president's neck. He has a little beard."

This was true, for Royo, the beige Lab-boxer with the gray Fu Manchu, had been situated clumsily around Nick's neck, under his stuffy jacket, for the speech. The dog needed fresh air, and also to pointedly remind Nick not to forget to say what he promised to add. Trying to communicate telepathically into such a full mind was like rowing through mud.

"*Get back in there*," the mic caught Nick whispering to him. "I'll tell them."

Royo wiggled back under the jacket, which knocked Fake Teddy's mask askew, which in turn prompted the audience to snicker and point again. At their table, Kip Thorne giggled at Octavia Butler's crack about a cross-species mutant. The pretend POTUS cleared his throat for his ending remarks, just the same.

"One quick aside," he said. "When in doubt, heed the purer species. And never again should we compel our dogs to wear reindeer sweaters at Christmas or deprive them of daily bacon. Indeed, if we were less arrogant, we'd realize it's not just cancer they can sniff out but thirty-seven other diseases doctors struggle to diagnose. The most evolved of pooches can even predict disasters and detect evil. How dare we insult them by baby talk?"

The eighty-member audience was now speechless, and Percy was done being patient. Back at the dais, he brazenly shoved Fake Teddy to the left, saying into the mic, "Okay, okay, show's over." Thinking it was, he straightened his tie.

But Fake Teddy snatched the mic from its holder, and when Percy tried wrestling it away, he hopped to the side. "A last thought from my bully pulpit. As I told your YMCA in 1911: remember, not all movement is necessarily progress."

Percy lunged to retake the mic, yet Fake Teddy shuffled farther to the left, stretching the cord. "In honor of my friend Lilly Busch, I say, *"Ich bin ein Pasadenan!"*

Fake Teddy then dropped the mic, which produced a burst of ear-splitting feedback, and started walking the direction he came. Percy picked it up, trying to be the consummate pro. "We thank," he said, "the Doo Dah Parade for sending us a representative to talk hogwash. Mr. Mayor, the stage is yours."

LAST CHANCE WITH THE CONCRETE DAME

BACK AT THE ALCOVE, Nick was torn down the middle. He was electrified by how Fake Teddy spoke up for the dead and against myth sugarcoated as history, and also mortified he'd made himself *persona non grata* in his birthplace, last days here and all.

Though night was falling, he was clammy under his mask and jacket. So, he removed them both, and leaned down to allow the whiskered sidekick on his shoulders to hop onto the bench. "That, weirdly, went well," he told Royo. "Now what?"

"You tell me," Royo said with restored telepathy. "I'm not your cheat sheet."

Everywhere around green and red Christmas lights sparkled, including on a church bell tower near the old Turner & Stevens Mortuary.

"So long as you know that, one way or another, we're still blowing town."

"Sure, Nick, sure."

"That sounded patronizing."

"Harsh as it is to say, you're not awake yet. I wouldn't have needed to assault that float to connect you with Reginald if you were."

"How did you know to do that?"

"Michael, the man in the Zep jacket, the one we called graybeard before, egged me on. Defiling Julie's calf was my initiative."

"I always sensed that guy was different. Mystical, even."

"Sorry to tell you. Sensing doesn't get you bubkes today."

They actually were inside the Southwest terminal at LAX when Nick realized they couldn't board their flight. No way. A dog speaking into your head and forming vowels on his forehead is a phenomenon smart not to blow off. Limo driver Al, fortunately, hadn't left, and pronounced himself happy to ferry them home. On the way, he let Nick use his Nokia cellphone to dial Loomer. After Nick notified him he wouldn't be arriving tonight, his PO-ed investor warned him he "better get his priorities straight."

In the backseat of the Benz, Royo returned to brainwave chatter, suggesting Nick press his head against his for a crash history lesson. Nick, with nothing to lose except a future, tilted forward. *Roll life!*

The past washed over him in jerky clips, where silhouetted people moved in a dream-like fog: a man riding an exotic animal along a trail, and then chasing a gaunt dog with a bag in his teeth; the same man speaking with a woman in pearls on a park bench, and later squatting on a hillside tinkering with a small lamp. The fog, however, lifted as quickly as it shrouded, and Nick felt like someone neither here nor there. There was but one definitive way to learn who he *might've* been, what this was about, and the geriatric he witnessed die had sprinkled breadcrumbs. "Go look it up," Reginald had said from his Sunny Slope Manor room.

Nick asked Al rush him to Eagle Rock Public Library before it closed. There, he went to the microfiche room and scrolled through the *New York Times* archives while Al watched his indubitably telepathic dog Royo outside. Sitting in a cubicle, the early century whizzed by at vertiginous speed. Eventually, a 1903 article about Theodore Roosevelt's trip to Pasadena shone from the white screen. On it, he read how one *Nick Chance* had stumped the United States' twenty-sixth president! You could've knocked him over with an ostrich feather. The ridiculous was now the irrefutable.

From the library, Al took Nick to his house; he wouldn't take a dime for his services. Nick inside ripped open a carton that he'd asked Fleet to donate to the Salvation Army, and dug out the Teddy mask and a secondhand hunting jacket he'd gotten for a 1990 Halloween party. Trusting his gut, he packed the things he needed into his Toyota and drove to the bridge. At the western steps, he talked his way onto the deck, lying to one of the cops that he was a doing a routine for the party. His migraine—and fear of heights—no longer tormented him.

Nick, as Fake Teddy, intuitively knew the message for Pasadena's elite. Where he went from here was less obvious, besides his awareness of two imperatives: positioning the solar projector on top of a balustrade, which was about fifty yards from where the disrupted ceremony was resuming behind banners and streamers, and withdrawing specific images from the Manila envelope.

"You know that you invented that gadget," Royo told Nick clairvoyantly. "Get it working and solve the riddle. E-I-T-D-I. No time to ramble on."

"I see what you did there. Geez: I was on to sun power before it was in vogue?"

"Let me rock your world some more, kemosabe. Today isn't only this gal's eightieth birthday. It's the eightieth anniversary of *your* murder, right here. You were trying to rescue me when you got shoved over. Close your eyes."

Once Nick did, he saw, again in foggy silhouette, a man up on the bench peering down as someone runs up behind him, arms outstretched. "So this is why she's had this effect on me?" he said. "It was there the day I was born. Who did it?"

"A man named Ernest, if you can believe it. Dark human. But you broke your word."

Nick clumped down on the bench next to Royo with more questions than there were wild oak trees in the Arroyo. He was about to nuzzle foreheads to tease out further answers when two things happened: the bridge's grape-bunch lamps flicked on and someone joined them.

"The fuck you doing, rough rider?" Percy said, swerving around a banner, listing bridge milestones in Morning Glory fonts. "This get you off, playing the subversive?"

Nick wasn't terribly shocked he desired a confrontation. "I'm not doing this for ego," he said. "I'm doing my civic duty. Finally."

"Then you'll be delighted to learn that your civic duty scared off Al Gore. He was our scheduled surprise guest. The Secret Service agent listening to your bullshit kiboshed that, though; proud of yourself?"

"Al Gore, really?" Nick looked at Royo in an are-we-sure-we-know-what-we're-doing manner. Gore was Pasadena's kind of Democrat. Plus, he invented the Internet.

Royo didn't know Al Gore from Al Bundy, learning the world, as he mostly did, through Nick's. Now, he only craved payback—payback on behalf of his tail-wagging brethren. He sprang off the bench to confront Pasadena's serial dog killer of 1913.

While Percy might've been your standard sleazebag in this life, the telltale aura of the man who chloroformed the stray dogs that growled in the presence of his malevolent soul still clung in Royo's nostrils. He'd executed them in the basement of his shadowy house on the Arroyo's eastern bluff. Royo knew that for a fact, being the mutt *he* was supposed to be.

On one of his exploratory jaunts outside Ivy Wall, Royo had followed the sounds of panicked barking to Percy's property. For an hour, he'd tried freeing the prisoners by kicking in the basement window with his hind legs. When Percy finally heard him, he came out dangling a slab of raw steak that Royo could smell was laced with poison. He fled, back to Ivy Wall, souring fast on humanity.

Citizens could've unmasked the real Percy behind the icehouse proprietor and civic big man. But distractions—Colorado Street Bridge fever, percolating racial tensions over a future public pool at Brookside Park, and other topics—shielded him from scrutiny.

This new Percy marched past Royo and up to Nick, unloading on him with a vicious slap across the face. "I don't know what grudge you have against Pasadena," he said. "I know the bad-mouthing ends today."

The slap left a red welt on Nick's face and more. It jogged a memory in his head of former Percy in a woolly winter coat on a misty day under the bridge.

Royo didn't care which iteration the creep was. He lunged at him with feral purpose, sinking his chompers through Percy's argyle socks and into his left anklebone

"*Owwwww*, you mongrel," Percy yelped. He leaned down, smashing his fist into the top of Royo's head. The dog unclenched his jaw and backpedaled, growling.

The same wicked smile Percy flashed the doomed dogs in 1913 returned in 1993. "You know what? The Rose Bowl's behind us. Field goal try!" The sandy-haired stockbroker then stepped back and booted Royo in the rib cage with an upward force that jettisoned him five feet onto the deck. Nick's muse thumped sideways, crying, *Er, er, er, errr.* Within seconds, his body was twitching.

"Hey, Percy?" Nick said, weaponizing Percy's vanity in a distraction ploy. "Isn't the mayor calling you over for an award?"

"An award?" Percy said.

When he pivoted toward the ceremony, Nick barreled into his waist and tackled him onto the roadway. The tussle was on, and they threw alligator-arm punches but Percy, the workout warrior, soon got the better of him. While one hand pinned Nick down, the other reached into his blazer pocket. From it he grabbed his commemorative letter opener, the one engraved "Pasadena-Centennial" on its chrome blade, and stabbed Nick above the belly button through his Barbara Bush Chia Head T-shirt. Nick shrieked, grasping the bleeding hole in his belly; he'd been impaled by a souvenir.

Percy cooly plucked the letter opener from Nick's stomach, which made a slurping sound and got to his feet. He cast off his blazer next—and speared himself in his left shoulder in a frame-up job. "Police!" he hollered, jumping onto the sidewalk in front of the bench for elevation. "*Help!* This wacko is trying to kill me."

Nobody heard his bogus plea with applause rippling from the bridge rededication.

"Don't stab me again," Percy shouted. "I have a family (an ex-wife and a bling-collecting, pregnant mistress, anyway). "I'll have to defend myself."

A spasm-ing Royo made eye contact with Nick, whose duodenum was punctured. "E-I-T-D-I," Royo said telepathically. "Percy's being the real him. Time for the real you."

Nick wobbled onto his legs while Percy scanned east, waiting for the authorities. "Dude, cut the pep talk and just tell me," Nick said. "We're getting our butts kicked." He spit blood.

"Don't call me dude, my hail fellow," Percy said with a cackle, believing Nick was speaking to him. "You're going to jail. And your fat-ass dog is roadkill. Get it?"

The dimmer setting on Nick's listless spirit cranked past manufacturer recommendations hearing the term "roadkill." He spun Percy around and jammed the letter opener into his shoulder. Percy screamed, "*Youch!*" and Nick, the southpaw, round-housed him in his haughty jaw.

The punch staggered Percy backward into the concrete bench. And more. His upper body clanked into the re-soldered portion of fence subjected earlier to Reginald's principled vandalism, and the jarring caused the patch to shear off its fresh welds and drop. It crashed on top of the plywood deck over the shattered condo skylight in a bang that everybody on the deck heard. Everybody.

To their left, Pasadena PD started ripping down the banners separating the battle and the star-studded party, which still hadn't gotten to that red velvet Federico's cake.

"I've seen enough police shows on TV to know the guys with big guns are coming," Royo thought. "What rhymes with learn? Not that you do it proficiently."

"At least I don't bury yoga pants or behead a kid's doll," Nick said. Then across his wan face his eyes brightened. "*Ooh*, I figured it out," he said. "E-I stands for earn it. Yeah, that's it. But earn what?" He spun the knob on the projector, and gears whirled.

"I'm not telling," Royo said via brainwaves. He coughed blood.

Captain Crum, Lieutenant Figgle, and three sharpshooters now jogged over, joining the other cops about thirty feet away. "Everybody freeze until I sort this fiasco out," Crum said. "And why is everybody bleeding?"

"Officers. Thank God," Percy said from the bench. "This anarchist and his rabid dog double-teamed me. I had to fight back. Shoot 'em."

"You talk too much," Crum said. "Hands up, everybody."

Percy, trying to demonstrate how compliant he was, whipped his arms upward with ill-considered zest. The tip of his right hand caught the razor-sharp edge of a severed fence post and, as well as any QVC-sold Ginsu knife, the movement sliced off his two middle fingers at their knuckles. They became the next objects to bounce off that condo's roof, which was taking a drubbing today.

Blood spurted from Percy's new stumps, and he rolled off the bench and onto the bridge sidewalk. He writhed there before he clutched the Fake Teddy mask and wrapped his hand in it like a plastic tourniquet. He then curled into a ball, sniveling like the coward he was.

Crum shook his head, jawing to Lieutenant Figgle, "Back to FUBAR territory, I guess." Then louder, he said, "If anybody has any weapons, throw them down. I mean it, you guys."

Nick slowly raised his arms to show he didn't have a gun and slowly lowered them back onto the antique solar projector. It took every fibrous strand of want-to for him to deposit the first postcard into the slot. On the periphery, SWAT sharpshooters were kneeling.

"You any closer?" Royo asked. "I'm seeing myself as a teething puppy. Hurry."

"Nick. Please," Crum said. "Show history some respect."

Nick, be it the Alternative Nick or Current Nick, just then understood that he once hung from a strap stories above here. He thrust the postcard down into his fully charged machine. Instantly radiating out over the south side of the bridge, with a slight 3-D effect, was a billboard-size image of Vroman's Colorado Street store from 1913.

As it brightened the twilight, a woman in an old-lady mask, long, frilly dress, and gray wig scampered over, waving her arms. She'd sweet-talked her way into the event, too, never expecting it was the table-setter for this. The police wouldn't allow her to get any closer.

"Nick. It's me!" said Julie, yanking off her Lilly-Bush-esque mask. "Whatever you're doing, give up. We still can have a future."

Nick, weakening by the second, gaped at her. "Really? But why are you here?"

"Well, I can't write about something if I miss its party, can I? Now stop. This bridge has seen enough tears. I love you."

"After today, I may transfer to San Bernardino," Crum side-mouthed to Figgle.

"San Berdoo?" Figgle said. "I wouldn't. More felons out there than San Quentin."

Nick's bloody hands pressed a second postcard into the slot. This one broadcast an image of Thaddeus Lowe and his sons on a breathtaking, snow-capped Echo Mountain.

Any pretense the ceremony could resume uninterrupted was over. The invited guests and others now were busy *ooh*-ing and *aah*-ing at the aerial-projected memories of yesteryear.

"Well, lordy!" exclaimed David Lee Roth, stupefied by Nick's device. "This is a *gen-u-ine* George Lucas." Close by, Kip Thorne scribbled an equation on his palm.

"As Robert Plant once sang," Royo told Nick, "the path you seek burns inside the light ahead."

"I'm still confounded, boy. Why did God recruit a fuck-up like me—a fuck-up selling plastic crap, underachieving every which way?" Nick fed the third postcard into the projector: a panoramic shot of upper Busch

Gardens that accentuated its grassy steppes and Gingerbread Hut, the Budweiser-eagle flowerbed and exotic cacti.

Julie and the police were mystified. To whom was Nick talking: an invisible friend? Voices in his head?

"Didn't you know that Jesus predicted fuck-ups will inherit the Earth?" Royo said. "Let the answer come."

Nick eyeballed the image and turned to Royo. "He never said that. I'm an ex-Presbyterian." He gulped. "I'm *supposed* to be a truth shiner, aren't I?"

"Warmer," Royo answered by brainwave.

"A truth shiner that'd, *um*, rather die for the best of something's aims—than live dishonestly in its fables, no matter how beautiful the lie."

"Getting there, human. And whatever happens from here, I apologize for shredding your couch. Tasty as that foam was, it was no excuse to go Royo Asswipe."

"Forget it." Nick said, stepping over bawling Percy and grunting, scooping up his fading dog. "We have all some Royo Asswipe inside. Looks like, though, we're not making it to San Francisco, after all." He cradled Royo in his arms, barely able to return to where he'd stood while sharpshooters clicked their automatic rifles at them.

"I'll take Pasadena anyway," Royo thought. "Prettier. And better grass to roll on."

Holding his dog in his right arm, Nick used his left hand to load the final image into his whirring projector. But this one wasn't a postcard. It was far better: a photograph of a smiling, dark-haired man atop a plumy ostrich with a dog hoisted up on its front legs beside them, as the trio watched the bridge under construction from patchy ground. Inexplicably, A. C. Vroman's photo spread wider than the others. One of its borders spilled over to the side of the alcove, right to where the exposed hole in the fence was.

"*Holy mackerel*: that's us!" Nick said. "And I think she's extending us an invitation, catch me?"

Both were dripping blood all over the bench.

"I do. What you never understood was that *she* always needed you as much as the city needed her," Royo thought. "If you're really awoken, what's E-I-T-D-I?"

Nick, in this time of dying, smiled truer than he had since he was a kid in Mac's garage. "Sure sunny, this awareness, this high of knowing who you really are. Knowing who you're supposed to be is the ultimate high. Ready?" He then shouted the answer to Royo's acronym riddle, though only one person heard it—the person designated to—over the police walkie-talkie chatter and rising confusion. "Shall we, muttenheimer?"

"Call me the butterscotch wolf," Royo thought. "Last one to Buford's buys."

"Like you ever bought a sandwich in your life," Nick said. "Or lives."

Nick, clutching Royo in his arms, ducked through the gap in the fence perfectly sized for them. A stunning white flash, like the flash of a hundred old-fashioned cameras, exploded in the night air as they stepped into nothing. When the flash petered out, they were gone.

"*Nicccck*! No," Julie wailed, so loudly she sprained her esophagus.

"Oh, my god," Sally Field said from the table area. "What's happening?"

"I'm definitely taking some personal time," Crum said.

Nearly simultaneously, the mourning women on the bank, and only them, saw something as jaw-dropping as Nick and Royo's disappearing routine. Brilliant streaks of purple light illuminated the spots below the bridge where each one of the people they lost landed after jumping from the deck. Each woman only saw the purple light related to her tragedy, rather than the entire spider web of intersecting beams reminiscent of a Griffith Park laser show. Each in their own way implicitly knew that it was a recreation of a loved one being lifted up and jetted home a trillion-trillion miles above the stars.

Some of the ladies fainted. Some howled thanks. Connie Prunell wept euphoric tears of relief. There'd be a good deal of inebriation, laughter, and joyous reminiscing over photo albums later that night.

Even so, the following weeks were a muddle. Initially, none of the eyewitnesses could agree on what they'd witnessed, debating whether it was a miracle, prank, or something defying categorization. One bunch, including most of the police closest to the white flash, suspected it was an elaborate, David Copperfield-like hoax involving mirrors and fossil-fuel-protesting actors. Two months later, someone claimed to have seen Nick and Royo in the snowy parking lot of a Chili's restaurant in Indiana. False rumor.

Across the world, religions with long-held beliefs in reincarnation enjoyed a record surge of new members and donations. In Nick's honor, a Caltech physicist sketched the plans for a spectrometer to capture light escaping the departed.

⍦⍦⍦

THREE YEARS LATER, IN the afterglow of her blockbuster book about the true history of the Colorado Street Bridge and its connection to deathless endings, Julie was the keynote speaker at the dedication of a plaque for the men who died during the bridge's anything-but-immaculate conception. Her knees trembled when she noticed a vaguely familiar gent in the back of the admiring crowd. Seeing his twinkling eyes, she veered off her prepared comments, describing a recurring dream she was having: that sometime in 2050, with the Earth unraveling, Pasadena's concrete queen would brook more than the Arroyo Seco.

"People," Julie said in closing, "frequently ask me if I expect Nick and Royo to return to this gem of a city. To them I say we have to earn it to deserve it."

ACKNOWLEDGMENTS

A S A NATIVE PASADENAN, I've spent most of my life living within a few miles of my famous subject. Yet, memories of teenage mischief there and an evolved appreciation for the light-dark paradox that is the Colorado Street Bridge only served as raw inspiration. How fortunate, then, I was to have my wife, Kate, and two daughters, Samantha and Lauren, pushing me forward, never doubting I could weave the loose threads of imagination and reality into narrative whole cloth. I love you all to my depths. My big brother, Paul, sparked my premise years ago when he encouraged me to write about a special dog using the organic smart-ass in me. My editor, Seth Fischer, performed his usual magic by helping me situate my boundless ideas within a manageable universe. Steve Eames, another terrific editor, added his insights on all things grammar and logic. Gary Cowles, Ann Scheid, Ann Erdman, Sue Mossman of Pasadena Heritage, the Pasadena Museum of History, and the Pasadena Central Library were generous with their support. Fellow writers Kimberly Kindy, David Kukoff, David Rocklin, and Kevin Uhrich were always there with a positive word (or kick in the butt), as well. Your kindness shall not be forgotten. Finally, an arch-sized thank you to the wondrous people at Rare Bird Books, who continually produce literary miracles and support us neurotic authors on incredibly little caffeine. No one loves books or recognizes how they transport us as much as you do.

RESEARCH

BOOKS

LUMMIS, CHARLES F. *A Tramp Across America*. Lincoln: University of Nebraska Press, 1982; Waddell, John Alexander Low. *Bridge Engineering Volume 2*. RareBooksClub, 2012; Phillips, Cedar Imboden, and the Pasadena Museum of History. *Early Pasadena (Images of America)*. Charleston: Arcadia Publishing, 2008; Perlin, John, and Amory Lovins. *Let It Shine: The 6,000-Year Story of Solar Energy*. Novato: New World Library, 2013; Ebershoff, David. *Pasadena (a novel)*. New York: Random House, 2002. Conyers, Patrick, Cedar Phillips, and the Pasadena Museum of History. *Pasadena 1940–2008 (Images of America)*. Charleston: Arcadia Publishing, 2009; Conyers, Patrick, Cedar Phillips, and the Pasadena Museum of History. *Pasadena: A Business History (Images of America)*. Charleston: Arcadia Publishing, 2007; Wood, J. W. *Pasadena, California, Historical and Personal: A Complete History of the Indiana Colony*. Pasadena: J. W. Wood, 1917; Scheid, Ann. *Pasadena: Crown of the Valley*. Northridge: Windsor Publications, 1986; Heckman, Marlin. *Pasadena in Vintage Postcards (Postcard History Series)*. Charleston: Arcadia Publishing, 2001; Arthur, Anthony. *Radical Innocent: Upton Sinclair*. New York: Random House, 2006; Thomas, Rick. *South Pasadena's Ostrich Farm (Images of America)*. Charleston: Arcadia Publishing, 2007; McWilliams, Carey. *Southern California: An Island on the Land*. Salt Lake City: Peregrine Smith Books, 1946; Walsh, Tim. *Wham-O Super-Book:*

Celebrating Sixty Years Inside the Fun Factory. San Francisco: Chronicle Books, 2008; Crocker, Donald W. *Within the Vale of Annandale: A Picture History of South Western Pasadena and Vicinity.* Pasadena: Pasadena-Foothill YMCA, 1990. Thomas, Rick. *The Arroyo Seco (Images of America).* Charleston: Arcadia Publishing, 2008; Hernon, Peter, and Terry Ganey. *Under the Influence: The Unauthorized Story of the Anheuser-Busch Dynasty.* New York: Avon Books, 1991.

NEWSPAPERS, INSTITUTIONS, PERIODICALS, AND WEBSITES

ALTADENA HISTORICAL SOCIETY, ANHEUSER-BUSCH.COM, Arroyoseco. org, Biography.com Brainhistory.com, city of Pasadena, Bissellhouse. com, Bizarrela.com, Eagle Rock Sentinel, Engineering Record, Hardesty & Hanover, Historic American Engineering Record, Facebook, Flickr.com, Fortune, Google Books, Hometown Pasadena, KCET, Laacollective.com, L.A. Curbed, Ladailymirror.com, Lompoc Journal, Los Angeles Herald, Los Angeles Magazine, Los Angeles Times, Mentalfloss.com, Mountlowe.org, Oldradio.com, Onthisday.com, Pacificelectric.org, Pasadena Daily News, Pasadena Digital History, Pasadenagardens.com, Pasadena Magazine, Pasadena Now, Pasadena Post, Pasadena Star, Pasadena Star News, Pasadena Weekly, Rolling Stone, Southwest Contractor and Manufacturer, Slate, Structure magazine, Thaddeuslowe.com, The New York Times, The People History, Tournamentofroses.com, University of Southern California, Waterandpower.org, Westways, Wikipedia, and Youtube.